IN THE WAR AGAINST HITLER,
THEY WERE SECRET, LETHAL WEAPONS . . .

For a moment, nothing happened. Then the air was filled with fire and noise.

Whitney looked for Sister Bernadette and Sister Magda through the dust and fire, located Sister Magda, saw her leap onto the running board of the only surviving Nazi truck. As Whitney watched, Sister Magda seized the driver's hair, yanked his head out through the window and slit his throat.

Magda smiled as she wiped the blade on the man's shirt, then pulled him out and got behind the wheel. Whitney began to climb down. Suddenly, a searing pain in her right thigh tumbled her down toward the road. Her arm looped over her head, protecting it from the rocks and bushes that lashed out at her . . .

The Butterfly AVENGERS

BARBARA ATLEE & BRYN CHANDLER

POCKET BOOKS

New York   London   Toronto   Sydney   Tokyo

An *Original* Publication of POCKET BOOKS

POCKET BOOKS, a division of Simon & Schuster Inc.
1230 Avenue of the Americas, New York, NY 10020

ISBN: 0-671-65776-3

First Pocket Books printing December 1988

10 9 8 7 6 5 4 3 2 1

POCKET and colophon are trademarks of
Simon & Schuster Inc.

Printed in the U.S.A.

A TOAST
TO THE IMPORTANT MEN
IN OUR LIVES

Barbara Atlee:
> Howard Atlee
> James H. Schumacher, Jr.

Bryn Chandler:
> Rod Collins
> Jay Christgau

The Butterfly AVENGERS

PROLOGUE

September, 1940

"WHO IS SHE? How did she die?"

Donohue ran his palm over his thick hair and squared his sunglasses. He reflexively scanned the empty tarmac and the distant fields then looked at Whitney, who stood beside him, composed and regal, even in the misty morning of the remote English airfield. "You look fit, healed. I believe you may have even gained a bit of weight. Did you enjoy your vacation?"

She arched a thin brow as a puff of air teased the top layer of golden hair in her shoulder-length pageboy. "In one sense it was lovely, particularly in contrast to the last two years." She paused, shifting her deep blue eyes to meet his. "And for the same reason it was torture. I'm afraid I've lost the knack for relaxation. The Duchess, however, was a gracious hostess and I did a great deal of catching up. Is the Duchess one of ours?"

"It's not polite to ask."

She tipped her head to look at him. "Politeness is not a requirement for our occupation."

Donohue sighed. "Apparently you have had a good rest. And yes, the Duchess opens her estate to us as a safe house. You were quite well protected."

1

She nodded. "As was Erik. He was playing tennis when I left. And now it is time to get to work." She gestured toward the coffin which waited, draped with a Czech flag, next to the cargo hold of the U.S. Army plane. "William, who is she and how did she die?"

He sighed. "In some ways, her story is not unlike yours. Her name is—was—Cara Waldheim. She was from Cologne most recently, but her parents were both Czech, and she had been raised in Prague. They died in epidemics in the thirties and she lived alone. From her file we gathered that she spent some time in Berlin, then Brussels, and finally Cologne. When Czechoslovakia was invaded, she returned to Prague, apparently to form a resistance unit. Her French friends weren't particularly surprised, I gather. The reports say she was independent and strong-willed."

Whitney tossed her head back, her hair glinting gold in the sun. A smile teased at the corners of her mouth. "This is what makes us *alike?*"

William reached into his pocket and pulled out a pack of Camels. He shook one out, tamping it on his thumbnail, and stuck it into the corner of his mouth. He lit it with his Zippo lighter. "Yes," he said through the cloud of smoke, "and it is a great compliment to both of you." He took another drag. "She was captured while sending a radio message about the activities of the Nazis from a tenement in Prague to the Czech Free Army in England, and we assume she stayed at her post to finish the message even though it meant capture. She had a lot of grit."

"When was she taken?"

"Eighteen months ago. Like you, she spent a long time in the hands of the Germans. Like you, she escaped."

Whitney's eyes returned to the flag-draped coffin.

"And?"

Donohue ground his cigarette into the tarmac, then said flatly, "This is where the similarity ends. She was recaptured and tortured, then dumped outside Resistance headquarters in Prague. Our man there, Vota Rajic, had been her . . . close friend, and claimed her body. An empty coffin lies under her headstone in Prague."

2

Whitney stepped to the box, resting her hand on it lightly, then removed the flag and folded it carefully, presenting it to him, her jaw set. "We have one other thing in common. We'll both spend eternity as someone else."

She strode past him to the steps of the plane, then turned. "Let's go, William. I don't want to miss my funeral."

1

THE LANDSCAPE OF the Greenspring Valley of Maryland flashed through the parted curtains of the limousine, a blur of autumn's death colors replacing the fresh greens of memory's summer. Whitney Baraday Frost-Worthington, Countess of Swindon, raised an ironic eyebrow at the appropriateness of the image.

"Hurry, driver," she muttered, perversely enjoying the black humor, "or I'll fulfill my mother's predictions and be late for my own funeral."

"Don't worry, madame, we'll be on time," his voice responded from the speaker next to her ear. She glanced through the glass separating them at his neatly clipped, tightly curled black hair under the chauffeur's cap, then chuckled.

"I should have known you'd be able to hear me, since Colonel Donohue sent this car. Are you with the OSS?"

"The OSS, Countess? I'm not familiar with any such thing."

She watched as the muscles under the skin of the back of his neck tensed slightly, reflexively. "Of course."

Whitney raised a black-gloved hand to the window and began to pull the curtain aside, then hesitated. Donohue had been adamant about her not attending the graveside service at St. John's, until suddenly he had caved in, agreeing, even encouraging her while cautioning her repeatedly not to risk revealing herself. *Why the quick change?* she questioned silently, now conscious of the driver's prying mechanical ears. *Donohue never takes any action without at least three obvious reasons and ten hidden ones.*

President Roosevelt had trusted Colonel William Donohue as the head of the Office of Strategic Services, the nation's foreign intelligence service. The breadth of his power was unknown, even to Roosevelt himself, but Bill Donohue was the sort of man the nation could trust. He'd just square his broad shoulders, run a hand across his close-cropped salt-and-pepper hair and do the right thing. Whitney realized her father, Nelson Dowling Baraday, had been the same kind of man. She was overcome with the pain of missing him and her eyes stung with tears.

The car slowed and, almost unconsciously, she slid the pale gray jacquard fabric slightly to one side to look out the window. *Ten years,* she thought, excited about the home-coming but frightened that she wouldn't recognize anything.

"Sagamore," she said immediately as she saw the white fences and stand of silver poplar, "the northwest corner near Warfield's back acreage. Butler Road." With a gasp, she yanked her hand back, allowing the curtains to close out the sight, then pulled off her gloves to distract herself from any further reflection. She was, she had to admit, astonished at the depth of pain she felt. Unconsciously, her hand dropped to her wooden leg.

The car slowed further, then hesitated, and the door on the opposite side snapped open then quickly closed as William Donohue entered.

"Colonel! What an unexpected pleasure." Whitney quickly smothered her pain with the formal pretense they maintained.

"Countess." He nodded. "Please forgive the intrusion, but I wanted a few moments alone with you." He saw her eyes move to the back of the driver's head, then continued, "Cesar? Believe me, you need have no concerns." He reached into his jacket and pulled out a small notebook,

6

extending it to her, then caught her eye. "Are you certain you haven't put yourself in a difficult position? You can still back out, you know. I have others there."

She shook her head, her golden hair grazing the shoulders of her stone-blue Harris tweed suit, an ironic smile tracing the corners of her mouth. "How often does one have an opportunity to anonymously observe one's own funeral? I'll be just fine." Her smile grew firm. "What is this notebook?"

He proffered a smooth oxblood leather notebook gleaming with gold corner-wings. "Risking stating the obvious, Whitney, it is for notes."

"Oh, you spies are so clever. Nothing is ever as it seems." She smiled to ease his obvious discomfort with her flippancy. "Thank you," Whitney said, turning it over. She enjoyed the smooth feel of the leather.

William Donohue examined his fingernails. "I wanted to . . . perhaps . . . commemorate . . . would be the right word . . . the beginning of your . . . your new life."

"Seems appropriate timing." She glanced at him, a twinkle in her eye.

He shook his head. "Well, I see you haven't lost your sense of humor." Whitney felt an edge of disapproval in his voice.

She sighed deeply, then put her hand lightly on his arm. "William, you will recall I've seen my husband brutally murdered by his own nephew. I've played spy for you in Vienna and in Istanbul. I was a prisoner of the Nazis for two years, and after escaping, was running and hiding in wine barrels, brothels, and sewers for three months. I've lost two men I love and nearly a third, more friends than I care to think of, and my right leg to a war our country hasn't even entered and, now, I'm officially dead. How could I possibly lose my sense of humor? It's all I have left." She studied the worried look on his face. "Oh, come now. Wasn't it you who told me a sense of humor was required for this job?"

He shook his head. "I would never have said that."

"Well you should have, for it is. Don't you remember how amused you were when I played spy in Vienna?"

"I never thought it was amusing. I told you it wasn't a

7

game. And now with Hitler's armies spreading like a fungus across Europe, it's even less so. Whitney—"

"William," she interrupted, steel framing her words, "it is the ultimate game, and I believe you are the consummate player. Don't destroy my illusions."

"Countess, I did not join you to debate the nature of the espionage business. We are about to be late for your funeral. Now . . ." he hesitated, then cleared his throat.

"Yes, Colonel?" she prompted. "You were saying?"

"I was . . . saying"—he covered her hand with his—"welcome back. I truly did miss you and that dangerous humor of yours. But please make certain it doesn't turn on you."

She ran her fingers through her hair, pulling it back from her high cheekbones and aquiline features. "Thank you for the caution. I do want to stay alive, now that I'm officially dead."

"Good. Now if I may continue, it is my expectation some of your German 'hosts' may be in attendance today and, frankly, that was why I decided it was better for you to attend. You're the only one who might recognize the people from the Austrian hospital or the Swiss train station or Paris . . ."

"Or the Basque or Madrid. Or, for that matter, either of the bordellos. Yes, I understand. I suppose it would be logical for them to confirm my death. Do you suppose they'll demand to view the corpse?"

He thought for a minute, then slowly shook his head. "I can't imagine how they would carry it off. They wouldn't want to draw attention to themselves. I surely hope they don't." He paused. "I would assume they would be looking for some sort of slip of phrase, or other clue."

"They can't possibly think my leg would still have . . . anything in it?"

He shrugged. "My guess is they may not believe it's you at all and will be watching carefully to see who's in attendance; to see if they can view the deceased; to learn whatever they can. We haven't ruled out the possibility of a leak in Madrid or among our friends in the mountains. These times breed excess in both good and evil, and we cannot

8

monitor each of our sources. You're a much-wanted quarry, Whitney."

She smiled slightly. "More accurately, my leg is a much-wanted quarry. I'll make careful notes on anyone I recognize."

He nodded with businesslike brusqueness. "Good. But no heroics! Stay in the car. Keep the curtains closed. Cesar will photograph anyone you think might be significant. Are you positive you can handle this?"

Whitney tipped her head and studied him. "William, one thing adversity teaches: you can survive anything you can survive."

He took her hand, patting it paternally. "I wish Perry could see you now. He told me you had 'real grit,' but I don't think he knew how much."

Whitney felt the sting of tears, but pushed them back with a force of will. "Thank you. Perhaps, however, had he lived, I would never have needed develop it."

The turns in the road were as familiar as yesterday and she could see the passing scenery projected in her mind, but as they crested the hill and began the descent to St. John's church, she saw the neat, white sign, its carved letters filled with navy blue: "Winfield Farms. Senator and Mrs. Nelson Dowling Baraday." Her eyes tried to penetrate the brush at the edge of the road, to go beyond the white fences and low growth and trees up to the house, the Georgian dignity dominating green pastures, white stables, and autumn-brown fields of her childhood home. She wished the car would turn into the cobble drive and carry her up to the house and her cozy room, back through time to the safety of childhood.

As they passed the drive, she saw a black limousine approaching the road and the flash of a white face in one of the rear windows. Whitney quickly released the curtain and pushed herself back into the seat before her mother could catch a glimpse of the daughter she was going to mourn.

Lucille would be every inch Boston reserve, Whitney was certain, made ready for this funeral by having buried the Senator only three months before. Whitney shook her head

9

sadly. She had spent a great deal of time thinking about her father's death. It was unusual that he was driving toward Fairfax, Virginia, when he was supposedly coming home to the Valley from Washington. It made no sense that he was driving himself, for he'd always made a point of using time efficiently and he considered the trip from Washington to the Valley a time to work while Phillip drove. Something about the explanation they'd gotten wasn't right, but she was hardly in a position to determine what had really happened, particularly not today.

She felt the car slowing for the right turn toward the church and retreated further into the seat. *Perhaps,* she thought, *this will help close the door on the past once and for all. After all, how can someone with a shiny new life have any bad memories?* As the thought crossed her mind, she shook her head, sadly certain of the answer.

Patrice Rigby longed to open her bag, remove her passport and confirm that she was, indeed, no longer sixteen, but she was afraid she might actually have to explain the gesture to the very sources of her feelings who bracketed her in the back of the family limousine. She settled for removing the small gold Cartier compact that had been a gift from Stephen and studying her reflection.

In the small circle of mirror, she could see the light brown curls which framed her brow, a lacy accent above her slightly arched eyebrows and wide-set eyes. She touched the powder puff to her small, finely chiseled nose, removing only for an instant its persistent shine, then pulled her lipstick from her purse, tracing the generous lines of lips with color.

She pulled the compact back slightly to allow the whole of her heart-shaped face to appear. Certainly not sixteen anymore, she thought, studying herself through her dispassionate reporter's eyes, but a woman of character and achievement. Who, she added in her head with a mental chuckle, was still the child of her parents.

Jeanette Lawson Rigby patted a lacy handkerchief to her nose with one hand, while clutching her daughter's arm with the other. "Oh, Patrice, darling, we do so wish you were home under happier circumstances, instead of this terrible tragedy." She sighed pitifully again. "We had so long suspected our dear Whitney to be gone, but one hopes, one hopes . . ." Her voice trailed off, but Charles Rigby took up the thought.

"Now we have confirmation." He snorted. "What I don't understand is why those Turks suddenly decided to dig her body out from under that damned—pardon me ladies—bridge! After three years of inestimable pleas from the Foreign Affairs Department fell on deaf ears, suddenly Nelson dies in an accident and they dig up Whitney."

Both women turned to stare at him, their similar faces identically horrified.

"Perhaps that was a bit crass, but it does seem curious. Nelson must have sent them two hundred personal letters, along with those from other officials and dignitaries. After all, Whitney knew her share of diplomatic celebrities from her time at the embassy in Vienna. She never had an enemy in this world, that lovely child, and *now* she's truly gone. Perhaps it's a blessing, though, for now Lucille Baraday can lay everything to rest."

Patrice and Jeanette shook their heads in unison.

"Oh, bother. You know what I mean."

Patrice put her hand on her father's arm. "Of course, Father. It's been a terrible shock to all of us." Patrice felt trapped by the closeness of the car, the pressure of childhood friends and memories and, most of all, by the lie she was forced to perpetuate. She had just become accustomed to the idea that Whitney was alive when she was forced to attend her funeral. Life, sometimes, was just too complicated. She set the thoughts aside, reminding herself of the role she had been asked to play. "I am just glad I could come home for the service."

Jeanette sniffed pointedly. "We were rather hoping you would be coming home permanently. It can't possibly be safe in London right now, and I shudder to think of the other places you go. Don't remind me how old you are or how important this career business is to you. Careers may be fine for young ladies who have just graduated, but time is moving on and it's about time you settle down with a proper man and have your children. Patrice, life is passing you by."

Patrice compressed her lips to suppress the smile, reminding herself of her mother's perspective, but she couldn't stop herself from responding, almost defensively, "Mother, some people would think being a correspondent for the *Sunpapers*, stationed in London, following up on all the major European and African stories, is being right in the middle of life. And I have met the man I plan to marry when the world gets right again. You will like him, Mother. He's a fine man from a good family who believes in sharing his medical skills with those who desperately need them."

Jeanette raised her eyebrows, a gesture Patrice knew well to indicate skepticism. "The political unrest in Europe is terrible business, Patrice, but I wish you wouldn't use it as an excuse for not marrying and having children. I want you to have the sort of life people in the Valley have come to expect for themselves and for their families." She sighed. "I see my friends with their grandchildren and I feel great sadness that your life is empty of such joy."

"My life has a great deal of joy," Patrice replied. "I have a job which is fascinating, friends who are caring, and a man of character with whom I will eventually make the sort of life you would like for me." In the silence that followed she heard the firmness in her voice and wished she'd been more gentle.

"Patrice," her father interrupted sternly, "please do not take such a tone with your mother. You can imagine how dangerous we believe your job to be. We do, after all, read your articles."

Patrice was tempted to add, "and you should see the ones which get censored," but decided that would only fuel their fires. They didn't need to know about the exposés she'd written on the Jewish ghettos which had nearly put her into a Nazi prison, nor the raids she'd ridden on with the Spanish guerrillas where they'd fled through the mountains, chased by bullets. Instead, she chose a safer route. "You will meet Stephen very soon, I promise. He can't break away from his work in Spain just now, but soon . . ."

Jeanette's face showed her disapproval. "Well, it seems

improper to us. We know nothing of the young man or of his family. If this were a proper engagement, we would have entertained them and he would have asked your father for your hand. It's all a bit too progressive and avant-garde for us, dear. And this business of your young man using his medical degree to work in the mountains of Spain with sheepherders . . . well, this does not sound like the sort of life we'd hoped our only child would have."

Patrice shrugged, longing to be out of the car, done with the charade and back on the Pan Am Clipper to London or even a bus to Washington. "Mother, these are difficult times. I respect Stephen's work. His family is from San Francisco and I am certain you will meet them when they are out here . . . or," she added pointedly, "when you travel out there." She was greatly relieved when the car came to a stop and Winston opened the door. Patrice took a deep breath as she emerged into the gray drizzle and damp chill. *A funereal day for a funeral,* she thought. She tugged at her black pigskin gloves and buttoned her coat as she waited for Winston to unfurl the umbrellas. She turned away from his frustrating battle with the stubborn appliances, looking instead up and down the line of somber black automobiles, limousines, and touring cars shiny with the moist air, clogging the lane beside the old cemetery behind St. John's.

How much of my life has centered here, she thought, her eyes tracing the outline of the old stone church and its yard. *So many beginnings. I was christened here, confirmed, and graduated into the world. We started each Thanksgiving, outside the church on horseback, ready to ride to the hounds at the Thanksgiving hunt. It was here Tessa and Howland Kenney were married and their two children christened.* She sighed. *And now,* she thought ruefully, *we begin the endings. How did it all get so complicated when it was once so very simple?*

"Come along, Patrice," Jeanette Rigby said as she swept past, her umbrella clutched in one hand, her other arm firmly on her husband's. "Winston has an umbrella for you."

"Thank you, Winston," Patrice said, taking the heavy wooden handle, then turning to follow her parents toward the Baraday family crypt near the center of the small ceme-

13

tery. At least, she reminded herself, she'd always be a child to her mother. Perhaps that was the fountain of youth.

Cesar guided Whitney's limousine to a stop on the roadside next to the churchyard, angling it to give her the broadest view with the least possible chance for exposure. He shut off the engine, then turned slightly in his seat, sliding the glass window open between them. She was surprised at his finely chiseled features and light golden brown eyes. She realized she hadn't even looked at him when he'd held the door for her that morning outside the house in Annapolis where she'd been staying. She chided herself to be more observant. Her life could depend on it.

His voice was low and soft. "Madame, I hope this will be the optimum spot."

Whitney leaned forward and pulled the curtain slightly to the side. "We're a bit far away."

Cesar nodded briskly, extending a brass tube to her. "That's why I brought a spyglass."

She looked up quickly, caught the humor in his eyes, and smiled. "Seems the perfect implement," she said, setting the glass to the window, scanning the panorama in the cemetery.

The glass limited her field of vision but brought everything closer. She scanned the line of vehicles, noticing the drivers reading newspapers or smoking or staring as drivers did, then hesitated at the insolent, cheerful, wonderful fire-engine red MG punctuating the gloom.

"Howland Kenney, if I weren't dead, I'd kiss you!"

"I beg your pardon, madame?"

"Oh, nothing . . . just a nice tribute from an old friend."

She returned her eye to the glass, focusing on the vivid reminder of their school days at Goucher and Johns Hopkins. The MG embodied the fun, freedom, and practical jokes which had seemed would last forever. Howland had been one year older and two years smarter, graduating from both high school and college in three years and beginning medical school at Johns Hopkins before transferring to Cornell's veterinary school to follow his true calling. He'd been the first to come to the end of his youth, yet now, the red

14

MG blazing in the line of cars indicated that he'd found it again. She wished she could hug him just once more. Quickly she pulled the glass away from the memories, reminding herself firmly that this was a job in her present life, not a visit to her past.

She scanned the cemetery, glimpsing familiar names in marble, tasting the remembrances they stirred, until the crowd of people suddenly filled her view. She raised the glass slightly and the marble and ivy of the family crypt appeared. BARADAY, the stone proclaimed over the grillwork door which stood open. She shuddered, aware of how close she was to being macabre.

"I hope the rain stops," she said to break the feeling.

"It would be easier if the umbrellas were lowered," Cesar said, and she glanced into the front of the car. He held a small, oblong camera fitted with a very long lens.

"What a strange camera," she observed. He extended it to her and she cradled it. "Leica. Isn't that German?"

Cesar nodded. "Unfortunately, yes. It's brand-new technology. It's called a 'single lens reflex.' What you see is what the camera sees. I bought it in Berlin."

"That's what I like about war," she said, returning it. "All issues are always so clearly black and white." Whitney assumed his small smirk was all the smile he'd ever manage, so she was inexplicably grateful for the compliment.

"There are so many things to like about war, it's hard to choose," he replied, returning his attention to the crowd.

Smiling appreciatively, Whitney turned to her glass in time to watch her mother, back straight, head high, steps sure as she walked to the crypt. "Mother," she said quietly, wondering as she had all her life what was going on behind the façade.

Her mother was joined by a small form, and Whitney wondered how Patrice would carry off her difficult role. Probably, she thought, warmly, with flair. She pulled the glass away for a moment, thinking, *Being dead is difficult enough; without Patrice this would be the worst possible nightmare.*

*   *   *

"Mrs. Baraday, I just arrived late last night from London. Please accept my condolences."

Lucille Baraday's eyes were clear of tears. Patrice was not surprised.

"Patrice. How good of you to come. Your parents must be pleased to have you home. How long will you stay?"

"I am only here for a few days, unfortunately."

"Perhaps you will call on me before you depart, Patrice. I would be most interested to hear about your life in London. I read your articles and you seem to have a fascinating career."

"Thank you; I shall call." Patrice had stepped to the place her father had indicated as she reflected on Mrs. Baraday's emotionless eyes. She wondered if the façade ever cracked, ever opened the slightest bit. Perhaps, she thought, even the tiniest crack would bring it tumbling down.

Patrice heard a muffled sniffle and turned to see Tessa, her arm through Howland's, her eyes puffy with weeping, pressing a damp hanky to her pinkened nose. She slipped away to give the tall woman a hug, then one to Howland.

"I hate this," Tessa said, her voice quavering. "We've all known for years that Whitney was . . . had been . . . didn't . . . survive, but this just makes it all so . . ." Two tears teetered on her lower lashes, then plunged down her creamy cheeks.

"I hate it, too. Everyone on the Pan Am Clipper thought I was crazy, but I couldn't stop sobbing. Now I seem to have run dry." Patrice looked at the couple, so matched and perfect, and felt a terrible longing to belong so completely to someone. Suddenly Stephen's dedication and her career seemed but playing at life. "The only good to come from this is that we've managed a reunion. I think Whitney would like that."

Tessa attempted a wobbly smile and Howland nodded his agreement. "I think she'd like us to play a joke in her memory, but I haven't been able to think of anything that wouldn't be just horribly bad taste."

Patrice turned her back on the assembly as she struggled with her smile. "Can you imagine? I'm certain you're right.

16

It seems like I saw her only last week." *It's not much of a joke, Whitney,* she thought, *but it'll have to do.*

"Actually, I'm afraid the last time I really saw Whitney was that terrible Thanksgiving hunt. Christmas of that year, we went to Virginia and then I was at Cornell. It seems so long ago when you think of what's happened . . . and it seems like yesterday."

Tessa was staring at her husband, astonished. "Why, Howland, how . . . poetic."

He shrugged uncomfortably, patted his pocket, took out horn-rimmed glasses to polish them as both women watched on.

"You're exactly right," Patrice concurred, giving his elbow a squeeze. "Tessa, Howland, I feel certain Whitney knows we're here, together again, and is glad for it. Perhaps we can spend some time together before I go back Monday."

Tessa hugged her again. "Please, Patrice, come to the farm. We live at Knollwood, you know. Howland's parents are retired to the farm in Virginia. The property demands less attention and the weather there seems more . . . ." She hesitated, realizing she was rambling. "Anyway, please promise you'll come over."

"I promise, Tessa." As Patrice walked away she thought Tessa Warfield Kennedy had turned out to be the real beauty. No longer the gawky girl whose parts seemed only rarely to be attached to the same controlling brain, she was now slim, graceful, and elegant, even with puffy eyes.

Patrice resumed her place beside her parents and Lucille Baraday, glad the drizzle seemed to have stopped and the umbrellas lowered. She caught Colonel Donohue's eye for a fraction of a second as she skimmed the assembly, but he didn't acknowledge her as her eyes moved on with abrupt secretiveness.

The senior Warfields had joined Tessa and Howland. Patrice was surprised to see how much Tessa had become like her mother and how little her mother had aged, still straight-backed and vigorous, her hair ungrayed. Patrice could imagine the missing member of the family, Buckingham, Whitney's childhood sweetheart, though both had vehemently denied it, who had joined the RAF and been shot down over

France. The RAF had sent a cable the preceding May to the Warfields saying he was being held in a prison camp, but they had heard nothing since. Jeanette had told Patrice the Warfields were optimistic he'd be just fine.

If, Patrice thought with irony, *anything about this war would be just fine.*

"Beloved friends, we have gathered here today to bid farewell to our dear Whitney, daughter of Nelson and Lucille Baraday, a true child of this valley."

Patrice watched as everyone turned slightly to face the Bishop, rustling, then quieting, leaving only the leaves to whisper around his rich voice.

"Whitney, the golden-haired child of constant surprises, left this world in 1937, a perilously short life into which she managed to inject a great deal. Her life seemed complete as she traveled the world with her late husband, the Earl of Swindon, Peregrine Frost-Worthington, whose own life ended in tragedy. After his untimely demise, she could have retreated into grief, but instead accepted a position on the staff of the American Foreign Service, managing the social functions at the embassy in Vienna."

Patrice blinked hard at the tears which stung and threatened to spill down her cheeks, reminding herself that Whitney was still alive. Yet the Whitney about whom the Bishop spoke was gone and would never be again. Her demise deserved to be mourned, for it was a spiritual death if not a physical one. Patrice looked down and the tears slid. To regain some decorum, she glanced at the other faces around the crypt, then caught her breath at the group of figures who approached from the road, led by Boyleston Greene.

Tie askance, hair mussed, suit rumpled, Boyleston marched unsteadily through the marble stones as the leader of an unwelcome parade. Quickly, Patrice glanced back at the Bishop, who continued speaking, either unaware or unacknowledging, and then at Donohue, who followed the dart of her eyes back to the approaching group.

Boyleston had been a funny drunk when they were young, six or seven years older than the group but welcomed for his outrageous antics. He'd lost favor when he'd allied himself with Harold Smythe and his overt German sympathies. Now

18

he'd become a complete pariah. He looked old and mean and disgusting. Patrice wanted to order him away imperiously, particularly when she saw the rest of the tardy mourners.

Harold Smythe stood next to Boyleston, placing himself between the obviously intoxicated man and Mrs. Smythe, who looked gray and wispy in a black coat and hat. She didn't seem to know where she was, looking first at her husband, then at Boyleston, with gentle puzzlement as though awakening in a strange room. Patrice felt sorry for the woman who had been such a welcoming hostess to Whitney, Patrice, and all the others when they were growing up with her own daughter, Laurel.

Patrice resisted showing her distaste as the Smythe party joined the rest of the assembly. She was most astonished by Harold Smythe's enormous girth, his body misshapen with rolls of fat, noticeable even under his coat.

Patrice looked back to their car, which was parked, engine running, in the middle of the lane. Two blond men stood beside it, their arms behind their backs, their eyes scanning the cemetery. Patrice wondered what had become of the Smythes' driver, Willie, who'd given each of them patient driving lessons when they were teenagers. Willie couldn't have been retired, she felt sure, for he'd be in his late forties or early fifties. The strangers made Patrice uncomfortable, and she wondered why they were behaving like guards instead of drivers.

When Patrice looked back to Harold Smythe, he was joined by a redheaded woman waving gaily to Patrice. Laurel Smythe Pugh! Patrice turned her head away as though she'd not seen the inappropriate gesture. The two strangers had to be Helmut Pugh's watchdogs, since Laurel's wealthy German industrialist husband didn't seem to be with them. How dare Laurel come to Whitney's funeral. They were hardly friends, particularly after the accident on Thanksgiving so long ago that Laurel had not only caused but gloated over.

There had been a tight knot of children in the Valley when they were young: Tessa and Buckingham Warfield, always the tallest, Buck with his long legs and sly sense of humor, Tessa always thinking she was too tall and always in love with Howland Kenney.

Buck had joined the RAF and was listed as missing in action. Whitney had told Patrice of their coincidental meeting in Paris when both Buck and Whitney were being smuggled out by the underground. Buck had not survived, and Patrice's knowledge of this secret seemed a more terrible burden than the truth that Whitney still lived.

Whitney had always been the ringleader of their mischief—the sprite of games and good times who could take nothing seriously except her beautiful Edgewood, the magnificent horse she loved. Whitney and Edgewood had been a unit, thinking and moving as one through the field of the hunt, Edgewood sure of his footing and careful of his burden, Whitney trusting the instincts of the giant horse.

Laurel had been a chubby, freckled, redheaded girl, an outsider from the moment of her birth to a mother who was a child of the Valley and a father who was not. Laurel had been a spoiled only child, never deprived of the things she wanted, but never able to have the love of her father and the unconditional acceptance of her friends.

Still, Laurel had been included, given a ride home from school for holiday weekends, invited to the parties until the terrible Thanksgiving Day hunt when Laurel had deliberately ridden her horse in front of Edgewood just as he began a jump, distracting him and sending him into the stone wall, breaking his neck.

After that there had been no effort to include Laurel. Her exclusion had paralleled the ostracism of her parents as Harold Smythe's financial shenanigans with the Germans during and after the Great War became too blatant to be politely ignored.

Laurel's wedding to Helmut, the son of the owner of the enormous Pugh Machenwerks, had been a further embarrassment to the people of the Valley as she paraded him around and bragged openly of his wealth and association with Hitler. Patrice glared across the churchyard at the redheaded woman and her family, now more than an embarrassment as their open support of Hitler bordered on traitorous.

". . . her love of horses and her beauty as she rode. None of us will ever be able to erase the picture of Whitney

20

bending over her fallen steed on that terrible Thanksgiving hunt, and perhaps now some will see that as a portent of future pain in her life: the death of her husband on a hunt and her own fatal accident while hunting boar in Turkey. Do not look for signs and symbols in a life, my friends, but share in the delight Whitney showed for everything. . . ."

Patrice could see Laurel moving around the edge of the group, her gaze fixed on Lucille Baraday, who stood beyond Charles Rigby and his family. What, she wondered, could that bitch be up to now?

". . . lay to rest the joy and laughter she shared with all of us, but she will be here forever in our minds and hearts. This is not truly good-bye as much as it is adieu, for we will find our laughing, golden Whitney, I am very certain, in heaven." The Bishop hesitated, watching Laurel, who felt the eyes of everyone on her, and paused. "Let us now pray. Our Father . . ."

Laurel didn't bow her head, but looked around at the faces in the circle, their eyes piously lowered. Her lip curled derisively as she remembered how the world was here— those who were from the Valley on the inside and those who were not from the Valley forever on the outside. Laurel knew that well, being on the outside. She'd felt it her whole life from all of them, hurting as that bitch Whitney had led the others in laughter, teasing Laurel for her red hair and her freckles, acting as though they were better than she, as though their fathers' business deals were better than her father's just because he used the war as an opportunity to increase his fortunes with his German contacts instead of profiteering from the Americans.

They'd hated it when Laurel had married so well. They'd used her successful marriage as an excuse to sever all pleasantries with her family.

Her mouth formed a bitter smile. Well, they had their vengeance, and she was having hers. She knew Whitney wasn't dead, that this was all a sham, but it was a pleasure to see the rest of them mourning and feeling a tiny bit of the pain she'd felt her whole life. She hadn't felt so satisfied since that Thanksgiving when Whitney's horse had died.

Laurel hadn't meant for Edgewood to die. She'd just

21

wanted Edgewood to throw perfect Whitney over the wall so she'd get mud in her blond hair and maybe scratch up her little face. The ruckus everyone had made when the horse had died was ridiculous. It was only a horse, after all, but they'd acted as though she'd taken out a gun and shot one of them.

Now it was only a matter of time until this disgustingly poignant scene could be repeated for real. Whitney would be found and perhaps Laurel would have the honor of attending her funeral twice.

As the senile old priest droned on, beseeching the Lord to take an unavailable soul to his bosom, Laurel lowered her eyes, shutting out the ridiculous assemblage in front of her.

As she bowed her head and listened to the Bishop's words, Patrice was intensely curious about Laurel's motives in being here. She had to know she would not receive a warm welcome, yet Patrice had seen that look of determination many times before, and it wasn't usually a harbinger of good.

". . . amen." The Bishop sprinkled holy water on the casket, paused to clasp Lucille Baraday's hands in silent compassion, then moved toward the church. Mrs. Baraday watched for a moment as the attendants moved the coffin toward the open door of the crypt, then turned to take Charles Rigby's arm. Before she could move away, Laurel approached.

"Such a tragedy," Laurel gushed, taking Lucille's hand. "I just couldn't believe it! What a disaster. You must be devastated."

"Well . . . yes," Lucille replied, seeming uncertain how to respond graciously.

"Whitney was such a beautiful woman. So dear to all of us. I always thought we would all be together again someday, but now she's been taken from us. I can't believe it." Laurel sobbed, patting her handkerchief to her dry eyes. "It's simply devastating. We shall all miss her so. How I long to see her beautiful face just once more."

Mrs. Baraday's discomfort became obvious, and Patrice clenched her jaw to keep her mouth from falling open.

22

Ignoring their reactions, Laurel glanced quickly into the crypt then plunged on. "I know this will sound strange, Mrs. Baraday, but would you object if I opened the casket just for a moment to see our dear Whitney once more? She was my dearest friend and I shall miss—"

"Mrs. Pugh"—Lucille Baraday's voice was arctic—"you know my daughter has been dead for several years and her remains would hardly be viewable. Your unimaginable bad taste is exceeded only by your inestimable nerve. Do you think I am senile? I remember quite clearly your involvement in the death of my daughter's beloved horse, Edgewood, and your intemperate words afterward. This, however, is beyond discussion, beyond even imagination. Please leave immediately."

"Well, I never," Laurel huffed, spinning on her heel and stomping away. Patrice couldn't wait to tell Whitney.

"Can you imagine what that witch is up to?" Whitney mused, pulling the glass away. "Did you get a photograph of her bodyguards? Neither seems familiar, but . . ."

"Several shots. I think we should go now." Cesar started the car as he spoke and Whitney took one last glimpse at her mother, still the picture of dignity and reserve as she walked from the crypt. "I wish we'd liked each other better, Mother. Well, at least you're in good hands with the Rigbys."

The limousine slid out of the churchyard and Whitney released the curtain. The car turned south and began to climb the hill which formed the southern boundary of the Valley. As they crested the rise, Whitney whispered, "Good-bye, Whitney. Rest in peace." She sighed deeply and settled back into the seat, fighting a pall of gloom which had threatened all day, then suddenly chuckled. Her thoughts of the Valley had made her think of riding to the hunt, and of the term they used when the fox hid and seemed to just disappear. "Whitney Baraday has 'gone to ground.' What a ghastly pun," she added after a moment, her mood lightening a bit. "Well, on to my new life. I wonder how I'll like it."

2

Enveloped in the comfort of the automobile, Whitney dozed dreamlessly as Maryland slipped past the still-closed curtains. She awakened as the car slowed, and reached to pull back one of the curtains.

"Washington, D.C., madame," Cesar's voice said over the intercom speakers. "We'll be at the house in Georgetown soon."

"Thank you." She yawned and stretched, then fumbled in her purse, reapplying her lipstick and running a comb through her hair.

Obviously, they weren't returning to Annapolis, and she was relieved. She still felt wary of staying in any one place for too long, fearful of the ominous, unseen pursuers. She'd been in much greater danger running from the Nazis who chased her through France and Spain, but she knew America wasn't safe either. Not now. Not with the world the way it was.

The car slowed, made a sharp turn, and angled downward. Whitney heard a rumble of a garage door closing behind them as the car came to a halt. Cesar alighted and moments later opened the door for her, extending his hand to assist her, and she was, for the first time, conscious of his slender build as he towered over her.

"Thank you."

"If you'll follow me," he said, striding across the deserted, echoing room to an elevator. Whitney stepped in, suddenly aware of how weary she was. They rose silently, slid to a stop, and Cesar opened the padded door, then the outer gate.

"Thank you," Whitney repeated as she entered into an elegant living room. She surrendered her gloves and umbrella to Cesar, then strolled into the vast room, admiring the luxury. The walls were covered with creamy ecru peau de soie. Heavy Wedgwood blue drapes covered the windows. Two couches upholstered in ecru and Wedgwood fabric flanked the fireplace, with wing chairs and loveseats making other intimate areas in the room. An ecru grand piano dominating an alcove at the back of the room displayed a huge arrangement of fresh flowers, adding a splash of soft colors to the soothing blues and creams.

Whitney settled onto one of the couches, set her bag on the glass coffee table in front of her, and resumed her inspection of the room. She noticed over the fireplace a large portrait of a woman, her beautiful, strong face framed with dark hair and centered by huge green eyes. The woman, dressed in formal riding togs, stood with relaxed confidence, two fox terriers at her feet. A smile teased at her mouth and eyes, and her air of vibrancy made her seem about to move. Whitney found herself smiling back at the painting.

"No chiffon gown for you, I see. Well, I think we would be friends."

Her attention shifted to the back of the room. Next to the piano alcove was a large wet bar, crystal gleaming in the soft light, and Whitney thought how good a drink would taste. She was about to get up when Cesar reappeared, this time clad in a white jacket and black pants.

"Would you care for a martini up, olive?" he asked, and she nodded, not as much surprised that he knew as at his altered role.

"Most decidedly yes," she said, watching his economy of

motion as he mixed a pitcher of drinks then poured one for her into a gleaming glass.

Whitney twirled the olive through the drink before taking a sip. "Perfection," she purred. "Absolute perfection."

"And might madame care for canapés?"

"Please," she replied, suddenly aware of how hungry she felt.

He proferred another silver tray. "Dinner will be served at eight. If madame would like, I can show you to your accommodations and you might rest until then."

"And bring the martinis?"

He smiled slightly. "And the canapés."

"Thank you, Cesar."

"My pleasure," he responded, transferring the napkins and olives to the canapé tray and picking up the pitcher. "If you will follow me."

They returned to the elevator, ascending two floors, and Whitney followed his formal, graceful strides down a hunter green-carpeted hallway.

"Colonel Donohue trusts you will find this comfortable, madame. He will look forward to seeing you at dinner." Cesar swung open a door and stepped aside as Whitney entered a tea-rose–colored sitting room, the furniture upholstered in chintz, the room seeming filled with flowers and sunshine. "The bedroom is through that door." He placed the tray on the low table between the loveseat and chairs, bowed slightly, and exited.

Whitney slid out of her shoes, refilled her glass and wandered through the warm, welcoming room into the bedroom, which reflected the rose colors and femininity of the sitting room. She felt sure the woman in the portrait had decorated the house, and liked her even more. Whitney shrugged out of her suit jacket, then reached to unbutton her skirt.

"May I draw a bath for madame?"

Whitney gasped and jumped, then, hand over her thudding heart, turned toward the voice. "My God, you scared me half to death."

The little, round, pink girl seemed to fit perfectly into the room. "I'm so sorry, madame. I didn't mean to startle you.

I'm Cynthia, and I'll be your personal maid while you are here. The Colonel has taken the liberty of having your closets stocked, if I may show you."

Curious, Whitney followed her into a small cedar-scented room lined with mirrored doors. She tried not to look at her gaunt figure as Cynthia opened the doors.

"Dresses, sport clothing, blouses, suits, intimate wear, lingerie," Cynthia intoned, opening doors in sequence. "Shoes, boots, accessories. Formal wear. Please let me know if there is anything else you'll need and I'll purchase it for you."

Whitney looked at the racks and hangers of clothing, colors and fabrics she would have chosen for herself, each garment brand-new. Curiously she slipped her foot into one of the shoes and it fit perfectly.

"This is a little like being Cinderella," she muttered, and Cynthia looked at her wonderingly. "Sorry. This is quite overwhelming. Would you mind drawing a bath, please? I like the water quite warm with—"

"With English rose salts."

Whitney took off her skirt, draping it over a chair, then removed the rest of her clothes. This was all very nice and very thoughtful, but it was also a bit unsettling. These people seemed to know everything about her, even to the extent that someone had bought clothing and shoes for her and was right in every choice. She shook her head to drive out the eerie feeling. Part of the job, she reminded herself.

As she reached for a bathrobe in the closet she looked at herself in the mirror, her slim frame sinewy after the physical trials of her escape from the Germans, the clumsy appliance which held her wooden leg onto the stump of her right leg seeming to be the only thing holding her together.

She began to turn away from the mirror, then hesitated and finally turned to face the reality fully forward.

Somewhere inside the form she saw still lived the gangly child whose thin legs seemed as though they would never assume the curves of womanhood. They'd been perfect legs for riding, long and strong, perfect for running through the fields and playing with the foals.

She smiled at the memory of the tall thirteen-year-old

whose body was beginning to change and who finally became the debutante who flowed gracefully into the stream of Maryland society and womanhood at Goucher College.

The whole world had been her oyster then, a time of limitless possibilities and great joy, marred by two terrible events. First her darling Edgewood, the horse who had been almost an extension of herself, had been cold-bloodedly murdered by Laurel. The second event was a consequence, she had to admit, of her own thoughtlessness.

Patrice had won her first entrée into the world of journalism in which she was now so successful. She'd been hired by the *Baltimore Sun* to write a column of advice to the lovelorn, and the comic possibilities were irresistible to Whitney, who created a few lovelorn letters and sent them in to the paper. She truly had thought Patrice would understand, but when Patrice found out, she'd been furious.

Whitney had gone to tour the continent and Patrice had gone to work full-time at the paper without their ever resolving their feud. During her time in Europe, Whitney had met and eventually married Peregrine Frost-Worthington, the Earl of Swindon. She'd invited Patrice to the wedding, but Patrice never responded.

The feud was finally resolved when she and Patrice had been reunited in, of all places, Madrid three months before when Patrice had been part of the team who rescued Whitney from the Germans.

Whitney's hand dropped to her appliance. In between her marriage to Perry and the reunion in Madrid, life had compounded those early, terrible events. Perry had been murdered after only two years of their perfect marriage and Whitney had lost the baby she'd been carrying at the time of his death, the child wrenching away her heart and her ability to ever have another baby.

She'd been drafted by Donohue out of her grief and into the social whirl of the American Embassy in Vienna where she'd once more opened her heart and fallen in love with a man who was also mysteriously snatched from her. But this time she knew more about why Perry had been killed, and she followed him into the spy business.

From Vienna her new trade had taken her to Istanbul, but

28

this time in pursuit of the man who had killed Perry. She'd been assigned to work with an explosives expert to stop the flow of military matériel from Germany through Turkey.

Whitney's hand traced the straps holding the false leg against her real one, the weight of the wood and metal a constant reminder of that ill-fated mission. In her thoughts she could smell the dry hills through which she and Phoenix had ridden to get to the bridge spanning a wide gorge. She could feel the cold bridge's beams against her back as she slid along, connecting the explosives with wire.

They could hear the trucks coming and Phoenix had urged her to hurry with the wire and the last of her explosives. She felt the tug of the tangle around her right ankle, felt the wire relentlessly holding her against the steel beams, felt Phoenix desperately yanking to free her.

The bridge began to rumble as the first explosions began ripping away its supports. Phoenix and Whitney were scrambling desperately up the hill to escape the rain of metal and roadway that fell all around them when suddenly they were overtaken.

Whitney gasped, feeling the pain again as her leg was hopelessly crushed, grabbing for the support of the wall as she felt the remembered edge of black unconsciousness smothering her.

"Madame!" The voice was sharp in her ear and Whitney tried to pull away, but Cynthia's hands were firm on her arms. "Madame, what may I do to help you?"

Whitney stared at the momentarily unfamiliar face, took a shaky breath. "Thank you. You have done the right thing already." She squared her shoulders and the maid released her arms.

"Your bath is running now," Cynthia said, turning to lead Whitney to the waiting water.

Whitney took another breath, still shaky, and turned toward the filled closets. She took a mauve wool robe from its hanger, then followed the roar of running water into the spacious, old-fashioned bathroom, tiled and echoey, the bathtub oversized, standing imperiously on lion's feet.

She unbuckled the waist harness of her prosthesis, then sat on the chair to remove the leg from the harness. Sud-

29

denly, she had the uncomfortable feeling of being watched, and looked up. Cynthia stood at the end of the tub, staring at her wooden leg and the stump under it. When the maid realized Whitney had noticed, she flushed bright red and turned away.

"Don't be embarrassed," Whitney soothed.

"It must be terrible," Cynthia replied, her back still turned as she fussed needlessly with the water controls.

"At first I thought so," Whitney replied, "but now I have become quite accustomed to it. I didn't mean to shock you."

Cynthia squared her shoulders and turned. "I'm sorry I gave you the impression I was shocked. May I take your . . . limb, Countess?"

Whitney hesitated for a moment, then realized it was important to the girl and nodded. "Thank you." She slipped out of her robe and into the warm scented water, sighing with pleasure.

"It's very nice to be home. Wherever that is."

Cynthia retreated, leaving her alone, and Whitney languished in the soothing bath, letting the scent of tea roses fill her nostrils. Absently she ran her hand over the end of her stump, finally healed after her escape, but lumpy with scar tissue both from the amputation and from reinjuries.

As she touched the healed skin she thought of how it had been when she'd awakened in the German hospital in the Austrian Alps, drugged on morphine and surrounded by people who wanted to keep her that way. It had seemed hopeless she'd ever be anything but a morphine-addicted cripple until Erik von Hessler appeared one day.

Whitney chuckled slightly. Erik. For so long she had thought Erik had murdered Perry, and that assumption seemed confirmed when Erik suddenly appeared in Vienna. When Dragi, the man she'd come to love, disappeared as well, her rage with Erik bore the fruit of vengeance, and that was why she'd become a spy. When Erik came to her bedside at the hospital, he seemed to confirm the desperation of her situation.

In truth, he had been the instrument of her healing, giving her the strength to suffer the torments of morphine withdrawal, helping her learn to walk, then to run, with her prosthetic leg, planning her escape, while all the time keeping the Germans believing he had turned her to work for them. It had taken a long time for her to trust Erik, especially because of his friendship with her husband's nephew Sydney, a man she'd never trusted. Sydney, too, appeared at the hospital and Whitney began to realize she'd been blaming the wrong man for her husband's death.

She ran her hand over the stump again, remembering the day of her escape, crossing the border into Switzerland on a passenger train disguised as a peasant, but held as a prisoner. She'd made them believe she moved slowly, encumbered by her false leg, but when she saw the opportunity to escape in the Geneva train station, she'd shown them how she could run. She'd fled into the ladies' room, woman's eternal refuge, where God had intervened on her behalf.

Whitney turned the faucet and allowed more hot water to run into the bath, then leaned back again. She let herself drift back to that tiled haven in Geneva. Outside she could hear the SS guards frantically looking for her. She'd looked around desperately, finding each possible escape route closed: bars on the windows, no air ducts to hide in, no way to get out without being seen.

That was when the miracle had happened. A group of nuns had come rustling into the room, their wide white mantles buttressing their sturdy, smiling faces. Before she knew it, Whitney had found the courage to ask for help and found herself in a habit and being hustled to safety, rescued by the Sisters of Mercy.

She drizzled more salts into the water, swishing her hand to mix them, shaking her head as she remembered the horrible hours at the American Embassy, where she'd gone hoping to be flown home. Instead they'd told her she was dead and imprisoned her as a spy. She'd stolen some painter's coveralls and escaped once more, fleeing into France and back into the chase with the Germans.

French Resistance fighters got her to sympathetic Basques who were her escort to an escape from Madrid. She rubbed the lumpy mass, recalling the horrible pain it had given her as they rode and walked through the rocky peaks. One night she'd removed the leg to wash out the tattered lambswool

31

pad which was the only protection her stump had and found a secret compartment in the leg. As she opened it, a sparkling slither of diamonds filled her hands—and immediately the hands of one of the guides. As he fled with the stones she realized what the Germans had been intending for her to do in Geneva.

Just as she thought she was going to die from the pain in her leg, she'd been saved by an American doctor working among the Basque freedom fighters. Whitney shook her head at the memory of Stephen, who the fighters called *El Doctore Miracolo*. The Doctor of Miracles had been that for her—and, she later found, for Patrice as well.

"Small world," she said aloud, the room echoing her voice. She looked over at the leg which Stephen had made for her as he worked at repairing and mending her body and her spirit. Eventually she was ready to go on to Madrid.

As she had many times before, Whitney wondered if she would have left the safety of the mountains if she had known what was waiting for her. She had been sent to meet one of Donohue's agents in the center of the Plaza Major at night, and to her delight, that agent was Erik. Before they could flee, however, the night brought one more terror—Sydney, her nephew by marriage, had plunged a knife into Erik, trying once more to take away a man she loved.

Whitney's rage was still fresh, months and miles later. In the water, her right hand closed around the memory of the knife she had pulled from its hiding place in her "Stephen" leg. She could remember stabbing Sydney again and again, her hatred for him making her arm strong as she finally got the revenge she'd sought for her husband and her baby.

Strong hands had pulled her back then, the strong hands of William Donohue, who had carried Erik away from the center of the square—into that astonishing reunion with Patrice, who'd been looking for her as hard as the Germans had been—and finally to her own funeral.

She sat up in the cooling water and briskly scrubbed soap onto a cloth.

"It's very nice to be home."

*   *   *

"I hated your funeral!" Patrice said again, taking another sip of her scotch. "I hate lies, you know, and it was just one big lie. But you would have loved what the Bishop had to say about you, and you really had quite a nice turnout."

Whitney sipped another of Cesar's perfect martinis, letting Patrice wind down.

"You haven't changed, you know? You're still jousting with injustice at every chance."

"Of course! And I *have* changed. Anyway, Tessa and Howland were there and—"

"And came in the MG," Whitney interjected quietly, putting a spoonful of caviar onto a toast point.

"Yes. And you'll never ever guess who else showed up!" Patrice continued, oblivious to Whitney's interruption.

Whitney gave a moment's thought to replying, then decided she couldn't take the wind out of Patrice's sails so ruthlessly. She'd done that once and it had cost their friendship ten years. "No, who?"

"None other than Boyleston Greene, drunk as you please. . . . And Harold Smythe, who is positively obese and disgusting. . . . And"—her eyes quickly saddened—"Virginia Smythe, who looked just awful. Oh, Whitney, I'm afraid something terrible has happened to that dear woman. She was always so good to us. Oh, and their car wasn't driven by Willie, but by two men I'd swear were perfect Aryans. Creepy!" She took another sip of her scotch, then leaned closer to Whitney. "But the *pièce de résistance* was the appearance of none other than our dear old enemy, the redheaded horror, Laurel Smythe Pugh! Can you believe she had the nerve to show up at your funeral? And—you won't believe this—she had the nerve to pretend she was deeply upset. And—you won't believe this—she actually asked your mother if she could . . . this is so morbid . . . could see you once more!"

Whitney's glass stopped halfway to her lips. "I wondered what she was saying, but I never imagined . . ."

"You wondered . . . how did you know?"

Whitney sipped, then set her glass down. "I was there. In one of the limousines."

Patrice shook an admonishing finger at her. "I should

33

have known you wouldn't be able to resist the ultimate practical joke." She popped a caviared toast point into her mouth. "That must have been a very strange feeling. Why?"

Whitney shrugged. "Just wanted to see how the turnout was." She took a large swallow of her drink. "And because we thought something might happen. Have you seen the Colonel? Did you tell him what Laurel asked?"

Patrice nodded. "I rode down here with him. His reaction was about the same as yours, almost as though he expected it."

"He did. How did my mother bear up?"

Patrice sighed. "Better than anyone else. Tessa, my mother, Mrs. Warfield—well, just everyone—and I, of course, were sobbing and snuffling, but she was just impassive, as though she were hiding behind a mask. What a strong woman she is."

Whitney finished the rest of her drink quickly and Cesar stepped to refill her glass. Before she could comment, Colonel Donohue entered the room, accompanied by three people Whitney didn't recognize and one she did.

"Dr. *Miracolo*," Whitney said, returning the kiss he placed on her cheek. "How nice to see you in a civilized situation. And how surprising. When did you come in from Spain?"

Dr. Stephen Forrestal was obviously trying to maintain his dignity, but his eyes kept jumping to Patrice as he took Whitney's hand. "Just this morning, as a matter of fact. I must say, you're so much lovelier when you've had a bath, Limping Lady. This seems a far better setting for you than Basque shepherds' huts or Madrid sewers. I never thought you fit in very well over there."

She smiled. "I couldn't agree with you more, though I don't know what I would have done there without you."

His expression became serious. "How are you feeling?"

"Fine. Are you here for training as well?"

He shook his head. "No, William asked me to design a couple of special appliances for you. He seems to think one leg isn't enough."

Whitney chuckled. "Sometimes two hardly suffice. Now why don't you greet Patrice before you both burst."

Forrestal actually giggled as he swept Patrice into his arms and out of the room. Whitney smiled a greeting at Donohue. "Colonel." She extended her hand and he bowed low over it. "Isn't love grand?"

"Countess. Indeed. And Dr. Forrestal is correct. You do seem quite at home here."

"It's a lovely house. Beautifully decorated."

"Thank you. My wife, Laura, was responsible. Though she didn't spend a great deal of time in Washington, this house received her special attention. That is her portrait over the fireplace."

"I regret I never met her," Whitney said, recalling that William had once revealed his wife had died of polio years before. Now she could see the profound influence she'd had.

He nodded. "You would have liked her," he replied, abruptly ending the glimpse into his real life. "Now, if I may present some of our colleagues: Lady Primrose Benningham, an expert in firearms, explosives, and hand weapons, as well as communications; Andrew Collins, Raja Abichandri, an expert in codes and coded transmissions; and Paul Sanders Stewart, our expert in physical conditioning and training. Lady Primrose, gentlemen, your students."

"Lady Benningham, I'm so pleased to meet you," Whitney said, extending her hand.

"The pleasure is mine, Countess. I feel as though we've met, for my mother and Lady Elizabeth Langford are great friends. She has told us so much about you and your lovely Swindon."

Whitney smiled broadly. "Dear Lady Elizabeth. How is she?" Whitney's smile didn't reveal the pain she felt remembering those early days with Lady Elizabeth, who had been the one to introduce her to Perry and to a life she'd dreamed of having. Lady Elizabeth had been a dear friend as well as a splendid matchmaker, and Whitney longed for a chat over tea with her old friend. "Has she married yet?" Elizabeth's machinations to attract a husband were legendary.

"I believe she sees the war as the worst possible barrier to her quest for a husband," Lady Primrose said with a wry smile before turning to Patrice, who had just returned to the room, blushing furiously, her lipstick wandering a bit beyond the edges of her lips.

The Raja bowed over Whitney's hand. Tall and darkly handsome would be the best, if the most trite, description, she thought. Not at all what she'd imagined a cryptographer to look like, expecting rather someone doughy with thick glasses.

"I am most charmed, Countess, I'm sure," he said, his voice rich, his accent very British. "I have visited Swindon Castle and admire your restorations there very much. Now that I have met you, I can finally understand what the estate lacked with the absence of its mistress."

"Thank you. But Swindon! How I miss it. When were you there?"

"Several months ago. A cryptographers' training conference."

Whitney looked at Donohue and raised a questioning eyebrow.

"MI5 took advantage of the trust provisions to use the estate in times of national emergency, but don't worry. Frobisher spends each day scurrying about with a rag and a bottle of wood oil in his hands, wiping away any fingerprints in an instant. He overheard so much we finally drafted him. He's now Leftenant Frobisher, and no one ever wore a uniform with more pride . . . or more spit and polish."

Whitney laughed. "You drafted my butler? William, will you stop at nothing?"

Paul Sanders Stewart was tall and slim without the bulk Whitney would have expected in someone in charge of physical conditioning, but she had to admit he exuded an air of good health. His handshake was firm.

Patrice looked at the confidence on his face, the eagerness in his eyes and wondered if she'd ever been so young and so innocent, so filled with more enthusiasm than common sense. Immediately she reminded herself that not only had she been young and innocent and wildly enthusiastic, but it had only been a few years before. What a gulf the things she had seen and done had created between her and this man only a few years her junior.

His grin was positively boyish. "Actually, I'm a graduate

36

of Yale Law School, but the Colonel doesn't seem to need any lawyers right now. Or at least he doesn't think he does. And I'm not at all sure either of you needs me."

Patrice giggled. "Not certainly as a lawyer. I, however, would appreciate some exercises."

Cesar approached and rang three tones. "Dinner is served."

William offered his arm to Whitney. "Tonight we will socialize. Tomorrow you begin training. Perhaps if you genuinely learn to be a spy, you won't think it's such a game."

She smiled, sliding her hand to the inside of his elbow. "And perhaps it will seem all the more so."

"Forgive me, Countess, but if you stab a man in such a ladylike fashion, it's quite likely he'll survive at least long enough to kill you. If I may," Lady Primrose said, taking the combat knife from Whitney, then turning abruptly and expertly thrusting the knife under the rib cage of the dummy and upward. "This motion has much more economy, doesn't take any more energy on your part, and is always instantly fatal if done properly." She returned the knife to Whitney with a bright smile. "Now, Countess, Miss Rigby, again if you please. And this time I should like to see real venom in your thrusts. Imagine the dummy is someone for whom you bear a great animosity. It might add sincerity to your actions. Again, please."

Whitney gripped the knife as Lady Primrose had drilled them, found her balance, then attacked the dummy, envisioning Lieutenant Baer's face over that of the straw victim.

"Lovely, Countess, simply lovely! Now, Miss Rigby, if you please. On our toes; find the balance and let it rip."

Patrice wrinkled her nose, but followed the instructions.

Lady Primrose clucked. "Miss Rigby, you must do that with a truer heart."

Patrice sank to the floor, sighing. "Lady Primrose, I have a lot of trouble murdering anything, even a dummy."

Lady Primrose smiled sweetly, patting her dark curls into place. "Now, now, Miss Rigby, one must not think of this as murder but as self-defense. I hope you'll never need to use it, but should you encounter something which cannot be

37

subdued with logic . . . well, I am certain I need not explain the advantages of having been trained.'' She extended her hand to help Patrice to her feet. ''Now please, Miss Rigby, just once more. Try to think of our dummy as a personal enemy or a vicious assailant, seeking to take your life.''

''Laurel Smythe Pugh, you rotten, evil, traitorous *bitch!*'' Patrice yelled, decisively terminating her target, then turning to the teacher. ''Better?''

''Well, I should say.'' Lady Primrose smoothed her khaki fatigues. ''Indeed. I certainly shouldn't care to be this Pugh woman. You both seem to have . . . grasped the . . . basics, shall we say, of stabbing. I believe we can proceed, in the hour we have remaining, to other objects which might be used should a knife not be available. If you'll make yourselves comfortable, we can begin. Good. Anything with a point makes an excellent defensive weapon. Scissors are an obvious choice; hat pins, a traditional weapon. A sharpened pencil can be quite effective, as can a fountain pen. Knitting pins are most effective, particularly if they are steel; and one must not ignore . . .''

''. . . can't break a hold, just go limp. Your weight will throw the attacker off balance and you can use the opportunity to remove yourself from his grasp. Make sense?'' Paul Sanders Stewart looked at Patrice, then Whitney.

Whitney sighed. ''That may be fine for someone who has both legs, but I am not necessarily as agile or as flexible as I once was no matter how proficient I have become.''

Paul nodded. ''True. You do have an advantage, however, because your leg makes you weigh more than you appear to. An attacker will size you up before he hits you, if he's smart and, frankly the dumb ones won't use Chinese ju jitsu. Anyway, the smart attacker looks at you and his mind registers about one hundred ten.''

''One hundred, actually. I weigh less without . . .''

''Of course. But to look at you, he'll set his body to expect the force and struggle of a woman of one hundred ten pounds. Do you know your weight with your leg in place?''

''About one twenty.''

"That extra ten pounds will disrupt his balance, and you can use that to your advantage. Would you like to try?"

"Whitney, I don't think that's a good idea. What if you hurt yourself?" Patrice fussed solicitously.

"Patrice, I think Paul would be hard pressed to do more in training than his predecessors have done in earnest. Yes, let's try."

"Fine. I'll approach you from the back. Using what we studied, try to break my hold, then disable me." Paul moved off the mat and Whitney turned her back on him, bracing herself.

He ran at her, grabbing her roughly, his arm around her throat. Whitney relaxed immediately, felt him fighting for balance and abruptly brought her elbow back into his ribs, hitting him hard, feeling his breath expel forcefully. She then shifted her weight and swung her good leg in a mighty kick, heel centered on his shin. As he howled, she rotated her shoulder sharply toward her left, then back to her right, breaking free of his grasp. She spun to face him, tucked her head low and butted him in the stomach. With another sharp exhalation, he sat on the mat with a plop. She was about to follow up with a kick when he held up his hand.

"Uncle!" he managed to croak as he fought to regain his breath, lying on the mat, clutching his stomach.

Whitney lowered herself to the mat. "I'm sorry. I thought you wanted me to really try."

"I did. I'll never make that mistake again," he whispered, rubbing his sore ribs. "Let's take a break before I work with you, Patrice. You baited me into this, didn't you? You set me up just to humiliate me. It's not enough I join this crazy organization as a lawyer and end up teaching ju jitsu, but now you couple of smarty-pants ladies set me up. Funny."

"That's exactly what I keep telling William: you've got to have a sense of humor to be in this business," Whitney said sweetly, then added, "I hope I didn't really hurt you."

Paul pulled himself to his feet. "Nothing permanent. Except perhaps my ego. Patrice, are you ready?"

She laughed, raising her eyebrows. "The question is, are you?"

*　　*　　*

Whitney had her towel draped around her neck and Patrice was blotting her face as they boarded the elevator, riding up from the training rooms two floors below the garage.

"Don't you wonder how many other things are hidden in this house?" Patrice said, her voice muffled by her towel.

"And how many microphones listen to every word you say?" Whitney asked, her voice teasing.

Patrice glanced around the elevator, then shrugged. "It's all so . . . Mata Hari." Her face brightened to a grin. "Or maybe Greta Garbo. Did you see that movie? Do you think she ever went through any of this?"

Whitney laughed aloud at the thought of Greta Garbo learning Chinese ju jitsu from a blond Yale law school graduate and weapon use from a young Miss Marple. "I should suspect not. I think Miss Garbo's talents were simply the results of a Hollywood fantasy, and Mata Hari's talents were more horizontal. I don't think they expect that of us."

"Whitney! I should hope not."

The elevator stopped on the floor on which their suites were located, and they went to Whitney's sitting room. Propped on the coffee table were two long, white envelopes, one addressed to each of them.

"What do you suppose?" Patrice said curiously, holding it up against the light from the setting sun.

"Why not open it and find out, dizzy. Patrice, I repeat, you haven't changed one bit in ten years!"

20	23	15	12	1	4
9	5	19	6	18	15
13	7	15	21	3	8
5	18	1	14	4	7
18	5	5	14	19	16
18	9	14	7	1	14
4	12	15	14	4	15
14	13	21	19	20	12
5	1	18	14	3	15
4	5	19	15	18	4
9	5	20	18	25	9

14	7	23	5	19	20
1	18	20	20	15	13
15	18	18	15	23	

COLLINS

"What in the world do you imagine this might mean?" Patrice said, staring at the page.

"I rather suspect it's the beginning of our lessons in cryptography." Whitney glanced at it, then set it down.

"How strange. What do you suppose it means?"

"I think revealing that might be lesson one." She pulled the bell and Cynthia appeared instantly. "Might we please have a pitcher of martinis?" Cynthia curtsied and scurried out as Whitney settled into one of the wing chairs. "Well, before the drinks arrive to addle our brains, let's see if we can work it out. I think he'd hate it if we did."

Patrice's brow knitted. "He's so elegant and so courtly, but there's something about him. . . . Well, he's just strange. And where do you suppose he gets his title?"

"I asked William. His father, Lord Dennis Collins, was a British colonial officer in India, where he married the daughter and only child of the local raja, who then adopted Lord Dennis as his son so the title would not fall to his wicked nephew. Doesn't it all sound like a dime novel? At any rate, our Andrew's mother and father are also sister and brother, which makes him a . . ." Whitney hesitated, looking puzzled. "What do you call the offspring of a brother and sister?"

Patrice giggled. "In this case, Raja Chan-something-or-another."

"If you don't mind, perhaps we could have our brandy in the conference room. Andrew, I understand you will not be joining us this evening."

"Regrettably, I have some business outside with respect to an upcoming series of concerts I will be giving," Collins said, including the group in his explanation.

"A concert tour!" Patrice responded. "How exciting. What instrument do you play?"

"I attempt the piano."

41

"Attempt!" Lady Primrose interjected. "Hardly an adequate description, Raja, if I may say so. Masterful has been said, brilliant, even virtuoso. I have long been an admirer of the Raja's talents at the concert grand!"

"Lady Primrose, you are too generous. At any rate, my American representatives have managed to organize a concert at Carnegie Hall in New York and another one or two in other locations over the next three months."

Whitney was even more curious now about the mysterious man. "Perhaps you will grace us with some of your rehearsals. I should very much enjoy hearing you play."

Andrew rose, bowing to her. "It would be my pleasure, Countess. If you will all excuse me."

Colonel Donohue stood and the others at the table were quick to follow him to the elevator. Patrice continued her conversation with Paul Sanders Stewart about the legal rights and protections for journalists as Whitney listened to the latest gossip from London as related wittily by Lady Primrose. Andrew Collins took his coat, hat, and briefcase from Cesar, then moved toward the front door.

"Oh, Mr. Collins, just a moment," Whitney called, removing a folded piece of paper from her purse. "We two ladies from Goucher and Greenspring and London who must learn codes or die trying would like to present this response to your message." She extended the paper, and he took it with a sardonic smile and a small bow.

"With your permission, I shall decipher the code when I return. Unless, of course, anyone else would care to try in the interim. Is this a form of your own devising?"

Whitney's smile mirrored his own. "It is only a small effort and I'm sure you will find it no challenge at all. We're looking forward to tomorrow morning."

He bowed once more, then exited through the front door.

When everyone had entered the elevator car, Donohue took a ring of keys from his pocket and inserted one of them in the control panel of the elevator. They descended, passing the garage level, office floor, and training floor before stopping. Donohue selected another key, unlocking the grating and solid door and sliding it aside.

Patrice caught Whitney's eye, a quick look of puzzlement

crossing her face, and Donohue said, "No, Miss Rigby, there are no limits to my secrets."

Patrice blushed furiously. "I hate being so obvious."

William took her arm, walking her across a large carpeted expanse to a glass wall in the opposite corner which glowed with light. "Perhaps it is not that you are so obvious as that I am skilled at my profession."

Whitney looked at the desks covered with phones, lamps, and papers, which indicated they weren't unoccupied all the time, and wondered how many people came and went from this building during the day; how many people were privy to the secrets here; what secrets the room hid. The maps which graced the walls carried slashes of colors—obvious plans of attack, as though the people who worked here were already at war. She shivered. *Fate's control room,* Whitney thought as they passed the glass wall and into another, smaller room with more maps and more phones, centered by a large oval table with three lamps hanging low over it. Two figures sat at the table, their backs to those entering. Whitney proceeded to a chair when she glanced up then squeaked with delight.

"Erik," she said, rushing into his open arms, thrilled to again see his handsome face, his tall form, his soft blond hair. "My darling. You look wonderful. Is the pain all gone? Has the wound completely healed?"

He kissed her tenderly, then said, "Yes, I am back to work, which is why I am here."

William was smiling paternally as he came to shake Erik's hand. "Good to see you, my boy. Ladies and gentlemen, by way of introduction, Baron Erik von Hessler has long been a member of MI5 working inside the Nazi intelligence organization. I do not need to mention to any of you the importance of keeping his affiliations completely confidential." His eyes roamed the room, stopping on each face, waiting for agreement. "Erik was instrumental in Whitney's escape from the SS and her return, for which we are most grateful. This gentleman," he continued, turning to the dignified man sitting next to Erik, "is William Stevenson, my counterpart in MI5.

Stevenson nodded briskly, then returned to his seat, and

the rest of the company quickly sat down. Donohue moved to the end of the table, spread his notes in front of him, then looked up.

"Before we begin, I did offer brandy. Would anyone care for some?"

"Oh, yes, quite," Stevenson said, and Cesar appeared immediately with a silver tray, a decanter and some glasses, pouring for each person who requested.

When he'd finished, Donohue nodded to him. "Join us, won't you?"

Whitney and Patrice both looked surprised as Cesar removed his white jacket, poured himself a brandy, and joined the rest at the table.

Donohue waited until he was settled, then said, a twinkle in his eye, "In this business nothing is as it seems, ladies. Cesar Ball is one of our most senior operatives. Remember this lesson: reality is only believed illusion. Now, on to our business. First, let me set the background. When Whitney left the Nazi hospital in Austria, they felt they had turned her, so she was acting as a courier for a large fortune in diamonds being moved to a bank in Geneva. The diamonds were hidden in her false leg. Instead of cooperating, however, she slipped away from her guards and escaped. Through some bureaucratic bungling in the American Embassy in Geneva, she felt threatened there and left before we could help her, and fled, chased by the Nazis and us through France and finally into Spain. During her journey, the diamonds were stolen from her, but she accidentally discovered an additional hiding place in her leg which contained a microfilm, which she surrendered to me when we were reunited in Madrid. During her flight from her pursuers, her father, Senator Nelson Dowling Baraday, was killed in an automobile accident. Erik?"

Erik rose. "Thank you. After Whitney's departure from a safe house in Britain, I returned to my post in the German organization, still giving the illusion I was pursuing the Countess and the microfilm which Germany believed she did not know she carried. I was able to find out what that microfilm contained and why it was so important. Before I

44

explain that, however, I must give you some background information.

"In the twenties, several German industrialists developed a machine to keep their corporate communications secret while transmitting documents. This machine, named Enigma, appears to be a typewriting machine but is special in that it was able to translate normal language into a random code which can only be translated by another Enigma machine programmed for the same code. The codes are complex but can be changed by simply moving a lever. It could be said the machines are able to think. I do not need to tell you of the value of such a machine to an intelligence organization, and the German intelligence organization was quick to adopt it, making their codes unbreakable. The existing machines are guarded more carefully than Hitler himself, but there has been a persistent rumor of two machines in the possession of the Allies, which makes Hitler frantic." He grinned slyly. "These rumors are true, but he doesn't know that. In an attempt to keep the Allies from ever deciphering his messages, he commanded a revised machine be built with a different set of encoding instructions, which would render the rumored Allied machines useless.

"The microfilm Whitney surrendered to Donohue contained the only copy of the completed parts of the plans for the improved Enigma. The Nazi scientists working on the machine destroyed their original documents once they had been microfilmed. Eventually all the microfilms would be gathered under the eyes of Hitler himself, and it was there the machine would be assembled. The microfilm Whitney carried was the plan for the encoding tables, the most important part, and the scientist who devised them was mysteriously murdered before Whitney and her cargo disappeared. Therefore, the microfilm is more than urgent to the Nazis—it's irreplaceable."

Whitney gasped, her hand dropping to her leg. "No wonder they have been so interested in where I was."

Erik nodded. "You are the number-one priority. The ruse of the funeral was not believed at all. We have managed to send them scurrying to Australia to look for you with a false lead, but it is only a matter of time until they are back on

45

your trail. Your cover is going to have to be a good one, for they call the search Operation Limping Lady."

Whitney couldn't help looking over her shoulder warily, then shuddered. "How I hate that nickname," she said.

Erik put his hand on her shoulder. "You are quite safe here, and I feel sure William will keep you that way even when you have completed your training." Erik sighed, fiddling with his pencil. "There is an additional piece of information I have gathered which may be painful for you, but must be told." He held her eyes with his own intense blue ones, her hands hidden inside his. "I'm sorry, Whitney, but I have every reason to believe your father was murdered by Nazi agents searching for the microfilm."

Donohue nodded. "His office was broken into the night he died and it had been searched thoroughly. We had hoped it might be random coincidence, but now at least the focus of the Germans' campaign is revealed."

Whitney listened numbly, Erik's hands forgotten on her own, tears stinging her eyes. *Now,* she thought, *the game has become deadly serious.*

46

3

LUCILLE BARADAY SHIVERED slightly, then drew her robe more tightly around her, glancing up at a sudden flare in the fireplace of her sitting room.

She sighed, reaching for the pot of tea, but she could tell the liquid would be cold even before she poured, for the pot felt chill to her touch. "Hrumph," she snorted, tucking her silver place marker onto the top of the page she'd been reading and placing the book on the table. She rose and moved to the bellpull beside the door. She rang twice, long rings which should certainly have summoned either Matthew the butler or one of the upstairs maids. She waited for acknowledgment, tapping her foot, and finally rang once more.

She turned to the fireplace, adding a small log, then fussing with the poker to adjust it properly. Nelson had once mortified her by telling someone she was the best fire-tender he'd ever met, as though it were a talent to be respected or even discussed.

Lucille shook her head. How very different they had been, she and Nelson. He had loved pounding across fields and fences astride a horse no matter the weather or temperature, and she hated everything about horses and riding, including

47

the clothing. He had adored sailing and that terrible boat he kept on the Chesapeake, which to her had never seemed to be anything but nauseatingly choppy and deadly boring. Nelson was adroit at social functions but truly hated what he called the "phony necessities," while she adored entertaining. She loved the theater and concerts and opera, and he invariably fell asleep. They had both known and acknowledged their differences, and he'd once observed the only two things they had in common were Agatha Christie and Whitney. She sighed. It had been true. He hated chowder and scrod and her Boston accent, she loathed Maryland terrapin soup and soft-shell crabs, and yet they had loved each other beyond expression.

"Oh, Nelson, darling, I miss you so much," she whispered to his silver-framed photograph which graced her mantel, caressing his black-and-white smile briefly with her fingertips. "Now, where is Matthew? Minnie? I am growing impatient."

She pulled the bell again, then opened the door to listen for footsteps. The house was still, the lights of the hall glowing softly.

Lucille spun on her heel, swept to the table, and retrieved the tray. "One is hard-pressed to find good help these days," she muttered as she strode down the hall toward the stairs. "And one of them is going to be hard-pressed to find other employment without a reference from me," she added, irritated by the unbalanced heaviness of the tray as she descended the dimly lit staircase, her steps silent on the thick carpeting. As she reached the bottom, she sighed with a bit of relief at having navigated the stairs so well with the tray. The tea had become a secondary consideration; now the issue was simply being answered promptly when she rang. As she crossed the foyer, she determined that if no one else were about, she would rap on cook's door when she reached the kitchen. It was bad enough to have to carry a tray downstairs without having to make the tea as well. Lucille hesitated for a moment, realizing she had no idea how to properly make tea.

A strange noise coming from the Senator's office halted her progress. It had only been a slight scraping sound, but

48

Lucille felt certain it was not one of the natural noises of the house. She slid the tea tray onto a hall table and opened the door to his study.

"Who are you? What are you doing here?" she demanded loudly of the three men who turned at her voice. For one moment, the four of them were frozen in a tableau of mutual unexpectedness. "Get out immediately," Lucille added, trying to recover, but her voice was barely a small squeak.

With silent deliberateness, two of the men sprang toward her, grabbing her roughly before she could pull the door closed, dragging her inside the room, yanking her arms behind her.

"No," she cried out, "please. Please, you're hurting me. Matthew, help!"

One of the men punched her and as her face turned with the force of the blow, she saw Matthew, his head bloody and misshapen, lying behind the couch.

"No," she screamed, twisting, trying to pull away from the hands which restrained her, kicking backward. She felt her foot connect with something, heard a gasp and, to her surprise, found the hands holding her loosen for a moment. She kicked back again viciously and was rewarded with a grunt of pain and a further momentary release. It was all the encouragement she needed to pull free. As she spun away, she grabbed the chunk of Wyoming jasper Nelson had brought back from one of his outdoor adventures in the Rocky Mountains. She clutched it tightly, then swung her arm in a wide arc, striking one of the men who rushed toward her. She watched, fascinated, as he seemed to melt into unconsciousness before her eyes. A second man was approaching her headlong and she threw the rock at his face, pleased but astounded to see blood blossom on his forehead as she scurried between the leather couch and Nelson's desk, seeking refuge.

Directly in front of her one of the French doors stood open, and she plunged through it into the night, pulling up the skirt of her robe and fleeing out onto the back veranda of the house. *Run,* she urged herself—for the first time wishing she'd been more interested in some of Nelson's physical pursuits—*run!* She could hear the third man behind her as she rushed into the back garden, feeling the lilac branches scratching her face and arms, wrenching one way then the other as she fought to escape her pursuer and the boughs.

Lucille could hear the man chasing her as he crashed through the hedge and she paused, unsure of where to go, but knowing she had to hide. Frantically she looked first one way, then the other, hearing only his cursing and breathing. In the dim starlight she could see the white frame stables to her left, seeming miles away, but then her eyes fell on an immense evergreen nearby and she thrust herself toward it, scrambling through the tangle of spined branches to crouch, cowering, behind it, for the first time tasting the salty copper of blood in her mouth.

The man paused not twenty feet from where she hid and she tried to hold her breath so he wouldn't hear her. It seemed an eternity he stood there waiting for her to make a mistake, but she was determined he would not do to her what had been done to poor Matthew.

"Forget the woman," a voice called from the direction of the house. "She can do nothing before we get out. Come back."

The man started to move, and Lucille had almost been tempted to rise when he paused again and she held herself still. Finally he began to move away, his steps thudding on the soft ground, but she stayed, shivering uncontrollably, hiding in the hedge until she was certain he'd gone. Then, slowly, cautiously at first, she rose, peering into the hostile dark. When she finally decided she'd not been deceived, she fled across the driveway feeling very vulnerable in the open. When she reached the door of the stable, she flung it open, throwing herself inside and running down the brick walk between the stalls.

The horses, roused by unfamiliar steps, began to move in their stalls and make noises. "Hush, please," she whispered. "Don't give me away. Don't tell them I'm here."

"Madame?"

Lucille spun, a scream bursting from her. "No!"

"Madame, it's me. Herbert. What's the matter?"

50

"Oh, God, Herbert. They're in the house. They've killed Matthew and they're after me. Hide. We've got to hide."

Old Herbert, teetering on the brink of seventy-five, loyal groom for the Senator and his father, stared at her, convinced Madame had finally succumbed to the pressures of the disasters of the past six months.

"Herbert, now!" Lucille commanded, and he was finally inspired to action.

"This way, Madame, and mind your step," he said, scurrying with her back toward the door she'd entered, but she hesitated.

"No. Don't you understand? They're chasing me and they're out there."

"Madame, we won't go outside. Now please, Madame, come with me."

She paused, then they both heard a sound outside and she rushed to follow him. Herbert opened one of the stalls. "Here, Madame, and please keep quiet. I'll see to the intruders."

Before she could object, he closed and latched the door and she heard his steps as he rushed to the door. "Who are you? What do you want?" Lucille heard him say, then, to her horror, a gunshot and tires spinning on the gravel drive.

"No, no, no, no," she repeated, cowering in the corner of the stall, afraid to move and afraid not to. "No, no, no, no, no."

"Has it really been six weeks?" Whitney asked, reassembling the Sten gun for what seemed the ten thousandth time.

"Yes, hasn't it flown by?" Patrice chirped, snapping the barrel of her gun back into place and rubbing it down with oil. "I can hardly believe how fast it's gone."

Whitney looked up from her task. "Years ago, in another lifetime we shared, I told you the one major flaw in your character was your unfailing cheeriness. You've gotten worse, I think."

Patrice pursed her lips. "Whitney, haven't you had a good time? I think everything we've learned so far has been fascinating."

Whitney smiled, easing the harshness of what she'd intended as teasing. "Actually, yes, though I shudder to think we may have to use all this."

Patrice stopped polishing her weapon. "And I shudder to think we may not have learned enough," she said quietly.

"I didn't mean for you to go from cheery to terrifying," Whitney responded, feeling a chill slide down her insides.

Patrice sighed. "I meant that more for myself. Remember, I have to leave this afternoon to get back to work. I've more than exhausted my vacation allowance and Colonel Donohue says Raven has begun sending very nasty cables to the *Sunpapers* office in Baltimore asking where and who I think I am. I spoke to them today and they would like me to be in New York tonight to cover a big end-of-the-campaign dinner for President Roosevelt." She shook her head. "I'd completely forgotten this was an election year."

"I was living in Europe when he was elected for the first time and now he's trying for a third term," Whitney said, almost to herself. "How strange that seems." She shook her shoulders, pulling back from a sensitive area.

Patrice waggled her finger at Whitney. "Now stop that! It's only eight years, not the lifetime it sounds like, and besides, you'd better be cheerful. I don't want to recall you being glum. After all, who knows when we'll see each other again."

Whitney smiled and raised her eyebrow. "I feel certain it will be soon. They wouldn't have spent all this time teaching us all these things just to ignore us." Her smile grew to a grin. "And if we don't get to see each other, at least we can send our gossip encoded."

Patrice's return grin was mischievous. "Knowledge is, indeed, power."

Patrice was running down the platform of National Station in downtown Washington, D.C., looking for the parlor car where she had a private compartment, very conscious of the near-to-departure activity around her, when she heard a familiar voice calling to her.

"Here, Patrice. You've almost passed it."

She stopped abruptly, turning around, but there were no

familiar faces on the platform. "My mind is going," she muttered, turning to resume her search.

"Patrice, up here," the voice said again and again she turned back. "No, up here."

Her eyes followed the sound and, to her surprise, Paul Sanders Stewart was leaning on the frame of an open window, grinning.

"Paul! It's nice to see you, but I can't stay. I have a compartment booked and I'm trying to find it before . . ."

"You have this room, Patrice. And you'd better get aboard, because I think we're about to leave." He gestured toward the end of the car where the porter was beginning to lift the step stool inside.

"Wait," she called, running toward the door. "Just a moment."

A man in the blue-and-brass uniform of the B&O Railroad hesitated, then extended his hand to help her up. "Welcome aboard, miss," he said as she passed him. "You just about didn't make her."

"I didn't even hear them call," she explained breathlessly, "and I couldn't find my car, but my friend is in the parlor, and if he hadn't called . . . well, never mind."

"Yes, miss," he said, turning back to his task.

"Paul," she said as she swept into the room, "Donohue didn't tell me you were going to New York today, too."

He took her briefcase and pocketbook as she talked, helped her out of her coat, hanging it, then gestured toward a seat. "Oh, yes. And New York is only the beginning."

"Really? Where do you go then?"

"I have been assigned to be your partner. I hope that will be agreeable."

"Actually, it would be a pleasure. What cover will you use in London? Can you get a job there as a lawyer?"

He sighed. "Do what I've been trained for? Hardly! This is the part you might hate. It seems our good Colonel has pulled some more of his magic strings and, voilà, Paul Sanders Stewart, cub reporter! Seems I'll not only be your partner but I'll also be your errand boy."

"But you don't know anything about the newspaper business. And I don't ever work with a partner. And I go lots of places where it's much better if I'm alone. And Raven won't stand for it, Donohue or no Donohue. And . . ."

Paul shook his head. "I'm sorry, but it's a *fait accompli*. Raven, you, and I were not consulted."

"Well, then, we'll have to make the best of it," Patrice said, then quickly added, "Please don't think I don't welcome you. It's just not what I'm used to, but I'm sure we'll have a lovely time. Do you drink scotch?"

"Scotch? Why?"

"All reporters drink scotch. You'll just have to learn. As a matter of fact, we can begin your training now, in the club car."

"Political affairs are so boring, but since we're so close to the end of the campaign, maybe there will be some good quotes. From what I understand, *Sunpapers* wants this story written for European . . . well, free European readers, so there will have to be some background on the candidates, their views, and so on."

Paul smiled. "At least *something* I studied is finally coming into my work. My undergraduate major was politics."

Patrice grinned. "Maybe we're going to be great partners."

"Don't jump to any conclusions. I got a C in the one creative writing course I took."

"And then again . . ." Patrice smiled quickly to soften her words. "Remember, we're here as workers in addition to diners. I think we should sit at separate tables. Keep your ears open for anything that isn't common knowledge."

"Do I have to dance with any of the local matrons?"

Patrice grinned. "All of them. And ask plenty of questions. And write things down—verbatim." She reached into her bag, then rummaged. "Oh, nuts. I've left my little notebook in my room. I guess I've lost my edge in the past six weeks. I'm going back to retrieve it."

"How am I supposed to dance and ask questions and write things down verbatim all at once?" Paul sounded genuinely confused.

"Old reporter's tricks," she said. "And if you're going to be an old reporter, you'll have to learn how to do them.

Don't worry, you'll manage just fine. You're such a good talker that you'll be able to get all sorts of inside scoops on the local politicos. Now go be charming and take notes, and I'll be back in a minute."

He looked so cute in his tuxedo—rather like a high-school boy at his first prom. Patrice shook her head quickly to drive that thought away, reminding herself sternly that if she continued to think of how young he was, she would begin to think of herself as old.

Patrice returned to the elevator banks and rang, pulling her room key from her bag, tapping her foot with impatience at her disorganization.

The brass doors slid to the side and she stepped into the car, still looking into her bag as though the notebook would magically manifest itself.

"Eleven, please," she muttered.

"Patrice, is that you?"

She started and turned. "Laurel," her voice was flat. "I expected you'd be in Berlin."

Laurel, red curls piled atop her head, wore a green sequin dress which clung unflatteringly to her generous curves. On one arm was draped an opulent stone marten stole, on the other, a Nordic-type man, blond and handsome with arctic eyes and chiseled features, but, Patrice noted, rather broad hips pushing against his fitted tuxedo jacket. "Patrice, imagine the two of us, you living in London, me in Berlin, meeting by chance like this in New York. My, my what a small world we live in."

"Lucky us," Patrice said, still eyeing Laurel's companion, decidedly not her husband Helmut.

"Patrice Rigby, I'm proud to present one of Germany's brightest young leaders, Reinhard Heydrich. Reinhard is very important to the future of all of us. Reinhard, Patrice is one of my dearest friends from childhood. Oh, I have a wonderful idea," Laurel continued, speaking right over the others' formal greeting. "Why don't you come up to Reinhard's suite in the Tower and have a glass of champagne, and you and I can get caught up. I haven't seen you in ages."

Patrice was about to decline, but her long-dormant reporter's instinct kicked in. "Marvelous," she said.

Laurel was still as poor at holding her champagne as Patrice had remembered, beginning to slur her words after her third glass. Still, Patrice had to admit, though Laurel got louder and gigglier, she wasn't foolish enough to lose control completely, glancing frequently at Heydrich, who hadn't drunk any of his champagne and sat silently watching the two women.

"It's so interesting to hear about what's going on in Berlin and Paris," Patrice finally said, "but you still haven't told me what you're doing here."

Laurel's eyes shifted to Heydrich before she gushed, "Why, I thought you knew. Reinhard came to meet with certain enlightened American businessmen who understand the Reich is the future of Europe . . . and of the world. They'll meet tomorrow here in the hotel."

The champagne in Patrice's mouth turned to dust.

"So what room did you go back to? The one in Georgetown? I've danced with every woman in this room, twice, and not one of them will ever be Ginger Rogers. And the chicken à la"—Paul stopped abruptly. "What's the matter?"

Patrice glanced around them. "I have a scoop which will knock Mike Raven's door right off its hinges." In a low whisper she told him about the meeting, ending with, "and I asked at the desk where the meeting was being held, and I even visited the room."

"You can hardly just walk in. I'm sure the press won't be welcome at something like that."

"Oh," she grinned, "we'll be there. I hope you don't mind getting up early in the morning."

"You can't be serious. What if they find us?"

Patrice shrugged. "Then we'll end up in jail. And someone will come and bail us out. And we'll both have to find something else to do with our lives. Now hurry up." Patrice gestured to the grating covering the heat duct which was conveniently hinged and standing open. "It's going to be a tight squeeze, but it's just too big a story."

"I hate this business already," he said, sliding his feet in ahead of him.

"Hurry up. Someday I'll tell you stories about some of my adventures, which should make you really hate it."

"Politics, gentlemen, should not be the major consideration. We are businessmen, pragmatists. Our job is to keep the nations running so the politicians have something to govern." Heydrich surveyed the faces seated around the conference table. "Mr. Martin, does General Motors care about the political affiliations of the drivers of Chevrolets? And Mr. Jack Arrenson, do you care if the proud owner of a Ford is a Republican or a Democrat? I would venture not, judging from the number of Ford automobiles I see in Berlin and Paris. And the number of Chevrolets. And Mr. Jason Carter, does Texaco have any guidelines for whom may purchase their products?" He shook his head and his motion was reflected by the men around the table.

"I believe you will remember, Mr. Heydrich," Mr. Martin began, "that I have been in negotiations with the President to shift our allegiance to Germany. It is clear to all of us who have lived in Europe that Britain will not be able to hold against the power of the Reich. It would not be to the advantage of America or her business community to lose our holdings over political maneuvering."

"My point precisely, Mr. Martin. I had understood that was the position of General Motors."

Frederick Strass nodded. "I have a number of major investments in both Germany and France, probably amounting to millions of dollars. I'd be foolish to wish those forsaken. It is, as you say, business. And we are not the only men who agree with you. There are many others who admire the way in which Germany rebounded from the Great War and the Depression. An ambitious, proud nation, Germany—much to be respected."

Patrice was astonished and glanced at Paul, whose face was ridged with anger.

Heydrich continued, "My friends, we hear of this support

and it gladdens us, for all too often we see Roosevelt and his corrupt ally Churchill, who try to convince us that the United States is unanimously on the side of England. We laugh, knowing even the American Ambassador to the Court of St. James believes England cannot last. We think two, perhaps three months under the current blitz and England's leaders will topple, leaving the people free to make the obvious choice. But we have come here to ask for your help: continue to pressure Mr. Roosevelt. Take independent action. Delay shipments of matériel to England when you can. Send less than they order or the wrong supplies. Help your true allies win quickly so we can go forward together to the new order.''

Patrice felt sure he was going to snap the Nazi salute and shout, "Heil Hitler," but instead he went to shake hands with each of the men and the meeting ended.

The man Heydrich had identified as Mr. Martin hesitated beside a man who'd not been spoken to during the meeting. "So, Colonel Brecht, now you and ITT will have to make a choice since you've been manufacturing weapons for both sides. Which will it be?"

Colonel Brecht looked at him wordlessly for a long time, then stepped around him. "I am not the only person involved in such a decision. Just as you're not. I have stockholders to think of."

Martin snorted. "Stockholders! How much stock do you have in public control? Twenty percent? Twenty-five, perhaps. You are the president of ITT. You are the man who makes the decisions. Which will it be?"

"Time, Mr. Martin, will tell," Colonel Brecht said, moving away.

The room had been empty for ten minutes before Patrice felt safe enough to swing the door of the grating open and crawl out. She was still horrified at what they had heard, and she could tell by the storm in Paul's eyes that her rage was not unshared.

"These men are selling our country to the enemies! For money!"

Paul leaned against the table, brushing the dust from his clothing. "It's the world's second oldest profession."

"This is the hottest story of the century," Patrice said, excitement mixing with her anger, "and the way to get them punished for what they are doing. It's perfect. Let's go get notes down before we forget."

Paul put his hand on her shoulder. "It's a hot scoop, but I think the only person who will ever hear it is Colonel Donohue."

"Donohue! The only one! You want me to sit on the biggest story of 1941! You're nuts, Paul."

He shook his head. "No, I'm a spy. Just like you."

Patrice slammed the door to the grating. "I am going to hate this business," she sputtered, knowing he was right.

He grinned, putting his arm across her shoulders conspiratorially. "Sometime I'll tell you stories that'll make you really hate it."

"Paul, you are a bastard!" She turned to leave. "Maybe Donohue will let us run it anyway."

"I wouldn't count on it. But think what a wonderful cocktail-party story it will make when this is all over."

== 4 =====

MIKE RAVEN STOPPED to allow a lorry laden with shattered wooden beams to cross in front of them.

"They only skipped once—November second. Otherwise it was a barrage for seventy-six nights in a row. Lately it's been more sporadic."

Patrice shook her head slowly, her eyes never leaving the devastation which scarred every block they passed. "I had read about it, of course, and seen pictures, but . . ." She sighed, then turned to look at him. "How powerless words are in the face of this."

Raven re-engaged the gears and the car cautiously crept through the pocked street. "Pictures, too. Even movies. You saw the newsreels, didn't you?"

Patrice nodded and he continued. "It's perhaps the most frustrating thing about our business. People expect us to see something and, with our words or pictures, take them there to experience it." He turned his head slightly to include Paul, who leaned on the back of the seat, listening intently. "Take notes, kid. This is Journalism I."

"Yes, sir," Paul said, and both Patrice and Raven laughed as he reached for the notebook, then looked embarrassed

60

when he realized Mike had not been speaking literally. He shrugged, then grinned.

"You might just be all right, kid. Now, back to my point. When a newsman is confronted with something like the Blitz, his temptation is to try to capture the whole scene, to give the reader the broad scope. Worst mistake he can make. The most devastating news is intimate; it's one person; it's one family; it's one house burning." He shrugged. "The only one who remembered that during the worst of the Blitz was Murrow."

"We listened to those broadcasts, sir," Paul said. "I had chills." Patrice could hear the excitement of discovery in his voice. Maybe Paul Sanders Stewart could be a newsman, she thought, then couldn't help smiling at the ironic twists of fate which guided people's lives.

"Murrow stood on the roof of a building with bombs whistling down and talked about how he felt and what he saw. Put that narrative under a film of what those bombs did and you have real life coming across to the people in the movie house. Capture that same flavor in words and you've got yourself a Pulitzer." He chuckled. "Murrow scooped all of us, right under our noses. We were out there gathering the 'important story' and he got up on a roof and admitted to the world he was scared to death and nothing anybody else got meant a tinker's damn. And don't call me sir. End of lecture."

Patrice lit a cigarette, struggling to control the shakiness in her fingers—part excitement, part fear. The feeling of security she had from the training in Georgetown evaporated, and was now replaced with the fear brought by the knowledge that it was probably far too little to cope with the reality they were facing. *No, Whitney,* she thought. *Spying is not a game at all.*

She sought facts to corral her fears. "You said the bombing is sporadic now?"

Raven brought the car to a stop again as a figure in a brown overcoat and helmet held up a mittened hand to halt their passage. The first of several overloaded lorries growled into lumbering motion and out of a debris-filled pit.

"Home Guard," he said. "They're women and girls and

vets of the big war and they take their jobs very seriously. If they tell you to do something, do it. Their word is law. About the air raids, some weeks there's nothing. Other times, there will be three or four nights in a row of pounding. The safest place to be is in the underground stations. If you choose the right station, you'll find yourself in the middle of a fine party."

"A party?" Patrice was incredulous.

"You know the Brits . . . stiff upper lip and all. Strange as it seems, this has truly been, in the words of Churchill himself, 'our finest hour.' Charing Cross station had one party that went on for three days, bombs or no bombs. The first three sets of bobbies they sent in to break it up joined in. And if there's not a party, there's certain to be singing or charades or lively conversation. I hear romance is in bloom as well."

The woman Home Guard waved them through with a cheery smile.

"Having seen this, I don't need to tell you that if you hear the sirens, you need to get out of your house and into a shelter." He glanced sideways at Patrice. "Is that clear, Miss Rigby?"

"Why shouldn't it be clear?"

Raven chuckled, directing his comment to Paul. "This innocent act of compliance is a façade, kid. Did you see the wide eyes? Did you hear the tone of submission? Don't believe it for a second." He shifted his gaze to Patrice. "Look, Rigby, I'll make you a deal. Go to a shelter the first couple of times until you understand how the Blitz works; how the bombs sound and how to tell where they're going to hit. Then you won't have to lie to me."

Patrice fluttered her lashes. "Lie, Raven? To you?"

He pointed a cautionary finger at her. "Rigby, I'm not kidding. This is real war and I need you around for a while."

Patrice waggled the pencil between her fingers. "The message that's getting through at home isn't strong enough. My point is this: America's not in this war . . . yet, and there are people at home," she glanced at Paul, "who don't

62

necessarily believe we ought to come in on the side of the British.''

Raven snorted. "Nobody takes Lindbergh seriously.''

She shook her head. "It's gone far beyond Lindbergh.'' Patrice could feel Paul's tension and struggled for a moment between her two loyalties.

"Who? How do you know? How much influence do they have?''

Patrice lit a cigarette, avoiding both of their eyes, vacillating. It had all seemed so clear in Georgetown, but now she understood how very foggy questions of trust and loyalty could be. She sighed. " 'Reliable sources,' Mike," she said, her tone flat. Paul's sigh of relief was almost audible.

Raven picked up a pencil from his green blotter and rolled it slowly between his incongruously graceful hands. "How reliable?''

Patrice felt eight years of trust between them begin to crumble and lowered her eyes to conceal the sting of tears. Suddenly she hated Whitney and Donohue and Paul . . . and herself. She took a drag on the cigarette and let the smoke out slowly. So this was the "greater good of the nation.'' It surely didn't feel good.

"Beyond reproach.'' She hesitated for an instant, then added, "I can't give you specific names, but I can tell you the men who are unconvinced are in positions of strong influence over major corporations.'' Her gaze slipped to Paul. His mouth was compressed, but he didn't try to stop her.

"What are their reasons . . . according to your source?'' Raven too had felt the crumbling, Patrice realized, as his concession to her secrecy seemed an attempt to patch the larger cracks.

"The obvious, I'm afraid. Money. If they choose the wrong side, it will cost them millions.''

Raven sighed. "It's what makes America the best . . . and the worst. Aren't they reading the papers? Watching the newsreels?''

"I think that's the whole problem. The question becomes one of who's winning. Not just now, but next month, next year. Politics and philosophies aren't important. It's prof-

63

its." She leaned forward. "And the rest of America, maybe even the majority, seems to feel that we're safest staying out of it entirely. I think they're seeing the pictures and reading the words and thinking, 'Thank God it's not here.' "

Paul nodded. "I have the impression that many of our countrymen may even believe if Hitler gets Britain, he'll be satisfied and quit and things will be able to go on without change at home."

"So, what do you propose?"

Patrice plunged quickly. "You said it in the car when you picked us up from the Clipper. It has to be intimate. People at home have to begin to believe they're next."

Raven leaned forward. "Isn't that what we've been saying from here for the past four months?"

Her gaze was as strong as his. "Apparently it's not enough."

He leaned back in his chair and Patrice had a terrible premonition that she had finally pushed him too far, but he burst out with a rumbling laugh and she was relieved. Their relationship had always been stormy on the surface, with a tradition of door-slamming and ashtray-throwing as a fitting ending to an argument. They may have fought, but they also made good journalism together.

"Welcome home, Rigby. I hadn't realized how much I missed you." He sat forward abruptly, pointing his pencil at Paul. "Now don't go getting any ideas that this is how reporters are supposed to act. I couldn't stand having two around like Rigby."

Patrice rose abruptly, turned on her heel, yanked the office door open, then hesitated. "It's nice to be home," she said, slamming the door with a resounding crash before Raven's bellow of protest. She couldn't see the grin that spread across his face, but she knew it was there. It was nice to be home.

"Helmut," Laurel hissed in English through her bared-teeth smile, keeping her eyes on the German officer across the table who had been glowering at her husband's drunken state, "if you have any more wine, I will be forced to discuss your drinking problem with your father."

"Yah, Liebschen," he mumbled, reaching for his glass. "So then he will spank me and send me to bed without my dinner."

"Damn you," she hissed, still forcing her smile. She dropped her right hand, quickly reaching under the tablecloth, finding his elbow and jostling it so the wine sloshed from his glass and onto the creamy linen. "Oh, Helmut," she said aloud, deftly removing the glass from his hand, "you didn't spoil your suit, did you?" Solicitously she patted at his lapel with her napkin, turning to face him. "Don't defy me, you sniveling pig. Do as I tell you or I'll ruin you."

He stretched forward to plant a loud kiss on her pursed mouth. "Don't be angry with me, Liebschen," he whined. "I hate it when you're angry with me. I'll be good." He folded his hands in his lap, a contrite little boy, and Laurel turned away in disgust, once more conscious of the contemptuous stare of the officer across the table.

Laurel tapped her long, red nails on the edge of the table, impatient with Helmut Pugh's weak personality. His father was strong and commanding; his uncles were powerful and successful; even his sister had some spine. Helmut, however, was a jellyfish. She glanced at him. He was staring at the molding along the top of the wall, humming some inane folksong under his breath. At least he wasn't drinking, she thought with little satisfaction.

"Dear friends," their host said, rising and tapping his water goblet with his knife. "Welcome." He raised his wineglass and there was a pattering of applause from the forty guests along the table. "Lisle and I are happy to welcome you to our home tonight to celebrate the glorious progress of the Reich." The guests stood, raising their glasses. Laurel yanked Helmut to his feet, firmly planting his water glass into his hand.

"Hear, hear," voices rumbled around the room. Laurel clutched Helmut's elbow to stabilize him, her smile grimly fixed.

"And now, if you will join me in the salon, we are very fortunate tonight to have some entertainment." He waited politely at the door as the guests obediently filed into the

65

drawing room, then supervised the serving of cognac and brandy. Laurel managed to steer Helmut into a wing chair, then stood guard over him. Refusing an after-dinner drink for her husband, she ordered double cognac for herself.

"My dear friends," their host said over the conversational buzz, waiting until it quieted before continuing. "We are fortunate indeed to have so many gifted officers in the army of the Reich, talented not only in their military skills but in the rich culture of our beloved fatherland. Tonight we are honored to have one of the brightest and most gifted officers of the Reich among us, and he has agreed to share his exceptional talent with us. My friends, I give you Reinhard Heydrich."

Laurel glanced quickly at Helmut and was relieved to see his closed eyes and flaccid mouth. At least he couldn't make a scene if he was asleep. As she turned her attention to Reinhard, the ice in her eyes softened and a warm smile danced across her lips.

With a slight bow, he tucked his violin under his jaw, then caressed the strings with the bow. Elegant, wistful music began to fill the room, twisting through the motionless audience. Laurel was captivated; Heydrich's music was so contradictory to the power he wielded in pursuit of his military career. He was amazing, Laurel thought. A giant among his peers, a personal protégé of the Führer himself; a man on whom greatness rested easily. Helmut snorted in his sleep, breaking her concentration, and she glared at him. If she could only meld the two men: Helmut's money and Reinhard's personality. Then, indeed, she would be assured of a stellar future.

Her eyes swept the audience, then hesitated at the passive, doughy face of Lina. Her "dear friend" Lina Heydrich, Reinhard's wife. Lina and Helmut would have been the perfect match; the dumpy little frau and the chubby drunk could have owned a rathskeller in Munich.

Laurel sighed. All things would happen in their time, she assured herself, caressing Reinhard with her eyes. She was destined for greatness and nothing would stand in her way. Nothing!

*   *   *

66

"Chocolate! Ooh, Swiss chocolate!" Patrice took her time selecting a piece of candy from the box Raven offered, inhaling the rich scent. Finally she settled on a fat, dark pillow, swirled at the top, then took a tiny bite. "My favorite. Raspberry cream. How did you manage Swiss chocolates in the middle of the Blitz in London?"

"We have a bureau in Geneva, you know. Actually, I bring it in every chance I can, but not for totally selfish purposes. When people work as many extra hours as the staff in our office does, there must be some rewards."

Patrice licked her fingers, one at a time. "Such selflessness!" she teased, eyeing the box again. "And from someone as addicted to chocolate as you. It's a pleasure to be around a philanthropist."

Raven quickly waved the box under her nose, then offered another selection to Paul. "Far from it, I assure you. I told you my purposes were not totally selfish, but that doesn't mean they're totally unselfish. One more?"

"Ten more," she said, taking one. "Now, before I pass out from too much pleasure, tell us about these mysterious broadcasts. Have you a shortwave radio so you can listen to the Nazis' secrets?"

"Yes, in a sense." Raven glanced at the clock. "I just want you to listen." Raven turned on the radio, waiting while it warmed up, then adjusting the dial. "You don't exactly need a shortwave for this. Unfortunately."

When will the British come to their senses? The people of England have listened to the whining of Churchill and believe that their spirit will survive in the face of a superior power in the hands of the Reich and its allies. The Jews whisper in Churchill's ear that Britain must succeed and he listens to their drivel, not caring that hundreds of good British citizens are dying to save a few slimy Jews.

America and England must begin to see the truth; must begin to muzzle the whining Jews, that inferior race of subhumans; must begin to listen to rational voices who have seen the truth. The British Empire could be great again, could rise with the help and protection of the Reich to its former glory. America could ally herself with the future, rid herself of the Jews who steal the money from her banks and the food from her children, and open her mind to the glories of the time ahead when the whole world will be united, rid of the Jew menace which now threatens to rip it apart.

Surrender, England, not in defeat but to your future. Make war not on your German brothers with whom you have so many ties through history and even through the royal family, but on those animals who want only to steal your money. Listen, America, and realize who the real enemy is. Wake up, Canada, and declare war on the traitors within. . . .

"Who . . . is . . . he?" Patrice blurted, having heard as much as she could stand of the deranged vitriol. "And who allows him to speak on the radio? This is outrageous."

"Pound. Ezra Pound. He's an American writer who lived in Paris after the Great War, then moved to Italy, where he turned his talents to touting Mussolini. For a while it worked, until Italy invaded Ethiopia and the rest of the world began to see what Il Duce was up to. Pound, however, stayed on in Italy. Now he's been given radio broadcasts to spread his madness. They began earlier this month. He calls it the 'American Hour,' but it seems to be less than ten minutes. He's not on every day. Thank God."

Paul had been listening intently. "Damn traitor," he spat, his face glowering darkly.

Raven nodded. "Technically, in fact, he's not. America's still a neutral nation and he's merely expressing his opinion as is his right. Don't mention him at the American Embassy unless you want to lose your head, however, for his harangues have them in a dither. And Pound's not the only one. After the 'American Hour' from Rome, we have an additional treat. Anybody need a drink?"

The Reich would be delighted to help the courageous people of London rebuild their city, and with the technical skills Germany possesses, London would be far more beautiful than ever before. It won't take much, just pressure on the corrupt government of England, to bring London and her brave people under the protection and care of the Reich.

Just think: Germany and England united again as they have been through all of history, standing strong, side by side, building rather than destroying. Believe me, dear friends, our beloved Führer weeps at your agony, prays nightly for the people of England to rise up against their contaminated leaders and strike them down in the name of freedom and racial purity.

Don't be fooled by all their talk of courage and victory. England cannot resist the power of the armies of the Reich; cannot but fall to the might of the modern and skilled Luftwaffe. Believe me, we don't want you to be hurt. We don't want your homes to burn or your children to die, but your leaders do. The time has come, dear friends, to make up your own minds; the time has come to make a choice. Rid yourself of these old men and join with the youth and purity of Germany. Come home.

Patrice had been staring at the radio, at first perplexed, then incredulous, and finally enraged.

"That hopeless, insufferable bitch!" she spat as the broadcast ended, rising to pace across the room in an effort to disperse some of the tension her anger generated.

"Actually, she's more of a threat than Pound. No one here knows who she is, but they'd love to. It's theorized she might be a child of a German diplomat or businessman who was raised and educated in the U.S. Her accent is certainly American." Raven extended the bottle of scotch toward her, and she quickly poured a generous splash and drank it.

"I know who she is," Patrice said, her voice heavy.

Paul and Raven leaned forward, startled. "Who?" they demanded in unison.

Patrice poured another drink, took a large swallow, then said quietly, "She's an American, not a German. I've known her since childhood. Her name is Laurel Smythe Pugh." She set the glass down deliberately, then turned to Raven. "And I want this story more than I've ever wanted anything."

Raven's brow furrowed. "Frankly, I don't think you have the distance to write it."

She spun toward him. "Laurel is mine, Mike, or you have my resignation."

"Jesus, Rigby, who the hell is in charge of this bureau?" He held up his hand. "Never mind, don't answer that. How do you want to handle it?"

"I'll figure that out as I go. Meanwhile, I need tickets to Berlin. And I'd like to take Paul with me. He speaks German and nobody knows him there."

Raven sighed. "My only hope, Rigby, is that someday you have to run a bureau."

Laurel glanced at the back of their chauffeur, then shrugged to herself. If Klaus didn't know everything about their life by now, she'd be astonished. Certainly he was more than aware of Helmut's indiscretions and, she added in a burst of honest appraisal, her own. She dismissed him with a small snort. He was paid to be deaf, dumb, and blind, and if he forgot that, he could find himself on the Eastern front, stubby leg or no stubby leg.

"Helmut," she began, managing to insert both authoritarian threat and wifely concern into the same tone, "please remember who we're dining with tonight and try not to compromise either of us." Although it made her skin crawl to touch him, she briefly caressed his cheek. "After all, we both can gain much from an association with men like Himmler and Heydrich."

The schnapps he'd consumed while dressing had begun to sour his breath, but she didn't flinch as he turned to face her.

"Do you think Pugh Machenwerks needs to pander to Himmler to get business? Himmler has to pander to us." He gripped her wrist tightly. "So what you really want is something for yourself. Yah? Like always, yah?"

Laurel pulled away, rubbing her wrist. "Helmut, don't do that," she whined, "you know how easily I get marks. I just don't understand you, sometimes. You know very well your father is most careful with these people, doing everything he can to please them. I don't think you have any excuse to be less gracious than he, no matter how secure you think your business is with the Reich." She waggled a finger at him. "After all, we want to be in the right position when the English and Americans finally come to their senses. Can't you imagine it, Helmut? Pugh Machenwerks in Moscow and Liverpool and Pittsburgh. Offices in Paris and London and New York. We will have the world."

He cocked his head and studied her. "We and our children," he said slowly. "What about our children, Liebschen? You are always so concerned about what my father wants. Well, you know he wants grandchildren, so what about that? When should we begin having our children?"

Laurel could just imagine how quickly Reinhard would tire of a fat, pregnant woman, but she was also pragmatic enough to know that her continued access to the Pugh fortune depended upon producing grandchildren. She shuddered at the thought not only of her body being misshapen for nine long months, but also at the process necessary to achieve pregnancy. Helmut's drinking had precluded any such activities for a long time and she had no interest in resuming them now. Perhaps she should encourage him to drink, she thought, and continue to manage as she had.

"Helmut, how can you think of bringing a child—our child—into a world at war! Once victory is ours and the world is safe, we will make your father the proudest grandfather in all Germany. We will have darling little Aryans to carry the Reich forward." She managed to elude his grasping fingers. "Not now, Helmut, you'll muss my gown. And you know how easily I mark. Besides, I think we've arrived." *To my relief,* she added in her head.

They mingled with the elegantly uniformed officers and their elegantly gowned and bejeweled wives, making small, optimistic talk about the successes in England and North Africa, basking in the secure pride of being associated with powerful victors.

Mrs. Himmler was notorious for her adherence to social forms and for the strict timing of her parties. As the ornate grandfather clock struck the first tone of eight, she fluttered

71

around the edge of the gathering, herding the guests into the dining room.

"Please now, Herr Goring, Frau Goring. Look for your places. And tonight we have no husbands sitting next to their wives. Frau Hess, where is your husband? Oh, yes, I see him. If I remember, I put you next to Herr Pugh on the left side of the table. You'll see the cards. General Reicheman, Frau Reicheman. Good. Ah, Frau Pugh, Frau Heydrich. Now hurry along."

Laurel sauntered along the table, noting the careful consideration which had been given to seating pairs. She glanced across to see Helmut settling the excessive curves of Frau Hess into a chair and, momentarily, felt sorry for both of them. She'd talk his ear off, and he'd get very drunk.

"Oh, look, Lina, here you are. And right next to Herr Goebbels." She lowered her voice to a whisper. "Try to stay awake."

Lina giggled, but glanced over her shoulder to see who might have overheard. Satisfied that Laurel's impertinence hadn't caused either of them to be viewed askance, she rested her hand on the damask covering of the backrest, waiting in her patient, bovine way for Goebbels to pull out her chair.

Laurel continued her stroll along the table, watching not only for her place card but also for Reinhard's. He'd been closeted with Himmler, disappearing without even a nod in her direction as she and Helmut entered the party. Her heart leapt at the sight of him, but she'd taken her cue from his behavior and her face had remained impassive.

As she neared the end of the table, she spied her name and glanced to see who her dinner companions would be. A sly smile tugged at the corners of her pouting mouth. Reinhard Heydrich would be sitting on her left. Admiral Wilhelm Canaris on her right.

Interesting, she thought. Canaris, as chief of counterintelligence, was a wonderful font of tidbits for her broadcasts if only she could get him to give them to her. She owed him a debt, she acknowledged, for his approval had been required before she'd been able to broadcast. Still, he certainly had to acknowledge the contributions she'd been making to winning the British and Americans over to the side of the Reich.

Laurel jumped at the hand on her shoulder, but recovered quickly, smiling up at the officer. "Admiral, how delightful to see you again," she purred, placing her hand in his for the gallant kiss she expected. He shook her hand with firm dignity.

"Frau Pugh," he muttered, holding her chair, then turning to Greta Schultz who waited on his right.

The tart, Laurel thought, glancing sidelong at the flamboyant, blond actress who had wormed her way into the inner circle with no commodity but her body and her willingness to share her favors. Laurel smiled across the Admiral's beribboned chest.

"Greta, how marvelous to see you. You look wonderful, as always."

Greta turned, her brow furrowed with puzzlement, then, just as Laurel's teeth were beginning to hurt from clenching them, said, "Oh, Lili? Lila? Ah, Laura, of course. Nice to see you."

"Laurel," she hissed, her smile in place.

"Of course, Laurel. Forgive me my small memory for names. And my worse English." Her mouth parodied a smile. "Of course, perhaps you are not comfortable to speak German—even here in Germany." She took a cigarette from a tortoise and crystal case, tamped the end, then inserted it into an ebony and gold holder, glancing up at Laurel through her exaggerated eyelashes.

Laurel was about to respond when Reinhard seated himself to her left, saving her from voicing the catty reply which teetered on the tip of her tongue. "Frau Pugh," he said briskly, "you look well."

"How gracious of you," Laurel purred, pointedly turning her back on the actress. "How have you been? Lina and I were enjoying a lovely chat before dinner. I'm sorry you weren't there to join us." She laid her hand lightly on his arm, holding his eyes with hers.

"Perhaps you can give me the details later," he replied, and Laurel felt her heart leap again.

"It will be my pleasure," she said, her voice low and

husky, leaning forward to afford him a glimpse of her cleavage.

"Admiral," Reinhard said, leaning past the proffered temptation without acknowledging it, "I appreciate your support for my plan to control our problems with the Jews."

"It is difficult to disagree with something which cannot but improve not only the present but also the future for all good Aryans. I have long objected to the Reich's paying good money to simply contain them. After all, no matter how one considers it, they have limited use in building the Reich. I understand, Mrs. Pugh, your husband's companies have been victimized by some of their subversion."

Laurel was aware that the others around them had abandoned their own conversations and she glanced down the table to see if Helmut was listening. His head was bobbing with metronomic regularity as Frau Hess's mouth wrapped itself in an intricate ballet around her inaudible conversation.

"I have been shocked," Laurel said, "by the many incidents we have discovered. I believe they have all had to be removed from any contact with production facilities and now are only useful for cleaning, which hardly covers the cost to maintain them." She watched carefully to assess the reaction of the powerful men around her. They were intent. "Theft within the factories has escalated alarmingly and Helmut has said they must be watched every moment and searched thoroughly before being returned to the ghetto each day. It's scandalous."

Heydrich nodded. "You see, they continue to undermine the German people. Thus, we must find a more permanent solution. From evidence such as this, I am certain there will be more than ample support for my idea."

Himmler, sitting as host at the end of the table, leaned forward. Laurel had always felt he looked a bit like a turtle with his jutting nose and sharply sloping chin. "The Jews and gypsies and filthy homosexuals seem to increase with each state which joins the Reich." He drained his wineglass, then glanced at the other men around the table. Laurel could feel the challenge in his posture and attitude. "Once we have brought Russia into the fold, we will have more undesirables. Why must the good Aryans of Germany spend money which could be used for better causes to simply isolate these bad influences from the pure races? It makes no sense. There is no point to include them in the future of the Reich, so why incur expense now when the treasury must focus on the war? Your idea is brilliant and I feel quite certain the Führer will fully endorse your plan. My compliments, Reinhard."

Reinhard snapped a brisk acknowledgment with his head. "I am grateful for your approval."

Laurel opened her mouth to ask what this brilliant idea was, then closed it again, not wanting to reveal her ignorance. She was angry with Reinhard for keeping such a big coup from her when, out of the corner of her eye, she saw Helmut lurch to his feet.

"But why would any of us be surprised to find our Reinhard had devised another brilliant idea?" he slurred, swaying. "Is he not the liebling of the Führer?" He lunged for his glass, sloshing some of the wine onto the damask tablecloth and his jacket sleeve. "Let us raise a toast to Reinhard Heydrich, planner for the Reich, darling of the Führer, lover of all good Germans." His vicious glare drew all eyes to Laurel.

The room was stunned into silence, the only sound a loud slurping noise as Helmut drained his glass. Laurel saw the room through a red haze of fury as she rose.

"My husband has not been well," she announced as she rounded the table. "Please excuse us."

"Not well, my *Liebschen*? Do not lie to these people whose status you always consider to be so important. I have never felt better in my life. How could I be ill when I have such a good wife to care for me?" Helmut sneered defiantly as he watched Laurel approach. She grabbed his arm, digging her fingers deep into the vulnerable nerves on the inside of his elbow.

"We will say good night now," she spat, her voice flat with rage, yanking him back, toppling the chair. Helmut stumbled, but she held him on his feet with sheer will. "Please excuse us." Laurel propelled him toward the door, feeling the knives of amusement slicing her treasured status to ribbons.

"I have never been so humiliated," she exploded as Klaus sped through the streets of Berlin."

"I said nothing wrong," Helmut pouted, propped in the corner of the seat. "If you had not made a scene, no one would have made any note, but *your* guilt . . ."

"Shut up!" Laurel leaned forward, stabbing at the button which opened a speaker in Klaus's compartment. "Stop the car." Klaus did not respond and she pommeled her fist against the glass partition. "Stop the damn car!" She was thrown off the seat as he slammed on the brakes, but simply grabbed her purse and flung the door open, crawling backward to stand in the street. Klaus, stunned, had only managed to get one foot out the door before she grabbed his collar. "Take him home and make certain he stays in his room."

Laurel pulled her coat around her and clicked off through the empty street, not looking back, but listening intently until she heard the engine start and the car pull away. Helmut was rapidly becoming more of a liability than an asset. Despite his money, something would have to be done.

"Lina, I must return to my office. Himmler has requested it." Reinhard bowed slightly as she passed him, entering their house. "I shall be home when I can. Please do not wait up for me."

"Reinhard," she began, a tentative tone in her voice, "about Helmut Pugh . . ."

"Do not trouble yourself over something which does not concern you," he said firmly, turning away from the door. Lina stood, watching him descend the stairs, then sighed and let the door close slowly.

Heydrich strode across the courtyard toward his car waiting outside the gates, his swagger stick tucked under his arm, his boots gleaming in the dim light which invaded from the street, his thoughts on the unpleasantness with Helmut Pugh. The sudden blow that glanced off his shoulder broke his pace, but he recovered instantly, compressing himself and whirling toward the unseen assailant, ramming his shoulder deeply into his attacker's lower abdomen. The two of them crashed to the ground, Heydrich rolling quickly away, leaping to his feet and drawing his pistol. The other man lay on the ground, however, drawn into a moaning ball, clutching his stomach. Heydrich used the toe of his boot to turn the man's head, then reholstered his weapon.

"Pugh," he said, his voice heavy with disgust. "Haven't you done enough for one evening?"

Still clutching his stomach, Helmut struggled to his knees, then looked up at his adversary. "I came to kill you," he slurred.

Heydrich snorted. "Obviously, you have not succeeded. Perhaps I should kill you."

Pugh began to sob, his voice catching on his emotion. "You . . . have. Why can't you leave . . . her alone?"

Heydrich reached down, yanked Pugh to his feet, then slapped him. "Be a man, Pugh. And do not intervene in things you do not understand and which do not concern you. No, I shall not kill you, for you do not deserve such a manly death." He turned Pugh toward the gate, pushing him. "Go home and sleep off your wine and do not trouble me further. Next time I may not be so charitable." He brushed at his jacket, picked up his swagger stick, and strode past the sniveling Pugh to his car.

"Was there trouble, *Obergruppenführer?*" his driver inquired.

"Nothing important," he said, climbing into the car.

Laurel had chuckled to herself as she soaked in the bath laden with French scented oil. Helmut had given her the perfect excuse to absent herself without one of the tedious explanations she usually had to think of in order to escape the house. *The fool,* she thought, ladling the softening fragrance over her body with her cupped hand. He deserved everything he got.

She emerged from the bath, toweled dry, then slipped the slinky silk and lace negligee over her head, enjoying the sensual tickle of the fine fabric on her skin. Reinhard had brought it to her after his last trip to Paris, along with the bath oil, a bottle of perfume and a case of Dom Perignon Brut. *To the victors,* she thought, *do indeed go the spoils.*

She opened the closet, selecting a pair of royal-blue silk

pajamas and a burgundy smoking jacket, laying them out on the bed carefully, then going into the small kitchen of the hotel suite to open a jar of Beluga caviar and a tin of English cream biscuits. She heard him enter the suite as she spooned chopped onions onto the plate beside the dish of caviar; heard the bath running as she placed the biscuits carefully, fanning them onto the plate. She emerged from the kitchen with the tray in her hands just as he entered the room.

He waited until she had set the tray on the table, then bowed low over her hand, kissing it before taking her in his arms, entwining his hand in her hair to pull her head back, enveloping her mouth with his. "So," he said, pulling his head back from her eager mouth, "you think I have come here to eat caviar?"

Laurel laughed low in her throat, but before she could respond, there was a rap at the door. Reinhard's face clouded with anger. "I told them not to disturb me," he said, striding to the door, returning in a moment with a large envelope in his hand and a slight smile.

He took a glass of champagne from Laurel, settling himself in the corner of the sofa, flipping open the envelope and removing a musical score.

"What is it?" Laurel said, craning over his shoulder.

"Obviously, it is music," he said, glancing at her out of the corner of his eye before returning his attention to the notes on the page. "A gift from my dear friend the concert-master."

"Written just for you? How marvelous! Please, play it for me," Laurel gushed, rising quickly from the couch to retrieve the violin he kept at the suite. "Please, darling."

He ignored her, continuing to study the score until he had read all of it, then extended his hands for the instrument.

With casual expertise, he touched each of the strings, adjusting two of them slightly, then tucked the violin under his chin, holding it there as he tightened the bow. Not glancing at the music, he played an intricate sonata, the music romantic and strong.

Laurel was enchanted with the beautiful piece, and more so with the magic her powerful lover could create. She

78

watched him, rapt, as he played, then applauded heartily as he finished.

"It's wonderful! Exquisite. Was it written for you?"

"For us," he replied, setting his instrument atop the still-closed score and reaching for her.

Dawn began to gray the sky as Laurel hurried into her clothes. Reinhard sat propped against the pillows in the bed, the covers pulled to his waist, watching her dress.

"Your next broadcast is this evening, yes?"

She nodded, reaching for her brush to try to tame her hair. "Yes. At seven." She caught his eyes in the mirror and smiled. "I wonder if the English will assume the joy in my voice comes from living under the Reich."

"Hah," he responded with a slight smile, then added, "You should be careful of the jokes you make, Laurel. There are those who do not understand your American sense of humor."

Her expression sobered quickly. "Have I done something wrong, my darling? Have I offended you? Have I made a bad joke that the Führer objects to?"

"No, and you must not. Not if you plan to keep rising in the Reich."

She smiled, pleased at the acknowledgment of her contributions. "You know I am dedicated to the Reich."

"Or at least to your position in it," he added. "I will be at your broadcast studio at six. You need not worry about a script. I will provide it for you."

She sat on the edge of the bed, leaning to kiss him. "I hope the day will speed by in that case, my darling. Until we can be together again."

"Of course," he said, mussing her hair as he pulled her to him.

5

WHITNEY FIXED HER eyes on the top of the wall as Lady Primrose had coached, then began to run, gathering speed as she approached the barrier. She thrust her hands upward to grasp the wall's surface, pulling up with her arms at the same time and pushing with her legs. As she twisted to sit, victorious, atop the wall, she grinned.

"Like the real thing," she said, patting her newly fitted calf. "Light as a feather, but it sits firmly. Did you see me running? I haven't been able to run without pain since . . . since I lost my real leg."

Erik extended his arms to help her down, but she waved him away. "I've got to be able to jump down, too, you know." She looked down at the ground five feet below, then pushed forward, landing with her knees flexed. Grinning, she stood, extending her arms. "Tah-dah."

Erik and Lady Primrose applauded dutifully.

"I would never have believed I could be so comfortable. I must thank Stephen once more."

"All in due time, my dear," Lady Primrose agreed, striding beside her. "You still have a great deal of work to do here and time is slipping away."

Whitney shivered, pulling on her gloves, then shoving her

hands deeply into her pockets. "It's so hard to believe time exists at all. Or a war. Or anything besides these hills and trees and fields. It could be any winter day at my grandfather's farm . . . or at Winfield."

Erik put his arm around her shoulders. "Regretfully, I assure you there is indeed a world beyond here and time is only one of our enemies."

Whitney leaned her head against his shoulder, then said softly, "With all that in mind, I'm very glad you're here."

He hugged her, then teased, "And that's the only reason?"

"Absolutely. Come on, let's run again. It feels wonderful." She took a few steps, then halted, turning with a bright smile. "You know, I'll bet I could dance again, too. And ride; maybe even hunt. This is wonderful!" She turned, trotting away from them. "Truly wonderful," she called over her shoulder.

The imaginary wind of the familiar nightmare pulled at her hair, drawing away the warmth of the sun on her cheeks and forehead. Beneath Edgewood's hooves, the ground smelled of green summer freedom as the two of them fled the constraints of the exercise ring.

They moved as one, woman and horse, no communication necessary as they cleared a fence, sailed over a brook, launched themselves over a fallen tree, not so much defying gravity as ignoring it.

Suddenly, they emerged from a thicket, and there it was, unexpected but dreaded, always appearing without warning: the wall, its stones menacing and contemptuous.

Whitney pulled back on the reins, and Edgewood surged forward in confusion.

Then, as always in her nightmare, the wall exploded, dust and rocks and metal raining down on her and Edgewood as they desperately fought to get away. As she had so many nights before, Whitney awoke, drenched in sweat and shaking. She clutched at the quilt covering the bed, chanting "dream, dream, dream" in her struggle with the shades of the distant past.

Finally her breathing became more regular, and she forced

her fingers to release the comforter, then turned toward the window, seeking a reinforcement of the reality of the present. Early light had begun to gray the sky to the east. She glanced at the clock.

"Oh well," Whitney said aloud, "at least I only lose half an hour of sleep this time."

She reached for her robe, shrugging it on as she swung her foot over the side of the bed and leaned to pick up her "Forrestal foot" as she'd begun to call her new prosthesis, carefully sorting out the harness straps to attach it to her thigh.

She brushed her teeth and hair vigorously, reaffirming her alertness, then washed her face in cold water to drive away the last of her sleep terrors. Returning to her room, she chose a warm Irish sweater and twill pants, warm socks, and sturdy walking shoes. Grabbing her jacket, she left the room quietly.

Dawn backed the hills to the east with pink promise when she emerged from the kitchen door and, pulling on her gloves, strode briskly along the path toward the wooded hills. Her feet rustled the leaves on the path, and over her head a crow barked a warning of her presence. Suddenly she stopped, cocking her head, trying to capture the phantom sound only a part of her consciousness had heard. At first there was only the crow and the wind, but then she heard it again—hounds.

Whitney quickened her pace, breathless as she topped the hill, where she could see down into the valley. Her heart leapt as she saw first the pack of hounds, then the riders, emerge from a wooded cover far across the fields below.

She felt her spirit race to join the hunt, her sensory memories awakened. She stepped forward, waving, when suddenly she was grabbed from behind and yanked backward.

As Paul Sanders Stewart had taught, she relaxed completely, letting her weight throw off her attacker, then took advantage of his momentary imbalance to gain her footing and spin as she pulled forward, throwing him to the ground. Her hand was reaching for the knife in her pocket before she'd even focused on the sprawled figure.

82

"Colonel! Oh, I'm so sorry. Why did you grab me like that?"

William Donohue sat on the ground, shaking his head. "Well, I see you have absorbed the training we've given you." He raised himself to his feet, brushing himself off.

"William, you scared the life out of me!"

"And you have more than retaliated, Whitney. But I didn't want you to draw attention to yourself . . . or to us. The neighbors in this area believe the occupant of this house is an elderly recluse."

"I had no idea. I'm certain they didn't see me."

"However, had you persisted, I'm certain they would have. We can't risk the safety of this operation by even casual contact with the outside."

"Somehow I have trouble believing you have come all the way from Washington just to prowl the borders of your secret installation." Whitney gestured toward a fallen tree nearby. "Care to join me in the salon?"

He nodded, offering a hand for assistance.

"No, thanks. I'm getting more independent by the hour with my new limb . . . and all this training."

He chuckled, lowering himself next to her on the log. "So I've noticed. Not, of course, that you ever were dependent to begin with. And you are right. I didn't come down just to 'patrol the borders.' I've brought something you might find interesting."

Whitney unfolded the sheaf of thin papers he extended. "Oh, from Patrice." She began skimming the text, then her brow furrowed with a frown as the report involved her. "Obviously," she said as she finished, "the Germans didn't believe the funeral for a moment."

Donohue shrugged. "It was a long shot."

"Is Patrice *positive* it's Laurel doing these broadcasts?"

Donohue nodded. "I know few other people who make her as angry, and she's furious about the references to the 'Return of the Limping Lady' to Europe."

Whitney nodded. "The only consolation is that their information is not correct since 'The Limping Lady' is sitting here with you in the Virginia hills, not in Europe."

"Oh, it's most decidedly a fishing expedition on their part.

Regardless, it will make life more difficult for you once you are in the field again."

"And should I infer that won't be long?"

He turned to look directly into her eyes. "How do you feel about it? Are you ready, or have you lost your fervor for the spy game?"

Whitney tugged at the fingers of her gloves, taking them off. "William, I have never had a 'fervor for the spy game,' as you put it. My motivations are far more personal." Her hand dropped to her leg.

"That's the worst possible reason to be in this business. No matter how angry you are, no matter what you do in the field, you will never bring your leg back."

Whitney sighed. "Or Perry. Or the two years I spent as a guest of the Reich. No, William, I am not trying to avenge those things which have happened and I'm not certain I can explain in words why it's so important to me to be in the middle of this conflict." She paused, staring at the trees, then sighed and shrugged. "Who knows, maybe it's fate." She grinned.

"If it's any consolation, I'm not averse to accepting that as your motivation. As long as it's not some misplaced sense of adventurism driving you."

Her smile took an impish turn. "That's it, exactly. The adventure of it all. After all, my life has been so very dull up to now."

He chuckled. "Based on that, I'd hate to hear your definition of lively. But let's go back to Laurel's broadcasts. As you can see in Patrice's report, she mentions you in every one of them."

"But you said it was a fishing expedition."

"Yes. And no. The point is, they know you're alive and they're hunting you. Or, more accurately, they're hunting what you brought out with you. I can't tell you how important those plans have turned out to be."

"You mean the improved Enigma machine?"

Donohue nodded. "The second generation of the unbreakable code machine which Hitler treasures above all else. British MI5 has a team working on it now, and it won't be long before the Enigma is just another typewriter. Believe

84

me, it will prove a turning point in this war." He turned to face her. "The strength we have right now is that the Germans don't seem to believe, or don't want to believe, perhaps, that you found the secret compartment with the microfilm. I'd guess they're assuming the diamonds they'd put in your leg would satisfy you."

"Actually, it was a good ruse. It was only pure accident that I found the other compartment."

"That's the crux of their hunt for you. That, perhaps, and their arrogant belief that we really are inferior. A smile tugged at his mouth. "So, I've cooked up an idea that may keep them looking for a long time. Come on, let's go back to the house and get some coffee."

"Rigby, does *no* ever mean anything to you?" Raven lit a cigarette, then snapped his Zippo lighter closed. "We've tried to get visas for you three times, and the German embassy, which seems to have a fairly good, fairly long, memory of your past visits, has declined three times. We've used all the normal channels and are batting precisely zero. So, the assignment is now canceled."

"What do you mean, canceled? So we don't succeed using normal channels. You know normal channels are only where you begin. Now we'll try our abnormal channels."

Raven shook his head. "Not this time, Rigby. We've got something much more important in mind for you."

"What could be more important than exposing a traitor? This is our chance at a major scoop and you tell me the assignment is canceled. Honestly, I can't imagine what the people running this paper—if there is anyone running this paper—are thinking. Aren't we known for being on the cutting edge of the news? And here we are with the biggest scoop of the century, and suddenly it's no longer important."

Raven leaned back in his chair, crossing his hands over his stomach. "I suppose you think you could do a better job?"

"You bet your boots!"

"Okay, you run the bureau, then."

"Oh, very funny," Patrice said, standing abruptly. "If

85

you will excuse me, *Mister* Bureau Chief, I'll just go back to what passes for my office and see if I can think up something which might top the scoop you just yanked out from under me."

"Don't slam the door, Rigby," Raven said, bracing himself for the explosion. "And when you've returned to reason, I'll be happy to tell you about your new assignment."

She hesitated with the doorknob in her grasp. "There really is a new assignment?"

"If you're interested." He leaned forward and stubbed out his cigarette.

Patrice closed the door and returned to the chair opposite his desk. "So?"

Raven pulled a tear sheet from a file on his desk and extended it to her. Patrice read it, looking puzzled.

"Why is Monkton congratulating me and wishing me luck? Come on, Raven, spill the beans."

He grinned. "Maybe some background would help. As you know, I feel very much at home here in England. After all, I've lived here almost as long as I lived in Baltimore. I've gotten pretty tired of the Jerries bombing the hell out of my adopted nation and figure I owe her something in return. The RAF has decided they might be able to teach me to fly a plane, so I'm joining up."

Patrice felt shocked. "Mike, really? Are you certain you want to do this?"

He nodded. "Positive. Besides, that leaves the job of bureau chief open and you just told me you could do a better job, so have at it."

"Me? Bureau Chief?"

Raven nodded his head. "Monkton's managing editor of overseas bureaus and he refused to even consider anyone else for the job." He smiled warmly at her. "And I agreed wholeheartedly. You're the best reporter *Sunpapers* has."

"Being a reporter is one thing, but I don't want to be tied to a desk watching everyone else getting the scoops."

Raven laughed. "And you think that's going to be the case? Monkton'll be really furious to hear that, after all the time he spent training you. Monkton's the king of the newspaper business, and you'll soon find out how much of a working reporter you'll still be. Especially with the war getting worse and the growing need for more correspondents. Oh, maybe you won't be trooping into the desert for six weeks at a time, but you can plan on continuing as a reporter. Now, however, you can take only the big stories, the ones you really want, and assign the Queen's teas to other people." He leaned his elbows on the desk. "I think you'll be great in the job. And I'll be watching you."

"Bureau Chief," Patrice repeated, then nodded. "Yes, that does have a nice ring to it. Bureau Chief Rigby, *Sunpapers,* London." She grinned broadly, then sobered again. "But I'm worried about you, Mike. Are you certain this isn't just some spirit-of-the-day impulse?"

"No, but it's too late now. Leftenant Raven, reporting for duty, ma'am. One week from today, to be precise. So we'd better get to work. First I had to teach you how to be a reporter. Now I'm stuck trying to teach you how to run this joint, Rigby."

She grinned across the desk at him. "That's *Bureau Chief* Rigby, to you, soldier!"

"And that's Leftenant, to you, Yank."

"Before I tell you about the assignment, let me tell you a bit about Yugoslavia," Donohue began, settling into one of the library's comfortable chairs, cupping his hands around the coffee mug and blowing on the steaming liquid.

Whitney curled into an armchair opposite him, sipping her coffee. "Is this a general geography lecture or shall I assume my activities will center in Yugoslavia?"

He nodded. *"Based* would be a more appropriate term, I guess. Have you been there?"

She shook her head.

"Yugoslavia is about the size of New York State, with an extension of the Dalmation mountains occupying most of the central part of the country. Along the coast of the Adriatic are a number of towns which have been trading and fishing ports for centuries. Belgrade is the capital, up in the mountains." He stopped, sipping his coffee. "Yugoslavia wasn't even created until after the Great War when the Ottoman Turks were defeated. Before that, the country was really six regions and, frankly, the creation of the nation has had little effect on their separatist notions. Yugoslavia's national groups have too much historical separation to overcome. The largest of the republics is Serbia, where Belgrade is located. The Serbs, as well as the republic called Bosnia-Hercegovina, were under the influence of the Ottoman Empire for centuries and you see Turkish influence everywhere, including the fact that many of the people are Muslims. The other republics were not part of the Ottoman Empire, but had their own influences. For example, Slovenia is very German even though it's physically closest to Italy. It will remind you very much of Austria in the foods, architecture, even the accents. Croatia, on the other hand, is very Slavic. As a matter of fact, they consider themselves to be the true Slavic homeland. On the other end of the country is what was in ancient times called Macedonia, and you would swear you're in Greece when you're there. The last of the republics is Montenegro. They were violently anti-Ottoman, holding off the Turkish armies again and again in the mountains and from the sea.''

"It sounds like they're still at war," Whitney said, fascinated by Donohue's recitation.

"They are in many ways. For example, three religions hold a dominant position in different parts of the country. I've told you about the Muslims, but they're only about ten percent. The two biggest religious influences come from Roman Catholics, primarily in Croatia and Slovenia; and from Serbian Orthodox, which is as different from Roman Catholic as it is from Greek or Russian Orthodox. And, if that doesn't make getting along complicated enough, each region also has its own language. Italian is spoken along the Dalmatian coast in Slovenia, where you will also find German spoken frequently. German is also spoken in Croatia, but there you will also find Serbo-Croatian. And most everyone speaks French as well. Obviously, a lot of Turkish influence lingers in the language in Bosnia and Serbia, and just to make it worse, Macedonians often speak Greek.''

Whitney looked up from her coffee. "Please tell me I don't have to learn all of them."

Donohue laughed. "By the time you did, the war would

be over. No, your French will be fine, along with your English and German.''

"And my Morse code, let us not forget."

"I understand you're pretty good with that. And with the radio. You're going to need it all, Whitney, and a great deal more. This is not going to be an easy assignment."

"So I'm beginning to see. How strong are the Nazis there?"

"Like everywhere else in Europe. They'll just bully their way in and kill anyone who objects. It's a brutal system, but it's been entirely too effective. And the Yugoslavs will be very bad at responding to it. They're so busy fighting amongst themselves that they can't seem to solidify a pan-national resistance. That, however, is not something you will have to concern yourself with, at least not directly."

Donohue paused to take another sip of his coffee and Whitney asked, "What, directly, is the problem?"

"Basically, you will coordinate and lead a group of your own against the Germans, sort of a free-lance resistance group. You will work with a couple of people we trust in the country, but not as a part of their operations. Your group will gather information, about not only the Germans, but whatever might be of use to us."

"So you really expect we will be in the war?"

He sighed. "We're already in, Whitney. No declaration has been made, and there are still a few voices in this country which persist in suggesting that America should keep out, but no one can believe for a moment that this won't turn into a global conflict. We've all been focusing on the Nazis in Europe, but we should also be keeping a careful eye on our friend Emperor Hirohito. We understand he's been studying the German advances and victories and can't help but be seduced by the ease with which Hitler has moved into Europe. It's becoming obvious Hirohito wants the other half of the world, and if we don't get in on our own, something or somebody will push us in. I want my group to be ready. We can prevent a shooting war only if we take the initiative to win the subversive war, and you're one of my generals."

"If I'm a general, who do I command?"

89

Donohue pulled a paper from his pocket, unfolded it, and extended it to her. "Your troops will arrive tomorrow for four weeks of training. It should be quite a challenge."

Whitney stood next to Donohue, watching two limousines slide up the drive. Cesar emerged from the first one, then stepped aside to allow four women to emerge. The second car was also filled with female passengers. Whitney watched them, shaking her head.

"Donohue," she muttered, "you have a strange sense of humor." She thought he'd not heard her, until his chuckle rumbled low beside her, but before she could pursue the subject, he stepped forward to shake Cesar Ball's hand.

"Major, glad you're here. And with all your charges . . . intact, no less."

Cesar took Whitney's hand, giving it a firm shake. "Countess, good to see you. You look well."

"And you, Major Ball. Do you have any last-minute advice?"

His serious eyes belied the slight smile. "I only wish I did."

"If it would be helpful, I can make the Major available to you for the balance of the training," Donohue said.

"Helpful! I think it might approach miraculous! I'd be most appreciative."

"Done, then. And here's someone else who might be helpful." Donohue stepped aside and Whitney gasped, thrust backward in time and far away to the scrub and rock hills of Turkey. Again, she felt the terror of the approaching explosions, smelled the dust and burning metal, heard her own screams mingling with the crashing of the bridge they'd been sent to destroy. "My God, Phoenix," was all she could choke out before sagging against Donohue's shoulder.

"I'm sorry, Whitney," Donohue said, taking her elbow. "I thought you would have recognized his name from the list I gave you."

She shook her head. "There was no reference to Phoenix on that list."

Donohue put his hand to his head in self-disgust. "Damn,

you never knew Phoenix was really Ross Robbins. I'm so sorry."

"No, I should be the one to apologize," Whitney said, squaring her shoulders, then extending her hand. "Mr. Robbins, please don't mistake my surprise as rudeness."

He took her hand, bowing over it formally. "I've never had the chance to say I'm sorry for the accident at our last meeting." He glanced down at her leg, then pulled his eyes away in embarrassment. "I'm very glad to see you . . . did . . . okay."

"Better than okay," Whitney said softly, "and the accident had nothing to do with you. I got caught through my own inexperience and frankly feel quite lucky to have survived at all. I'm very glad we'll be working together again," she added, not certain if she really meant it.

His grin made her feel a bit reassured that she hadn't revealed her trepidations. "At least we can't do any worse," he said, turning to retrieve his gear.

"It is only to be hoped," she responded very quietly.

Whitney stood beside her chair at the head of the dining table, Lady Primrose to her right, watching her troop file in.

"You will find namecards at your places," she said with a smile. "I apologize for not knowing who you are already, but this will help."

The first of the women to enter was tall, seeming even leaner in the black trousers and sweater she wore. Her hair, cropped close to her head in a bob, was, in startling contrast to her youthful face, silver gray. "Magda Maddingly," she said, her voice low and whiskey-rough. She located her place and slouched into the chair.

Whitney nodded her greeting. "Welcome aboard, Miss Maddingly."

"Yeah," the woman said, reaching for her wineglass.

"Regina Small," said the woman who stood behind the chair next to Magda Maddingly. Her smile seemed genuinely warm and Whitney returned it as she sought to fix the name with the long, plain face, dishwater-blond hair, and athletic form of the petite woman.

"Miss Small," Whitney said, linking the short stature

with the last name and hoping it would help aid her memory later.

Ross Robbins stepped to the chair beside Miss Small, pulling it out, then turned to the woman on his left, who gracefully flowed into the chair. "Judith Jones," the woman said to Whitney, then turned her shockingly lavender eyes to Robbins. "Thank you," she purred, her long fingers grazing his cheek briefly. Tossing her luxuriant blue-black curls off her shoulders, she returned her gaze to Whitney, who had to admit the woman was a stunning beauty. Her eyes were large and widely set above elegant cheekbones and a graceful nose, her facial perfection completed with a generous, sensual mouth. "Radcliffe, '34; Olympics, '36."

"Murder, '37; prison, '38," Magda Maddingly added. "Can I get a beer here?"

Whitney's smile felt tight. "I'm certain Philip would be more than pleased . . ."

"Now," Magda declared, glancing at the befuddled butler.

Whitney nodded and he scurried into the kitchen. She turned back to the table just as the last two women entered together, chatting in Spanish.

The first of them seated herself to Lady Primrose's right, then turned to Whitney. *"Señora,"* she said demurely, a dense row of dark lashes fluttering over her velvet-brown eyes, her classic Spanish face and olive complexion seeming exotic and mysterious, *"mi nombre es Leona Pinto."*

"Welcome, *Signorita*. Do you speak English?" Whitney added, hopeful.

"Yes, but poor, I think."

"I'm certain you'll do fine," Whitney said, despairing.

"I'm Bernadette Logan, and I do speak Spanish. I'll be delighted to help Leona all I can. I'm also a nurse." She smiled brightly, her pixie face folding her eyes into crinkled laughter, as though being a nurse were the most amusing thing possible to be. "I'm sorry we were so slow, but we got to talking about the Civil War in Spain. I was there for a little while as a volunteer, but my goodness, Leona was right in the middle of it all." Her face knotted around another smile. "I think we have a genuine heroine in our midst. Why, she even used guns and everything."

92

Magda drained the beer from her glass. "And you only used a needle, sweetheart. Just how many people did you poison before they caught on?"

Bernadette's fashionable French-rolled hair bobbed her indignation. "How dare you! I was framed."

Magda lounged back in her chair, dangling her empty glass over the back. "Me, too, honey. We were all framed, right? Those six guys I knifed would have been happy to defend me in court if they'd lived."

"I certainly wasn't framed," Regina Small said blithely. "But there was a reason I broke into all those houses. They had money and my family didn't, and my husband left me, and I never learned a trade. I just found a different way to use my gymnastic talents. But I never hurt anybody." Her gaze shifted from Magda to Judith.

"It was an accident," the beautiful woman purred. "Mark slipped and fell."

"Right out of the window and ten floors to the street, right?" Magda sneered. "Over the ledge of your penthouse terrace and, splat, right onto the cement of Park Avenue. What a clumsy son of a bitch."

Whitney's voice was steel. "There will be no further discussions of this type. I am more than aware that you have joined our group because you have been promised a full pardon from your prison terms at the end of the war. I am also aware that Leona's political affiliations make her undesirable in her own nation." She leaned forward, her eyes meeting each of theirs. "I am also more than aware, as you are, that I have the power to return you to prison with one word, and I want you to be equally assured that I shall not hesitate to use this power."

Whitney calmed herself with a deep breath, then continued, "We can accomplish our mission in one of two ways: either we work together as a team, helping each other, or I will make this experience pure hell. And believe me, I've been to hell and am completely familiar with how things are done there. So I will now offer each of you the opportunity to consider your position here. If you decide you would rather snipe at each other and undermine this mission, then I will be more than happy to return you to the custody of the state from which you came." She turned directly toward Magda. "And I suggest you enjoy your next beer. It will be the last for a very long time." Their eyes held, challenging each other until Magda broke the deadlock.

Whitney pulled out her chair and sat. "Phillip, you may begin. Now, to start, from this moment on, I encourage you to forget not only the last name of everyone here but also your own. Your life and the lives of the other members may depend upon it."

6

WHITNEY TURNED SLIGHTLY in her seat, glancing down the aisle of the Pan Am Clipper at her charges. They had been given stern orders not to speak with any other passengers and, so far, had complied. She turned back to the window, watching the French countryside below and the two German Luftwaffe fighter planes which flew beside the Clipper, escorting them, the pilot had explained tensely, until they reached the Swiss border and neutral airspace again.

She tried to reassure herself that a couple of German fighter pilots could not possibly recognize her—one little face in the window of the Clipper—but finally surrendered, closing the drape over the porthole, and turned to Lady Primrose.

"Do you think we have a chance of actually pulling all this off?" she muttered, carefully hiding her words in the steady snoring of the man in the seat ahead of theirs.

"Sometimes I think our chances are roughly the same as that of a snowball which finds itself in the Congo, but then I think of your escape from the Nazis and, frankly, anything seems reasonable after that." She patted Whitney's hand reassuringly. "And, to their credit, they do seem to have developed some semblance of discipline. Judith actually offered to help Bernadette the other day. One simply never knows with these sorts of operations.'' Her tone was airy, light, as though discussing the potential fate of the dahlias she would plant in the spring rather than one of the most dangerous clandestine operations Whitney could imagine.

As Whitney worked with Lady Primrose in their months of training and organization, she realized how little she knew of the woman herself. Prim's steady and predictable nature made her seem open and warm, until one day when Whitney had realized she knew nothing of Prim's background or personal life—not even if she were married. It was as though Prim lived only in the present; as though her past had never existed. The reserve which declared her noble background also built an effective wall against personal questions. Their friendship, though trusting and loyal, existed in the immediate. Whitney wondered if, after the war ended, Lady Primrose would simply disappear.

Whitney pulled the window drape aside and saw, with relief, the outline of the Alps against the horizon. The fighters still flew beside them, however, and she let the drape hide them again. There would be plenty of Germans to watch soon enough. These were still the problem of Pan American Airways.

Geneva's stuffy aloofness had, it seemed to Whitney, changed from a subtle undertone to an overt obsession virtually screaming, "We are neutral; don't ask us to get involved." But it was more bravado than confidence she soon observed as they drove through the city. People watched carefully. Smiles were cautious, eyes wary. Whitney wondered how many of the covered faces masked other secrets; how many of the watchful eyes belonged not to neutrality, but to one loyalty or another, how many gathered information to be relayed to Berlin or London or Rome.

The taxi pulled up in front of the Hoffman Inn, the small guesthouse where Whitney was expected, or more accurately, where Julia Belding of Omaha, Nebraska, held reservations. Each member of the team left the plane, went through Customs and Immigration, and exited the airport alone, ignoring the others, each safely and reliably on her way, Whitney fervently hoped, to a small guesthouse like the Hoffman Inn where they had been instructed to act like tourists and wait until someone inquired, "Have you ever visited the New York Public Library?" Then, one by one, they would be gathered and assembled for one last essential week of training during which their metamorphosis would be complete.

The proprietress of the Hoffman Inn stood in the doorway as the driver removed Whitney's luggage from the taxi. She nodded a brusque acknowledgment when Whitney said, "I am Julia Belding."

"We are expecting you," the woman said, turning away as Whitney paid the driver and picked up her cheap cardboard suitcase from where the cabbie had left it.

The smells of sauerkraut and bread and smoked sausage hung in the air like an old pomander, held securely in the velvet drapes and brocade on the walls and furniture, but the house was clean, as was the small, spartan room to which Whitney was escorted by the dour woman.

"There are two meals a day, breakfast and dinner. The bathroom is down the hall. No lights are to be on after eight unless the drapes are closed tightly. No men in the rooms," she said before entrusting the room key to Whitney.

"Thank you." Whitney sat on the corner of the narrow, creaky bed, her expression neutral, inoffensive, and innocent, she hoped.

The woman surveyed Whitney once more with suspicious disapproval as though deciding whether or not it would be necessary to lock up her few remaining treasures, then sucked at her gapped teeth and closed the door.

Whitney listened to the woman's retreating footsteps thudding on the worn carpeting, then sat motionless, absorbing the feeling of the house, its small noises. She could hear snatches of what seemed to be a Viennese waltz, but the music had an ethereal quality because she couldn't identify its source. Finally Whitney stood and began a detailed survey of the room, examining the undersides of the lamp, the small table and chair, even lowering herself to the floor

97

and sliding under the bed, but there did not seem to be any of the listening devices for which she'd been taught to look.

The drapes covering the window felt dusty and old, their floral print faded to colored shadows, and the rod complained bitterly as she moved them aside. Not surprisingly, however, considering the Swiss penchant for cleanliness and order, the glass in the window had been polished to a gleam. Whitney stepped back into the shadows of the room, her eyes systematically surveying the windows in the houses opposite the inn. Most were dark squares backed by anonymous white, but two that were naked of curtains contained splashes of red geraniums, bright defiance of the gloom which filled Europe. "Good for you," Whitney whispered.

The narrow street below was cobbled, bordered by small strips of flatstone walks, the stoops of the houses rising sharply, looking as though they had been shoved up against the brick of the buildings, then whitewashed into submission. The windows on the street level were all graced with window boxes, tidily emptied and awaiting the flowers of spring.

The street was peppered with people, bundled against the chill, walking with purpose and ignoring each other. None of them seemed interested in the Hoffman Inn or the observer in one of its windows. There was a car parked at the end of the street, a black pre-war coupe. Whitney leaned forward a bit to see if it was occupied. As she did, the driver's-side door opened and a uniformed man emerged.

Whitney gasped and stepped farther back into the shadows of the room, trying to keep him in her sight, her heart pounding as she watched him stride to one of the stoops, where he hesitated, looking up at the windows. Suddenly one of them opened and a beaming face surrounded by white curls emerged.

"Fritz," Whitney could faintly hear the woman call as she thrust her arms outside in a long-distance embrace. The uniformed man bounded up the stairs and through the door of the house as Whitney chided herself.

"What a secret agent you are. Terrified at the first uniform you see, and it turns out to be someone's grandson." She pulled the drapes across, then stretched out on the bed. "Of course," she reminded herself, "Hitler is probably somebody's grandson, too."

A sliver of sunlight penetrated a worn spot in the floral drapes. Whitney could not help but remember the last time she'd been in Geneva as she dressed. Though it had been only the previous July, it seemed a lifetime ago that she had fled from the SS to the American Embassy, then, finding bureaucracy and suspicion where she had expected refuge and welcome, she had run through fear and pain to the lakeshore and the boat that helped her escape into France. She shook her head at the memory. She had hoped France would fulfill her dreams of rescue and freedom, but the Nazis' occupation foiled that plan as well.

"Funny," she said to herself, "how different things appear when one is not running from invisible demons."

Geneva was many things at the same time. To some observers, it took the role of guardian of the world's money, secret fortunes jealously guarded by anonymous numbers. To others, particularly in the present political climate, she was a sunny refuge from the black clouds of Nazism. And—Whitney thought as she strolled past shops which displayed Swiss watches and Belgian diamonds and French couture and Italian glass and German cameras with determined neutrality—Geneva was also the temptress, seducing not only the pocketbook but also the mind into believing that what was going on outside her borders was perhaps just an unpleasant dream.

A threadbare old man had followed her for several blocks along the edge of the park, slowing when Whitney slowed, resting when she did, but each time moving closer. She stopped to buy a warm apple turnover and coffee, glad for the bustle and homey smells of the small food shop. She wasn't surprised when the old man settled himself at her table.

"Excuse me, young woman, but you seem to be an American."

Whitney glanced up, assessing his crinkled eyes and the deep grooves time and winter had etched into his skin, then nodded slightly.

"Ah," he said, shaking his head and smiling in remembrance, "how I loved America. I was there many years ago to study at Columbia University, where I took a degree in engineering. There were many beautiful sights in New York, and I, a young man from the mountains of Switzerland, stared in wonder at all of it."

Whitney smiled again, glancing around quickly to see if anyone was watching them, but the other patrons in the shop seemed absorbed in their own business.

". . . emotional feelings when I first came to America. It is a great nation."

"Yes, it is," Whitney said softly.

"All the best things of Europe, but new. Everything so new. And so grand. The buildings, the streets, the parks, the museums. Everything for people to enjoy and to learn. Oh, how much I learned at Columbia University. Not only engineering," his eyes twinkled, "but also life. We sat for many hours and spoke about freedom and women and all the great problems of life, which we knew we could solve in but a moment—even faster if we had one more bottle of wine." He chuckled, and Whitney couldn't resist joining him.

"Yes, Americans have so much, and not only of material things but also of ideas and energy and youth. The nation is young and filled with spirit. At that time, the president was Mr. Roosevelt. Oh, not this Mr. Roosevelt, but his uncle, Teddy. 'Bully,' he used to say about everything. He was a vital man, and we all admired him for the courage he showed. He was like so many other Americans who had money and liked to do things for the people. That man with the railroads, Mr. Carnegie. He gave money for libraries so people could read and learn. Have you ever visited the New York Public Library?"

Whitney had to keep herself from laughing aloud, instead keeping her tone low and courteously distant as she had been.

"Many times. I like the Greek collection there."

She waited, wondering if it was only wildly improbable coincidence.

"I preferred the studies of the Romans," he replied and

100

Whitney once more respected Donohue's subtlety and finesse.

"Is there a good library in Geneva?" she asked, keeping to the script.

"I know of an excellent private one which you might enjoy very much. It has a magnificent Greek collection. I'm passing there now. May I escort you?"

"I would be most grateful," Whitney said, rising and offering him a helping hand; to the casual observer, or even the acute one, she was a well-mannered woman assisting an elderly friend. The man put her arm through his and guided her gently onto the sidewalk.

"Let us be certain we have no escorts," he muttered as they crossed a street surrounded by a crowd. They stopped in front of a book shop and he took a long time explaining a subtle point of leather binding, but his eyes never rested, watching the reflections of the passers-by as he spoke. They stopped again in front of another book shop before they moved on.

"If we are being followed," he said, propelling her around a corner abruptly, "they are very good." His voice sounded younger, suddenly, and Whitney realized he was probably not quite as elderly as he'd originally seemed.

They hesitated in midblock, the man facing her, nodding and talking as though concluding a discussion. He continued to watch the street from which they had come until he felt they were safe.

"Three stoops ahead you will find a small gate. It is not locked. Follow the path to the alleyway behind, and there you will find a small truck. Be certain you are not observed, then climb into the back. God bless you."

Before Whitney could thank him, he crossed the street to return to the main road, and she turned toward the direction he'd indicated, quickly finding the gate, the alleyway, and the truck parked under a small shed. She was alone, she saw, and climbed into the back, settling herself among the boxes inside.

She was just beginning to wonder if she'd chosen the wrong truck when it coughed to a rumbling start and lurched, first backward then forward, and bounced down the lane. Whitney could hear traffic around them, then fewer and fewer noises as they left the smooth streets of the city and embarked on roads which were bumpier. And curvier, she thought, regretting the sweet turnover which now thudded back and forth with each twist. Her ears popped and she realized they were also climbing up into the mountains.

Just as Whitney feared she and the turnover were about to part company, the truck stopped and the engine quieted. She heard the truck's front door slam, then retreating footsteps crunch on gravel. The long silence which followed seemed endless, and Whitney considered opening the door, when she heard footsteps approaching. With a rush of chill air the door opened.

"Sister Camille."

Whitney looked up, squinting in the bright sunlight into a smiling face framed by an outrageously winged white wimple.

"Welcome to the Mother Convent of the Sisters of Perpetual Trust."

"Thank you," Whitney said, accepting the woman's assistance. "Have any of the others arrived?"

The nun took Whitney's arm as they walked along the packed snow path toward the austere chateau that dominated even the mountains surrounding it. The wind whispered through the dark green pines blanketing the hillsides. Whitney took a deep breath of the bitingly cold air, then coughed.

"Sister Camille, our air here is quite thin. You would probably be more comfortable if you avoided brisk activity or deep breathing until you adjust. You are the first to arrive, but I expect the others will be here soon. I am Mother Joseph, superior of this convent. You will eventually meet Mother Evangeline, the Mother Superior of our order, but we would like to spare Mother Evangeline any confusion about your presence or that of your associates. She has been our Mother for many years, and temporal matters are not her forte."

"I understand."

Mother Joseph smiled, nodding. "I feel certain you do." She gestured gracefully, her wide sleeve arcing against the icy blue of the sky. "I have been here since I was eighteen, yet each day has its own character, its own beauty. Sister Camille, I hope very much that should you ever find yourself in grief or difficulty, the remembrance of your days here will bring you peace and strength."

Whitney sighed. "Those are elusive commodities in these times."

"Indeed they are," Mother Joseph said, "but not impossible to find."

"What the hell do you mean, nuns, for chris'sake? Nuns!" The newly, temporarily ordained Sister Magda crossed her arms and glared at Whitney.

"Nuns," Whitney repeated firmly. "It will be our cover and our protection."

Sister Bernadette muttered something in Spanish to Sister Leona, who looked aghast.

"Please, Camille, this is not possible for me to be a nun." She shook her head as she spoke.

"Sister Leona, we will not truly be nuns, but only seem to belong to the order so we can hide," Whitney spoke slowly, assuming Leona had simply misunderstood, but Sister Leona shook her head again, then beckoned Whitney to one side.

Still shaking her head, she whispered, "I have too much sinned to take the veil."

Whitney put her arm across the Spanish woman's shoulders. "We all have, Leona, but I have told you, we will not really take any vows."

"God will make a punishment to all of us for this lie," Leona said, still frowning.

Lady Primrose had heard Leona's last statement as she joined them. "Perhaps he will bless us for our work, Sister Leona."

Sister Leona shook her head once more. "I do not want to go to hell, Sister Ruth."

"Oh, tish and piffle, my dear. Now let us join the others." With a wink in Whitney's direction, she shepherded Sister Leona away.

Mother Joseph was standing at the front of the room, her arms folded, her fingers idly tracing the long strand of beads with a large ivory cross which swung lightly against her black robes.

Whitney went to join her. "Ladies, if you will please take a chair, we have a great deal of work to do."

Sister Magda lounged into one of the chairs and lit a cigarette. Whitney glanced at Mother Joseph, but she seemed lost in her own thoughts. Sister Bernadette pulled Sister Leona to two chairs as distant from Sister Magda as possible. Sister Judith, elegantly clad in a creamy wool suit, settled next to Sister Regina who had assumed the lotus position on her chair. Sister Ruth came to the front to stand next to Mother Joseph and Whitney.

"Well, Sister Camille," she muttered, "now we shall find out whether or not this little scheme will work."

"Prim," Whitney began, but the woman held up her hand.

"You really must get used to calling me Sister Ruth and I to calling you Sister Camille. Remember, you cautioned our girls about forgetting the past, and it is good advice, particularly for us."

"Sister Ruth," Whitney began again with a smile, "I wonder if we will *ever* know if this little scheme, as you call it, will work."

"We are prepared to teach you the external behaviors of our order," Mother Joseph began, looking at each of the women in the room. "Perhaps a bit of history first, to aid you in understanding our involvement. The sisters of our order have been assisting refugees from the Nazi terrors for a number of years. We consider it to be part of our service to God and man. It is also the reason we have agreed to cooperate with your organization, not only in this training but in your future endeavors. We will not, however, welcome any public compromise of our order or its reputation." Her gaze settled on Sister Magda. "Nuns do not smoke cigarettes."

Magda took a deep drag, letting the smoke drift from her mouth. "I am not a nun."

Whitney put her hand lightly on Mother Joseph's arm. "Magda, in consideration of the arrangements which have been made for you to participate, it seems to me you will be anything we tell you to be. Unless, of course, you would rather return to the custody of the State of Georgia. Don't they have an electric chair in Georgia?''

Glaring at Whitney, she ground out the cigarette on the polished hardwood of the floor. ''Aren't you supposed to call me 'Sister Magda'?'' she mumbled sullenly.

Sister Bernadette raised her hand and Mother Joseph nodded in her direction. ''I'm really sorry, but I don't believe I'll be able to do this.''

''Why is that, my child?'' Mother Joseph asked gently.

''Because I'm Jewish. I know nothing about Christianity. No one would ever believe I'm a nun. They'd know just by looking at me.''

Mother Joseph permitted herself a small smile. ''My dear child, you above all of us have every reason to want this deception to work, for the consequences of the truth emerging could be very grave. Believe me, my child, by the time we finish our training, the Holy Father himself will be calling you to give him proper instruction in the ways of this order.''

''How the hell do you expect us to learn all this?''

''Sister Magda, nuns do not curse.''

Sister Magda glared at Mother Joseph, slouching further into her chair.

''Now, if there are no further questions, we shall begin.'' Mother Joseph clapped her hands once and two nuns appeared, wheeling a rack of black robes. ''The most obvious sign of our order is our habit and wimple, which do take some practice to wear convincingly.'' Her gentle expression became grave. ''And you must, above all else, be convincing.''

''Paul, this article is not bad at all. Not great, but not bad. You're still sounding too much like a lawyer. Can you get a more . . . I don't know . . . human touch?'' Patrice took a sip of her tea. ''I would commit small murders for real coffee. The ersatz stuff just doesn't make my mind work.''

Paul grinned. ''Are you suggesting that if I brought you some real coffee, the article would be all right?''

''Of course not,'' Patrice said indignantly before noticing the twinkle in his eye. ''Oh, Paul.'' She hesitated. ''Well, that is a thought.''

"I know better than to think you could be bought," he said. "Then again, it might be worth a try."

Patrice balled up her fist and punched his shoulder playfully. "Come on! Doing rewrites is the fun part of reporting. And I'll bet you thought it was getting to go to those teas and interviewing the man in the street."

Paul sighed. "Silly me," he said. "I thought being a smart lawyer and Yalie would make me a natural for those big stories."

"My friend," she replied gently, "out there, where the real war is happening, is where I have to assign real reporters, not smart Yalie lawyers using this business as a cover."

"So if I'm not going to write real news, why do I have to write anything?"

"Now you not only look like a high-school kid, you sound like one. You're here, you're working for me as a reporter, and I think you ought to be as much of a reporter as you can. Who knows? Maybe you won't end up being a lawyer or a spy!"

"At least I know you're teasing. Seriously, I'm not sure how much humanity I can find in aircraft engines."

"It's not the engines, it's the people who are building them. How many of the workers in the plant are wives of soldiers? of flyers? or mothers or widows or sisters? How many of the men working there fought in the first war? Get beyond the mechanical process of building the engines and find the people, and you will have a great story. You've begun to do it here in this paragraph about the man with one hand who holds the bolt with his teeth until he begins to turn it, but then you backed away from the story."

"Has it occurred to you how bizarre that sentence was?" Paul asked, chuckling.

"That's our business: the beautiful from the bizarre. Man bites dog. Robber delivers victim's baby. At least, anyway, that's the feature business. Hard news is another matter. But don't be discouraged because you've begun by writing features. I began working for *Sunpapers* by writing a lonely-hearts column, then I covered teas. I got a big break when I accidentally uncovered a white slave ring in Baltimore that sold young girls to sheiks in the Sahara, but that is for

106

another time. My point is, you're stuck playing reporter for the duration, so you might as well learn the business."

Paul stood. "Right you are. But, please, I beg you, no lonely hearts and no teas."

"No promises," she replied. "Incidentally, have you continued to follow the 'Traitor's Hour'?"

He nodded. "I'm coming to hate her as much as you do. How does she manage to look herself in the mirror after suggesting that Americans are being foolish to ignore the 'opportunities of the Reich?' "

"Let's not talk about Laurel or I won't get any of this paperwork done. Suffice it to say, she's certainly taken advantage of the 'opportunities.' "

Paul walked to the door, then hesitated. "Maybe it's crazy, but I truly do believe people get what's coming to them, eventually."

Patrice leaned back in her chair, sighing. "I've felt that way too, but I'm not so sure anymore."

Paul slipped out the door, closing it behind him, and Patrice reached for the packet of Luckies on her desk, fitting one into the holder she'd begun using, then lighting it with Raven's parting gift, his treasured Zippo.

Running her thumb over the smooth surface of the lighter, she picked up the rumpled, folded piece of paper and smoothed it out on her desk.

My Darling Patrice:

How I miss you and wish we could be together, but the work here seems to grow more desperate and more necessary with each passing day.

They come streaming over the mountains to us, and so many times I wonder how some of them have managed to hold onto life even long enough to arrive. Others, of course, are simply fleeing the dreaded Gestapo or SS, but their psychological wounds are perhaps more grave than some of the physical ones I have seen.

And the stories they tell, the things they have heard through the Resistance grapevine, are horrifying. The talk of "concentration camps" and "death squads" was viewed at first as propaganda, but I have heard them too many times, and, if they are even in part true, mankind has reached a new low.

I'm trusting this letter to a dear friend and hope it won't be read by unfriendly eyes. These stories trouble me so much, however, that I can't not tell you.

Meantime, I am fine, though I fear I'm losing my sense of humor.

"My darling Stephen," Patrice said softly, "I think we all are." She stared at the familiar scrawl of his handwriting and tried hard to remember what it felt like to kiss him, to hold him in her arms, finally shaking her head in frustration.

It had been a very long time since they had been together regularly, an ocean and war ago. Now he gave everything he had to refugees, and what little might be left, he put into a letter which would be given to one of those fleeing wretches to be passed along, hand to hand, until it reached her. He hadn't even bothered to date the letter, she noted, feeling anger and frustration and not sure with whom.

"Perhaps we are star-crossed," she whispered to the tiny shred of his soul on the paper. "Perhaps your beliefs in giving your life to others and my passion for writing their stories will keep us apart for all time. Would that bother you, Stephen, or would you just shrug in that way you do and go back to fixing one more broken life?" She sighed, dragging deeply on her cigarette. "And would it bother me any more than it would you?"

The bells of the convent tolled, echoing among the twilight of the mountains. Whitney stood next to Mother Joseph, her head bowed slightly as she watched the Sisters of Perpetual Trust file into the chapel for evening prayers. Sprinkled among them, she could see the faces of her girls, each blending seamlessly with the nuns around them.

During the service, she tried to spot her girls among the others, but no flaws emerged, and she began to relax. Just maybe they were going to be fine.

After the prayers were concluded, she beckoned each of her operatives to the side as they emerged from the chapel, then turned and led them into the privacy of Mother Joseph's office, where they rustled into chairs, still maintaining silence, heads bowed demurely, some fingering their rosary beads.

"I am very proud of each of you," she began, "and you should be proud of yourselves. The transformation is astonishing. Tomorrow we will put all this to the test."

Sister Magda looked up from the beads she'd been fiddling with. "Why? Are we going to go save a few little wayward boys?"

"I think that might be a waste of all our special talents, don't you? No, tomorrow we're going to travel to our base of operations." She hesitated. "We will be living and working in Nazi-infested territory and there will be no room for even the slightest slip. You must be constantly vigilant, constantly aware, constantly on guard, but not seem as though you are."

Sister Judith raised her head. Her stunning beauty was undiminished even by the lack of makeup and by the severe wimple which hugged her head and the wide starched wings of the mantle which extended as wide as her shoulders. "What will we be doing, exactly?"

"You'll be told as the operations come up. Perhaps that seems vague, but the less you know, the safer you will be. I guess you could think of us as instruments of vengeance against the Nazis."

Sister Judith nodded. "I see. Christian soldiers," she observed with irony in her voice.

"Or God's avengers," Sister Regina proposed.

"Well, look around you," Whitney said. "We don't look so much like anything so much as butterflies. Hardly the image of avengers." Suddenly she grinned. "Donohue has been asking me to come up with a code name for this operation, and now I think we've done it. We are the Butterfly Avengers."

The wood paneling and plush upholstery of the Orient Express, for so long the symbol of old European money and luxury, seemed an incongruous setting for the covey of nuns who scurried aboard. But they were invisible to the rest of the passengers, many of them, to Whitney's terror, German officers. Whitney kept her head down, and the travel documents transferring Sister Camille, Sister Bernadette, Sister Judith, Sister Magda, Sister Ruth, and Sister Leona to the convent of the Sisters of Sacred Trust in Dubrovnik, Yugoslavia, firmly at her side. The papers were authentic, courtesy of Mother Joseph's long-standing relationship with Mother Leo in Dubrovnik.

"Nuns, my daughter," Mother Joseph had said when delivering the papers, "are quite invisible. Many people feel it is disrespectful to look directly at us, though I have many times heard titters of laughter at our rather distinctive headgear. Keep your eyes down, read your Bible, speak little, and you will find yourself to be invisible. God Bless you, Sister Camille, and your Butterflies."

The train seemed to stop and start constantly, lurching to a halt for no particular reason, standing for a time, then just as suddenly lurching to life again. Whitney had watched the mountain valleys of Switzerland sliding past the windows, memorizing the serenity and freedom they represented, aware of how soon they would leave it all behind. The Butterflies, too, seemed introspective and wary. Each time a German officer passed their compartment, their eyes darted to inspect him, then just as quickly pulled away, as though their gazes might draw attention to them.

Once more the train lurched to a halt, but this time when Whitney looked out the window she could see Italian soldiers boarding. Her heart seemed to freeze, then race, and she hoped the color she felt rising in her cheeks would subside before the soldiers reached the compartment. Quickly she glanced at the other women. Sister Judith was looking impassively out into the small station, watching the activity there. Sister Regina's fingers flew along her rosary beads as her mouth formed silent prayers. Sister Leona, too, was obviously praying.

Next to Whitney, Sister Ruth was calmly reading a biography of Saint Joan of Arc, but she felt Whitney's gaze and reached out to pat her hand reassuringly.

Sister Magda was the only one who seemed completely unaffected by the approaching soldiers. She had pulled her passport and travel documents from her habit and was holding them as insouciantly as she did her cigarettes.

"Buon giorno. Documenti, per favore," the soldier said as he appeared in the doorway of the compartment. Whitney extended her passport and papers as the others did, then looked up and directly into the eyes of a black-uniformed German officer wearing the double lightning bolts of the SS on his collar. At first he nodded in disinterested dismissal at the anonymous faces framed by the stark wimples, but then his eyes returned to Whitney's face, and she saw a flash of puzzled recognition in his eyes.

Quickly she returned her gaze to the unintelligible book in her hands, but her whole being was focused on him.

"Give me the papers," he said in English to the Italian soldier.

Whitney heard the rustling of the documents like razors slicing through the little strength she had left.

"Sister Camille, you are American," he said, and Whitney knew she would have to meet his eyes again. She took a breath, reminding herself about the nearly two years she had spent in the SS hospital, recalling her hatred of each of the SS doctors who had tormented her with addiction to morphine and endless questions, pulling up the memories of her fearsome flights through France and Spain to freedom. By the time her eyes raised to his, she was magically infused with a great calm.

"Yes," she said, smiling slightly.

"How long have you been in this order?"

"I joined when I was very young and took my vows when I became eighteen."

He studied the passport and travel documents minutely. "Why have you kept your American nationality when you live in Switzerland?"

"Why should I give it up?" she responded, her voice neutral.

He stepped closer to her, studying her face closely. "What color is your hair?"

"Brown," she lied.

"Remove your hat," he ordered.

Before Whitney could move, Sister Ruth, frowning, spoke

111

up, her voice laden with authority. "Young man, you must not ask this of Sister Camille or of any nun. It would be most improper."

The SS officer's face clouded with anger and he turned to Sister Ruth. "Keep silent," he snapped, then turned to the Italian soldier, who was looking horrified. "Is this true?"

The young soldier nodded. "*Sì*. It is against the law of the church. It would show most bad respect."

The SS officer lounged against the door of the compartment, a sardonic smile on his face. "I know I have seen Sister Camille before somewhere, but she wasn't a nun then."

"Sister Camille has been part of our order for many years. Perhaps she looks familiar to you because she resembles Greta Garbo, a famous actress from your country, I believe." Sister Ruth put her hand atop Whitney's. "Sister Camille is just recovering from tuberculosis and she shouldn't be distressed like this." Her voice was firm.

The SS officer studied Whitney closely, then shrugged. "Perhaps she does look like Garbo, though not as pretty. He extended the bundle of documents to Sister Ruth. "Are you certain she is well enough to travel all the way to Dubrovnik, or should we make arrangements for her to be hospitalized here?"

"She will be fine with us," Sister Ruth said firmly, "but she should not have to suffer such questioning."

The SS officer nodded, bowing slightly. "Then she should not travel." He turned on his heel and moved to the next compartment. The Italian soldier quietly closed the door to their compartment, looking embarrassed.

"You were magnificent," Whitney muttered.

"Oh, tish. There isn't a man in the world, SS or not, who can stand up to a nun who takes a stand."

Whitney gestured toward the book lying open in Sister Ruth's lap. "I'm not sure that worked so well for Saint Joan."

"If she'd dressed like a nun, she would never have had all the trouble she did." Sister Ruth gave her hand one more pat, then busied herself with distributing the passports.

* * *

Patrice heard the knocking on the door through her sleep, and had pulled on her clothes and grabbed her purse almost before she was fully awake.

She yanked open the door, prepared to dash to the nearest shelter, but Paul put his hands on her shoulders and pushed her gently back into the room.

"Is it an air raid?" she blurted, pulling away from him.

"Sorry, no. Just me. I apologize for the late hour, but I've got something big and we need to get a report to Donohue. Where's the coffee?"

"Is this big enough for real coffee?" Patrice asked, yawning in spite of herself as she went to the kitchen to find the precious tin Paul had received from some unnamed source. As she put the water into the coffeepot, he joined her.

"I had dinner with an old buddy from law school tonight. He's a Canadian whose family was Russian. Now he's with the Canadian intelligence service and has been undercover on the Russian front. I think he's being sent back to Canada for a long rest. He was in the town his family came from and he's been shaken badly."

"Why? What happened?"

Paul opened Patrice's liquor cabinet and removed a bottle of brandy he'd brought her, pouring a healthy dollop into each of the coffee cups.

"Remember the man who spoke to that meeting we attended at the Waldorf?"

"Heydrich?"

"The same. It seems he's been a busy boy since he left New York. Apparently he's one of the prides of the Reich because he's in charge of 'controlling' the cities the Germans have invaded in Russia, and his idea of control is pretty odious."

Patrice poured the steaming coffee into the cups and they carried them into the living room. "How odious?"

Paul settled onto the couch. "Mass executions of the populace."

"Oh my God," Patrice said. "What are they doing?"

"Lining the people up along a trench and machine-gunning them," Paul said bluntly. "Men, women, children, everyone. My friend said one town was completely wiped out.

Three thousand people murdered in one afternoon. He, along with the others in his town, were forced to watch. Then they were told the same thing would happen to them if they did not cooperate with the Germans. He said he hasn't slept since, and to look at him, I can believe it.''

Patrice got up and went to the bookcase, removing a copy of *Winnie the Pooh* from the shelf.

"This is hardly the moment for a story, Patrice," Paul said, his voice conveying his irritation.

"Code book," she said, thumbing through the pages, then reaching for the phone and dialing a number.

"Eeyore," she said after a moment, then paused. "The honey is in the pot." She listened for another moment, then hung up.

"Eeyore?"

"The donkey who's Pooh's good friend."

"Of course. Makes perfect sense. Who am I? Tigger?"

"Actually, you're not in this code book. I suppose I could ask if you really want—" Before she could finish, the phone rang. She picked it up, listened for a moment, said, "Honey is very nice on scones," then replaced the receiver. "Donohue will be here shortly. More coffee?"

As she poured an additional cup for each of them, adding a generous shot of brandy, she tried to shake the ill ease she felt. It was one thing to assume the Nazis were murdering innocent civilians, but something else entirely to hear absolute confirmation. As she returned to the living room, there was a knock on the door.

Donohue and Cesar Ball entered, looking concerned as they surrendered their coats and hats. They settled into the chairs facing the couch while Patrice busied herself bringing the coffee and brandy to the living room, pouring them each a cup.

"I'm sorry to disturb you at this hour, but Paul has discovered something which may be very important." Briefly she recapped the information he'd given her, as well as the connection between Laurel and Heydrich.

"You were right to call," Donohue commented before turning to Paul. "This Canadian friend of yours, does he work for MI5?"

Paul shrugged. "I'm not sure. I know he's with Canadian intelligence."

"Well, he's a security risk to his agency, but I'd like to talk to him. Could you get him over here tonight?"

"I can try." Paul removed his address book from his coat pocket then dialed a number. "Tom Murphy, please," he said after a moment, then, "This is a friend of his. Why?" His face clouded as he listened, then hung up looking stunned. "He's dead," he whispered.

"Dead?" Patrice said incredulously.

Paul nodded. "The desk clerk at his hotel said he'd been struck by a hit-and-run driver in front of the hotel about three hours ago. That would have been right after we spoke."

Donohue ran his hand through his hair. "Damn. I'm sorry. Obviously I wasn't the only one who thought he was a security risk. Now the question is, who killed him? The Germans . . . or MI5 . . . or Canada?" He paused, obviously thinking, then said, "Paul, for the time being I'm going to put you on a special detail outside London. We can't be certain you wouldn't be the next target since he'd spilled his guts to you. We have a joint operation with the Brits working on German codes. You could serve a couple of purposes down there for me and be pretty safe."

"Unless it was MI5 who killed Tom."

Cesar Ball leaned forward. "Even then, I think they'll leave you alone as long as they can watch you closely. Maybe it would help you to understand a bit about this business. The art of gathering intelligence is constructed on a foundation of paranoia which is our best protection and our worst vulnerability. None of us trusts anyone else's operatives, and many in this business don't even trust their own. People get turned away from their loyalties. Sometimes it's money, sometimes blackmail, sometimes a woman—a thousand reasons. Knowing this, and using it on the enemy's agents as often as we can, makes us all suspicious of our own agents."

Donohue nodded in agreement, adding, "We also don't trust our allies' services. They, and we, would sell our mothers to preserve the greater good. Did your friend know you are working for us?"

Paul shook his head. "No. You told me not to tell anyone."

"Good for you, but even worse for him. That means he was willing to identify himself as an agent and give an outsider very important information just because he couldn't carry the burden of it by himself. If it were MI5 or the Canadians who liquidated him, it was because they'd found out he was giving them away. If, on the other hand, it was the Germans, it gives us two pieces of important information. First, what he had is not only true, but also something they don't want revealed. And second, it means there's a German agent, who has the latitude to make kill decisions, working in London." He sighed. "I'm going to go around to William Stevenson at MI5 on this one. He probably won't tell me if they liquidated their own agent, but he will owe me one if it is a German they don't know about."

"It seems to me there might be one other possibility," Ball interjected. "They may be very much aware of the German and let him clean up their mess for them. Or he might be a double agent."

Donohue smiled ironically. "You can see this is neither a clean nor logical business. However, all this is simply instructional and doesn't address what we need to do." He yawned. "One other thing about this business: it only seems to happen at night and on weekends." He refilled his coffee cup. "Tell me about your friend Laurel. How close is she to Heydrich?"

"I got the impression in New York that she's probably intimate with him. If not, she takes a great many liberties." Patrice conveyed her disapproval clearly.

Donohue shrugged. "What drives her?"

"Money, certainly, and power, I'd suspect. She has always liked to be the center of attention and to be around people who make decisions."

"Could she be turned?"

Patrice looked disgusted. "She has been. To them. She's the one who does the broadcasts from Berlin."

Ball nodded. "We've listened. One principle of this busi-

116

ness is that someone who has been turned will either become a fanatic or be easier than most to turn back.''

Donohue nodded. "She would seem to be the most direct route to our friend Heydrich.'' He leaned back in his chair. "You see, Reinhard Heydrich is not a new player to us. He's Hitler's golden boy and right under Himmler in the SS, at least on paper. In reality, he's the power in that organization. The profile we have on him is interesting—full of contradictions. He's cruel to the point of sadism but married, with three kids. He's in the highest echelons of the Nazis and a concert violinist. There was a story which came from a Polish Jew, who'd escaped from one of the ghettos, who said Heydrich had ordered that Wagner be played over the loudspeakers in the streets. We'd like to get more inside information about him, but he's as much a phantom as he is a public figure. So, Laurel Pugh could be a very valuable asset.''

"But how do we reach her? She's in Berlin and I'm certain she's watched pretty carefully.''

"Weren't you planning a trip to Berlin this spring?'' Donohue raised his eyebrows quizzically.

Patrice's face curled into a grin and she raised her eyebrows. "Of course I was. Hadn't we just talked about my trip? When do I leave and what do I do once I'm there?''

"What you do best, Miss Rigby. Talk, look for a weak spot, then pounce.''

"Everything here is old,'' Sister Magda sneered as she walked beside Whitney through the narrow, cobbled street leading from the cathedral where they had been polishing wood, back to the convent in the Bishop's palace, inside the old, walled city of Dubrovnik.

"And you don't see the charm in that?'' Sister Judith inquired from behind them.

"Charm! Have you used the toilet? The damn thing was probably made in thirteen hundred.'' She grinned evilly over her shoulder. "I forgot. You rich society bitches don't piss, do you?''

"Sister Magda!'' Whitney said firmly. "Nuns don't curse.''

117

"Bullshit, Sister Camille. Nobody can hear me but you and you know the truth."

Whitney took her arm, digging her fingers deeply into the small notch between the two bones of Sister Magda's elbow. "This, Sister Magda, is absolutely the last time I intend to caution you. Should you continue to ignore me, you will find yourself sitting on a very uncomfortable seat in Georgia. You have two choices. Do it my way, or go back." She applied a little additional pressure and felt the woman's arm jerk. "You must be a nun inside and out for the duration of this mission or you risk compromising all of us. And I, for one, do not care to spend any time with the SS just because you refuse to take responsibility. Is that clear?"

"Yeah."

"What?" Whitney snapped.

"Yes, Sister Camille," Sister Magda replied and Whitney heard, to her surprise, actual contrition in the woman's voice.

"Thank you."

As they approached the gate to the Bishop's palace, Whitney was surprised to see a tall, dusky-skinned man wearing the traditional garb of the Turkish Muslim lounging against the wall.

"Sisters," he said in a heavily accented French, "help a poor beggar."

Whitney paused in front of him, responding in French, "What is it you need?"

"Food," he said, patting his stomach. "And water."

"Come inside. We will help you."

He waited until all the nuns had passed, then followed them inside the gates to the budding gardens of the palace, closing the gate behind them. Whitney led the group to the convent entrance, letting the Butterflies pass inside, but stopping Sister Ruth with a glance. When the sisters had disappeared inside, she nodded and turned toward the kitchen. The three of them entered, and she motioned the man into a chair, then went to the door to make certain they were alone.

"Major Ball," she said, returning to the table, "this is an outrageous getup."

118

He shrugged. "Sister Camille, although I am light-skinned in comparison to many of my race, I would draw attention if I did not assume a common local persona. Sister Ruth, you look fetching."

Whitney and Lady Primrose settled down at the table with him. "I assume you have something critical," Whitney said.

He nodded, reaching into his caftan and pulling out a map of the country. "Erik has provided us with the routes the Nazis are using to get matériel into Yugoslavia. Apparently they are building up a strong cache of arms here and we feel you and your Butterflies could effectively disrupt some of the stockpiling." He looked from one to the other. "Donohue believes you will devise the best way to make use of the talent you have here. We'll provide as much information as we can about the important sites, but leave the operations up to you. The first site we'd like disrupted is here." He pointed to an area of the mountains just outside Dubrovnik.

Whitney looked at Prim, getting her concurrence, then nodded. "We'll do our best."

Cesar Ball smiled. "Then good luck to the Germans."

7

THANK YOU, *mein Führer*," Laurel said breathlessly into the telephone, her eyes aglow. "Thank you, I shall do my best to continue to convince them. . . . You are too kind, sir. . . . Thank you." She replaced the receiver almost reverently, then turned to face her father-in-law, smiling broadly.

"The Führer is pleased with your radio broadcasts?" he inquired.

"He says my programs are making a real difference. Many of their pilots are surrendering and asking to fly for the Luftwaffe. He also said there is still much support for the Reich among the powerful in America."

"We are proud of the contribution you are making to the advancement of the Reich, Laurel. We are proud to have you in our family." He rose, indicating their conversation was over, and Laurel turned to leave the room. She hesitated at the door, wondering if his genial mood might help open the conversation she had hoped to have with him about Helmut's drinking, which seemed to grow worse by the hour.

"Was there something else you wanted?" he asked, and Laurel could hear the edge of impatience in his voice.

"No," she said, turning back to retrieve the door to close it. "Nothing. Good night."

She climbed the wide, curving stairs slowly, savoring the compliments of the Führer, basking in the glow of her own rapidly expanding circle of influence in the Reich. It even seemed as though her father-in-law, Gerhard, was beginning to respect her, and she didn't care that it was because of her friends instead of for herself. As long as he knew there were others who thought well of her, she could count on his acceptance. Soon it would not matter if Helmut drank himself to death. She hesitated next to one of the stern family portraits that lined the stairs. Actually it would be very handy if he did. What a wonderful role: the grieving widow, rich, powerful, and unencumbered.

Quietly she opened the door to their suite, hoping Helmut would still be sleeping. She glanced inside and saw him sprawled across the bed, his breathing noisy but regular.

"Good night, Prince Charming," she whispered, pulling the door closed. Hurrying into her bedroom, Laurel laid out one of the lovely new gowns she'd bought on her last trip to Paris. She undressed and slipped into a scented tub, then put on a black lace teddy, sheer silk stockings, and the black gown Reinhard had told her he thought made her look very sexy. She slipped into black moiré pumps and put her official pass and money into a small evening bag. Wrapping her black loden wool cape over her gown, she crept through the suite and slipped out the door into the broad hallway. Laurel looked up and down the deserted passage before hurrying to the back stairs, and scurried down and out through the kitchen.

Klaus, as she'd instructed, had removed the car from the garage and parked it far enough away from the house so it wouldn't be heard. When she rapped at the window, he emerged quickly to open the door to the back seat.

"The *Bistro Franchen*," she said before leaning back into the comfort of the seat, still savoring her conversation with the Führer. Finally, after all the years of playing second fiddle to Whitney and Patrice, after being the outcast, now she was the star.

*   *   *

Reinhard rose as she entered, following the solicitous maître d' to the ringside table they always occupied. He looked so handsome in his full-dress black uniform with the twin silver lightning bolts sparkling from his collar. He clicked his heels and bowed formally when she reached the table, then kissed her hand before allowing the maître d' to seat her.

"You look very beautiful tonight," he said, resuming his seat and leaning across the table, taking her hand.

"Reinhard, the Führer himself called me to thank me for my broadcasts." Laurel felt again the exhilaration.

He smiled briefly. "He is very taken with you. He listens often. I will give you something tonight for your next three broadcasts."

Laurel felt an edge of panic. "You're not leaving again, are you?"

His smile faded. "You are starting to sound like Lina. I thought you were proud of my role in the Reich, but perhaps you are as selfish as she is."

"No, no," Laurel said quickly, fear rising in her throat. "No, please don't be angry with me. I am proud of you. But I miss you very much when you're away. But you know I understand. Please don't be angry."

He quickly finished his drink, turning away from her to signal the waiter while Laurel struggled to control her fear of his potential rage. He kept his face turned away from her until the waiter arrived with the replacement drink, which he swallowed quickly before he turned back, his eyes cold. "I am bored here. We will leave now." He stood abruptly, peeling some reichsmarks from a carefully clipped wad of money in his pocket, then walked away from the table, leaving Laurel to gather her purse and scurry after him. She rummaged for the coat check while Reinhard stood, staring out the glass doors at the street, then preceded her outside, signaling for his car.

He was silent on the way to the hotel, drumming his fingers against the leather armrest that he'd pulled down between them. Laurel wondered if she should simply go home, but worried that her departure might make things worse between them.

At the hotel, he opened the door of the car for her but made no effort to help her out. "Wait," he commanded the driver before striding into the lobby, leaving Laurel to follow him up to the suite.

He closed and locked the door, removed his uniform jacket, replacing it with the silk smoking jacket Laurel had given him for Christmas, opened a bottle of schnapps, and poured himself a generous portion. Laurel had removed her cape, but stayed standing in the foyer, watching him intently.

"Come here," he said, finally breaking his extended silence. His voice was harsh.

Laurel took a deep breath, breaking into a smile she hoped looked both alluring and unintimidated, and walked to the couch with the slow sensuality she knew he liked.

"Did you pour a drink for me, darling?" she purred.

"Sit," he replied, the anger still sharpening his tone.

She desperately held her smile, curling up beside him. "If you didn't make a drink for me, let me have a sip of yours, darling," she said, hoping he couldn't hear the fear in her voice.

"Don't call me 'darling,' " he replied, pulling the glass out of her reach. "And stop pretending you're my wife. I don't like my wife. You are my mistress and that's what I want you to be. Don't nag me. Don't whine when I go to do my job."

"I'm really sorry," Laurel said with exaggerated contrition, hoping the outburst had released all his anger and her submission would soothe him.

"Don't do things you must be sorry for," he said, suddenly slapping her hard across her face. "Now I must punish you and you know I hate having to do that. But it is not my fault. You have brought this upon yourself." He slapped her again and Laurel burst into tears, not only from the shock and pain, but also because she knew what would come now as it had several times before.

"Please don't hit me again," she sobbed. "Please don't hurt me."

"You are whining again," he said, exasperated. "Why do you make me do this?"

He grabbed her hands, wrenching them roughly around

123

behind her, tying them with the sash from his smoking jacket. Laurel squirmed, trying to get away from him until he put his hand around her throat, squeezing until her vision clouded with stars. "Hold still or it will only get worse," he spat, yanking the cord tight with his free hand, then pushing her back onto the couch.

"No, please," she whimpered.

"Shut up," he said, grabbing the low neckline of her dress with both his hands and ripping it open, then yanked at her lace teddy, freeing her breasts. Laurel turned her head away, steeling herself, unable to watch the maniacal delight she had seen on his face.

He traced gently around her nipples with his fingers, then suddenly pinched them hard, twisting roughly when Laurel gasped in pain.

"Do not whine. Do not nag me. Do not demand. You are not my wife." Each phrase was punctuated with a sharp, painful twist.

Laurel feared she would pass out from the pain, then feared she wouldn't.

He slapped at her breasts with his open hand, hitting them until they were scarlet, the nipples a deeper hue. Laurel turned back and looked down helplessly, watching as he again twisted and tortured her nipples. She was horrified, through the searing pain, to see blood seeping from one nipple, but relieved when he suddenly stopped.

"My poor darling," he cooed, covering the bleeding nipple with his lips. She could see him sucking on it, but could feel nothing until his hands began to remove the rest of her torn lingerie, his fingers probing and stimulating her. She felt nothing but the residual of the pain, but forced herself to respond, wanting to prevent another outburst of anger and torture from him, and more, wanting at any cost to keep the access to the power he afforded her.

"My darling," she whispered, hoping he'd be convinced.

Reinhard was sleeping, his breathing even and deep, his face a peaceful antithesis to his violent behavior only a short time before. Laurel winced in pain as she rolled away from him slowly, not wanting to wake him. She sat at the edge of

124

the bed, gathering her thoughts and her strength, then wobbled to her feet, each bone aching, her skin recoiling from even the gentle caress of the silk robe she wrapped around herself, knotting it lightly at her waist.

In the living room of the suite, she poured a large glass of cognac and drank it quickly, then refilled it, this time sipping more slowly as she bent to pick up the remaining tatters of her dress and the teddy she'd worn. She tossed the destroyed garments into a corner, then eased herself onto the couch. "Oh, ouch," she muttered.

"I hurt you, didn't I," Reinhard said from the doorway to the bedroom.

Laurel gasped, turning abruptly to him, then away again. "Yes," she whispered softly.

He came to stand beside her, then, surprisingly, caressed her hair gently. "I'm sorry. Do you forgive me?"

She nodded, then said, "Please promise it won't happen again."

His hand stopped its motion and she froze, instantly regretting the admonition in her tone.

"You don't understand, do you," he said, far more softly than she'd expected. He turned and walked to the window, staring out into the deserted street through a small slit in the drapes. "No one understands." He sighed. "Sometimes not even those closest to the Führer himself." He shook his head. "We are changing the world, making it new and clean again, giving the future a chance to be unpolluted by those who are unfit decimators of all that is good and right in humanity." He turned abruptly to face her. "People don't understand that such drastic changes demand extreme measures. They can't see beyond today, they can't understand how order and right will emerge from what seems to be chaos." He slammed his hand against the table. "They don't see that the common good of all people may sometimes mean ignoring the needs of one or two individuals."

His eyes glittered in the low light of the room as he walked to pour himself a cognac, then stood, looking out beyond her. "I carry so much of this by myself, you see. I have had to make decisions which seem to be cruel, but are kind to humanity." He paced back to the window, then turned again to face Laurel. "The Führer is really the only one who understands the great plan. When he speaks of a Reich to last a thousand years, he means not as it is today with war and anger and hatred, but a blessed utopia in which a clean, pure race of superior beings will thrive and grow. This is why we have taken a bold step and begun to deal with those who are weak or sullied. It is not from a hatred of gypsies or homosexuals or Jews but a love of mankind that we have devised the Final Solution."

"The Final Solution?" Laurel asked softly.

Reinhard grinned. "I have been working on this. It is a brilliant clarification of the first paces to utopia. You see, for years we have been holding these undesirable, polluting elements in ghettos, not knowing what might be done with them. Of course, we have found some small uses for them in building our unstoppable war machine, but the war will not continue forever, and the need for these societal contaminants will soon disappear. Are we to spend time and money maintaining them when we know they have no place in the Reich of tomorrow? Are we to use the hard-earned reichsmarks of the true Aryans to feed and house them? Obviously not. With each country won to the Reich, their numbers have grown, and our soldiers, who must be used to guard and maintain them, could be better used for the glories of the fatherland." He quickly gulped the cognac and nearly danced across the room in his excitement.

"There is only one obvious solution to all this, but you cannot imagine how much resistance I meet, even among those high-level officers who profess to believe in the Reich but are afraid to act. The Führer, however, who has the vision to see into the future and the imagination to do what needs to be done to achieve it, is fully behind me, and the others see they must join us so as not to be left in the past."

Laurel felt his contagious excitement. "What is your idea?" she asked.

He shrugged in a parody of self-depreciation. "It is so simple and obvious that I can hardly claim it as visionary. For the good of all people, for the benefit of tomorrow's utopia, those undesirables must simply be eliminated. We have devised a humane and swift way by using a painless

126

gas. The financial pressures of maintaining the undesirables will then be removed." He strode to her, taking her hands in his with a passionate excitement. "Do you see now why this is all so important? Do you understand now why the work we are doing is the beginning of such a beautiful future? You are so lucky to be a part of all this."

"If the Americans and the British could hear you speak like this, they would come to our side immediately. I will try to incorporate some of your brilliance and passion in my broadcasts, but I'm afraid I don't have your gift."

"Believing and understanding will help a great deal to overcome that," he said gently, taking her into his arms. Laurel, intoxicated by his power and vision, surrendered completely.

". . . you only see the war and what you believe to be hatred, but if you could only look beyond today and understand Germany's—and the Führer's—great love of humanity, you would quickly and freely join us.

"Stop listening to the self-serving prattle of your weak and selfish leaders, who only want to preserve their power and influence, and let your heart listen to the cries of future generations, who want and deserve a perfect world in which to live and grow. Give reason and truth a chance to prevail over greed and lies.

"Germany's National Socialists want you, and much more importantly, your children and their children, to live in a world where there will be no fear. No fear of the banks taking your hard-earned money and closing, leaving you without even a dime of your sweat. No fear of a Communist government taking away all your rights is an important part of the beautiful utopia which awaits us all, not in the far-distant future, but tomorrow, if you make the choice.

"Choose tomorrow. Come home to the future."

"I won't recruit her, I'll just kill her," Patrice hissed, snapping off the radio with a vicious twist.

Donohue glanced up from his notes. "Admittedly, it's a temptation, but her rhetoric, beyond being inflammatory, is

127

truly the party line. It's obvious she's connected right to the top, and she'd be a valuable asset to us."

"I don't mean to be a gloomy gus, but the more I listen to her, the less I believe we could ever find a way to turn her. You don't know Laurel like I do. She's a terrier. Once she gets hold of something, you practically have to shoot her to get her away from it."

"Are you losing your enthusiasm for the assignment?" Donohue asked quietly.

"Hardly! I'm simply making sure you understand her."

Donohue favored her with one of his lightning grins. "Just call it my Boston grandfather's stubbornness and my prospector-great grandfather's optimism . . . and my Irish blind luck. I still believe we can make her into a valuable OSS asset." He rose. "I'm on my way to pick up Paul from the safe house, where we've been giving him some quick lessons in cryptography, and get him out to his new job."

"And when do I go to Berlin?" Patrice asked, retrieving his raincoat from the stand in the front hall.

"I'm not certain yet. We don't want to move precipitously. Call it Irish luck again, but the right timing has always managed to make itself known. Just keep your suitcase packed and keep doing your job."

Laurel left the studio elated after her broadcast, ignoring the gray and gloomy rain which seemed endless in Berlin's spring. Klaus was waiting at her car with an umbrella as she swept from the building into its luxurious security. Surely there would be another call from the Führer tonight, she thought, happily reviewing the power and passion of the words which had flowed so easily tonight.

Klaus pulled the car under the portico at the side of the house, opening the door to the limousine just as the door to the house swung open. Laurel had become accustomed to the anticipatory service of the mansion and swept into the receiving foyer, shrugging out of her coat without looking, confident that, as always, someone would be there to receive it. She entered the central core of the house before the uproar around her penetrated her afterglow. She hesitated

128

for a moment, then was rudely grabbed and spun to face Gerhard Pugh.

"Let go of me," she snapped, infuriated at his presumption.

The man, his face a chalky, mottled mask of rage, yanked her toward the stairs, propelling her with the force of his fury instead of physical pressure.

"What is the meaning of this?" Laurel sputtered, outraged at this rude treatment.

At the door to her suite, he shoved her backward against the door, then reaching into his pocket produced an envelope.

"What is the meaning of this?" Laurel said again, but this time her tone was moderated, her anger penetrated by the expression she saw in the senior Pugh's eyes.

"Take this and get out," Gerhard said, his voice quavering with fury.

"What do you mean, 'Get out?' I am a part of this family, if you recall." She took the letter and opened it, then stared at the figure which marched across the check inside. "Why in the world are you giving me five hundred thousand dollars and telling me to get out? Has Helmut made you do this?" Finally it seemed clear. The bastard was too cowardly to confront her, so he'd let his father pay her off. "What has that sniveling little bastard done?"

"What has *Helmut* done?" Gerhard spat into her face. "The question is not what my innocent son has done, but what evil you have brought to this house. I want you out, forever."

"Does Helmut know of this? He will never agree to such a thing."

Abruptly her father-in-law reached past her, opening the door behind her, then spinning Laurel around, he pushed her into the room. She stumbled crossing the threshold, sprawling inside the door. When she looked up she found herself staring into the unblinking eyes of her husband.

"Helmut," she said furiously, "do you know what your father is trying to do?" Laurel pushed herself up to her knees. Suddenly she screamed, scurrying backward to get away from the lifeless form of her husband lying in a pool of

129

blood, his head smashed into a deformed, oozing blob on the floor. Laurel spun toward Gerhard. "Who did this? Who killed my Helmut?"

The senior Pugh grabbed her arm, yanking her to her feet. "You did, whore. You and that SS pig, Heydrich."

"I did not! And Reinhard isn't even in Berlin. You're lying."

"Get out. Take your blood money and get out." He yanked her away from the room, then flung her toward the stairs. The force of his thrust sent her running toward the stairs. Desperately, Laurel grabbed for the banister, holding herself up as her feet stumbled on the stairs. She could hear Gerhard thundering behind her and struggled to regain her balance.

When she reached the bottom of the stairs, she turned to see him standing on the landing, staring hatefully at her.

"What about my things?" she demanded.

"Get out," he shrieked. "Get out."

Laurel turned, fleeing. Klaus waited beside the car, which was laden with suitcases. Wordlessly, he opened the door. Laurel hesitated, then folded the check and put it in her purse before smoothing her rumpled suit and raising her head.

"To hell with you, Gerhard Pugh," she said, stepping into the vehicle.

She left Klaus to manage her luggage. As she climbed the steps to the hotel's lobby, it occurred to her that Klaus may very well have been more than a passive participant in providing reinforcement to Gerhard Pugh's store of information about her activities. *A whore indeed*, she thought, outraged.

She was still fuming as she strode down the hall to the suite. At least she had a place of refuge after being so unceremoniously thrust from her home. Laurel opened her bag to find her key to the rooms and saw the check. She removed it, unfolding the paper and staring once more at the enormous figure written in Gerhard's bold, precise hand—$500,000. American. Drawn on the Chase Manhattan Bank. *Well*, she thought, *this will necessitate a small trip to Swit-*

zerland. After all, one would hardly want to put such a large amount in a bank controlled by a nation at war. One can be loyal without being stupid.

She tapped the paper against her fingertips, thinking. Why would he call her a whore and then pay her such an enormous sum? If he truly believed she had something to do with what had happened to Helmut, he would either have had her arrested or put her out penniless. She smiled slightly. This, above all, was proof of the power she'd cultivated, a power which Pugh obviously thought far exceeded his influence.

She found the key and put it into the lock, then stopped abruptly. What if he refused to honor the check once she presented it? Laurel felt a wave of panic rising. What if it had just been a way to keep her quiet until she was out of the house? No, she thought, soothing herself. He must know how unwise it would be to dishonor his word to someone with her kind of connections.

She turned the key and entered, surprised to find the lights on in the suite. The hotel porters appeared with her luggage piled on a cart and she gestured toward the larger bedroom.

After they'd left, Laurel closed the door, turning the lock, then removed her coat and hung it in the closet. She felt exhausted, disjointed, out of step with her life, and she didn't like the feeling. She walked to the bar and poured herself a glass of cognac, drinking it quickly, then refilling the glass and swallowing half, hoping to dispel the ill ease which had begun to creep into the silent room.

She turned away from the bar, then gasped. There was a strange man sprawled on the couch, sleeping soundly. Laurel backed away, staring at him and the mess of papers and music sheets which surrounded him. As she stared, his tanned face transformed into Helmut's, his head became misshapen and bloody. Laurel's hand flew to cover her mouth as she watched the face of the creature on the couch quickly mutate from a stranger to Helmut and back. She felt the pressure of the wall against her back but continued to push backward, trying to distance herself from the monster. She slid slowly along the wall to the door of her bedroom. Helmut's dead face seemed to watch her, grinning with death's delight at her fears.

"No," she whispered, "no, no, no, no. I didn't kill you. You know I would never have killed you. No, I didn't tell anybody to kill you, either. You did this to yourself, Helmut. Now leave me alone."

Laurel felt the door frame pressing against her back and rolled around into the safety of the bedroom. When she reached the door, the figure on the couch stirred, and the scream she'd been stifling burst from her mouth. The figure sat up abruptly as she slammed the door and turned the lock, her heart pounding.

Laurel turned to hide in case the creature could come through the door, but suddenly she felt an overwhelming wave of dizziness and disjointedly observed the pile of suitcases pitching upward to meet her.

The man on the couch sat up, rubbing his eyes, trying to decide if the woman really had screamed or if it had been part of the horrid dream he'd been having about blood and death. He ran his hands over his coal-black hair, glancing at the closed door to the bedroom. Reinhard did find the strangest women, he mused, gathering up his papers.

"Laurel, open the door," Reinhard's voice commanded sharply. She opened her eyes, looking around, mystified at first how she'd arrived in the suite, then horrified that she might have overslept and not gone home before dawn— finally remembering as she stirred against the uncomfortable locks and handles of the luggage.

"Ouch. Oh. Just a minute," she said, pushing herself off the pile of suitcases, clutching the spasm in her back with one hand and her pounding head with the other. "Good lord," she said as she reached for the lock.

"What the hell are you doing here?" Reinhard stormed, striding into the room. "And what the hell is all this?"

Laurel continued to massage her back. "Pugh threw me out. The driver brought me here."

"With all this?" His arm swept to indicate the jumble on the floor.

"It wasn't my idea," she said peevishly, irritated with him that he wasn't delighted to see her. "I got home and he was crazed. Helmut had been killed and . . . it's all not very clear.''

Reinhard raised his eyebrow as he studied her. "Your husband is dead?''

"Yes. And Pugh accused—'' Laurel stopped abruptly, realizing with horror that she had been about to indict Reinhard.

Reinhard's face tensed. "Accused what?''

"Accused me of being a whore,'' she said warily, watching him closely to be certain he'd accepted the substitution.

"Who killed him?''

She shook her head. "I don't know. It was all so much yelling and''—she shuddered, remembering the creature on the couch and her husband's form on the floor—"blood. Pugh made me look at him, then threw me out.''

"Well, you can't stay here.'' Reinhard kicked at the suitcases, then turned to go into the living room.

Laurel followed, conscious of the stiffness in her back and legs. "Why not? I have nowhere else to go and—''

Reinhard spun to face her. "Because I say you can't stay here.''

"Well, how am I supposed to . . .'' Laurel stopped, seeing the seeds of anger sprouting from the furrow on his brow. "I'll try to find an apartment today, though you know how little housing is available in Berlin. Is it because of the man who was here last night?''

Reinhard spun to face her. "Did you speak with him?'' His voice was hard.

She shook her head, unwilling to reveal the hallucinations she'd suffered, fearing he would think she had weakened. "He was sleeping on the couch. I don't think he even knew I'd come in.''

Reinhard smirked. "You are wrong.'' He stared at her. "Describe him.''

"Don't you know what he looks like?'' Laurel said with quick irritation, then immediately regretted her response. "He was dark. Maybe Italian. I don't know.''

"You will stay here,'' Reinhard said abruptly. "But you will tell no one where you may be found and you will tell no one anything you see here.''

Suddenly she wasn't at all sure she wanted to stay. "No, I don't want to create difficulties for you. I'll go to another hotel. It'll be fine."

He took her arm roughly. "I said you will stay here. Don't make me do something neither of us wants."

Laurel felt a cold chill at his words. "Fine," she said quickly. "If you insist."

His face was cold. "I insist."

Laurel rummaged through her suitcases and was not surprised to find most of her good clothing and all of her jewelry missing. Who cared? she thought, reaching for the telephone and ringing the desk.

"Send up a maid to unpack for me," she said when the concierge answered. "And send up breakfast."

There was no physical evidence of the man who'd been there the night before, but Laurel couldn't help wondering about him. She strolled across the living room to the windows, surprised to find the day bright and sunny when she opened the drapes. She thought, with irony, that this was the first time she'd seen the view from the suite in daylight. It seemed prettier at night in the soft glow of the streetlights than it did with the sun making the gray, imposing buildings across the square seem more formidable.

Germans, she thought, loved power and all its trappings as much as she did. Every chance they got, they built monuments to it which not only glorified power but radiated it, dominating the city. She was turning away from the window to return to the bedroom when she noticed a sheet of paper under the couch. She stooped to pull it out, then realized it must have been left by the mysterious visitor. It was a sheet of music, the notes, black splotches on pale lines, meaningless to her. She tossed it onto the coffee table, drumming her fingers impatiently at the delayed maid and breakfast, staring at the sheet.

"Let's see," Laurel said, positioning her fingers on an invisible keyboard, trying to remember her childhood piano lessons. "C sharp, F, G, B, C sharp, C sharp, A." She tried to hum the tune, but it sounded atonal. "Sorry, Mrs. Sauberlich, but apparently it didn't sink in." The music was unusual because it was all written in quarter notes, if she remembered correctly what quarter notes looked like, but what did she know? She'd have to ask Reinhard to play it for her.

The maid rapped then entered, pushing a breakfast cart.

"Where will madame have breakfast?" she asked in heavily accented English.

"At the table. And please unpack the suitcases in the bedroom and put everything away. If anything requires pressing, do it."

The maid curtsied, quickly setting the table.

"I shall leave after breakfast. Please be certain everything is done properly."

The maid curtsied again. Laurel rejected the ersatz coffee and dry, doughy pastry, then picked up her purse, making certain the check was inside. Getting it into a Swiss bank was her first priority, she thought. She could get the travel papers today, then go to Switzerland the morning after next, right after her broadcast. She rummaged in her purse again, finding her American passport and the special passes she carried.

"I expect to be gone only overnight," Laurel said to the uniformed young man.

He continued to study her papers with a mixture of disbelief, suspicion, and condescension.

"You are American," he said, holding her passport up to confirm his accusation.

"Yes, but I've lived in Berlin for many years. My husband . . . my late husband," she amended, "is . . . was Helmut Pugh. Of the Pugh Machenwerks family." She'd learned the power games of German bureaucrats early in her residence. "And you will note that my special pass is issued by the Führer's office."

He raised a skeptical eyebrow. "That is for curfew violations. You are requesting travel documents. It is a different department."

"Look, I have some small business in Geneva which will require only a short trip. I don't understand why this is such a problem."

He squared his shoulders. "Madame, Switzerland is not part of our network of allies. You are an American living in Berlin requesting to travel to a neutral nation. Perhaps you are a spy."

Laurel's eyes flashed fire of indignation. "Hardly. Don't you know who I am? I do three broadcasts a week to non-aligned nations to help them see the right way. The Führer himself has complimented me many times on my work. Laurel Pugh a spy? What a ridiculous thought."

The man rose from his chair. "Please have a seat. I'll return in a moment." Laurel remained standing defiantly, but he continued to stare at her until she finally retreated into one of the stiff wooden chairs in the room, then he left.

Laurel waited impatiently, tapping her nails on the arm of the chair and her foot against the marble floor until the young officer returned, accompanied by an older man whose uniform wasn't quite as flattering.

"Mrs. Pugh," the older man said with bureaucratic conviction, "I have consulted with the office of the Reichsminister of Travel and Documentation. Unfortunately, we will be unable to issue travel documents to you at this time. We will, however, retain your passport until such time as you are permitted to travel. Here are the rest of your documents."

"Not permitted to travel!" Laurel flared, jumping to her feet. "Who has said so?"

"I believe the order came from *Obergruppenführer* Heydrich's office, madame. Perhaps you should consult with him."

Laurel stared at her passport clutched in his doughy hand. "I shall do precisely that," she spat, turning and storming out the door.

As she stood in the street outside the ministry office, Laurel felt betrayed and abandoned. Why would Reinhard suddenly be holding her prisoner, first in the hotel and now in Berlin? What if Gerhard Pugh had been right? Could Reinhard have killed Helmut?

"Mrs. Pugh, if you'll just fill out this lost-passport application, we'll be happy to issue another. When do you plan to leave Berlin?" The American consular officer smiled accommodatingly.

"Thank you so much. I'm not sure when I'll be leaving, but one doesn't want to be without one's passport."

The man sighed. "Mrs. Pugh, I know your husband was German, but you might consider making your plans to depart soon. Berlin is not a safe place for Americans right now."

"Well, I'm certain you feel far more pressure about political things than I do," she said with sympathy she didn't particularly feel. "I am quite at home here. How long will the new passport take?"

He sighed again. "Everything takes longer now. There's almost no one here anymore and the mail is very slow. The Germans . . . well, just between us, sometimes I think the Germans open our diplomatic pouches and take out anything they don't want us to have. Your new passport will come in a pouch from Washington, and it can take anywhere from two weeks to four months."

The words seemed to echo in her head. If the Germans opened the diplomatic pouches, they would find a new passport in her name and would certainly remove it. She felt a wave of panic rising. "Two weeks might be all right, but four months! Can't you just give me one here?"

She saw suspicion in his eyes. "I didn't think you had travel plans, Mrs. Pugh."

She pursed her mouth petulantly. "You were just telling me how important it was that I be prepared to leave on short notice."

"And you are absolutely correct." He shrugged. "It is, however, completely out of my hands. You see, the passport files are maintained by the State Department in Washington and they have to look up your passport number and—well, frankly Mrs. Pugh, with all the people trying to get out of Germany, they also have to make sure you really had one in the first place." He held his hands up to stem her retort before it began. "After all, Mrs. Pugh, we certainly wouldn't want our government to issue passports to anyone who claims to be an American." He smiled, then shrugged again. "I really wish I could be of more help, but . . . Well, I'm sure you understand."

Laurel snorted. "I do *not* understand. Listen to me. I have no accent. I was born in Baltimore, Maryland, and my parents are still there. Just phone the passport office in Washington and make them look it up while you wait and *give me a passport.*" She reached into her purse. "I'll make it worth your while."

The man shook his head. "Mrs. Pugh, even if I took your money, it wouldn't make any difference. I can't do anything from here. It might be faster, if your family wouldn't mind, to have them go down to Washington and get the replacement for you. I'll give you the forms and you can send them to your family."

Laurel thought for a moment, then shook her head. "No, my mother has been ill and my father is too occupied with his business to take such a large time away. Oh, never mind," she said, turning away abruptly.

"But Mrs. Pugh, without somebody making an application, you might be stuck here when—if—things change, which I think they will."

She spun around. "Oh, all right, give me the forms." She pushed a wire basket on his desk to one side and snatched the pen out of his hand, filling out the form hurriedly then pushing it back across the desk.

As she left the American Embassy, Laurel felt a rising wave of panic. If she were to admit to Reinhard that she knew she was on the no-exit list, he would know she had tried to leave and it could create a very ugly scene. He'd never understand why she wouldn't want to put the $500,000 into a German bank. She stopped in the middle of the sidewalk. If she put the check into a German bank, they might find a way to take it all from her. And she could hardly send it to her parents to deposit at home because she'd have to explain why she had the check.

"Oh, hell!" she said aloud and two soldiers passing stopped to stare at her. She smiled, nodded briskly, and walked quickly in another direction, her heart thudding.

A check for $500,000 was only paper unless it could be converted to cash, and cash was about to become a very serious consideration for the first time in years.

The black market, she thought, brightening. She'd just

buy documents on the black market and go to Switzerland. Her optimism quickly faded. How could she pay for the documents? A check?

Reinhard held the key to everything and she would have to find a way to manipulate him into giving her back not only her passport but also the right to use it. And quickly.

8

"BROTHER MARK," WHITNEY said to Ross Robbins, "I understand your missionary work proved quite successful."

Robbins glanced around the secluded balcony of the Bishop's palace, then reached into the neck of his robe, producing a packet of Luckies and a wooden match which he struck against the stone wall, lighting the cigarette with a sigh of pleasure.

"Wish I'd known when I took this assignment that monks don't smoke," he said, shaking his head as he took another drag. "And, yes, I think we may have found the mother lode. Incidentally, Sister Magda and Sister Leona are damn cool under pressure."

"Good. Now tell me about what you found."

He reached into his robe again, pulling out a map and unfolding it on the small table between them. "Right in this area," he began, stabbing at the map, "the local priest said he'd seen a lot of 'tank trucks' coming and going into a cave outside the village, and always at night. So we took a look and, sure enough, there were a lot of tank trucks—you know, the little ones that carry water and milk and whatever around those mountain roads—going in and out of the cave. And the entrance was guarded by what looked like half the

140

German army, so we figured the trucks weren't carrying milk or water. So, back we go to Father Jeruszik, and I'll be damned if he hasn't already gotten a little party together for us."

He stopped to light another cigarette from the first before stubbing it out, and Whitney said, "A party?"

"Seems the good father has a bone to pick with the Nazis and is the head of the local resistance unit, which is composed of a pretty international group: two Italians, three Sicilians, and a guy from Barcelona, as well as a couple of local talents. They had been keeping an eye on the cave but don't have the equipment necessary to solve the problem more than temporarily." He cackled. "I figured a little teamwork was in order, so I left the good sisters there, which made Sister Magda pretty happy because she could keep wearing civies and smoke and drink. Sister Leona is going to set up a radio post and teach the local talent how to do it right so they don't get caught sending messages. And I figured I could travel faster alone."

"What's your plan?"

He looked slightly surprised. "To take the damn thing out. What else? I figure the Jerries have been trucking gas or oil in there for a couple of months, so they must have a pretty good stash by now. Might as well blow the damn thing up."

Whitney stared out across the Dubrovnik harbor, thinking. "Could you seal the cave without destroying the oil? It might come in handy at some time to have a reserve."

Robbins' eyes twinkled. "I like it. I'd have to get inside to see how deep the cave is beyond the passage, but maybe some of the locals know." He hesitated, rubbing his chin. "Also, maybe there are other entrances the Jerries don't know about." He nodded. "It's worth the old college try."

"What do you need?"

"Sister Bernadette," he said promptly, then added, admiration in his tone, "That girl could blow out an apple core and leave the skin. She has a real nice touch. And Lady P— oh, I mean Sister Ruth. Wild Bill Hickock would have loved how that one can shoot. I suppose Cesar Ball's not around?"

Whitney shook her head. "Sorry. I can try to get him, though."

"No time. That'll do it, I guess."

"Not quite," Whitney corrected. "I'm going too."

Ross lit a third cigarette. "I suppose there's no point in suggesting you don't."

"None whatsoever."

He nodded, shrugging with resignation to the inevitable. "Okay, you're the boss. And Boss, we need supplies. We need dynamite sticks, big ones and lots of them. And wires. And timers—maybe six. And we need three trucks—tankers."

Whitney chuckled. "Are you sure that's enough? Maybe we could call in the RAF."

Robbins ignored her little jab. "Well, actually, we also need some Jerry uniforms, but those aren't so hard to come by. We'll just knock off a couple and take their clothes."

Sister Bernadette made a very convincing Yugoslavian truck driver, once she was behind the wheel, with her hair cropped close and a locally made cigarette dangling from her lip. Sister Ruth, coveralls bagging and her cap at a jaunty angle, also looked quite natural. Whitney, similarly disguised, rode with Robbins, who had little trouble assuming his new persona.

They had loaded the dynamite, wires, and timers into rubberized canvas bags, sealing them tightly, then putting them into the tanks and filling the trucks with water. Mother Luke, the real Mother Superior at the convent, had forged the travel documents they carried with them.

Robbins whistled an intricate melody as the little convoy left Dubrovnik with the early dawn. They had considered separating, but Mother Luke told them trucks owned by one company often traveled together, and reminded them of the lack of spare parts and the infrequent maintenance which could jeopardize a truck traveling alone. Robbins had chosen dawn as the best time to leave because the checkpoints would be filled with trucks and manned by tired soldiers.

At the outer edge of Dubrovnik, his instincts proved true. There were at least fifteen other trucks waiting at the barrier as two harried soldiers scurried among the irritated drivers. By the time they reached the first truck of the convoy, driven

142

by Sister Ruth, another fifteen trucks had piled up behind them.

Sister Ruth set her face into what she hoped was the appropriate expression of boredom, and the guard barely looked at her as he took the papers, glanced at them, and waved her through.

Sister Bernadette was also quickly passed, to Whitney's relief, but as the soldier began to approach her truck, he was called aside by a man whose bearing clearly indicated his authority. Whitney held her breath, hoping the officer was not replacing the soldier. The exchange between the two seemed interminable, but finally the soldier nodded, then saluted. Whitney could see tired resignation on his face, and she wondered if he'd just been told his replacement would be late.

Robbins was picking his teeth in the outside rearview mirror and, without even glancing at the soldier, extended the papers. The soldier took them, peered at Robbins then at Whitney, started to ask something, then tossed the papers back into Robbins's lap. *"Passen,"* he muttered, and Whitney unclasped her shaking hands.

Ross started the engine, then popped the clutch, and the truck lurched forward toward the gate. The soldier manning the portal, however, was talking to the same officer and Ross had to stop. The engine infuriatingly sputtered and stalled.

Both men at the gate turned to watch as Robbins struggled vainly to restart the truck. Finally the officer, a look of irritation on his face, strode to the truck.

Robbins quickly opened the door and stepped out, then hurried around to the front to raise the hood. The officer joined him, staring into the engine compartment as Ross fiddled with wires. Whitney could hear small bits of their conversation, the officer's clipped and precise High German and Ross's deliberately slurred, highly accented answers, but not enough to make sense out of it.

Ross swung back into the truck and pressed the starter again. The engine ground several times, but finally coughed to life. Ross started to get out again, but the officer reached up and slammed the hood.

" *'Schön,'* " Robbins called as he quickly pulled through

the open gate. "Shit," he added, relief in his tone as they cleared it. "Jeez, for one awful minute there I thought we'd had it. Damn guy's standing there telling me about his race cars while I'm trying to make this piece of trash work."

"His race cars?" Whitney said, incredulous.

"Swear to God, his race cars. And what a bunch of dumb jerks the Yugos are. I just kept tinkering and giving him more reasons to think the Yugos are fools." He grinned. "Who's the fool now, Herr Race Car?" He cackled, pulling a cigarette from his pocket. "As for this truck, it deserves to be blown up."

Whitney laughed, releasing some of the tension which had built up at the checkpoint. "Sounds like a good plan to me. How many more of those checkpoints do we have to pass?"

Robbins shrugged. "If they're set up the way they were when I came back to Dubrovnik, none. They change it all the time, though. It's a crap shoot."

"Oh, good," she said with an irony that escaped him. "Look, there are the girls." The other two trucks were pulled to the shoulder of the road, the girls waving as they approached. Ross hesitated, and the two others pulled out in front of him, their convoy restored.

"When will we get there?" Whitney asked, and Robbins laughed.

"Had enough already?"

"Nope. Just anxious to get started."

Sister Leona pulled the earphones from her head and greeted them with a broad smile. "Welcome," she said, pulling them inside the small stone house where she was practicing radio transmissions with the two local members of the resistance. "They will be very good. Who should be their contact?"

"Let them keep practicing, then we'll decide. Do they know the codes?"

"They are learning, but perhaps they should just transmit in Greek. They both know Greek."

"Unfortunately, so do a great many other people," Sister Ruth added. "We must devise a code for them to use. Can you do that?"

Leona nodded. "Of course. This is my job."

Sister Magda came into the room followed by five men.

"These are the group I told you about. Don't bother with names. They won't," Robbins hissed and Whitney nodded.

"What have you got?" Whitney said to Magda, who had ignored their presence in favor of a cigarette which she lit before answering. The five men disappeared into another room.

"I found a shepherd who knows a back way into the cave. He says it's a big cave with lots of underground passages and many rooms. He also says the Germans have explored the place pretty thoroughly and have guards posted at both entrances. There seem to be about fifty men stationed inside, and another ten who guard the entrances and patrol the mountains. They work twelve-hour shifts which change at three P.M. and three A.M. During the change, the guards double, but the patrols aren't around. And it's dark up there at night. What's the plan?"

"We'll outline it when it's ready. Were you able to see what the truck drivers wear?"

"German uniforms," Magda replied sullenly. "What would you expect?"

"Then we're going to need at least three of those. And six of the ones worn by the patrol guards, but not right away."

Magda nodded. "That can be managed. Dead men don't care what they're wearing."

Whitney offered silent thanks to Forrestal and his bioengineering skills as she climbed the rough path behind Robbins and their shepherd guide. Her leg was functioning comfortably and she felt sure-footed. At first, when she and Robbins had finished arguing about whether or not she should even attempt the climb, he'd been overly solicitous, stopping frequently under the flimsiest pretense. Each time, however, she'd waited impatiently for him to play his little role, then kept right on his heels as they ascended.

She saw the shepherd guide stop ahead and motion them into hiding places among the rocks. She followed his pointing finger toward the opposite hillside. He muttered something to Ross, who nodded, then turned to Whitney.

145

"The entrance is about halfway up that hillside. It's concealed behind that gray-brown chunk that sticks out. See it?"

Whitney scanned the hillside, then found the outcropping he'd indicated. "It looks narrow."

"Optical illusion. He says three men can enter side-by-side."

The shepherd muttered something else and Robbins nodded again, returning to Whitney with a grin. "There is, however, another way in the Jerries don't seem to have found. Or don't think worth guarding."

"Then let's have a look at it," Whitney whispered back.

Robbins mumbled something to the shepherd, who backed out of the rocks and motioned for them to follow.

The second part of the climb was more strenuous, but Whitney had no intention of showing any discomfort. She wasn't sure why she felt she had to prove herself constantly, particularly to the man who'd been partly responsible for her injury in the first place, but she never wanted him to think she was weak.

The shepherd led them up a twisting path which crested a ridge above the guarded back entrance, then down into a series of tumbled boulders and slippery gravel, through a small wooded area and into another jumble of boulders. Suddenly he stopped, pointing between two rocks.

Whitney and Ross stepped forward and found themselves looking down into a very small, very dark hole between the rocks.

"Well, now I see why they don't put a guard on this, even if they do know about it," Whitney said, discouraged, but Ross continued to stare down, then nodded and grinned.

"Looks like just the right size for little Bernadette," he said out of the side of his mouth, his words more a continuous hiss than real speech. "Little Bernadette and her toy kit." He turned to the shepherd. "Where does it go inside?"

The shepherd smoothed a patch of the dark brown earth with his hand, then sketched a rough map of the cave complex.

"Here is big tunnel where trucks go," he said, drawing with his finger. "Then makes two branches. One go up to

146

big room here. Is where maybe soldiers stay. Back door comes here. Other branch go down to three more branch. All go to rooms. One room has little lake, but water taste bad. Like eggs."

"Sulfur," Robbins said, scratching his chin. "Has anyone been inside since the Jerries have come?"

"My brother's boy. Look for lost lambs when they first start. He say many big cans."

"Oil drums?" Whitney asked.

Robbins nodded. "It would be a logical guess. Easier to bring the drums in and fill them than to truck the drums in full. Must be a helluva lot of drums."

"It would make a nice cozy fire, wouldn't it?" Whitney said.

"Maybe more than we know. If the lake tastes like sulfur, it may mean there's either oil in the rocks there or a vein of sulfur. It would fit the geology of this area. Sulfur burns." He paused for a moment, rubbing his chin again. "All the more reason to seal it. We could put the whole damn mountain on fire and the smoke from the fire would become sulfuric acid if it combined with moisture. Like in your nose or lungs. We don't want to kill off our friends, here." He turned back to the shepherd. "Where does this hole go?"

The shepherd returned to his map. "Into little room behind top big room. Hole is small, like for boy."

"So even if they know about it, they couldn't use it to get out," Robbins said. "However, it would let air inside and give the Jerries time and oxygen to dig out. We need to plug it, too."

"When?" Whitney asked.

Robbins erased the map with his foot, then pointed the shepherd back toward the path. "Soon," he said, following their guide.

Whitney, Ross, Lady Primrose, Magda, and Leona sat on one side of the small hut; the local resistance fighters with their international cohorts sat on the other. Father Jeruszik poked at the fire. No one spoke.

Finally the priest turned to Whitney. "I will drive one truck."

"Me," said one of the Sicilians.

"Me, too," added one of the Italians.

"Thank you," Whitney said. "Ruth will teach you how to jump from the trucks and roll away."

Magda was picking at her fingernails with the point of a knife. "I'll take care of any of the patrol guards who don't go back in time." She flicked the tip of the knife blade with her thumbnail.

"Fine," Whitney said, discomfited by the anticipatory smile on Magda's face. "Ruth will back you up with a sniper rifle. Ruth, you will also contain the guards at the gate. Father Jeruszik, your men will be divided evenly among Ruth's group, Ross's, and mine. We'll give you the details later."

Bernadette leaned forward. "What about me? And Leona?"

"You'll work with me," Ross said. "To seal the back doors. And to prepare the trucks."

"When?" Father Jeruszik asked.

Whitney looked at Ross, then said, "Tonight. No one leaves from now on. No one talks with any outsiders."

Suddenly the atmosphere in the room was charged, and Whitney, too, was caught up in the excitement. This was truly the beginning of their work.

"Please," Whitney said, climbing into the truck, "drive very carefully."

Father Jeruszik smiled. "Robbins said bumps would not trigger anything."

Whitney piled her hair up into the peasant cap. "Robbins has been wrong before." She looked out the door, surveying the other two trucks. "Everyone's aboard. Let's go."

The priest engaged the gears and the truck lumbered out into the small, cobbled street, the dark enveloping them but seeming to amplify the engines' sounds, which echoed off the darkened houses. Whitney was positive they would suddenly be set upon by hordes of Nazis, but the town remained dark and still as they left it behind.

"Why?" Whitney asked, looking across the cab at the nearly invisible features of the priest.

148

"More why for you," he answered. "This is my country, my village."

"But you speak four languages. You haven't spent your life here."

She could almost see his smile in the dark. "I'm a Jesuit," he said, as though it would clarify everything. "I studied at Georgetown University then was sent to work at the Vatican. When this all began, I couldn't stay there listening to the Holy Father trying to placate Mussolini and Hitler as though one could reason with the devil. I told them my mother was dying and I wanted to come home. I didn't tell them I had work to do."

Whitney reached across the dark between them, resting her hand lightly on his arm. "Please be careful. Get out of the truck and run. There's still a great deal more to do."

"I'll have some help, I'm sure," he said. "God protects His own."

The trucks stopped in a small woods as Ruth, Magda, and their four local back-ups disappeared into the dark of the rocks and the night. Leona, Bernadette, Ross, and three of the local resistance group had left on foot several hours before and Whitney wondered how they were faring, remembering the difficulty of the terrain in daylight.

"Waiting is always the hardest part of any operation," the priest said, and Whitney pulled back her sleeve to look at the dim radium glow of her watch face.

"Twenty-two minutes," she said, then jumped as a figure appeared beside her window.

"*Signora,* please, a moment," whispered the man, opening the door so Whitney could step down. "You have with you a traitor who is very dangerous."

"A traitor? One of my people? Who?"

The resistance fighter glanced into the truck at the priest, then pulled Whitney slightly away from the vehicle into the darkness. "You are good woman, good leader, but you have too much trust for too many. Will be good for you learn not trust nobody. Not one person is friend in wartime. Not one person is for trust."

"Then why are you trusting me?"

"I do not. I do not trust the priest. I have own reasons for

149

telling this to you. In war, always everyone has own reasons. Also, I like you. You have been to my country, with my people. You are known. We do not want you to die from traitor."

"Thank you," Whitney said, a bit nervous that he seemed to know so much about her, but grateful for his honesty.

Whitney listened to his story, thanked him again, then climbed back into the truck, checking her watch again, longing to be able to discuss her predicament with Donohue or Ball, but recognizing that she alone had to make the hard decisions about the administration of her unit.

"Let's roll," she said quietly. *One crisis at a time,* she reminded herself.

The trucks pulled out onto the approach road, Father Jeruszik pulling on the cap of the Nazi soldier, then slowing and finally hesitating just beyond the glow of the floodlights at the entrance to the cave so Whitney could climb down.

"Good luck," she said, "and run like hell!"

She climbed nimbly up the rocks, using her hands to make sure she didn't slip. Then she stretched out, keeping her profile low and flat, pulling the rifle from her shoulder and swinging it around to train on the gate. She could see the three trucks creeping up the incline to the first checkpoint. She raised her eyes to the hills, looking in vain for some sign of Ruth's unit.

As the first truck approached the gate, the horn sounded, bleating into the night. Whitney could see the German guards' irritation in their carriage as they went to attend to the unexpected arrival of three tankers just as the guard was to change. She held her breath, then saw the truck lurch forward just as she heard the first distant explosion. A moment after the roaring reached her ears, Whitney could see the compound around the mouth of the cave burst into a frenzy of activity. Nazi soldiers poured from the cave as the three trucks raced forward.

From the hills above, blazes and reports of gunfire erupted, and some of the guards who had been running crumpled onto the ground. She braced herself, firing at two soldiers who were raising their rifles toward the trucks. Several soldiers tried frantically to close the iron gates which protected the cave. Whitney raised her rifle a second time and fired at several soldiers who had come out through the checkpoint, firing again and again until all of them had been stopped. Quickly she glanced at her watch, wondering if anything had gone wrong with Ross's unit, surprised to find very little time had passed since she'd been dropped off. Then, right on the second, the mountain above the mouth of the cave was haloed with red fire and the thunder of explosions shook the ground beneath her.

Everything in the compound seemed to stop as the soldiers stared upward at the red glow in the sky. Another explosion, further away, shook the ground again and Whitney whispered, "Thanks, Ross," as she watched the race between the trucks and the closing doors. The moment of hesitation when the explosions had sounded had given the trucks an instant of advantage.

"Run," Whitney yelled as she watched first Father Jeruszik leap from his truck, then the other two resistance fighters follow. "Run, damn it," she said again, firing at the soldiers around the fleeing figures.

Suddenly everything froze in three instants of blinding fire and heart-stopping noise as first one, then the next, and finally the third truck were consumed by fire. The explosions rumbled and shook the earth. Then there was a moment of eerie silence before the mountain seemed to slide downward to embrace the gate and the compound in front of it in a roaring hail of rock and noise.

Whitney tried to see through the cloud of dust and rock, but she could hear only sporadic gunfire from the hills and screaming. Quickly she climbed down from her vantage point and, gun at ready, edged along the rock cut which framed the road. The black night was made more intense by the dust in the air, and she flattened herself against the rock as she heard someone coughing nearby.

The man coughed again, then moaned. She directed herself toward the noise, trying to walk quietly. Abruptly, a man's shape appeared and she raised the gun to her shoulder.

"The Lord is my shepherd," she said.

"Who is there?" a heavily accented German voice replied.

Whitney gritted her teeth and pulled the trigger. The man said, "Oomph," before he crumpled backward.

Whitney turned away quickly, fearing the gunshot may have attracted others of his company, but the road seemed to be empty. She hurried back to the shelter of the rock, moving forward into the clearing air.

"The Lord is my shepherd," she heard from the dark.

"He makes me to lie down in green pastures," she replied quickly, then added, "Who?"

"Magda," the voice replied.

"Come here, quickly," she said, urgency in her voice.

"There's none of them left," Magda replied, and Whitney heard the rasp of a match against a rock, then a flare of flame as Magda lit a cigarette. Her face and hair were covered with the red-brown dust of the mountain and she had her rifle slung over her shoulder. "Ruth sent me to look for you."

"Is everyone all right?" Whitney asked, falling in beside Magda.

"We lost one of the Italians. I haven't seen the drivers. And Brother Mark isn't back with his team. The rest are all okay." She took a deep drag on her cigarette. "Except, of course, for the Germans. You finished off the last of them."

Whitney shuddered slightly.

"That was your first one, close up, huh? First one's always the hardest."

Whitney's mind flashed back to the guard she'd killed with a knife while escaping from the Nazis, and her husband's nephew and murderer who she'd killed in Madrid less than a year before. She started to tell Magda, then stopped, reminding herself that Magda was far from the perfect confidante for any number of reasons. And, she admitted, in one way this was her first, for it was the first time she'd taken someone's life for simply being on the wrong side. It was hardly what she'd planned for her life's work.

Magda finished her cigarette and ground it into the road. "Guess we did pretty good for our first time out," she said. "It's a crazy idea, this whole unit, but it works. And it sure beats prison."

"I'm sure it does," Whitney replied. "Where are the others?"

"Over here. We found a truck that wasn't destroyed and they're inside. Here." She pointed toward the troop transport emblazoned with a swastika on the door, its canvas top tattered. Whitney could hear voices inside, their pitch and volume elevated by adrenaline. Whitney stepped to the rear of the truck.

"Do you plan to wait here for more Germans, or should we get going?"

Robbins jumped to his feet. "Jesus, she's right! Let's get the hell outta here."

He jumped down from the truck, followed by the others. Taking Whitney's arm, he began to move up the hillside, into the cover of the rocks. "They were great, all of them. Especially Bernadette. She's really something with a stick of dynamite. All finesse. Just enough blow in just the right place. The Jerries will be months digging that out. If they decide to dig it out at all."

"And Leona?"

Ross hesitated for a moment, then continued his climb. "She's a strange woman. Very complex. She wanted us to take the Jerries captive rather than kill them. I tried to tell her why resistance units didn't take prisoners, but it wasn't until Bernadette gave her the story in Spanish that she understood. I don't think she was pleased, though."

"Well, none of us, with the probable exception of Magda, enjoys the thought of taking someone's life, no matter how good the reason," Whitney replied.

"That Magda's an item, all right. That broad would make Dillinger nervous. She likes killing, which makes her good for this, but I hope they don't plan to turn her loose after the war."

"That's the deal they made with her. With all of them."

Robbins snorted his disapproval. "That's the best argument I've heard for this war going on forever!" He paused in a sheltering thicket, waiting for the troop to catch up. Whitney glanced up at the sky, which was rapidly lightening behind the mountains to the east. The devastation they had caused was hidden from her view, but she almost wanted to walk back and take a look at their handiwork, the first successful mission of the Butterflies. Instead, she turned to the assembled raiders.

"Thank you," she said softly, "for doing your jobs in such an effective and efficient way. I'm sorry we lost one of your men. He was brave and gave his life for something significant. Now, please separate into small groups and work your way back to the village." The local resistance group began to move away, silently blending into the rocks and woods around them. Whitney waited until they had disappeared. "Sister Leona, have you devised a code for them to use?"

"*Sì*, I mean yes, a simple code block which can be changed by turning the block."

"How creative. And how useful. Where did you learn such a system?"

"During the Revolution in Spain," Leona responded, puzzled.

"Are they ready to be operational?"

"Yes, they have three operators trained. All they need is know where to transmit. I will be happy to show them now."

Whitney shook her head. "Our work here is finished. We will be going back to Dubrovnik. Ross?"

He nodded, turning to lead them toward the truck he'd bought from one of the local farmers and hidden nearby. "Hope you girls don't mind a few smelly sheepskins."

Whitney would never forget the three hours they spent buried in cured sheepskins, certain the smell would linger forever in the backwaters of her sinuses if not in the pores of her skin. She stepped out of the bath where she'd been soaking, rubbed her skin briskly with the rough linen towels, reattached her leg, toweled her hair, and put on the habit. After all the excitement of the mission, it felt secure and comfortable to become a nun again.

Whitney climbed the narrow stairs to the unused bell tower and her secret radio. She had sent the message to Patrice four hours before and prayed the answer would be negative. She settled onto a small stool next to the receiver, turning it on and fiddling with the dial, searching for Patrice's blips. Like everything else about her old friend, Patrice's "hand" with Morse code was effervescent, a cheerful presence from far away.

Suddenly, there it was, as distinctive as her voice. Whitney carefully wrote down the random series of letters and numbers, then quickly signaled her receipt, and shut down the radio before it could be located by listening Germans. As always, she felt an intense sadness and increased isolation at the end of their "talks." *War, indeed, is hell*, she thought, packing the radio away among discarded suitcases and packing boxes which littered the abandoned tower.

Whitney pulled the small black book from its hiding place in the bell-ringing mechanism, translating the message.

"Cocoon confirms suspicion re blocks. *Miracolo* verifies subject to have bad connections and source to be reliable. All apologize for mess. Cocoon says he owes you one, but necessary to eliminate problem in definitive way. Leaves solution in your hands. I'm sorry, too. Know what this must mean for you. E well, sends love. Me, too."

Despite the unhappiness and betrayal she felt, she had to smile, feeling once more connected to Erik and Patrice, feeling the strong bonds of time, friendship, and trust healing, in advance, the pain she would feel at the trial ahead.

She sat, looking out the tiny slitted windows in the bell tower, their ancient glass distorting the azure and brown of the harbor and hills, then read the message again, finally burning it and grinding the ashes to dust.

"Eliminate problem in definitive way" left her with no other choices, she thought, descending the stairs and slipping out the small door into the hallway.

Whitney sighed, squared her shoulders then checked the stiletto in her sleeve. There was only one definitive way, but first she had to make sure they'd not been compromised already.

"Sister, would you be good enough to accompany me?" Whitney said. "There is a small matter with which I need your assistance."

Sister Leona looked up from her gardening, then rose, dusting herself off and removing her gardening gloves. *"Sì,*

155

of course," she said, following Whitney through the garden and into the old cathedral.

Whitney's eyes scanned the echoing church, checking the small nooks and niches. They were alone in the silence. "Down here, please," Whitney said, leading Sister Leona through an old wooden door and down a flight of stone stairs lacy with cobwebs. "Mother Luke tells me that this area was used during the Ottoman raids to hide resistance fighters and other heroes. It holds the crypts of the nuns and priests who have served here."

"Why do you need me?" Sister Leona asked, hesitating.

"Because there are some things hidden here which I need," Whitney lied, leading Leona further into the catacombs. Finally, they reached a small room lined with unused stone crypts, their lids open, lying at an angle across the tops of the oblong shapes. Whitney stopped, leaning against one of them.

"Let us rest here for a moment. Come, sit. I am afraid I still tire quite easily. You have been very clever in designing the codes for the resistance fighters in the mountains, Sister Leona," Whitney began. "I want to learn about how those code blocks work."

Sister Leona settled beside Whitney on one of the stone crypts, smiling with pleasure at being asked about her work. "It is very simple. There are ten lines of code, each thirty-one letters wide. It work like a calendar. On the first day of the month, the sender makes his code using the first line of the block. On the second of the month, he counts that letter and twenty-nine or thirty more, depending how many days in month, then makes code by use that letter. The next month, he begins from bottom."

"It's very simple, but very smart. Do you have the block you gave the resistance?"

Sister Leona nodded. "I have kept it in hem of my habit where it is safe." She raised her robe, pulling a square of fabric from her hem and extending it to Whitney.

"Reversible code blocks were used during the revolution in your country," Whitney said, her voice icy calm, "because they were taught to the Fascist forces by the Nazis.

156

Leona, you were in the right revolution, but on the wrong side. Am I right?"

Leona began to shiver. "No! I was with the Republicans!"

Whitney shook her head, then suddenly grabbed Sister Leona. "Who have you sold us to?"

Leona burst into tears. "They have my brother."

"Leona, that war has been over for a long time. That's a lousy excuse. Who have you sold us to?"

The woman's sobs increased. "No one, I swear it. Please, I beg you, no one." She slumped against the crypt. "Not yet. Someone is supposed to come for information."

"When?"

"I do not know. All I know is he will be priest. They tell me my brother would be let out of prison in Spain if I find you. They are looking all places with many agents. I am not the only one."

"How much do they know?" Whitney felt her rage rising, not so much with the woman as with the relentless pursuers. "What have you told them about our operation?"

Leona shook her head. "Only you are in Europe. I could not to tell them where we are this time yet because no contact. I was told to send message when we come to hiding place, but have not been able to tell them where we are."

"I don't believe you," Whitney said with icy calm. "When did you last make contact?"

Sister Leona leaned away from Whitney's cold anger. "I swear it was before we went the Switzerland convent. This is the truth. How could I make a message?" She smiled nervously, sliding away, but Whitney grabbed her arm.

"You had the radio in the village with the resistance." She dropped her free arm and moved her wrist, feeling the dagger slip into her hand. In an abrupt movement, she brought it up close to Sister Leona's face, eliciting a squeak of fear. "You had a whole week to send as much information as you wanted."

Leona's head moved back and forth frantically. "No! No! I made no message." Suddenly her voice quieted. "I try but no one hear. They have my brother. They will kill my brother." The woman was cowering, pleading.

"And I have you," Whitney said, putting the tip of the

knife against Leona's throat. "I don't care about your brother, Leona. I have lost many friends and relatives to this war. Your brother is of no concern to me, but my own life and this operation is, so I am going to ask you again: What have you told the Nazis about us?"

"Mother of God, Sister Camille, I swear on the grave of my mother. Yes, I did try to contact with the radio, but it was not sending. There was no other chance." Whitney pricked the skin of Leona's neck with the knife and the woman added quickly, "Please. In Switzerland before convent I told one man you were in Europe, but then I did not know where we would be."

Whitney felt at least relieved that the Nazis knew only that she was alive but neither where nor in what guise. "How was this message to be given to the priest?"

"He would find me. I was told to use code to make message." She pointed at the reversible block. "Please do not kill me, Sister Camille."

"How convenient for you to give the same code to the resistance fighters so the Germans would get a double bonus."

"Sister Camille, he is my only brother." Suddenly Leona wrenched away from Whitney, running toward the door of the room. Whitney gripped her knife, running after her. Leona reached the door, yanking at the heavy barrier, but it was slow to move and, hearing Whitney's footsteps approaching, she turned, pulling a small gun from inside her habit.

"I didn't tell them where you were even when I had the radio. Doesn't that matter? But now I have told you too much and betrayed them. Now my life is worth nothing on either side."

Whitney braced herself for the impact of the bullet, but Sister Leona raised the gun abruptly to her temple and pulled the trigger. As Whitney watched stunned, Sister Leona's mouth formed a smile and she crumpled to the floor.

Whitney knelt beside her, searching for a pulse she couldn't find, then rose and dragged the woman's body to one of the open crypts, struggling to lift her inside. Just before she closed the lid completely, she said, "God give you peace now, Sister Leona. You may end up being far more honorable than you ever dreamed."

"Sister Leona has gone on a long mission and will no longer be with us," Whitney said to the assembled Butterflies. "Sister Ruth will be assuming her responsibilities."

As she'd expected, there was little reaction from the others among the group except Bernadette, who blurted, "Oh, and she didn't even say good-bye. I shall miss her so."

"We all will, Sister Bernadette," Whitney said.

The brilliant stars over the harbor were distorted by the wavy glass in the small tower window as Whitney assembled the radio. She was tired to her bones, aching and empty, and wondered if her "hand" would even sound enough like her "hand" to verify the message.

She turned on the transmitter, then, finding one small reserve of energy somewhere inside, quickly tapped out, "Action taken, successful resolution. Love to E and you. Tell Cocoon he owes me a big one."

"Colonel Donohue, I think we've hit the jackpot," Patrice said as she joined him at the bar of the Dorchester Hotel. Like the others in the oak and padded-leather sanctity of the room, she kept her voice soft, but the excitement she was feeling was obvious.

"The jackpot?" he asked, signaling the bartender. "The lady will have J&B on the rocks, please."

"Thanks. I got this letter via a Swedish journalist friend of mine who just came out of Berlin. He said he was at a cocktail party to meet some of the big names in Naziland and this redhead cornered him, begging him to get her message to me in London." She offered a wrinkled envelope to him.

Dear Patrice:

I know you hate me, and I suppose it's for a lot of good reasons, but you're the only person I could think of who might be able to help.

Helmut has been murdered and his father has thrown me out. I'm being held virtual prisoner by Reinhard and I can turn only to you. This check was given to me by Gerhard Pugh when he threw me out, but I don't dare deposit it here. Please—you can even keep some of it—but put it in an account for me in England. Otherwise, I'll have nothing when I get out.

Please, please help me. I thought I was doing the right thing by coming here, but now I know it might have been a mistake. If Reinhard finds out I've contacted you, he will certainly kill me just like Helmut. I can't leave—they took my passport, and I can't get another one. Please, please help me.

Just so you know it's me and this isn't a fake, I remember Veesie and Room 427 at Goucher! Please don't think I'm exaggerating. They really will kill me!

He looked up from the paper. "How big is the check?"

"Half a million dollars! I was going to open a special trust account at the bank. It's a great deal of money. Do you suppose it's really good?"

Donohue shrugged. "What do you care? And what's this business about Veesie and Room 427 at Goucher?"

"Veesie was my horse when we were kids. And my dorm room at Goucher was number 427. And it does look like her handwriting."

He nodded. "Those things support the authenticity. Half a million dollars convinces me she's really in trouble. From all we know of Laurel, she wouldn't trust anyone with that sort of money unless she had no other options. And you are right—this is the jackpot, no pun intended. It's precisely what we've been waiting for. Now she has a reason to cooperate."

"So when do I go?" Patrice asked.

"Soon. First, I'd like to check to see if there's any other business you could take care of while you're there. Come on." He tossed some money on the bar, then escorted her to his car. "It's a nice day for a drive in the country."

The house, and the town of Bletchley itself, seemed untouched by war, or even the twentieth century. Patrice was surprised to see a woman in a Home Guard's uniform against the carefully tended Tudor homes and narrow, cobbled streets of Bletchley.

The house stood at the edge of town on a road with similar

houses, expansive but confined by the tidy gardens and ancient oaks. Even the gatemaster of the house appeared to be from another century, a classic caricature of the English gatekeeper, even to the gesture of offering a respectful tug of his forelock to Donohue.

"It's a beautiful estate. No wonder I haven't heard a word from Paul since you brought him here. I almost expect to see Queen Victoria strolling around."

Donohue chuckled. "Reporters are not supposed to have imagination."

When Patrice emerged from the car, she was struck even more by the mansion and its setting, high on a hill, looking over the clay pits in the valley on one side, the town and its busy train station on the other. "I can't wait to see the inside. I'm certain it must be lovely."

Donohue opened the door and Patrice preceded him into what had probably once been a gracious main foyer, but now looked as though someone had moved in and forgotten to unpack. Boxes, some opened and spewing papers, others stacked precariously, obliterated most of the marble floor and half the walls. Doors opened into what were probably meant to be a dining room, a library, and a salon, but they, too, were overwhelmed with boxes and machinery.

"Lovely, huh?" Donohue said, propelling her toward the door on the left. Just as they reached it, a tall, rumply, handsome man wearing a tennis sweater and baggy wool pants, clutching a sheaf of papers in one hand and what looked like ticker tape in the other, burst from behind one of the boxes and sent Patrice sprawling onto the floor.

The man dropped his papers and tapes into a pile on the floor, reaching for Patrice, hoisting her to her feet. "Sorry, after all. I suspect we need either a good cleaning or a bobby for traffic. Who are you? Oh, hello, Donohue."

"Alan, you're looking well. This is Patrice Rigby. Patrice, Alan Turing, the genius who runs all of this."

"Rigby, Rigby, Rigby," Alan replied, staring into space and ignoring Patrice's hand, then suddenly looking down at her and catching her hand just as she was about to pull it away, pumping it vigorously. "Rigby, of course. You some-how managed to find the Limping Lady and her microfilm in

Portugal. Right good find, I must say. You see," he said, plopping down onto one of the boxes, still holding her hand, "those blueprints have saved us more than a spot of work. The Polish scientists who'd worked on the old Enigma had gotten to a stalemate until you and that microfilm appeared. Now we know they've gone to four rotors and a new plugboard. But never mind. I think we're onto them." He leapt to his feet, shaking her hand firmly once again, then dropping to his knees to collect the papers and tape. "Off I go now. Good to see you. And you, Donohue." He scurried away.

"Is this the Mad Hatter's Tea Party?" Patrice said, befuddled.

Donohue laughed. "Turing's a genuine eccentric in a nation which prides itself on its eccentrics, but he's brilliant."

"What, exactly, did all that mean?"

"Briefly, Turing and his group—they call themselves the Baker Street Irregulars after Sherlock Holmes because they see themselves as detectives—are working on deciphering the secret German codes of the Enigma machine. It's a tricky electrical device that can encode something in one of about a hundred and four thousand alphabetical combinations and then uncode the whole thing."

Patrice smiled weakly. "Donohue, I think you've caught Mad Hatter fever, too."

He led her through the door. "It might be something in the air up here." They passed through a room filled with clacking machinery which issued mountains of the same ticker tape Turing had been carrying, then into another room, startling in its spareness. The boxes were not in evidence here, replaced by cupboards and huge library-type tables at which people sat, bent over their work.

"This is the cryptographers' room. The people here are attempting to design new codes for our side. The Germans seem to be able to crack our codes like eggs, so we're trying to find some new approaches. Well! Andrew, I didn't expect to see you here. I thought you were in Sweden."

Andrew Collins, Raja Abichandri, rose, bowing ceremoniously. "Miss Rigby, Colonel. I have just returned from a concert tour in that nation and had an idea, so I came down here. You see, it occurred to me while on this tour that music—written music, that is, could be quite a useful code. It's what we've been discussing."

"Music?" Patrice asked.

"Indeed. You see, music is actually quite a mathematical art, as are most codes. Of course, it would be of more help if agents had perfect pitch. Then we could simply play the notes and they could decipher the message. But we're working on a substitution code to set it up so it can be written. Now, if you will excuse me," he said, bowing again.

"Nice to see you," Patrice said, not sure how much she meant it. She still found his dark good looks appealing, but her lingering ill ease around him had not changed since they'd met in Georgetown.

Donohue rapped on a closed door at the back of the cryptographers' room, which opened first a crack, then fully. "Bill! And Patrice," Cesar Ball said, stepping aside.

"Major Ball," Patrice said, shaking his hand, his warmth dispelling the last of the discomfort produced by Collins and the confusion produced by Turing.

They settled into chairs and Donohue offered Ball the letter from Laurel. He read it quickly, then nodded. "The lamb to the slaughter, wouldn't you say. How much was the check?"

"Half a million," Donohue replied, and Cesar Ball whistled.

"Daddy Pugh really wanted her gone, didn't he? Say, do you think she means Heydrich killed Helmut? She says, '. . . he will certainly kill me just like Helmut.' Do you think Heydrich would actually kill the son of the biggest industrialist in Germany?"

"I wouldn't be surprised. What we know of Heydrich makes me believe the man would do almost anything. If the stories we got out of Russia are true, he's killed fifty thousand or more. Why would one more make any difference? You know he's Hitler's choice to be the next Führer, so I doubt Pugh could do much to influence Hitler's thinking about Heydrich." Donohue turned to Patrice. "This is part of the reason I wanted you to come down here, too. You must understand the man with whom Laurel has chosen to

164

ally herself is very dangerous and very wicked. I want you to have the chance to hear everything, then change your mind about going if you want to."

Patrice shook her head. "I'm the only logical choice. Laurel wrote to me, trusted me with her money, thinks I'm her friend. I'll have the best chance to get her out."

Cesar Ball rubbed his chin. "Get her out? Why should we get her out? What about if we offer her protection—maybe a couple of false passports and a connection to a conduit, and maybe even some money—but talk her into staying. Her radio broadcasts are a natural channel for messages, and it would be very nice to have someone right under Heydrich's nose who could tell us what he's up to. Do you think she'd stay?"

Patrice sighed. "I don't know. Laurel's not the bravest person who ever lived and she sounds frantic in this letter."

Donohue leaned forward, his elbows on his knees. "I think Ball's right. We're not in the traitor-rescue business. She's got to be willing to pay a price, and this is the price." He nodded. "I'd like very much to have someone right where she is. And the passports and conduits are no problem. How much money do you think it would take to keep her there?"

"Enough so she feels secure, but not so much that she feels independent," Patrice said, and Ball laughed.

"I like how she thinks, Bill. Incidentally, do you have anything for Whitney? I'm off tomorrow for a little adventure with the Butterflies."

"Just tell her Laurel's finally going to get everything she's had coming. It should brighten her day considerably."

Patrice felt certain the border guards would see through her false Swiss passport as quickly as they would her strawberry blond wig and broad Texas accent, but, to her astonishment, they were far too busy flirting with the outrageous expatriate American to doubt anything. As she batted her false eyelashes and wiggled her hips seductively, she was positive one of the guards would step forward, shout "Patrice Rigby" at the top of his lungs, and shoot her before she got out of Customs. Instead, one of them managed to secure a taxi for her.

"One adventure after another," she muttered as she settled into the car.

Just like Bletchley, Berlin showed few signs of a continent at war, save the overwhelming numbers of red-and-black flags and the many uniforms in the streets. Berlin housewives, however, still bustled along the wide streets carrying groceries in tidy baskets, and the city still had its imposing granite façade, proclaiming its Prussian heritage loudly and with swagger.

The hotel bore a huge Nazi flag which flapped against the building in the brisk wind. In the taxi, she had removed the wig and pulled a slouch hat low over her own hair, loosened the belt which had nipped her waist and removed, with relief, the cumbersome eyelashes. She had also slipped the Swiss passport for Trudy Weston Steiner, the American wife of a Swiss citizen, into the hidden compartment in her bag and removed the passport of Celestina Hernandez-Colon of Colombia, South America, who held the reservations at the hotel.

The desk clerk checked her documents with polite disinterest before issuing her a room key attached to a large brass disk. He summoned an old man who wheezed behind her across the lobby, up the stairs, and down the hall to her room. There he made a great show of carefully aligning her bags as Patrice rummaged in her purse for a suitable tip, which sent him on his way humming cheerlessly.

She unpacked quickly, then stretched out on the bed, pondering. Her goal had been to get to Berlin, but now that she'd arrived, she realized the next steps would be the most important. She closed her eyes, thinking about the other trips to Berlin she'd made, then suddenly snapped her fingers and sat up. Karl Foch, dilettante, writer, and acid-tongued observer of life, knew everyone who was anyone in Berlin and how to get to them.

She gathered up her purse and the room key, then paused. The two alternate passports hadn't been found by the men at Customs, but if her room were searched, they might be uncovered, along with the wig. Quickly, she pulled out the bottom drawer of the dresser, then, using her nail file, lifted up the liner panel at the bottom. As she'd hoped, there was enough space to tuck away the two passports, the wig, and the stack of reichsmarks she'd brought for Laurel. As a finishing touch, she filled the drawer with her lingerie and other personal items, then slipped out of her room, feeling more secure and very much the spy.

She found Karl listed in the telephone book and dialed his number, an anticipatory tingle creeping along her spine. The last time she'd seen Karl, they had shared an intimate night which years later still made her smile.

Karl Foch had been the darling of decadent Berlin, his melodramatic novels appealing to the dark romance of the German soul, but he was a true anachronism, loving puns and silly games, a merry twinkle in his blue eyes. His mother had been English, his father German, and he was equally at home in both nations and with both languages.

"*Ja?*" his voice crackled over the phone.

"Do you still change place cards at dinner parties to suit your own designs?" Patrice said, "and is your telephone tapped?"

His low laugh increased the pace of the tingle. "Probably yes on both counts. Do you remember where we walked the last time?"

"Yes."

"Half an hour," he said before hanging up. Patrice stayed on the line for a moment, listening for the click of an eavesdropper, but none sounded.

"Perhaps, Karl," she said as she replaced the receiver and left the phone booth, "they've grown tired of listening to your romantic assignations."

"You are as beautiful, maybe more beautiful, than the last time I saw you," Karl said, taking her arm and bending to kiss her warmly.

"And you are as good a liar as ever," she replied.

"Not that I'm complaining, but why in the world are you in Berlin when everyone is desperate to get out?" He propelled her gently into the small park, his eyes scanning the faces nearby.

167

Patrice studied his face, sad to see evidence of worry and fear. "Are you one of the desperate ones, Karl?"

He shrugged. "Perhaps not desperate as much as wishful. If you mean am I in trouble, no, no more than usual. If you mean am I unhappy, of course. The Nazis have no sense of humor and, unless you are willing to wear one of their silly costumes, no parties. I'm too old to be drafted, so I am under pressure to provide some other service to the fatherland, but it's a pressure I can bear." He smiled ruefully. "Perhaps the role of propagandist has taken its toll."

"Are you writing inspiring novels for the boys on the front lines or for their patient wives?" Patrice asked, trying to tease some of the humor back into him.

"Neither. I'm writing the daily history of the glorious Reich so not one word is lost. I am Hitler's official biographer. Can you imagine it? No, of course you can't. I can't, and I do it every day. He spends at least an hour a day dictating his thoughts and heroic deeds to several secretaries and once they type it verbatim, it is brought to me to 'organize' in the words of the Nazi masters." He glanced around them again, then added, "The man is crazy, Patrice. And he gets crazier by the day. You should see some of this." Finally a grin appeared, and she saw the old Karl. "I'm certain you would be delighted to see some of it. What a story that would make on the home front."

"So when do I get to see it?"

"You haven't been here in a while, have you? All the time I am working, a uniformed fanatic stands at my side. As soon as I finish a page of notes, he burns them. At the end of the work day, all the ashes are loaded into a truck, and the guard takes the manuscript." He reached into his pocket and pulled out a candy stick. "Want one?" Patrice shook her head, and he popped the stick into his mouth. "You see, they know the old man's dotty, but they also know on which side their bread is buttered." He ticked her nose with his finger. "I can hear your newswheels turning, Patrice, but I must ask you to wait with this story until the war is over."

"Why don't you just get out?" Patrice asked.

"German passports are not terribly welcome in most nations I'd like to go to these days. *If* I had a passport, which I no longer do. But this is far too depressing, and here we are together again after so very long." He stopped, turning her to face him, then gathered her into his arms, holding her tightly. "Here you are, the only breath of fresh, free air I've been around in ages, and I'm whining about the mess I've made for myself." He pulled the candy stick out of his mouth, tossing it into the bushes nearby, then tipped Patrice's chin and kissed her with a passionate intensity which, in spite of her loyalty to Stephen, she returned.

"A breath of free, fresh air," he said again, still holding her in his arms. "Not to be wasted. Come, we will have a fine time of it while you're here." He pulled back and looked at her. "Why, indeed, are you here?"

"Sort of a fishing expedition. You know, trolling for the big story. After all, it was a challenge just to get in, and my boss thought there might be something worth taking a look at in Berlin these days." She hoped her lie sounded convincing.

"Another intrepid reporter adventure piece? Well, you have had a record of producing those. Or at least you did when I last saw a paper in English. But why call me?"

She squeezed his arm. "Why do you think? A woman of our mutual acquaintance once told me you were a terrible candidate for a husband, but you would be the smile on my face when I was old that would drive my husband crazy."

He threw back his head and laughed, transporting them both back to a happier time. "I didn't know women talked like that." His expression sobered. "Any other reason?"

She nodded. "Because I trust you, and there's someone I need to contact, but it can't be done openly."

They strolled along for a moment, then he stopped. "Oh, don't tell me it's the widow Pugh."

"None other," Patrice said.

"About her radio broadcasts? What makes you think the darling of the SS is going to talk to you?"

"Just a premonition. Can you think of a way?"

He nodded slowly. "You might be in luck. If her friend Heydrich were around, never, but he's away from Berlin right now. She has called me a couple of times in the past— when he was gone—with only the flimsiest of excuses to get together, usually saying she wants to see some bon mot the Führer may have uttered. That woman certainly can drink!''

Patrice felt cramped in the closet, which was stifling with mothballs and filled with dusty clothing, but Karl had told her to be quiet. She wished she hadn't drunk the extra cup of tea and wondered how much longer she would be confined. She heard the doorbell ring and then, as Karl's footsteps approached, two light taps on the door, the signal that Laurel had arrived. "Alone, I hope," Patrice whispered.

Patrice leaned against the door, trying to hear what they were saying, hoping her decision to trust Karl was not misplaced.

". . . surprise," Karl was saying, when suddenly the door opened and she fell forward, sprawling on the carpet.

"Patrice!" Laurel shrieked, grabbing her arm and making it all the harder for Patrice to regain her footing. "My savior! Oh, thank God you got my letter. You did get my *letter?*''

"Yes, Laurel, it's in the bank." Patrice was trying to regain her poise and dignity, but Laurel's clutching was making it more difficult, and Patrice had to keep reminding herself why she had come.

"Have you told Karl everything? Does he know it all?" Laurel gushed.

"He hasn't been told, but he's a smart man. I am certain he can reason things out. But he's trustworthy." *I hope,* she added to herself. "Come on in here. We need to talk in private. Don't worry, Karl understands, *even if he doesn't know what about.*'' She hoped her message was getting through to Laurel. Patrice led Laurel into the dining room, closing the door behind them. Karl had set tea out, and Patrice deposited Laurel in front of it. "Pour," she said, "and listen."

Patrice settled into a chair opposite Laurel, watching the unsteadiness in her hands as she took her teacup. Patrice wondered again at the wisdom of recruiting her.

Finally she said, "Laurel, the money is in a trust account in the Bank of England. When you get out, all I have to do is sign some forms and it will be yours."

"Oh, I'm so grateful. But I plan to give you some—a lot—

170

of it. All of it, if you'll just get me out of here. I've never been so glad to see anyone in my life as I was to see you, even falling out of the closet. When do we leave?''

Patrice stirred her tea. "Well, we have a deal for you to consider first.''

Laurel's face fell. "You're not going to help me, are you?''

"I *am* going to help you, but the people I had to go to for assistance have certain interests as well, and they think a trade might be worked out. What they want is for you to simply keep an eye on Heydrich and gather anything which might be of interest to my friends, then pass it along.''

"Spy, you mean, don't you?'' Laurel's face suddenly transformed from a petulant pout to a feral smile. "A spy. Hmmmm, interesting.'' She sipped at her tea, thinking. "How am I supposed to transmit this information? You know how much trouble I had getting the letter out.''

"Two ways. First, if you agree, you will be provided with the name of someone who can get documents out. And you can work certain code words into your broadcasts, to which all of us listen ardently.'' She waited for Laurel to smile at the flattery, then added, "Not that you could exactly call many people fans, you understand.''

"People hate me, don't they?'' Laurel said quietly. "But if I'm right, I'll be a visionary.''

Patrice moved her teacup to the side. "Laurel, there is no room for pretense or games now. At this moment, in the eyes of the United States government, you are a traitor. What I am offering you is the only way you will ever be able to return to the United States.''

"What makes you so certain Germany won't win?'' Laurel sneered. "And why am I a traitor? America's not even involved.''

Patrice stood up. "Fine. Get out however you can.'' She turned and walked to the door.

"Wait,'' Laurel blurted, and Patrice could hear the panic in her voice. "I was just asking.''

"It should be obvious, Laurel. Now, are you going to cooperate, or do you have some alternate plan?''

Laurel sighed. "So, you're here to blackmail me with my own money.''

171

Patrice shook her head. "No, I'm here to do as you asked. To help you. This time, however, you're not in a position to dictate the terms of that aid. This time you have to give before you take. Now, are you in?"

"I hate you. I have always hated you. You and Whitney, the two most perfect girls in the Valley. Everyone's darlings. Always doing what was right. Now I suppose you're just going to hold all this over me, too, just like you always have everything else."

Patrice slapped her, hard. "How dare you? I risk my neck trying to help you out, and this is how you react? Look, I'm not here out of any love or friendship for you, Laurel, but I'm offering you an alternative to being shot as a traitor. Take it or leave it. But if you take it, we expect real cooperation, not just crumbs of information. Laurel, you can't expect to get something without giving in return, and particularly not now. Grow up, Laurel. Whining isn't becoming in a woman your age."

They stared at each other, their hostility open. Finally, Laurel pulled her eyes away. "All right, you win."

Patrice shook her head. "No, Laurel, *you* win. Now, for once in your life, don't destroy the only thing that can help you. Use your head." She sat down again. "Now, here's the arrangement. I entered Germany on a Swiss passport, wearing a disguise. That passport and the disguise will be available to you if you need it."

"Who will decide if I need it?" Laurel asked sullenly.

"The person who will keep it for you. Don't worry, it's someone we can both trust. Because it shows the bearer to be an American woman who is married to a Swiss and it has an entry visa, there will be no problem with having to get or forge an exit visa. Just be sure you look like the photograph. The trusted person will also hold for you reichsmarks, from which you will get monthly allotments until you leave, when you can take whatever is left."

"How much a month?" Laurel leaned forward, licking her lips.

"You'll be given an amount commensurate with the information you provide. Give nothing and you get nothing.

172

Think of it as piecework, Laurel, just like the factory workers your late husband employed."

Laurel jumped to her feet, reaching across the table to strike Patrice, then stopped and sat down again.

"Good. Self-control is very important," Patrice said coldly. "Now, the last condition my friends have imposed is that they would like a token from you—a bit of information to show that you are sincere. They've given me some guidelines on how to judge the information, and if it's good, you will be given the name of your contact here, and the list of codes they've devised for you to include in your broadcasts."

Laurel stared miserably at the grain of the wooden table, tracing the lines with her fingertip. "I hate being trapped like this."

Patrice sighed, almost feeling sorry for Laurel in spite of herself. She reached across the table, taking the other woman's hand. "Look, Laurel, no one's enjoying this war and the positions it has put people in. None of us has chosen what's happening in the world right now, but anyone who has a chance to affect the outcome has a moral obligation to try, I think. It's why I'm here, risking my neck to save yours. I know you must feel terribly alone and very helpless, but maybe if you can think about the greater good, it'll help."

Laurel's eyes rose to meet hers. "I didn't want anything different from anyone else. I wanted to be married, to be rich, to have a nice life. How did it all get so mixed up?"

Patrice shook her head slowly. "It's a good question, and I don't think anyone will ever know the answer. I'm sorry for the mess you're in, Laurel. Make it mean something."

Laurel pushed at the tear on her cheek with the back of her hand, then forced a smile. "And when it's all over, you and I will split Gerhard Pugh's blood money and . . . and . . ." Tears slid down her face, and she sobbed. "And buy Whitney a new horse."

Patrice rose and came around the table to cradle Laurel's shaking shoulders. "Great idea," she said past the lump in her throat.

Laurel's sobs quieted to sniffles, and finally she pulled

away from Patrice. "Now look. I've wrinkled your nice blouse." She rummaged in her purse for a handkerchief and blew her nose noisily, then squared her shoulders. "About that token of information. The last time I saw Reinhard, before he went back to Russia, he was bragging about a plan he's made up to fool the Russians into thinking their armies had been decimated after a battle. What he's going to do is take undesirables—prisoners from the re-education camps in Poland—and put them in Russian uniforms and then . . . kill them so when the Russians fly over they'll think their armies have been routed and they will surrender. He plans to do this soon. He told me they're manufacturing the uniforms now."

"Oh, my God. How can he think of things like that?" Patrice said, stunned.

Laurel laughed mirthlessly. "That's nothing compared to some of the other things he says." She shuddered. "Now do you still want me to have to stay here? Never mind, that wasn't a fair question. We've made a deal and that's my part of the bargain."

"Would it be any help to know that there are many other people who have made deals they hate in this war?" Her thoughts flew to Whitney. "And they're just as uncomfortable with them as you are."

"So I have a deal? I can get out if I need to?"

Patrice nodded. "You have a deal. Karl will let you know who your contact is to be. You can trust him, you know."

Laurel rose and picked up her purse. "One more thing. Tell Whitney they have known all along, and they still want her. Reinhard is obsessive about her. She must have done something terrible."

Patrice smiled. "Something wonderful," she said softly.

"And what about me? What's in this for me? I'd like to get out, too, you know." Karl swirled the snifter he held until the brandy formed a whirlpool.

"I don't have any other documents with me, but I'll do what I can. I'm sure my organization will try, especially since you've been so much help with this project. And you do have access to something important. I'm certain they would like to know how Hitler thinks." She nodded. "Yes, I feel sure something will be done for you."

"Then I will do as you ask. You can trust me."

Patrice looked into his eyes and smiled a sad, rueful smile. "I do. Anyone who'd switch the place cards at a dinner party can't be all bad." She kissed him gently. "You will hear from us."

"I thought the Turkish gypsy outfit took the cake, but Major Ball, you have outdone yourself as an Ethiopian Coptic monk." Whitney stood back to survey Cesar's quite authentic costume.

"If I might make the observation, Countess, neither of us is as we appear to be, but those secrets are ones we jealously guard." He gestured toward the kitchen garden and they strolled in that direction. "The Colonel will be delighted to know how well you look. Perhaps the religious life agrees with you."

Whitney chuckled. "Oddly enough, in many ways it does. These women, the real nuns here, seem so untouched by the world and its troubles. They don't seem to have any curiosity about us or our comings and goings."

"I don't mean to damage your illusions, but it's what they're paid for. I'm just glad to know the 'contributions' we're making to their coffers are not in vain."

Whitney looked puzzled, then laughed aloud. "Nothing is ever as it appears, is it?"

"I'm afraid not. Here, let us sit and enjoy the warmth of the sun and the beauty of this harbor, and let me tell you why I've come, and about the monk who's with me. Oh, but first, are you certain Sister Leona didn't betray you?"

"So far. Perhaps it's too soon to tell. She did seem sincere when she said she had not—right before she killed herself." She shook her head to drive out the memory. "I thought this spy game was supposed to be all parties and good times."

Ball chuckled. "That's what the recruiting posters say, but don't believe it for a moment. Now, on to the present. Abbé D'Astier is a genuine Franciscan monk from free France who is skilled in protective arts. The Colonel, and

175

the rest at Cocoon, feel that for the moment at least, you should have additional protection just in case Sister Leona did pass anything along to her masters. He will also fill your unit's need again for someone skilled in communications and codes." He paused, then grinned at her. "You should be flattered by all this attention."

"I would far rather be of no significance to anyone, but let us say I am grateful."

"The Colonel said to tell you that you can get out whenever you have had enough."

She shook her head. "Not yet. Probably not ever." She smiled. "I have begun to enjoy blowing things up."

"Then you will like this mission very much. He reached inside his robe and pulled out a map. In these mountains there are many deep ravines that are crossed by bridges built during the Great War. Tomorrow night a large German convoy plans to use two of those bridges to bring in supplies for their African occupation forces. The bridges are about a mile apart and almost impossible for the Germans to protect." He smiled, a glint in his eye. "Of course, Butterflies can go places others can't."

Whitney thought about Ball's joke as she clung to the thin tree and jammed her good foot into a crack in the rock below the bridge. She tried not to look down, or to think of how far "down" was, as she waited for Sister Regina to place three charges in a joint connecting several girders. Sister Regina, however, had swung hand-over-hand along the beam, then agilely up onto it, and was humming something as she attached the explosives. Whitney could hear her tune, which sounded a great deal like "California Here I Come."

"Wire," came the whisper above Whitney's head, and she gripped the small tree more tightly with one arm, then tossed the coiled loops. A small breeze caught the wire and moved it away from Sister Regina's reach, but before Whitney could react, Sister Regina flung herself out and neatly snared the wire, then pulled herself back up the safety rope she'd tied around her waist. Whitney struggled to keep from screaming or vomiting or both.

Whitney began climbing back up the side of the ravine as

176

soon as she saw Sister Regina swing down, meeting her at one of the pylons below the bridge where Robbins was just finishing laying the final charges.

"I thought you were a goner," Whitney said, still breathless.

Sister Regina shrugged. "Little trick I learned when I used to climb fire escapes in my past life. It's almost unconscious for me to tie onto something. I didn't mean to frighten you, but I have to admit it felt good to do a little gymnastic flying again. It wasn't a bad throw, incidentally, just a bad wind. But everything is fine up there."

"Good. We'll blow the joint first, then the pylons," Robbins said. "Sister Camille, you'll be the signal-passer to the other side of the ravine. We'll just have to hope both convoys are moving at the same speed so we get as many as we can." He looked at his watch. "Forty-five minutes—if the Jerries stick to their schedule, and if the guy gave us the real schedule. I wish I believed I had time to go across to the other side and check the set-up, but I guess I just have to trust Sister Bernadette to do her usual good job." He nodded. "That girl could blow the seeds out of an orange, so I guess I shouldn't worry."

"I wonder how Major Ball's team is doing." Whitney said, looking in the direction of the hidden bridge to their north.

Robbins sat on a rock. "I've known Cesar Ball for a lot of years. His'll probably go better'n . . ." He hesitated, cocking his head, then leapt to his feet. "Damn, there's the signal whistle. Damn Jerries are early."

Whitney turned and scurried up to her overlook, crouching between two large rocks and looking through her binoculars toward the opposite end of the bridge. As she watched, the first of the mud-green trucks rumbled onto the bridge. She could see the face of the driver as he leaned one elbow out the window and looked down into the ravine. Quickly, she pulled the glasses away. She didn't want him to become a person in her thoughts.

As the lead truck slowed to gear down for the sharp ascent, Whitney pulled her flashlight up and tapped the switch three times.

177

For a moment, nothing happened. Then everything happened as the air was filled with fire and noise. Whitney heard a screech as the girders began to fail under the pressure of the explosion and the weight of the trucks. The bridge began to tip, first swaying slightly, then suddenly raining trucks and debris into the ravine far below. In the distance, Whitney heard a parallel set of explosions and saw the red glow on the northern horizon.

She focused her binoculars on the far edge of the ravine, looking for Sister Bernadette and Sister Magda through the dust and fire. Finally, she located Sister Magda and was surprised to see her leap onto the running board of the last truck, which had not been on the bridge when it blew. As Whitney watched, Sister Magda seized the driver's hair, yanked his head out through the window, and slit his throat. Whitney grimaced, then was further horrified to see the smile on Magda's face as she wiped the blade on the man's shirt, then pulled him out onto the pavement and got behind the wheel.

Whitney had lowered her glasses and begun to climb down when she felt a searing pain in her right thigh and, an instant later, a shocking bump against her false leg, which gave way. She tumbled down toward the road, her arm looped over her head, protecting it from the rocks and bushes that lashed out at her.

Whitney heard feet thudding and said, "No, not again," but as she opened her eyes, she saw Sister Regina dashing past, then heard three quick shots and a scream. Whitney turned her head to see where she was and tried to get up, pulling herself up on her left leg, holding tightly to a pine-tree trunk, where Robbins found her, pale, her right leg soaked with blood.

He swept her into his arms and she clung to his neck.

"Just relax, Isis," he whispered, using the code name from so long ago. "This time we're going to do it right."

10

CESAR BALL SLID his thumb in an endless, reflexive caress of the smooth black stone in his hand, his brow furrowed. "Two things have bothered me all along about Laurel Pugh," he finally said.

Donohue swung in his chair to look at him with interest. Paul Sanders Stewart looked up from his elaborate doodling, and Patrice's gaze shifted quickly to his face. "Only two?" she said with an ironic lift of her brows.

Cesar's lips curled around a small smile, then sobered again. "We haven't the time to discuss all the things which bother me about Mrs. Pugh and her family, so I shall limit myself to our more immediate circumstance." His thumb circled the stone. "From observation I feel safe to say Mrs. Pugh may be greedy, power-hungry, an opportunist, and probably quite without compassion, but one cannot say the woman is stupid. She has been quite clever in her successful insertion of herself at the highest level of the Nazis' inner circles, and more remarkable, she has managed to remain there despite her rather public difficulties. Further, in the two months since she's allegedly been a member of our team, she seems to have strengthened her position with Heydrich, if her broadcasts are any indication."

Donohue nodded. "No one here would dispute anything you've said."

"Thank you. All this logic is my first concern. Why are we willing to believe her conversion was anything more than an example of her clever manipulation? She was in trouble; we bailed her out; she got what she wanted. What do we have in return? Very little. And what assurance do we have that we will get anything of value from her?"

Patrice leaned forward. "We've got her half-million dollars. That's a good bit of insurance."

Major Ball shifted his worry stone to his other hand. "Which brings up my second concern. Gerhard Pugh is a man known for his loyalty to the Nazis. Laurel, his daughter-in-law, noted for her powerful connections inside the same group, surfaces in a panic with a story about her husband's murder and mails Patrice a check for five hundred thousand dollars from Gerhard Pugh, drawn, no less, on an American bank, begging Patrice for help." The stone changed hands again as he paused. "How do we know we weren't being set up?"

Patrice sighed. "She certainly seemed terrified when I saw her in Berlin. Then again, she was always a convincing actress."

Donohue tented his hands, tapping his fingers together. "I think it's time to test Mrs. Pugh. Patrice, she's yours. What do you think?"

Patrice grinned, a gleam in her eye. "I think we'll get a good response if we tell her there's some difficulty in collecting her funds from the American bank which can only be resolved with her help. It's a big threat. That's all she ever understands."

"Why are you suddenly so interested in the Russian front?" Heydrich said irritably. "Are you thinking of volunteering for the siege forces around Leningrad?"

Laurel tickled his neck with a long fingernail. "Perhaps I shall. That way I could be close to you and be certain you haven't found yourself some Russian beauty to keep you warm at night."

He snorted, but she could feel the irritation disappear. "Perhaps I should take you to the front with me so you could see the Russian beauties you worry so much about. None of them are in danger of starving to death, and only their mothers think they are beautiful. And you do not need to worry about my being warm at night—summer in Russia is hot and humid. The tents are sweltering and the men smell like goats. Do you still want to come to Russia?"

No, Laurel thought, *I do not. But I must give Patrice something or I can kiss my half million dollars goodbye.* "I want to go anywhere with you. How much longer will they hold out before they realize they cannot succeed against the German army?"

Heydrich drained his glass of schnapps and refilled it. "The Russians are a stubborn, stupid race of people. Every other country we've liberated has quickly realized the benefit of joining the Reich. But these Russians and their damnable Bolshevism . . ." He made a gesture of frustrated dismissal. "They cling to their unreasonable system no matter what. If they would only realize they cannot stem the tide which flows around them, perhaps we would not need to resort to such desperate measures to convince them."

"Desperate measures! Why, it sounds to me as though you must be forced to do terrible things," Laurel cooed, tracing the vein standing out in his neck and wondering how long it would be before the man simply exploded.

Heydrich sighed deeply. "Years from now, we will be respected and admired for liberating nations which were held in the grip of the Jews and the Communists." He turned to encircle her with his arm. "I do not like to kill people who might be able to join in the brilliant future of the Reich. I want to eliminate only those who contaminate the society or the bloodlines of the Aryan race, to help the Führer in his dream of creating a perfect society. And unfortunately we have been forced to take many lives in the process of freeing people from the old ways."

"Is that the case in Russia?" Laurel asked softly, wishing she didn't have to hear the answer.

He nodded. "Many lives are lost in foolish resistance. They continue to ignore our warnings, so we must retaliate." He sighed again, drinking deeply. "A whole town. We were forced to eliminate a whole town when they refused to give up their Jews." He slammed his fist on the arm of the divan. "A whole town! Don't they know the filthy Jews brought this upon themselves? And why are they protecting the damn Jews? The Bolsheviks have no love for Jews and have tried to remove the problem, just as we have. We have done their work for them, and suddenly they all turn into Jew-lovers. Do you see what I mean about the mystifying stubbornness of these people?"

"It must be a terrible trial for you. Oh," she said, sitting up suddenly, "I know something which may make you feel better. Your friend, the one you call 'The Concertmaster,' has sent two large packages which I guess must be music. Perhaps if you played your violin . . ."

"Why didn't you tell me earlier?" he snapped, rising quickly. "Where are they?"

"Here," she said, fetching the unopened, oversized envelopes, "right here."

He snatched them from her and quickly opened them, withdrawing a thick sheaf of music from the first, and another of equal size from the second. He compared them, then put the second bundle atop the first. He placed the music on the table and leaned forward, staring intently at the pages.

"Interesting," he mumbled once, then quickly glanced at her as though he'd forgotten her presence. "The music is very interesting," he added quickly.

"I have no ability with music. Why don't you play it for me?"

"Play it?" he asked, sounding puzzled, then shrugged. "I suppose I could."

Laurel went to the closet and removed his violin case, setting it carefully on the table, wishing once again she'd paid better attention to her music lessons.

Heydrich opened the case and removed the instrument, running his hands lovingly over its polished surface, then plucking at the strings and adjusting their tune. "My father gave me this violin. He always hoped I'd be a concert violinist.'' He tucked the instrument under his chin, and began playing a mournful tune, never glancing at the scores before him.

Patrice opened the envelope and quickly withdrew the three sheets of paper covered with Karl Foch's generous scrawl.

My dear little friend:
　My house and ears yearn to hear your merry laughter, but for now I shall simply have to imagine it as I tell you of the news of Berlin.
　The trials of war seem not to have dimmed the social scene: the autumn social season seems to have begun early and in earnest—rather a pre-Oktoberfest whirl of parties at which one must not get very drunk but longs to. The conversational rules for the year seem to have changed: One may not speak of the Eastern Bear in any terms, but may endlessly recount visits to Paris—no longer 'occupied Paris,' for now it is ours—and mentioning the amazing bargains obtained is nearly a requirement. If I hear one more word about the house of Chanel or the scents of Coty, I believe I shall scream.
　Uniforms have replaced tuxedos, except for those unfortunate few of us unentitled to wear even the smallest bit of black or gray and medals. The women, however, are splendid peacocks, strutting their finery and the achievements of their husbands with equal assertiveness—a most un-Frau-like behavior. If all the stories I hear are true, the glorious Reich is but moments away from total victory.

Patrice could imagine how carefully he'd constructed the letter to sound victorious and smug for the censors. Knowing Karl, however, she could hear the irony ringing past the words. She finished scanning the letter, then rose and locked her office door.

Returning to her desk, she pulled open the bottom drawer, then removed the false bottom and took out the decoding fluid. Sweeping the desk clutter to the side, she laid the three sheets of Karl's letter on the blotter, then poured some of the fluid in the middle of the first page, brushing it to the edges with a square of linen. Leaning forward with intense interest, she watched the mystifying magic as Karl's gossip was replaced with another, far more important, letter. As the words became clear, she wrote furiously in a notebook, copying his information before the magic reversed and his original letter reappeared permanently. Somehow the five minutes she had to copy the page never seemed as though it would be enough. When the first page began to fade, however, she was already at work on the second, not really reading the words but simply copying them. The third page was just fading back when she replaced the "secret stuff" into the drawer.

Patrice:

Sorry for all the drivel. I think next time I do one of these, I'll write the invisible words first. Do you know how hard it is to write one thing over another?

But on to more important matters. Laurel must have more than believed your threat (which I tried to convey with deep concern and gravity, though I saw through your ruse immediately), for she has delivered three pieces of information she seems to think would move the Lord himself.

Piece one: Gathered from Heydrich directly. If you've heard of a whole town in Russia being murdered, believe it. Apparently Heydrich killed every man, woman, and child because he thought they were protecting Jews. She said she thought there must have been a great many of them, for Heydrich told her it took him three days. He's about as appealing as the Führer himself—and apparently his designated successor. Heydrich is treated with a reverence by the military that is second only to the master monster himself. He can do no wrong. If Laurel continues to his favor, you do indeed have a pipeline to the top, not only for now but in the future.

Piece two: Laurel, by observation of Heydrich. He has a mysterious communicant and occasional visitor he calls "The Concertmaster." Laurel has no idea who he is and has seen him only once, and that was the night Helmut was murdered, so she cannot describe him very well. He plays an instrument—piano, she thinks—and writes music prolifically which he sends to Heydrich on a regular basis. The scores have been coming more often lately and she has heard Heydrich mutter, "How interesting," while staring at the music. She wonders if the music is a code and, since the scores sometimes come in the mail from such places as Spain and Sweden, she wonders if the Concertmaster is a spy working on your side and sending back information to RH. Interesting possibility. Music as a code? What a thought.

Piece three: overheard at a party in a ladies' lounge conversation. She doesn't know who the women were, but one with a "Munich accent" was asking the other if she knew of any whores who called themselves the "Limping Lady." Apparently the woman with the "Munich accent" was suspicious because her husband had healed this woman and was now looking for her again. She said he had told her he needed to go on a trip and she had found out he was seeking this woman, perhaps in Austria. Laurel said you'd understand all this and would know who to warn. You must promise to explain all this someday when we have time and a large bottle of superb cognac!

Whitney waited until the real nuns had filed into the chapel before slipping from the pew at the rear of the cathedral. Her false leg, however, had developed a most irritating creak after the foray to the bridges. As she walked through the darkly shadowed columnary, the sound was amplified, echoing noisily and making her giggle.

Some spy, she thought, squeaking through the stone corridor.

Suddenly a figure emerged from the shadows, and Whitney gasped as the man appeared in front of her.

"We thought you were still alive," he hissed with a chillingly familiar accent. Whitney's hand tightened around her cane as vivid recollections flooded her memory.

"Who do you think I am?" she asked, trying to keep a tone of innocent confusion in her voice. "Perhaps you have mistaken me for someone else. I am Sister Camille of the Sisters of Perpetual Trust. Whom do you seek, sir?"

"Limping Lady, the time for charades is over." As the man stepped closer, Whitney could clearly see his features. She was staring at the face of the doctor who'd haunted her dreams for two years—the man who'd removed her leg and addicted her to morphine.

"You look well, Limping Lady. Much better than I have been since our parting. Your defection has caused much difficulty in my career. You have taken something which belongs to the Reich. And the only way I will ever recover my career and my life is to get it back. Give me your leg."

Whitney strained to hear her team around her, then, raising her voice, replied, "*Herr Doktor,* you and your Nazi masters are not so foolish as to believe I did not discover the diamonds." She laughed with a rough arrogance. "Don't be ridiculous. Those diamonds are now in the hands of people who will use them for right." She hesitated again, listening without appearing to, hoping the tiny hiss of fabric on stone was not her imagination. "Who sent you here, *Herr Doktor?* Have you come to take my other leg?" She could hear her voice echoing along the columnary.

"No, I have come to take your life. The diamonds don't matter. There is something else in your leg which does, and if I bring it back, I will be restored to glory in the Reich and able to take my place in the important research the Reich is conducting without me, using that pig Mengele to do my work. He has stolen my ideas and my position, but I will get it all back."

As he lunged, she raised her cane to strike him, but the cane was knocked aside by a blur of black and white,

186

followed by a solid thud as the doctor was thrown to the ground. Sister Magda, Whitney realized, was kneeling atop the man's chest as Sister Judith removed the braided silk cord which held the large rosary around her waist.

"Sister Camille," Judith said with a dignified smile, "has this man been bothering you?"

Sister Magda looked up from her position astride the struggling man's chest. "Is this the German creep doctor who kept you in prison in Austria?" As she spoke, she moved her lower arm suddenly and Whitney could see the gleam as the stiletto slipped from her sleeve. Without waiting for an answer, she spun, thrusting the point of the knife up under the man's chin. "Lie still, bastard," she spat.

Still holding the knife at his throat, she slipped from his torso as Sister Judith moved to his other side. Together, they leaned him up against one of the columns, and Sister Judith tied his hands behind it.

"I told you to be still," Sister Magda said, making a quick slice with her knife, leaving an instant red line which began to ooze blood onto his white collar. "Now, perhaps Sister Camille has some questions for you."

"Who sent you?" Whitney asked, her voice low and quiet.

The doctor's eyes darted from one to the other. "No one, I swear. I told you, I have been discredited. I came on my own to try to get back what belongs to the Reich." He glanced again at Magda, then at Judith. "I am not a man of violence. I could help you. I saved her life, don't forget that. She would have died without my skill. She would have bled to death, but I saved her. I could work with you now. I could be your doctor here. I can tell you much about what Mengele is doing."

"I thought you said he stole your work and your ideas. If what he's doing is so awful, you must have thought of it. Why would we want someone like you?" Whitney was surprised at her delight in toying with him.

"But I can tell you a great deal about the Nazis' plans. And I swear on my life no one knows I am here. I can tell you much."

Sister Magda nodded. "And you will."

"Who is this Mengele?" Whitney asked.

"He's a madman," the doctor said quickly. "He is using the people in the camps, but not the way I wanted to. You see, we want to understand why twins are the same and the special connection between them. I wanted to do some studies on them, but I swear I would not have hurt the children. Mengele is doing terrible experiments. He tortures one to see if the other can feel what is happening to his twin. He experiments on pregnant women to see when twins are formed. He does other things with diseases. It was not what I wanted to do."

"What are you really here for? What do you really want?" Whitney demanded, sickened at his revelations.

"There was a microfilm in your leg. Plans for some machine. I can show you where it is hidden."

Magda and Judith looked at Whitney curiously, but she stared down at the doctor. "What else?"

"Isn't that enough?" Whitney could hear the panic in his voice.

"How stupid you must think we are, *Herr Doktor*. We found the microfilm long ago. Now what else?"

His eyes widened with panic. "I have not been a part of the operations. I told you. I know only about Mengele and the microfilm. Isn't that enough? I can help you."

"And you came back to kill me so you could experiment on innocent children. I feel no mercy for you, just as you felt none for me." She looked at Sister Magda, then nodded.

With swift skill, Sister Judith stuffed the hem of her robe into the man's mouth, blocking the scream which was about to emerge as Sister Magda slit open the crotch of his trousers, then his shorts.

She knelt between his legs, ripping the cloth away. Cradling his testicles in one of her hands, she leaned toward him with an eerie parody of intimacy. "Ah, now we have come to the heart of the matter, dear physician. It seems you took something important from our dear Sister Camille and now you must give something in return. We can't have the world out of balance, can we?"

The man whimpered through the cloth gagging his mouth,

188

trying to pull away from her hands, desperately attempting to close his legs to protect himself.

Suddenly Magda made a quick, twisting motion with the knife, and her hands were covered with blood as the man's muffled scream filled the air. Magda turned to Whitney, extending her open hand to display two gray and bloody glands. "Now things are back in balance, Sister Camille. Perhaps you should retire to your cell to pray for his soul while we feed his body to the sharks."

11

WE HAVE, WHITNEY thought to herself during a momentary pause in the torrent of information and interpretation, *been living in a convent far too long*. She glanced at Lady Primrose, whose bright pink cheeks and rapt attention to their visitor indicated she was feeling the same way.

Erik sat beside Whitney on the uncomfortable bench in Mother Luke's office. His thigh was nuzzled against hers, further distracting her, but the feeling was so good Whitney didn't want to pull away. When the others were distracted, he leaned toward her.

"I've missed you very much. I was crazy when they told me you'd been shot. Are you certain you've healed completely? Do you want to be pulled out?"

She caressed his hand lightly with her own, longing to disappear into his arms but highly conscious of the presence of Mother Luke and the two novices who were passing teacakes.

"I'm really fine. I'll show you my scar later," she muttered. "And I most certainly do not want to be pulled out. All hell is breaking loose here, in case you hadn't noticed."

Dusko Popov waited until the door had closed behind the retreating novices, then nodded briskly. "Thank you for your courtesy, Mother Luke. Tea was certainly a welcome respite from the matters at hand.'' He smiled and an impish dimple flashed endearingly on his cheek. Lady Primrose's color deepened.

"Having given you an overview of the relative positions of the Nazis and the Allies, I will now proceed to some specifics.'' The dimple appeared again. First, the Church. Like so many other anomalies, the Church, and Pope Pius XII, seem to be playing a dangerous game of appeasing the lion. The Pope thinks that the Nazis will leave the Catholic clergy alone if only he can find the right distractions.'' He sighed. "Yet he appears to have also decided to ignore the numbers of Polish, French, Czech, and German priests and nuns who have been sent to the camps.'' Popov shrugged. "We know he's aware of their arrests, but apparently Mussolini has convinced the Holy Father that his missing clerics are ministering to the people in the camps.''

Erik leaned forward. "Tricycle, have you seen the camps?''

Popov nodded, his eyes focused on a distant horror. "Though I wish I hadn't. Ladies, out of respect for you I won't belabor the details, save to say that thousands a day are arriving by train in cattle cars. Many are Jews, but there are also gypsies and cripples and, as I have told you, nuns and priests.''

Mother Luke stood, obviously distressed. "Why can't the Allies stop them?''

"Regrettably, Mother Luke, the Allies can't, at the moment, seem to stop the Nazis from doing anything. If it were possible to neutralize the camps, we would, but one of the difficulties with that is getting the Allies to believe such things are going on. There is the Geneva Convention, which protects prisoners of war, but the Nazis do not view people in camps as prisoners of war.'' He drank deeply of his tea as though trying to chase a bad taste from his mouth, then continued. "I fear the Germany I love is gone forever, trodden into mud by Nazi jackboots and the blood of honest people.'' He paused, wiping at his forehead with a handkerchief. "And the England I love is lost as well, her innocence consumed by fear.''

Lady Primrose took his hand. "We all share your grief. This is a bad time for the human race."

With great elegance, he raised her hand to his lips. "Thus it is such a pleasure in this bad time to be able to be with dear friends." He held her hand and her eyes for a moment. "Now, to finish about the Church. I am here to warn you that the Pope's policy of nonacknowledgment has led to a great deal of political action for both sides within the Church. Trust no one, ladies, not even within the walls of the Bishop's palace. Of course, Mother Luke is an obvious exception, as is the Abbé d'Astier, but be very cautious. Don't take anyone at face value simply because he wears a clerical collar. Erik, would you like to address the political situation?"

Erik nodded. "You are well aware that Prince Paul of Yugoslavia played the same game with Hitler as the Pope: give him a little and hope he'll think it's enough. In April we learned how Prince Paul courted disaster. His agreement with the Führer was that the Italians were allowed access to the Greek and Albanian frontiers in exchange for which Yugoslavia regained full control of Macedonia from Greece. The Prince believed the Italians were less menacing than the Germans, but I cannot understand his reasoning, since Yugoslavia is now occupied by Nazis, which I scarcely need to tell you. There are more soldiers here than in Berlin, I think."

"And more arriving every day, bringing supplies and weapons with them," Whitney added.

Erik grinned. "Except, of course, for those unfortunate enough to encounter the Butterfly Avengers. Complicating the situation here, however, is also the presence of USTASHI."

"We thought they were relatively small," Whitney said, her brow furrowing.

"Not for long, I'm afraid. Yugoslavia's occupation by the Germans has brought in a great deal of money and support. Their leader, Andreija Artukovic, formerly Minister of the Interior, has, however, openly been a Nazi ally for a long time, and Hitler has great plans for Artukovic! You can trust

Tito and his guerrillas, even though they are relatively small."

"We know him." Lady Primrose nodded. "A very independent and intense young man, but idealistic, I think."

"And an intense nationalist," Popov added. "He chooses his forces carefully, not only for their skills and vitality, but also for their national spirit. He has great dreams for the Yugoslavs and is quite intent on carrying them out. Don't assume he's going to rush to help you, however, if your mission doesn't quite fit with his plans. He's quite particular about controlling his operations."

Erik nodded, then continued for Popov. "And Donohue is quite particular about controlling ours. Which leads me to an operation Donohue would like you to undertake. USTASHI has set up several highly efficient broadcasting stations that are pumping a great deal of information into Germany about local conditions inside Yugoslavia. I'm certain I don't need to remind you of the possible consequences if USTASHI agents happened onto you. One way to prevent that is to disrupt their broadcasting as much as possible. I've brought some jamming equipment, and USTASHI will make it a bit easier for us, since their stations are permanent installations. All you have to do is find them."

Lady Primrose nodded briskly. "That shouldn't be too difficult. We're a resourceful lot here."

Erik laughed. "Indeed you are."

Whitney smiled. "Thank you."

Erik returned her smile. "You know a compliment always precedes a special assignment, and this is no exception. In addition to neutralizing USTASHI, you are also asked to monitor the radio traffic between the German troops in Russia and Italy. Obviously, everything will be in code. Just write it down and get it out to us. A courier will come every few days." Erik reached into his tunic and pulled out a small camera and rolls of film. "In addition to radio listeners, you ladies will also become photographers. Write the code in clear letters, photograph it, and destroy the papers. The film goes to the courier, who will bring it to London for interpretation." He set the camera and film on the table in front of them. "The Russians don't seem to have any idea of what's going on in the Ukraine and we're hearing some pretty wild rumors about mass killings and extermination squads." He hesitated, then shook his head. "I might also add that the rumors in Berlin are just as wild. The Russians may be winning, but they seem pretty effective at confusing radio transmissions to Berlin. Which explains the Italian channel for communication. Which also explains why Donohue is so interested in having you listen to the radio constantly, since Dubrovnik is in a direct line from the Ukraine to Rome. We Germans, you see, have a weakness for layers of information, and this channel is being set up by Goebbels to confirm what is coming in from other sources."

"In other words, the Germans are spying on each other," Whitney said.

"Precisely. I'm certain everyone in London thinks the Germans' great strength is their unity. Hardly. Everyone on Hitler's councils is checking up on everyone else to be sure no one is getting more than they are. The Russian front is a psychological plum if you understand Hitler's fascination with Napoleon. He is determined to succeed where Napoleon failed, and is trying to get a foothold in Russia before winter. From what I hear, however, the Russian front is fragmented and chaotic. Hitler's got Heydrich in there trying to sort it out, but he's not meeting with much success, at least according to the rumors."

Tricycle nodded. "I hear the same things. Heydrich kills anyone who *seems* to be opposing him or Germany. I have heard about the elimination of an entire city's people by Heydrich's squads. But one must always temper such information with the understanding that Heydrich is doing a great deal to enhance his own mythic presence. He probably starts the rumors—or if not him, then that American woman who is his mistress. I would hate to have her against me. She is quite a tiger."

"I assume you mean Laurel Pugh," Whitney said flatly.

"You know of her?" Tricycle asked, surprised.

"I grew up with her. She is indeed a formidable opponent, in part because she is obsessed with herself. She's a dangerous, nasty woman."

"Indeed she is," Erik agreed. "But she's in for a rough

194

time. Hitler is more than a bit of a prude about married men who have mistresses. At any rate, now you at least have an idea of why Donohue considers the Ukraine broadcasts to be so important. The Russian operation is costing Germany dearly in men and in matériel and could reverse the fortunes of the Nazis if the invasion continues to be so thoroughly opposed."

"So we are to listen and relay information. That seems a simple enough request," Lady Primrose said.

"Simple but essential." Popov rose. "With regret, I must be on my way, since my mission for the Germans, who think I work for them, was one which should not have kept me long." He bowed to Mother Luke, shook Erik's hand, bowed low over Whitney's, then, with sweeping grace, took Lady Primrose into his arms for a passionate kiss. Mother Luke kept her eyes lowered, however, moving papers on her desk as the reunion continued. Whitney and Erik turned away, both of them struggling with an urge to giggle. Finally they heard Lady Primrose sigh deeply and Popov clear his throat.

"A pleasure to see you again, Dusko," Lady Primrose said, as though they had just shaken hands.

"I have prepared the painting," Mother Luke said, breaking the romance of the moment. "I shall accompany you to the gate and make quite a show of presenting it. Much as the words may stick in my throat."

"Painting?" Whitney asked.

"Political realities, I'm afraid," Sister Luke said, picking up a rolled canvas from her desk.

Popov said apologetically, "Hitler has a great love for art—especially that which he does not own. Sister Luke's gift is designed to placate the lion."

He turned toward the door, then spun again, once more taking Lady Primrose in his arms. "It's been a very long time, Prim," Whitney heard him say before he followed Sister Luke's retreating back to play out their charade.

"War is hardly glamorous," Lady Primrose said, adjusting her wimple and wide mantle before departing. Whitney was surprised to hear tears in her voice.

*   *   *

195

"Don't move. Please don't move one inch," Whitney purred into Erik's neck. "You feel so good exactly where you are."

"So do you." He moved the pillow under her head slightly.

"Whose apartment is this anyway?" Whitney questioned.

Erik smirked. "It belongs to one of our early recruits who is currently strutting around Berlin behaving like the perfect Nazi. If Hitler only knew how many men like Tricycle, and our host, and me he has in his ranks, he might begin to worry about the future of the Reich."

"Don't laugh like that again," Whitney whispered, and he gently moved to meet her lips.

"Don't worry, my love."

"Oh, but I do," she said, tracing his lips with her fingertip. "About both of us. Here I am in Yugoslavia playing spy with a group of extremely hardened criminals, and there you are, dashing in and out of Germany, playing a very dangerous game. Do you know what worries me most?"

"Besides my moving?"

"Don't make me laugh," she repeated. "What worries me most is what we'll both be like when this is over."

"I promise you we'll spend a great deal of time together finding out." He stirred against her, bringing a broad smile to her lips before he bent to kiss them passionately.

"I have to get back to the convent before curfew," Whitney said, and Erik turned, startled, then burst out laughing.

"Can you imagine how that sounds, my love? It makes me feel the complete rogue."

"As you are," she teased, pulling on her peasant dress. "At least I had the grace not to come with you in full habit."

"At least." He sat beside her on the rumpled bed. "One more bit of business. Sister Leona's death isn't known in Berlin, but there is some curiosity about why she hasn't reported in. Here's the name of the control who ran her. I've found out he's never seen her and expects she's posing as a whore. Her objective was to find soldiers with very loose lips. Could one of your girls do a convincing Spanish whore?"

196

Whitney nodded. "Probably all of them, but Bernadette is the most logical choice. She speaks fluent Spanish. And she was friendly with Leona, so may be able to behave convincingly."

"And you trust her?"

"As much as I do any of them."

Erik came to take her into his arms once more. "Don't . . . trust . . . anyone!" he said, emphasizing each word with a kiss. "Please, Whitney, protect yourself. You don't have to do anything to prove your reputation. Let the Butterflies take the chances."

She held him tightly. "I can't do that and you know it. I'm responsible for this operation. I don't put myself into things I can't survive, and neither will I do that with my women." She leaned back to look into his eyes, then smiled. "Actually, though I never would have thought it could happen, they are really quite a crack unit. They are good women, and they are loyal to me. I have to live up to that loyalty."

Erik caressed her hair then brushed her face with his lips. "And don't you forget that we have a life to spend together someday."

"Someday," she echoed, reaching once more for his lips with her own.

Whitney looked out across the harbor, through the slit in the abandoned bell tower, at the blue water, the colorful fishing boats, and the Italian battleship which lay at anchor midharbor, making no pretense about its presence. She blotted her wet brow once more, then stuck her lower lip out and exhaled, sending more warm, moist air up across her face. Summer held Dubrovnik like a possessive lover despite the mountain breezes which carried the gentle aroma of wild rosemary and lavender to scent the city like a gentlewoman's salon.

The battleship wasn't the first enemy ship to come in, but it was the largest so far, and the sailors seemed to fill the streets of Dubrovnik. They were polite to the sisters, tipping their caps or muttering a greeting. They seemed so young and eager—boys playing war.

197

Whitney shook her head to dispel the gloom which threatened to settle over her again. Erik's visits were so infrequent and made so much more difficult by his leaving. When he'd been away for an extended time, she could think of him with longing, but right after they had been together, memories only brought pain, loneliness, and depression, all of which made her vulnerable.

Suddenly the radio chattered to life and Whitney grabbed for a pencil and notepad, scratching down the coded message.

The radio stopped as abruptly as it had begun, just as Primrose appeared at the door.

"Time for a lovely cup of tea, my dear," she said, setting the tray she carried onto one of the decrepit stools, then pouring with natural elegance. "Was that another message?"

Whitney nodded, not distracted from her careful printing, hurrying to finish before the next transmission. "Things are heating up," she muttered. "There. I sometimes wish we could decode these so we didn't waste our time with orders for bratwurst."

Primrose sipped at her tea. "Or bullets." She sighed, then brightened. "Incidentally, Regina and Abbé D'Astier have just returned from installing another of Erik's jamming devices. They're busy congratulating themselves. Those devices are quite clever, you know. I should be very surprised if the Italians don't figure out they're being jammed for quite some time. Not only do the devices block transmissions, but the signal sends out a false marine beacon which just happens to be on the frequency used by the Italian Navy. Perhaps we'll net a few big fish as well as silencing USTASHI."

Whitney smiled. "Something has to go right."

"Oh," Lady Primrose said, nodding sagely, "you have the blues."

"Not precisely the blues, but . . . ." She was interrupted by an explosion of code from the radio which she quickly began to record. Suddenly, the first message was interrupted by a second, different, hand and Whitney's face lit. "Patrice," she said, writing furiously.

198

Primrose transcribed what there had been of the interrupted message as Whitney worked on the one from Patrice.

"This partial one is ready for the camera. What does Patrice have for us?"

"Bad news," Whitney replied simply, unable to expand before the radio again burst to life and she bent over the message.

The tea had become cold and cloudy in the cups and the light was disappearing from the harbor before they were relieved by Sister Regina. Whitney carefully photographed her transcriptions as Prim tidied up, burning all the papers they'd used, then mixing the ashes with tea and returning the mixture to the teapot, which she would empty in the kitchen.

Whitney stretched, twisting her tightened back muscles. "They've been transmitting like crazy all day. Things must be heating up in Russia."

"If the weather's the same there as it is here," Regina said, tying a cloth around her dripping forehead, "I'm not surprised."

Whitney followed Lady Primrose down the narrow stairs to the deserted corridor, then put her hand on Primrose's shoulder before she could open the door which led to the kitchen. "I know it's not my business, but I was born a busybody, and I've been waiting for you to tell me about you and Tricycle. And now I have to ask, because those kisses . . ."

Primrose chuckled. "One could be forgiven for such curiosity," she said briskly. "Though I do apologize for our rather public display. That's Dusko's character flaw, I'm afraid. He simply can't control those romantic, gypsy genes of his. Generally we try to be so much more subtle, but this time we had no opportunity to sneak off"—she glanced sideways at Whitney with a conspiratorial smile—"as did some others. Dusko's my husband."

Leaving Whitney open-mouthed, she disappeared through the door and down the stairs.

The chapel of the Mother Superior had been offered by Mother Luke as perhaps the only secure meeting place for the Butterflies. They had gathered, as always, after evensong for their daily conference, passing with quiet respect through Mother Luke's office to the small, windowless room, sweet with centuries of incense, candles, and wood oil.

". . . another broadcast station. Our only concern is that by blocking the three in this area we are likely to arouse suspicion. Maybe it would be better if we used the last two jamming devices up the coast a bit." Sister Regina paused, glancing at the Abbé, who nodded his agreement, his bald head gleaming with perspiration in the candlelight.

Nothing else about him seemed monklike to Whitney. He was tall and rangy and looked a bit like Abraham Lincoln. His monk's robes of rough wool padded his thin frame but did not disguise the hollows of his face and the thin arms and wrists which protruded from his sleeves. He was a man of few words and murderous skills, which he'd used against the Nazis invading his French homeland until the price on his head nearly matched that on de Gaulle's. Donohue had offered him assistance in return for his expertise.

Whitney nodded. "Your plan makes sense to me. Do you have a rough idea of alternate locations?"

Sister Regina smiled. "More than a rough idea. Abbé knows four precise spots."

"How far and how dangerous?" Whitney asked, shifting her gaze to the Abbé. "And how many reinforcements do you need to go with you?"

"We have not the need for reinforcements, Sister Camille," the Abbé replied in his rumbling, rich French accent. "The good Sister Regina is an excellent companion to both my work and travels. A woman of great resources," he added, bowing with Gallic courtesy at Sister Regina.

"But how far and how dangerous?"

"It is my belief we can manage this operation in four days," he answered, and Whitney surrendered to his evasiveness in light of his expertise.

"Sister Regina?"

"I agree."

"Good. Then I shall leave the matter in your hands. I want to remind you that we need to be extra cautious. Even here in the convent. There is a traitor among us."

"One of us?" Bernadette burst out.

"No, someone in the convent. Magda and Judith, I'll appreciate your help, and we'll talk about that later. One last thing: Bernadette, do you have a report on your mission?"

"I fear I was such a convincing whore that I nearly didn't return," she replied with a nervous laugh. "Anyway, my German control seemed convinced I was Sister Leona and asked many questions about the number and locations of whores in the city. I'm not certain he wasn't simply looking for a guidebook to brothels rather than information on his men, but I told him I'd not heard of anyone emptying their minds while satisfying their bodies. We will meet again in a week."

"Sister Madelaine, would you have tea with us?" Mother Luke said as her Croatian secretary moved to leave the room.

Madelaine turned with delighted surprise. "Thank you. It would be nice. Is there anything you wished me to do for you while we sit?"

"No," Mother Luke said, her voice kind and gentle. "We take too little time together in these days of chaos. Of course, you know Sister Camille, Sister Judith, and Sister Magda."

"Only slightly, I fear," Sister Madelaine said, settling primly into a chair as Sister Magda poured a cup of tea and passed it along. "I think it is wonderful that the American members of our order choose to join us here during such a difficult time."

"We just wished to be of service to God and man," Sister Judith said. "Teacake? I baked them myself."

"How nice. Are they American? Is this what you do in America?"

"I should think you'd know a great deal about everything we do," Sister Magda said. "You seem to be very much aware of where any of us is at any time. And of what's in our rooms."

Sister Madelaine looked puzzled. "What do you mean? Mother, am I under suspicion for something?"

"Not under suspicion, Sister Madelaine," Mother Luke replied in a soothing tone. "Will you excuse me for a moment?"

She rose, leaving the room quickly, closing the door firmly behind her.

"Have another cup of tea and a teacake, Sister Madelaine," Judith said, extending the plate to the woman, who quickly popped one into her mouth.

"Real tea is so rare these days," she said, looking uncomfortably from one to another of the American women.

"As Mother Luke said, Sister Madelaine, you are not under suspicion," Whitney said, not smiling. "Judgment has already been passed. Sister Magda has made a thorough search of your possessions and it is hard for us to believe a nun would find herself needing a code book, a contact with a German name, and letters from a certain Nazi physician thanking her for her help in locating one of his victims."

A puzzled look crossed Sister Madelaine's face and she rubbed her eyes. "I think I should leave now. I think I am ill."

Sister Judith put her hands on the woman's shoulders, pressing her into the chair. "I shouldn't be surprised. Sister Bernadette said rhododendron leaves would make a pretty powerful poison that you would not be able to taste in tea. Not very fast-acting, however. Before you die, we'd like to know who else you've been writing to."

"Die? Die? Are you going to kill me over a few reichsmarks?"

"No, we're going to kill you for being a traitor." Sister Magda held up a small glass vial. "Unless, of course, you tell us who else you've been writing to. Then we might give you this antidote to the poison."

Sister Madelaine lurched desperately toward the vial, and Sister Magda moved beyond her reach as Judith pulled her back into the chair.

"How did you know the doctor was looking for me?" Whitney asked, taking the vial from Magda and holding it up.

"I heard they were looking for an American woman with one leg. A blond woman. Skinny, like you. My sister is a nurse and she worked for the doctor. She told me. Please, it's the truth. I didn't tell anyone else but him. Really, I did not. Please, give me the medicine. My stomach." She clutched at her midsection.

"Who else did you write to?" Whitney continued.

"No one. Truly. I did it to help my sister."

"Then why do you have a current code book?" Magda asked.

"Because the doctor sent it to me. He told me to put my letters in code so no one in Berlin would know what he was doing. He was trying to find you to clear his name. He wanted to go back to do research. He wasn't going to kill you. He promised me. Please, the medicine. You're not going to let me die, are you?"

"Unfortunately," Sister Judith replied, "we have no choice. You see, drinking rhododendron-leaf tea is a very dangerous practice."

Sister Madelaine doubled over.

Magda stepped around the chair, inserting a gag into the woman's mouth just as she began to scream. "Don't worry, we'll give you as nice a funeral as your friend the doctor would have given Sister Camille."

12

"COLONEL, WHEN DO I get to be the bride?" Patrice sipped at the ersatz scotch and tried hard to convince herself she liked it, but failing miserably.

"I wasn't aware you were engaged, Miss Rigby," he said with mock innocence.

Patrice glared at him over the rim of her glass but controlled her urge to do something worthy of Hollywood. "All right, so being subtle isn't going to work. I'm getting very frustrated in both my careers at the moment. On the *Sunpapers* side of things, over which I am aware you have no control and in which I am certain you have little interest, I find myself writing only about ten percent of the time. The other ninety percent of my day is consumed with paper-shuffling and death-threat mediation among my staff." She paused for a breath.

"I'm sorry to hear that," Donohue said with frustrating understanding.

"Thank you, but it's not really your problem. What is something over which you *do* have some control, is that in my other role, I am collecting some astonishing information which it seems impossible for me to use to pursue my real career. Which I surmise will more than outlast my tempo-

204

rary position with your organization, unless this war goes on forever. If you follow my reasoning."

Donohue finished his drink and signaled the waiter with his glass. "Barely. Patrice, when we first struck our bargain you knew this would be the situation, so it shouldn't be such a surprise." Before she could object, he continued, "I can, however, give you some different perspectives on things which have already happened which you might be able to use."

Patrice grinned. "I thank you. *Sunpapers* thanks you. The readers at home thank you."

Donohue sighed. "Obviously you haven't been home for a while. No one there wants to know what's happening right now in Europe—or in any other part of the world, I regret to say. The tides of isolationism run stronger every day. Oh, of course people are upset and feel badly for Europe, but the prevailing sentiment is: just keep it over there and we'll be fine."

"Do you mean to say people can read about the Blitz and the Nazi invasions of practically every country in Europe and not understand just how small the Atlantic is? Is everyone just sitting there pretending nothing is going on?"

"It's not quite as simple as that. Certainly there are people who recognize just how perilous America's situation is. Quite frankly, under the guise of helping supply England, many factories have begun to retool to produce military supplies, but Roosevelt is still meeting with the Japanese as though he can hope to influence them to stay out of it. Meanwhile—and this is not for publication—the Japanese ambassador to Germany enjoys Hitler's ear and opulent hospitality."

"I'm getting discouraged before I begin."

"Don't. If you keep hollering down the rain barrel, eventually you'll get an echo." Donohue raised his glass.

"Somehow the image of you 'hollering' down anything is a difficult one to conjure up."

Donohue shrugged. "Who can ever predict what I'll do?"

"Who, indeed. Incidentally, I've had another letter from Laurel." Patrice rummaged in the chaos of her bag, finally

205

extricating a crumpled envelope. She extended the folded papers to him.

Donohue quickly tucked the letter into his pocket, glancing around the room. "Why didn't you destroy this immediately? And why hand it to me in a public place?" Seeing the crushed look on her face, he quickly added, "Patrice, I've had to remind Whitney a thousand times, and now, it seems, I must remind you. This is very serious business we're engaged in and anything you carry makes you vulnerable." He leaned toward her. "Please be paranoid about everyone and everything. I don't want either of you to get hurt." His eyes scanned the room again.

Patrice felt as she had in sixth grade when she'd peeked at an answer on Whitney's paper during a test and, to her everlasting horror, had been caught. "You're absolutely right, and I'm sorry." She laughed nervously. "I guess I just feel immune because I'm in London."

"Unfortunately none of us is. Now, let's put this behind us and go on. What did you hear from Laurel?"

Patrice covered her lingering embarrassment by gesturing for another drink. "At least she's providing things of value. Apparently, as always, money is a strong motivator for Laurel. The biggest bit of news is that Heydrich may be made 'protector of Czechoslovia' for the Nazis. Laurel seems to have recovered from her fears of him, for she says she hopes it won't happen because then he'd be moving to Prague." Patrice snorted her derision. "She also says there have been more musical scores than usual from the Concertmaster. She's going to try to pilfer one and send it along."

Donohue's brow furrowed. "Of course it would be most welcome, but I think that might be taking a risk."

Patrice's jaw set firmly. "In my view, it's about time she took some risks, just as Whitney does every single day. It's about time Laurel Smythe Pugh started to have to pay her way in this world."

Laurel stopped in front of the mirror in the reception area of the radio station, futilely attempting to control her wild curls. She finally surrendered to the heat and humidity, and applied fresh lipstick.

She was still furious about having to take the subway in the first place, furious with Reinhard for "borrowing" her driver, furious with the radio station for refusing to send a car, and furious with the Germans for sending all the taxi drivers to the Russian front. The subway! Laurel sniffed. She'd make very certain she never had to suffer that again.

She swept into the studio, extracting her script from her pocketbook, nodding in response to the greetings from the staff.

"Laurel, *mein Liebschen,* do not look so angry. I cannot stop the heat." Meyer Kolnitz, the director and producer of the series of broadcasts, held her chair, moved her microphone into position, and patted her on the shoulder, all in one motion.

Laurel was not in the mood for his antics. "Move the fan. How am I supposed to sound convincing about the wonders of the Third Reich if I am roasting?" she snapped, her mood deteriorating.

Behind her back, Meyer motioned to one of the crewmen, who went to move the large floor fan, then rolled his eyes in exasperation. Catching the eye of one of the technicians in the booth, he made a grotesque face before turning back to Laurel.

"Is that better? We don't want our brightest star to be the least bit uncomfortable."

Laurel turned, locking him in place with the ferocity of her gaze. "If you don't want your 'brightest star' to be the 'least bit uncomfortable,' you should have sent a car for me. I had to take the *subway* like a *hausfrau."* She shook a stubby finger in his face. "I think everyone here is forgetting who I am!" Her finger moved menacingly closer to his nose. "All I have to do is mention what a queer you are, Meyer, and the Führer will have you on a train to the Russian front faster than you can whistle!"

From what Meyer had heard, the train for homosexuals didn't go to the Russian front. "Sorry, darling. Really," he said quickly. "You should have called me. I would have driven over to pick you up. In the future I shall make certain you have a car and driver for each broadcast. Now, does the breeze feel good? Would you like some tea, perhaps?"

207

Laurel was beginning to feel better. "No, wine. *French* wine. And one of the *American* cigarettes you have hidden in your desk."

Meyer dashed out of the studio, reappearing with a carton of Camels. "Here, darling. I've quit anyway. Take them as a gift."

Laurel took the carton, opened it, removed one pack, counted to see how many packs were left, then put them in her purse. "Where's the wine?"

"Coming, darling, coming. Is your script ready? We only have a few moments. Is everything fine now?" Meyer was sweating profusely.

Laurel opened the packet slowly, put a cigarette to her lips, and leaned to the flame from his gold Dunhill, exhaling the smoke in a steady plume. "Nice lighter, Meyer. Did one of your little playmates give you that?"

"No, I bought it in London," he said, too quickly, then realized his error and extended it to her. "Why don't you keep it, Laurel, darling. I have quit smoking anyway."

She took it, dropping it into her purse. "Thank you."

Meyer turned as someone entered the studio. "Here's the wine, Laurel. Are you ready?"

She glanced up at the clock. "I will be when it's time."

Hello, again, my dear friends. I hear it's very hot in London these days. Unusual for London to be hot, even in the summer. But perhaps the heat you're feeling is from your stubborn leaders, who would rather see you die than see you unified with the future.

Here in Berlin cool breezes of hope for a wonderful tomorrow are blowing. We're sitting in our lovely outdoor cafés, enjoying a glass of good German wine and drinking to the day when you are partners with us.

Our two nations have a long history together. Your corrupt royal family was once a part of the proud German people. Come home, dear friends. Come join us for a glass of Moselle and drink to the passing of the old ways.

Don't you wish you could be with us right now? You can. It's ever so simple. Don't join the RAF, you'll only

208

be shot down. Don't support their war machine. Don't work in the war plants which are simply wasting your hard-earned money on useless weapons. Say no when they ask you to give up meat and eggs and butter and milk which your children need to grow healthy and strong under the new order.

It's really only a matter of time. The proud German army has liberated most of Europe, and it is flourishing, while England is quickly going bankrupt, wasting money and men, sending your sons and husbands and fathers to die because your corrupt government wants to hold onto the years of graft and corruption that are its history.

Say no, dear friends, to their abuse, and say yes to a bright future. Let us reunite, not in the shadows of evil and corruption, but in the sunlight of the Reich.

Good-bye for now, dear friends. Try to stay cool in the heat by thinking about the breezes in Berlin.

Laurel put the cork in the wine bottle and tucked it into her bag along with the script, then waited for Meyer to appear to pull out her chair.

"Wonderful, Laurel. Perfect. I cannot imagine how they could listen to such an impassioned plea and not follow your suggestions. You really are the strongest persuader we have, and I know the Führer must be proud of the contribution you make to the Reich," Meyer gushed as he helped her up and escorted her to the door of the studio. "I'll get that car and driver for you. Just stay right here."

She shook her head. "Never mind. I want to go shopping along the Kufurstendaam and then perhaps have a small lunch. I do want a car, however, before the next broadcast, just in case my own driver is . . . is not available again."

"Of course, darling," Meyer smiled nervously. "Anything you want is just fine with me. I'll send the driver an hour before the broadcast." He smiled nervously again. "About what you said about the train . . ."

Laurel put her hand up to his cheek. "Don't give it another thought, Meyer. Unless, of course, I become displeased. But don't worry. I know you know how to keep me happy." She felt much better when she saw the terror in his eyes. She'd never have to take the subway again.

She left the studio, but her brisk walk along the street of fashionable shops and massive government buildings was anything but a window-shopping stroll. She stood impatiently in a busline, then once more crammed herself in with sweating Berliners, enduring the press and smell of the crowd for the anonymity it offered.

When Laurel stepped from the bus into the cooler, tree-lined street, she hesitated, watching until a black staff car pulled away from the front of the house where she was headed. She scurried down the block and up the steps, ringing the bell impatiently until Karl Foch opened the door.

With a glance up and down the street, she hurried into the cool darkness of his house.

"Karl, I hate coming here, because I have to take the bus. The bus is always so crowded. I hate that. Here, I brought some wine. And some stuff to keep Patrice from stealing my money." She opened her bag and pulled out the bottle along with an envelope. "I hope it didn't leak in my purse."

"Nice to see you, too, Laurel. You seem to be in good spirits. How was the broadcast? Did you win anyone's undying loyalty today?" He took the extended bottle from her. "Chardonnay. Nice choice. And 1936 was such a good year. Come on in. Sit down. Relax."

"Relax! Do you know what that man did to me today? He took my driver and car. I had to take the subway to the radio station. And this heat! I don't remember it being this hot last summer." She plunked down into one of the chintz chairs and accepted a glass of wine.

"You were at the North Sea last summer with Helmut," Karl said mildly. "I remember reading about it in the papers."

"Was that only last summer?" She set her glass down, her eyes focused on the past. "Only last summer?"

Patrice pulled the sheet of yellow typescript out of her little Underwood as a voice cried out from her open door. Patrice screeched first from fright, then in joy, as she turned

210

"Raven! Oh, Mike, I'm so glad to see you." She jumped up and ran around the desk to throw her arms around him. "Look at you. Where did you get all this hardware?" She tapped at the ribbons on his chest.

"Just bad judgment on the part of the military. They think I'm actually flying those missions."

"I know better than to ask which missions, and, as long as you're all right, I don't really care. But do tell me what you're doing—or as much as you can. How about sharing the last inch of real scotch I have left?"

He set his hat on the corner of her desk and lounged in one of the chairs, grinning. "Still as articulate as ever, I see."

Patrice found the treasured bottle of Chivas Regal and two glasses. She poured the remaining liquor carefully, letting the last drops drain into the glass, then put it firmly into Raven's hand.

"So, how do you like being Bureau Chief?"

"All I can say is that it's no wonder you joined the RAF. You were just going from one war to another. How did you keep all the paperwork from taking over your life?"

Raven laughed, raising his glass. "To the paperwork."

"There is no way I will toast paperwork," Patrice said firmly, "especially not with the last real scotch I have. How about 'to old friends?' "

Raven raised his glass and they both drank solemnly.

"I'm really flying, Patrice. And I love it. I just wish we were winning."

Patrice nodded. "I know. It all seems so hopeless sometimes."

He shook his head. "I'm afraid, though, it will get worse before it gets better." He hesitated, looking at her. "Do you have a way out, just in case?"

"A way out? Of England?" Patrice was surprised at his question.

"Yes. A plan. Just in case. I don't mean to make you think it's right around the corner, but we don't seem to be able to do anything to even slow down the damn Jerries, and I wouldn't want you to get caught in the middle of it."

"You really believe it could happen at all?"

"Rigby, this is war. Don't take unreasonable chances. Oh, and about the paperwork?"

She leaned forward. "Yes?"

"Throw it away. If it's important, they'll come get it themselves."

13

"FORGIVE ME, FATHER, for I have sinned," Whitney muttered to the screen in the confessional, then waited for the heavily accented reassurances of Frather Antujelshi, confessor for the nuns and spiritual advisor to Tito and his resistance fighters.

"You probably have," said the crisp, British accent on the other side, "but haven't we all?"

Whitney stared at the unrevealing screen, astonished. "I beg your pardon," she finally said.

The deep laugh seemed to fill the tiny confessional. "I said, you probably have sinned, but so have all of us. It's a part of the business. Sister Camille, Father Tricycle absolves you of all your sins and encourages you to consider sinning again."

"Tricycle! We hadn't been told to expect you."

"My apologies. Seems the operation in London has been rather busy, but you'll hear about that later. For now, Father William wants you back in his flock. You and Sister Magda and Sister Ruth."

"When?" Whitney whispered through the screen.

"Tonight, after evensong. I've set it up for you three to provide nursing services to some poor souls who've caught typhus and are convalescing at Villa Drobic. Here are passes for you as well as one for Mother Luke, since someone really must nurse them. Wear your habits; we'll provide other clothing later."

Whitney took the documents he pushed through the small gap under the screen and tucked them inside her habit. "Just the three of us?"

"Yes. And put your house in order here. I have no idea how long you'll be gone, but I suspect it will be a while. Mother Luke will administer your team and their listening to the news from the Russian front. For the time being, that and Sister Bernadette's ruse of being Sister Leona will be the only activities here."

"But what are we going to do?"

Tricycle chuckled. "If I told you that, your surprise would be spoiled. Now go say your prayers of contrition, and I'll see you later."

Whitney could smell fresh air as they turned a corner. The moss on the steps gave way to a coating of salt and water, and the moldy fish smell was replaced by the scents of seaweed and salt water as they came slowly down the last few steps.

When they'd reached the bottom, Antonia led them to an iron gate which she unlocked. "I wish for you good luck," she said, shaking hands with each of them as they passed through the portal and out onto a rocky cove. Whitney heard the iron gate creaking shut above the hiss of the surf in the distance. She stood for a moment, letting her eyes adjust to the starlight. From the featureless gloom, she could finally see that they were in a small, protected cove. The white foam of the surf outlined the narrow passage through the protecting cliffs, and beyond, she could see the clear sky and the darker bulk of Italy on the distant horizon.

They waited on a narrow, rocky beach, surrounded on two sides by protective cliffs. Behind them stood the enormous bulk of the villa, its black shape rising to blend with the dark of the sky, no lights showing to relieve its overpowering presence.

"From one prison to another," Magda said, digging at the pebbles of the beach with her boot.

Whitney was looking out to the horizon, wondering if something had happened to their contact, when suddenly she felt a hand on her shoulder. She gasped, then clenched her teeth. She spun around to face the chest of someone dressed in a costume similar to hers. She looked up, then grinned. "Major Ball, a most unorthodox entrance."

"Sister Camille, Sister Ruth, Sister Magda. If you'll join me," he said, leading them away from the villa. As they progressed along the beach, Whitney could see a boat anchored, tucked in against the cliff. It had a round, wide shape and a small deck house, but carried a large crane on the stern.

Cesar Ball hesitated next to a skiff. "One at a time, I'm afraid. Sister Camille?" He helped Whitney into the skiff, then climbed in and took the oars. "I'll be back in a moment," he called to Primrose and Magda.

"I can hardly wait," Magda replied, and Whitney could see the quick flare of a match as she lit a cigarette.

Cesar set to the oars and they quickly approached the boat. Whitney could smell it, though, before she could see it clearly.

"Whew!" she said, her eyes watering.

"Charming, isn't it? I think this boat has caught fish every day for the past hundred years."

"Yes, but when do they plan to unload them?"

Major Ball laughed. "You'll get used to it."

"How far are we going?"

"Italy. Rome, actually, but only the first portion by sea." The skiff bumped into the side of the fishing boat and Whitney felt a hand reach down to take her duffel, then grab her wrists and lift her out. As her feet touched the deck, she grinned into the face of the Abbé.

"Bless you, my daughter," he said. "Welcome to the *Pescado*."

Whitney squeaked as she tried to avoid inhaling the strong smell of fish. Finally, need overcame common sense and she took a great gulp of the foul air, then gagged.

215

"You will find it useful to breathe lightly," the Abbé said with a small laugh. "Until we are at sea."

"When I'll be too busy getting sick," Whitney replied.

To Whitney's surprise, the crossing to Italy was remarkably smooth. She discovered that if she stood in the bow of the boat the smell wasn't as strong. Although the air was chilly, she pulled off her knitted cap, enjoying the freedom of the wind tugging at her hair. She'd looped one arm around the mast as she watched the coast of Italy approaching.

Ball stepped up beside her and she jumped, startled. "You must stop doing that!"

He smiled slightly. "Just testing your reflexes, Countess."

"What's all this about?"

"I don't really know. All I know is that I'm to deliver you and the ladies to Rome, where you'll connect with another operative."

"And you?" Whitney knew better than to probe about their mission. She felt certain Ball must know more than he was revealing.

"I've got a date with a camel jockey. Listen, do you trust Magda?"

Whitney nodded, shrugging. "Yes, oddly enough, I do. I don't particularly like her, but I do trust her. She's proven her loyalty several times. Why?"

Ball stared at the coastline of Italy, now looming to cover the horizon. Whitney wondered why he'd asked about Magda but decided against pushing him. *Spies,* she thought disgustedly, *are so enigmatic*.

"Major, do you know how my mother is doing?" she asked suddenly.

"She's fine. Donohue's men keep an eye on her, though I'm sure she doesn't know." He started to say something else, then hesitated.

"What? What were you going to add?" Whitney was losing patience with his spy game.

"Just an impression. I was in Washington last month with Donohue and he saw her at a party. Donohue said she seemed . . . reserved. Quiet. Distant."

216

Whitney nodded. "She's always been that way. I'm glad to know she was at a party."

"Perhaps I'm not saying it clearly. He doesn't want you to worry, but he thinks you should be prepared. She doesn't seem quite connected to the world anymore. He was sitting across from her at dinner and her conversation seemed to wander. Perhaps I shouldn't have told you. I don't want you to be worried."

Whitney sighed. "It's fine. I was never allowed to worry about my mother. Now there is nothing I can do, at least until this is over, so my worry would be futile. I'm glad Donohue is watching out for her."

Major Ball wandered back to the deck house, leaving Whitney alone. For the first time in her life, Whitney could see the faults which had made her mother seem so distant and uncaring as human flaws, and those flaws seemed very dear. She looked up at the sliver of moon in the sky and whispered, "Take good care of her."

The coastline of Italy filled the horizon, craggy and dark. Cesar stood in the front of the boat, his fingers looped over the lens of a flashlight so only a thin beam flashed a signal. Behind him, huddled together in an effort to chase away the chill that had descended with the darkest hours of the night, the women waited, feeling very vulnerable. Whitney's eyes scanned along the beach.

"There, to the right," she said, her voice low. She saw Ball's head turn as he raised the flashlight and returned the code. The engines of the small boat slowed to turn toward the beach and Ball gestured for the women to come forward.

"We'll need to be quick about this," he said, swinging a pack up on his shoulder. "I'll hand you down."

The prow of the boat crunched into the beach and immediately Ball grabbed Whitney's hand, pulling her up beside him, then lifting her over the rail to waiting hands below. The man who caught her turned, setting her on a rocky beach which, except for the castle, was very like the one they had left in Yugoslavia. Magda came next, nimbly vaulting the rail, her pack on her back, landing lightly without assistance. The Abbé followed her in the same fashion as Ball lifted Prim over to the man who had caught Whitney.

"Hello, darling," Whitney heard him say softly. Prim immediately gave a muffled whoop of delight which melted into a kiss.

Magda was standing next to Whitney, staring.

Whitney took her arm. "Local custom. Let's go." She turned Magda away from Prim's reunion with Tricycle, following the Abbé as he hurried into the shadow of the cliffs. Behind them the engines of the boat rumbled a bit louder as it backed away from the beach.

Tricycle, Ball, and Lady Primrose came to join them under the protection of the cliff.

"The place is crawling with Eyeties," Tricycle said, his voice blending with the noise of the waves on the beach. "And they changed the curfew passes today, too late for me to have some made for us. Which means we're going to have to either wait here and risk being discovered in the morning or take our chances cutting cross lots."

"How far, cutting cross lots?" Whitney asked.

"Three miles, plus or minus," Tricycle replied.

"Which course do you favor?" Ball asked him.

Tricycle, his arm across Lady Primrose's shoulder, shrugged. "It's six of one, half dozen the other, actually. If they find us here, they'll shoot us as probable spies. If they find us along the road, they'll shoot us as curfew violators."

"Lovely choices," Prim said.

"I hate the thought of being a sitting duck," Whitney offered. "I think we should move."

"I hate both choices," Magda said, taking a cigarette out of her pocket.

Ball took the cigarette from her hand. "Not here, please. That light would be a magnet for the beach patrols. I'd rather keep our options open. And I think I agree with Camille."

"I am also in agreement," the Abbé added.

"That's it, then. Off we go. Step smartly and watch your footing." Taking Prim's hand, Tricycle led them along the foot of the cliff, then turned onto a narrow path. "Mind your footing," he said again.

Whitney brought up the rear with Ball, following Magda,

218

who clung to the rocks with easy grace. Watching her, Whitney tried to place her feet on the narrow track with the same confidence, but each time she changed her weight, she felt the stones shifting under her until she recalled Juanito, the Basque guide who had helped her through one portion of the Pyrenees. "Keep your legs loose," he'd said, flexing his knees to demonstrate. "Think of yourself as part of the rock; move with it, don't fight it."

She hesitated, flexing her good leg, then pushing her hip forward, then the knee where her false leg joined her real one. Immediately she felt more in control.

"Are you all right?" Ball whispered in her ear.

"Thanks. I'm fine," she replied. She set her eyes on the tiny portion of path she could see in the dark and kept her legs "soft" as she followed the others over the crest of the cliff and into a cleft of boulders. Magda stretched while the others caught their breath.

"Now," Tricycle said, gathering them together, "we can stay along the edge of this road for a time. We'll come to an olive grove, and we can travel through that to the cemetery behind the church, where we have a safe haven. Be prepared at all times. The Eyeties are taking this business quite seriously. They travel in pairs and not always in vehicles. Shall we?" He eased out of the crag, looking along the small road in both directions, then motioned the others to follow.

The road, a rocky track, began to descend quickly as the small group moved away from the sea, the air filled with the mingling smells of earth and ocean. Eventually the scent of the ground began to dominate as the road wound downward toward the olive grove. Whitney listened to the sounds the team made as they walked, then beyond those for anything unusual.

"Halt!" A barked command came from behind them. Instantly Whitney whirled into the blinding glare of a flashlight.

"Hands up! Higher!" This time the order came from the other direction, punctuated by another flashlight beam.

"Oh, shit," Magda said.

"Enough!" the first voice said, moving forward, herding

219

them into a tight knot with his comrade forcing Tricycle and Primrose and the Abbé back as he advanced.

"*Guten tag,*" Tricycle said, a note of authority in his voice as he produced his Nazi identification. "These spies are my prisoners." Tricycle stepped toward the soldier in front of Whitney, but before he could take a second step the soldier behind him hit him smartly with the flashlight. Tricycle's eyes rolled upward as he fell into the dirt.

Suddenly, the two women moving almost as one, Primrose spun, raising her leg to smash Tricycle's attacker just as Magda sprang into the air, kicking the light out of the hands of the man who faced them. Without breaking her movement at all, Magda flipped the knife from her sleeve and lunged at the man, landing squarely on his chest, driving the blade home. Whitney heard a violent squeal from the soldier.

She turned abruptly to assist Primrose, but the Abbé had rushed to help her, quickly removing the man's gun from his hand, then pushing him up against the rocks.

"Mine's dead," Magda said matter-of-factly.

Whitney heard a sharp snap.

"As is this one," the Abbé said. As he lowered the man's lolling head to the ground, the Abbé mumbled a prayer in Latin, then made the sign of the cross over his victim.

"Let's get out of here," Magda insisted.

"No, wait," the Abbé said, going to the other man, mumbling the same prayer in Latin and again making the sign of the cross. When he had finished, he added, "First we must lay them to rest. If others find their bodies, we will be in more danger."

Primrose was kneeling in the dirt, patting Tricycle's face. "Come 'round, now, darling. That's better. Yes, darling. No, don't sit up quite yet. Let me have a look at those eyes." She took the flashlight from the ground, shining it in his eyes. "Good, no permanent damage, it would seem." She ran her hand over his head. "But you're growing an awful goose-egg. I hope we'll find some ice at this church."

Tricycle reached up to caress her cheek, then sat up, blinking. "Dizzy," he muttered, holding his hands on either side of his head. "Ball?"

"Taking care of our captors with the Abbé. Not too

220

quickly, darling," Primrose said, supporting him as he tried to rise. Whitney moved to his other side and they raised him to his feet.

"I told you those Eyeties were sneaky," Tricycle said, gingerly patting the back of his skull.

"I didn't hear a thing," Whitney added indignantly.

Ball and the Abbé returned. "We've got to hurry now," Ball said. "Are you all right?"

"I can manage. Off we go. And keep your guard up." Tricycle put his arm across Primrose's shoulder, and they continued on.

As they reached the olive grove, the sky began to gray with the first light of dawn. By the time they had crossed the vast planting of ancient, craggy trees, the sun had risen.

"This is good timing," Tricycle said as they reached the cemetery. "Curfew ends as soon as the sun comes up. This might be the best spot for all of us to change into our religious garb. The Eyeties are suspicious of ladies in trousers."

Whitney looked around for something which might offer a bit of privacy. With no obvious shelters, she simply retreated into the grove and opened her pack to take out her wrinkled habit and drooping wimple.

Dressed, she returned to the others just as Magda was finishing a cigarette.

"Nuns don't smoke, Sister Magda," she said reprovingly.

"Nuns don't kill people, either," Magda replied with a shrug. "Life is full of contradictions."

Ball and the Abbé, both dressed in monk's robes and sitting on one of the old headstones, were having an intense conversation. Whitney looked around for Prim and Tricycle, then turned back to Magda.

Before she could ask, however, Magda grinned. "What the hell. Getting hit over the head always makes me feel sexy, too."

Whitney opened her mouth to respond, then quickly closed it as Primrose and Tricycle appeared from a small crypt. Primrose was blushing furiously, but Whitney decided to ignore it.

Tricycle, dressed as a priest, led them through the grave-

221

yard to the back of a small stone church with a large bell tower. They walked in a file, Tricycle first, then the two monks, and finally the three nuns, heads bowed in contemplation to anyone who might have noted their unusual approach to the building.

Father Tricycle led them around the structure to the front where two huge wooden doors were flanked by two smaller doors bearing a crucifix. As they climbed the steps, one of the smaller doors opened to reveal an enormous man whose priestly robes reached only to the middle of his arms and the middle of his calves. He filled the entire doorway not only with his height but also with his generous girth.

"Padre Antonucci," Tricycle said as the man stepped out to embrace him in a warm welcome.

"I see God has brought you safely to my humble house," the Padre said, embracing all of them with his warm smile. "It gives me great joy to welcome you." He stepped aside and they moved into the dark, familiar smells of the church. The sun cast colors around the deep walnut walls and Whitney felt safe at last. *Strange,* she thought of her reaction, wondering for an instant if she were rushing headlong into a religious life, then laughing at the thought.

"Come, we will have a small breakfast," Padre Antonucci boomed, leading them along the side aisle and into his private apartments in the back of the church. "I have made a repast from the gifts of my parish: some lamb chops, a bit of fresh bread, some pasta. Sit, sisters, my brothers. Make yourselves at home in the house of the Lord."

Feasting first on the smells, they waited, trying not to seem too eager for the food, but they were unable to hide their anticipation as the Padre carried heaping plates to the tables.

Padre Antonucci folded his hands and bowed his head before offering a blessing over the food. Whitney thought she would faint from hunger and temptation before he finished, but finally he concluded with an amen which they all echoed.

"Now, eat."

Conversation was stilled as everyone ate with gusto, trying to savor the excellent flavors while still sating his hunger.

After he'd consumed most of his breakfast, Ball inclined his head toward Whitney and said in a low voice, "I'll be leaving almost immediately, as will Tricycle. The Abbé will conduct you to Rome tomorrow."

"And then?"

A small smile tugged at the corners of his mouth. "And then the adventure will continue. Fine breakfast, don't you think?"

14

R EINHARD, I STILL don't understand why you can't take me to Prague. It could be just like it is here. I could have my little apartment and you could have your clothes with Lina and the children." Laurel tickled his ear with the tip of one long fingernail.

Heydrich tossed his head impatiently, brushing her hand out of the way, then took a long drink from his schnapps. "I have told you, things are difficult in Prague and I will not be distracted from my work there. You are a distraction." He drank again from his glass and Laurel reached for the bottle to refill it.

"Have I distracted you here?" she whispered, letting her breasts brush against his hand as she leaned across him.

"No, but only because I do not allow you to. There, things are different. Prague is hardly Berlin. They have no sophistication, no nightlife. It is a city run by the priests, and the priests do not approve of mistresses, particularly flamboyant red-haired mistresses who do not know how to keep their mouths shut."

Laurel replaced the bottle on the table, then turned back to him, this time rubbing against his upper arm. She was determined not to let him intimidate her but also cautious not to let a rage build.

As though accepting his words, she changed the subject. "Have you listened to my broadcasts lately?"

He shrugged. "When do I have time for this? I am a busy man. Why do you ask, anyhow? Have you been saying anything out of the ordinary?"

She was relieved and disappointed at the same time. Though she did not use her broadcasts to relay information to Patrice and her friends, his not listening meant he wasn't aware of what else she was doing.

"Nothing special or unusual, darling. I just like to think I am speaking to you when I sit in front of the microphone. I try to send you my love over the air, you see." He glanced sidelong at her, disgust playing about his mouth.

"Laurel, I have told you many times that I do not love you. I love no one. Love makes a man weak and I must be strong for the glory of Germany and the Aryan race. Do not speak of love to me!" He drained his glass and she hurriedly reached for the bottle, but he shook his head.

"Enough now. I cannot fog my brain with schnapps. I am going to see the Führer tonight to receive the rest of my orders for Prague."

Laurel set the bottle on the table. Prague again! "What will you do in Prague?" she asked. Perhaps he'd give her a tidbit to pass along to Patrice.

He stretched his arms up over his head then laced his fingers behind his head. "I will carry on the work which has been begun. Even when we have liberated a nation from its corrupt government, our work is not finished. Not at all. Then we must root out the source of trouble and correct it. There is a highly active subversive network in Czechoslovakia which must be brought under control. That will be my first priority."

One for Patrice, she thought. "How will you do that?"

"How does one crush a resistance? I should think you would know this by now, for it is not unlike what we have had to do in Russia. We will find out who they are and we will eliminate them in a public way. I find this keeps other

225

people from volunteering to be replacements." He turned to look at her. "You must think I am very heartless."

Indeed! Laurel thought, but she smiled and caressed his cheek. "No, I understand that you are very loyal to the Reich and are only doing what must be done. But heartless? Never. I admire how much you give to the future. I know how large your heart is." She leaned to kiss him, nibbling at his lower lip playfully.

"Not today. No more schnapps and none of you, either. I have too little time before I see the Führer. I don't want him to think I had taken time away from my work to be with a woman."

"How would he know unless you tell him?" Laurel pouted.

"He would know. Tell me instead how you have been spending your time when I am not here." He moved slightly away from her on the couch.

"I read. I walk. I visit friends." She sighed. She could feel her power base eroding with his transfer to Prague. It was one thing to have him going back and forth to the Russian front, but with Lina and the children in Prague, and his having to use the Luftwaffe to make his trips to and from Berlin, she knew their visits would be limited. Not that she really minded. He was a terrible lover, either passive and disinterested or violent and sadistic, and she didn't enjoy either. Berlin, however, was bad enough with nothing left in the stores and all the soldiers taking over the nightclubs, but having Reinhard around meant Laurel could, at least, attend some of the glittering parties. With him gone, she'd have nothing to look forward to.

"Who are these friends?" he asked, bringing her back from her reverie.

"Just . . . friends. Just people I've known."

"Like Karl Foch?" he persisted, and Laurel felt a cold dread enclose her stomach.

"Sometimes. Karl is very amusing."

"Foch is half English and a parasite. He wastes his talent on pulp that keeps the people from thinking about victory; romance books to dull the minds of the women who must maintain Germany while their brave men are out advancing

226

the cause of the Reich." His lip curled into a sneer. "And he's an adventurer with women. How do I know you are not having an affair with him?"

"An affair with Karl?" Laurel laughed. "How could you even imagine such a thing? Karl is charming, but you are my lover. With a lover like you, why would I want another man?" *Except, of course, to be satisfied,* she added in her head, thinking about the stories she had heard from tittering women who had shared Karl's favors. "Besides, Karl works for the Führer."

Heydrich sat up abruptly. "How do you know this? What does he do?"

"He told me. It's no secret. The Führer makes notes in his log books and Karl's job is to combine those notes with other records to write a history of the Reich from its beginning through the eyes of the Führer. Every day a man comes from the Führer and brings the notes to Karl. Karl works all day on the history and then the notes are taken back to the Führer along with the history. If the Führer trusts Karl to be his historian, perhaps you should respect him more."

"He should never have told you about his work. If he talks about what he does, then he probably talks about what is in the notes." Heydrich rose and paced the floor. "The man is a parasite. I cannot imagine why the Führer trusts him."

"Perhaps the Führer feels he can make *some* decisions without consulting you first," Laurel sneered, pushing at a known tender spot, wanting to hurt him for his impending desertion and her resultant loss of status and power. As soon as the words were out, Laurel knew she'd finally stepped over the line. Heydrich wheeled around, grabbed her arm, and yanked her to her feet.

"Bitch," he spat. "You have tried my patience one too many times, nagging me about taking you to Prague, having an affair with Foch, and then denying it. Now you have gone too far. Perhaps you have not looked at yourself in the mirror lately, Laurel. You are fat as a pig. You think I do not want to make love to you because of my meeting with the Führer, but it is because you disgust me. You have

227

pushed me too far." He flung her onto the couch, then strode to the door and yanked it open.

"Lieutenant Schmidt," he called, and instantly his aide, a tall, cold Aryan in the sinister black and silver of the SS, appeared, snapping a salute.

"Heil Hitler."

Heydrich gestured in response. "Heil Hitler. Take her out of here."

"No," Laurel yelled, grabbing the arm of the couch. "Where? What are you doing to me?"

"Shut up. Lieutenant, take her to my second office. I'll relay orders later." He turned away in dismissal, his face a hard mask of disinterest.

"No," Laurel screamed at the Lieutenant, scooting away along the couch to evade his grasp. Suddenly she felt herself being lifted roughly from behind. Schmidt hoisted her to her feet and spun her against the wall. She felt cold steel encircle her wrists and heard the rasp of the handcuffs closing around her arms.

"No! No, no, no, no!" she kept screaming. The Lieutenant pulled up on the chain linking her wrists until her arms ached, then pushed her roughly out the door.

"Reinhard," she screamed as he propelled her down the hall, "you bastard!"

"Time for the bitch of Berlin," Patrice said, turning on the radio.

Paul Sanders Stewart was carrying a heaping bowl of mashed potatoes toward the table. As he set the dish down, he laughed. "Why do I feel you don't like your new little spy any better now than when she was a traitor?"

"Why are you willing to believe she's not still a traitor?" Patrice countered, fetching the meatloaf from the kitchen, then joining him at the table. "Laurel is loyal to herself and her interests alone. We have only the money to hold over her head, but if she found a better offer, she wouldn't hesitate to sell us just as she has sold out her lover, Heydrich."

The radio crackled, whined, and the now-familiar martial

music which always preceeded Laurel's broadcast filled the room.

Paul scooped some potatoes onto his plate. "I'm not defending her. I've never met the woman and I genuinely hate her." He extended the bowl to Patrice.

She laughed as she accepted it. "Oh you're just saying that." She took some meatloaf, then handed the plate to him. "I'll have you know this actually contains at least one ounce of real beef . . . along with about sixteen ounces of ground soybeans. Paul, my animosity toward Laurel started a very long time ago in a very different time and place. I have not trusted her for years, and I do not trust her now."

"Familiarity, in other words, breeds contempt."

"You sound like my grandmother." She tipped her head. "Well, here we go," she said as the march faded and then her expression changed as a familiar but implacable voice began speaking. "Who in the world? What is—? Well, where in hell is Laurel?" She rose quickly to increase the radio's volume, then listened intently, staring at the glowing dial. "I know who that is," she muttered, wracking her brain. "And where is Laurel?"

Paul shook his head. "What's this concern I hear?"

She turned. "Only professional, I assure you. She's probably blowing our Berlin operations wide open right now. She could be telling Heydrich and his associates about her association with me, and she could be turning in . . . Oh, no. I know whose voice that is." She turned back to the radio, shaking her head. "That's Karl Foch." She walked slowly back to the table. "Why Karl? And where is Laurel?"

Laurel paced the short length of the tiny room, crossing between the barred window at one end and the steel door with the small, grated window at the other, each time looking out the portal before wheeling to pace again to the other end.

Even after two days, her mind refused to make sense out of the circumstance or the location. How did this happen? And why?

She turned away from the window, beginning her walk to the door again, passing the filthy sink, the toilet bowl which

229

had no seat, and the narrow wooden cot with the thin pallet and itchy reprocessed wool blanket before she reached the steel barrier and peered out into the hallway. As always, all she could see was a solid gray wall. Laurel stood, listening. She could hear distant voices, footsteps, the clang of doors being opened and closed, but nothing specific, no one nearby, no one to help her.

She turned, striding back to the outside window again. It overlooked a wall, but gray stone filled most of her view. At the very top, if she leaned far enough into the window and pressed her face against the bars, she could see a small slice of sky. As it had been during the daylight hours for the preceeding two days, the sky was as gray as the stone.

Laurel turned away from the window, staring at the door. The Lieutenant had brought her here, still in handcuffs, and had turned her over to a harsh blond woman. Tears came to Laurel's eyes at the memory of the humiliating strip-search during which she had been forced to stand, naked and handcuffed, in front of three women, who had seemed far too curious for simple professional interest. Cold, terrified, and humiliated, she had been subjected to repeated searches, then finally dressed in this rough, shapeless dress. She was shoved into the cell. During the whole process nothing had been said to her, and since then, no one had appeared.

"Maybe they plan to starve me to death," she said, clutching her aching stomach. "Maybe they plan to torture me until I go mad." She stamped her foot. "Damn you, Reinhard."

Laurel had resumed her pacing when suddenly she heard a key turning in the lock. At first she wanted to run and hide, then she thought of trying to escape. Instead, she stood transfixed as her emotions raced from terror to delight and back.

The door swung open as a soldier leveled his gun at her. Laurel gasped and took a step backward. "What do you want?" she asked, her voice small and timorous, but the guard said nothing, simply stepping aside to allow one of the matrons to enter.

Quickly, Laurel backed away until she was flattened against the wall, between the window and the toilet.

The matron didn't even look at her. She set a covered tray on the bed and then stomped from the room.

Laurel stared first at the door, then at the tray. Suddenly she was aware of the aroma of food filling the room. She pushed herself away from the wall and scurried to the bed, pulling the napkin away from the tray.

"Meat! And hot bread! And fresh beets. Oh, and chocolate! Oh, it's so beautiful." She picked up the fork and knife, cutting off a large chunk of butter, and began to spread it on the bread, her mouth watering.

Suddenly the door slammed open again and the matron rushed back in. Before Laurel could react, the woman had snatched the bread and knife from Laurel's hands and the napkin from her lap, grabbed the tray, and left. Just as the door closed behind her, Laurel launched herself from the bed, trying desperately to reach it before it closed. By the time she got there, the lock was being turned.

Laurel stood, her face pressed against the grating. "Wait," she screamed. "Bring that back here right this minute. Do you know who I am? Do you know who I know? I am a personal friend of the Führer himself. You can't do this to me! I'm starving."

She could see the guard and the matron out in the hallway. As she watched, the matron finished buttering the bread and ate it slowly as the guard held the tray.

"Please." Her voice became a whine of desperation. "That's my dinner. Please, I'm so hungry," Laurel said again and again, tears streaming down her face.

"God damn you to hell, Reinhard Heydrich," Laurel screamed before sinking to the floor, sobbing.

Before you ask, I haven't the foggiest notion what the hell is going on around here. All I can do is to report what I know and hope I can get this out to you. I know you must be as confused as I am, but I'll bet you're not as scared!

Here's how it all developed. Laurel had been over here with her usual gossip on Wednesday. She couldn't stop talking about how angry she was that RH was refusing to take her with him to Prague. From what Laurel had to say, he's been back and forth to Prague, and apparently his experience in Russia has stood him in good stead, which is very bad for the poor Czechs. From what he has told Laurel, his *Einsatzgruppen*, that terror squad made up more of intellectuals than soldiers, is proceeding against the resistance there.

The thought of what they may be doing makes my blood run cold, particularly with what I have been reading in the diaries of AH. It seems Heydrich's other brilliant idea, the 'Final Solution' to rid the world of Jews, is going forward. Six death camps have been set up in Poland, and if what he says is true and not some gruesome fantasy, they are killing trainloads of people.

As I said, Laurel was here Wednesday. Normally, I would have seen her again on Saturday after her next broadcast. Early Saturday afternoon, however, a terrifying gang of SS men appeared at my door. I thought I would never be able to breathe again. Then I was certain they had somehow managed to read the invisible ink on one of my letters to you. Then I wondered whose husband I'd made furious this time. But, to my amazement, they were most polite, explaining that RH had sent them to ask me to fill in for Laurel. They presented me with a script and escorted me to the radio station.

I tried asking the SS men where Laurel was, but got nothing but polite smiles. Needless to say, I have no one else to ask, so I shall just keep my eyes and ears open. I don't think they have killed her. Not yet, anyway, but I don't have anything but instinct to tell me that. I hate to say it, but you'll be hearing my voice on the radio again, I fear. I also fear that Laurel will be happy to tell them in great detail about my role with you if they put any pressure on her.

Do I need to tell you how little sleep I've been getting?

Laurel was ready for them now. It had only taken two episodes of disappearing dinners for her to understand how meals would be served. She stood at the end of the bed, ignoring the matron, and waited until the woman had set the tray down, then lunged at it, grabbing what food she could, shoving it into her mouth until her cheeks bulged like a chipmunk's. When the woman returned in precisely thirty seconds to take the tray, Laurel would wait until she was out of the room, then spit the food back onto the blanket and make it last as long as she could.

She was fairly certain she'd been in the prison for two weeks and two days. It hadn't occurred to her to make marks on the walls for the days until long after she'd arrived; then she wasn't certain if it had been three or four days since the nightmare had begun. All the time she was finding a way to record the passage of time, she was convinced it would only be a matter of hours until Reinhard appeared, full of love and forgiveness, to take her back home.

She could barely stand the way she smelled. She had torn a ragged strip from the blanket to make a combination washcloth and towel, shivering as she took a sponge bath in the cold water from the sink. But without soap or toilet tissue, her scent was beginning to be overwhelming.

Laurel put her hands on the bars and pushed forward to stare out the window at the strip of blue sky. She wondered how long Reinhard could stay angry. It was obvious the man was crazy with hate, complete and total, not only for the Jews and Russians but also for her.

She pushed away from the window, setting her hands on her hips, and suddenly became aware of sharp bones under her knuckles and, for the first time in two weeks and two days, laughed. What if this was Reinhard's insane way to make her diet? She bit her lower lip, thinking about it. After all, no one had come to question her or torture her, except by means of the thirty-second meals, or even talk to her. In his rage Reinhard said she was fat as a pig. It would be just like him to do this to her, hoping to serve two purposes with one action—first, to make her lose weight, and second, to make her so frightened of him and his power that she would never question him again.

"All right, Reinhard Heydrich," she said, setting her jaw defiantly, "I'll let you think you've won. I'll play the timid little skinny mouse for you—and I'll hand your insane head to Patrice and her friends. My friends. My only friends in the world.''

Patrice sat in her office, fighting the mountain of paperwork. The blackout blinds tightly covered the windows against even a sliver of light escaping into the night. She glanced at the clock, then reached for the radio, turning the dial away from the droning on the BBC to the "Traitor's Hour." It had been nearly four weeks since Laurel's last broadcast, and the two letters Karl had managed to get out shed no light on her disappearance.

Karl was still doing the broadcasts, and each time she listened, her heart grew heavier. She could hear the strain in his voice as he read the prepared scripts with as much conviction as he could muster. At least he was still doing them, which meant that Laurel had obviously not talked her little head off. For once in her life.

The martial music heralded the program and Patrice leaned back in her chair. By now she had become familiar with the program format and knew there would be haranguing propaganda before the main event. She was afraid, however, either to close her eyes—positive she'd fall asleep in a second—or to go back to work and shut out the noise to the extent of missing the broadcast.

Her mind, left to its own devices, drifted to Stephen, and she felt the same sense of resignation and loss that she'd had since his last letter.

He hadn't said there was no future for them. He hadn't sounded much different, in fact, than he had in every other letter: refugees and injustice and pain filled his days with purpose. But he also hadn't said he loved her or missed her or that she was more to him than a correspondent.

Patrice wished she felt like crying. It would be easier if she could mourn the passing of her plans, but she had to acknowledge those plans hadn't existed for very long.

What she had come to realize since his last letter was how safe the very lack of solid future expectations made her feel. She had been able to point to Stephen and say "marriage" to her parents and friends, all the time knowing she could

234

pursue the life and career she loved. It had been a convenient charade. Now, however, the charade had to end.

At the end of his letter Stephen had mentioned, almost casually, that he had accepted an assignment in Canada at an RAF rehabilitation hospital. That wasn't really the problem—the Pyrenees and Canada were equally remote. What had made Patrice understand the place she occupied in Stephen's life was that he also said he'd turned down a similar assignment in London.

She sighed. He hadn't meant to be cruel, she was sure. He was just being his usual honest self—content with things as they were. To Patrice's surprise, she'd discovered he was no longer what she wanted.

"Ah," she said aloud, leaning toward the radio, "but what do I want in Stephen's stead?"

As the music faded and the voice began, Patrice's head snapped up and she spun in her chair, almost expecting to see a chubby, smug face surrounded by red hair in place of the dial.

"Good evening, dear friends. As you can see, I have returned from my vacation, rested and feeling at the peak of health. You see, we are eating so well here in Germany that I had gained weight and needed to go to one of our beautiful vacation spas to get thin again. I know you understand how hard it must be to refuse the temptations of delicious weiner-schnitzel swimming in gravy or the wonderful pastries for which our chefs are known. . . ."

Patrice grabbed for the telephone, quickly dialing the secret number which would connect her to Donohue. She waited impatiently as she was passed along, until finally, over the crackles and squeaks, she heard his voice.

"She's back. Laurel's back," she said without preliminaries.

Donohue's whistle was loud through the phone. "Well, I'll be damned. I hate to ask, but do you think you could safely—"

"I'll begin packing as soon as we're off the phone. Are you still hoping to go ahead with the plan as we've discussed?"

"Absolutely. Let's just hope she's still a willing player."

15

WHITNEY GRABBED PRIMROSE'S arm as they stepped off the plane. "Smell it? You can smell it!" Her face was wreathed in a brilliant smile.

Primrose looked puzzled. "You are perhaps the only person I've ever met who would wax ecstatic over the scent of the moors."

Whitney shook her head, tossing her blond hair in the chill of the breeze. "Not the moors, silly. Freedom."

Primrose tipped her head, studying Whitney curiously, then slowly nodded. "You're right. We have been too long in the shadow of that black eagle." She inhaled deeply. "I'm not certain I can smell it, but I am positive it feels very nice already."

Whitney, still grinning, descended the steps of the plane onto the packed earth of the remote Scottish moors where their small plane had landed, and looked around. "And now that we're here," she said, turning to the Abbé, "where, precisely, are we?"

"Perhaps here is someone who can tell us," the Abbé said, drawing his cloak around him and fighting back a shiver in the wind.

Whitney followed his eyes, spotting the square shape of the Land Rover approaching.

"I thought I'd seen the end of the world . . . until now. Where the hell is this place?" Magda pulled a cigarette from the pack in her pocket, then tried to light it. "Damn this wind," she said, retreating to the plane, returning a moment later, the cigarette sending out a thin plume of smoke. "And, while I'm asking and no one's answering, what the hell are we doing here?"

Lady Primrose clucked disapprovingly. "I should think after spending a week in the Vatican, Sister Magda, your language would have improved."

"How about that place? I've never seen so much gold in all my time! They act so uppity, as if there's nothing going on in the world. I couldn't believe it. There was only one good thing about it, frankly. It was the one time I've had that damned outfit on where I didn't feel as though people were staring at me and laughing." Magda took a long drag on her cigarette. "But they sure could use some help in picking out beds. I thought those mattresses in the convent at home were—" She stopped abruptly.

Primrose and Whitney, who had been only half listening to her, both turned. "At home?" Whitney said with a smile.

"I'll be damned," Magda said, staring off into space. "I must really be losing my mind. I called that convent 'home.' " She shook her head.

Primrose patted her shoulder. "Perhaps for all of us, in one way or another, it is home."

Whitney had been staring at the approaching Land Rover as it pulled up and stopped and its driver emerged. Suddenly she whooped and rushed toward the automobile, into Erik's welcoming arms.

The Abbé busied himself with gathering up their duffel bags, and moved the two remaining Butterflies out of the way so the plane could take off as Whitney and Erik enjoyed their reunion. Then supervising the distribution of the warm Scottish wool jackets he found in the back, he shouted, "Come, come! Let us quickly get out of this cold."

It wasn't much warmer inside the Land Rover, but at least

they were sheltered from the wind. Erik engaged the gears, retracing the narrow track over the hard, rocky ground.

"The question of the hour has been 'where are we?' " Whitney said, her voice joyful.

"And what are we doing here?" Magda added, suspiciously.

"You're in the Scottish moors," Erik replied. "Home of the Hound of the Baskervilles and other mysterious creatures of the night."

"I've had quite enough of creatures of the night," Primrose said, "with living in Yugoslavia under the Nazis."

Erik laughed. "Then you should feel quite at home here."

"Are we here to fight some monster?" Magda asked, a bit puzzled.

"Perhaps, in a sense, we are. You'll hear the whole story in good time. I can tell you the operation is still in planning, but because it is complex, Donohue wanted you to get started with some special training." His brow furrowed. "This is going to be a very important job and it must run without a hitch. But before you ask, it's far too complex to explain right now. I promise you'll learn everything as soon as possible."

"Are we going to another convent?" Magda asked, and Whitney could hear the desperation in her voice.

Erik shook his head, navigating the car around an outcropping of gray boulders. "Hardly," then smiled enigmatically as he turned the car onto another, unmarked track.

"Well, if not a convent, then where?" Whitney asked.

"There," Erik replied, pointing across the moor they were traversing.

Everyone in the Rover strained forward to see what he was indicating, then Primrose said, "Why, it's a castle."

"Castle MacGeorge, actually. It's an ancient property on loan to the Crown, at least in part, as a training center for special missions like ours. I think you'll find it quite interesting and most gracious. The owners, the Earl and Countess MacGeorge, still live on the property and are welcoming hosts."

From first glimpse, across the moors, the scale of the castle seemed small. But as they drew closer, Whitney saw it was an impressive structure carved from the gray stone of the moors, containing at least ten acres within its crenellated walls and high towers. The road approached a side of the castle with no entrance, then wound around the walls.

"It has a moat," Whitney said, amazed.

"With water in it," Primrose added, enthralled.

"It looks like a prison," Magda said, shivering.

"Does everything look like a prison to you?" Primrose asked, a bit irate.

"Pretty much everything *is* a prison," Magda replied flatly, "if you think about it."

"Well, I don't think about it," Primrose said firmly, still staring at the castle.

The road curled around one more tower then led onto the bridge over the moat. The massive chains were still in place as though the bridge might need to be raised. The chains swayed slightly as the Rover crossed into the inner gate of the castle.

"Oh, my, this is wonderful," Lady Primrose said, emerging from the Rover and surveying the small village of gray stone, thatched-roofed houses which surrounded the courtyard. "It's like a medieval city."

Erik came around the car to help Whitney out. "It was built in the fourteenth century and has been restored twice. The village is called St. George's."

Magda grinned. "And it has a pub! I think I will like it here!"

"And a lovely little church," the Abbé said.

"Something for everyone," Whitney said, taking Erik's arm and smiling up at him.

"These steps lead to the castle itself," Erik said, pointing them toward a stone stairway which began at the side of the small village.

Whitney looked up at the massive structure rising above the steps. "It's enormous."

"Perhaps the largest in the country," Erik replied. "Are you all right on these steps?"

"Perfectly. Dr. Forrestal's leg is a wonderful creation. Sometimes I forget it's not my own. How is he?"

"Fine, I imagine. He's in Canada."

"Canada? When did he leave Spain? Does Patrice know?"

Erik nodded. "He's there running a rehabilitation hospital for RAF flyers and others with serious war injuries. I saw him briefly in London when he came through on his way to the new assignment. So did Patrice."

Whitney laughed. "I'll bet she was very happy about that. Do these stairs go on forever?"

"No, just long enough to dissuade even the most sincere invader. I'm not so certain Patrice was happy. I think Patrice and Stephen have agreed to part as friends."

"Oh, no!" Whitney exclaimed. "I thought she was so much in love with him."

Erik shrugged, mystified. "I am not very clear on these matters of the heart. When Patrice talked about it, she told me she was sad but also relieved. She said Stephen is a man whose work is his consuming passion, which leaves no room for anyone in his life."

Whitney looked up into his eyes then reached to caress his cheek with her fingertips. "You are a man whose work is a consuming passion," she said softly.

He nodded. "But there is a difference. It is *our* work and a passion we share. We are not the same as Patrice and Stephen. You do not need to worry about that. What you do need to worry about is these steps which we must climb, but I shall give you a tour to distract you. These buildings are the stables. There are ramps on the back that allowed the horses to be ridden directly from the stables to the gates. That building was for armor, and there are some magnificent suits still here. This was a blacksmith shop, and the forges can still be operated." They ascended more steps. "This was the mill, and over here, the pens for small livestock."

"You have obviously been here for a while," Whitney said.

"Two weeks. We've been working on something very special, but I have managed to find time to explore."

"War is hell," Whitney teased, trying not to sound breathless from the climb.

"And here is the door," Erik said, reaching for the huge lion-faced knocker. It's sound reverberated even on the outside when Erik pulled it up, then released it.

The door opened after a brief moment to reveal a hearty man whose face was ringed by a full auburn beard. He wore a creamy wool knit sweater and a tartan kilt of red, green, and cream plaid. "Welcome to Castle MacGeorge," he boomed, his rolling brogue encompassing the words warmly.

"Lord Hugh MacDonald, Earl MacGeorge," Erik said, "it is my pleasure to present Lady Whitney Frost-Worthington, Countess of Swindon."

"My house is graced with your presence, Lady Whitney," Lord MacGeorge said, shaking her hand heartily. "Please come inside."

Whitney passed into the foyer, looking carefully at the beautiful details of the room, feeling more than a bit homesick for her own Swindon. The walls were covered with grand tapestries of hunters on horses, and dogs and stags. The center of the room was dominated by an enormous stone fireplace, the mantel of which was a whole log which had been polished to a high glossy glow. Three Scottish deerhounds, elegant in their grace and wiry power, slept by the fire, but raised their noble gray heads to inspect the arrivals. Then, sensing no danger, they again put their heads on outstretched paws. Surrounding the fireplace was a split stairway ascending to meet above the mantel in a wide balcony.

A fire crackled merrily in the grate. Whitney stepped toward its warmth, extending her chilled hands. She heard the others coming into the room, carried forward by the rolling brogue of their host explaining the history of the castle.

Suddenly Whitney heard a gasp above her and looked up.

"It is you. It really is you," cried a woman's voice, but before Whitney could focus on the face, it had disappeared. Whitney heard footsteps racing down the stairs and turned just in time to be hugged fiercely.

"Whitney, my darling friend. They told me you would be here, but until I saw your dear face, I could not believe it."

Whitney was mystified until suddenly she gasped and returned the hug. "Rowena!" She pulled back to look at the face of her closest friend from Swindon, the woman who had helped her after Perry had died.

241

"I was devastated when they told me you had died. I could never accept that such a courageous spirit as yours would be gone from this world. And then, just when I had lost all hope of ever finding such a wonderful friend again, Erik came to tell me you had, indeed, survived and wanted me to care for Swindon. Since I'm here, you know I can't be there, but please don't worry. Dear Uncle Harry is guarding your hearth and ours." Her grin widened. "And, of course, dear old Frobisher is still there."

They both laughed and hugged again. "You look wonderful," Whitney said. "And your castle is magnificent."

"And I see you have met Hugh," Rowena said with a gentle smile in the direction of her husband.

"He's wonderful, too," Whitney said, then hugged her again. "And obviously makes you so happy. What a joy!"

With her arm still around her friend's shoulders, Whitney turned to the others. "Of course you know Erik. I'd like you to meet my friend and cohort, Lady Primrose Benningham. Prim's as much of a mischief-maker as you and I."

Rowena extended her hand. "Welcome to our home, Lady Benningham."

"And this is Abbé d'Astier, our comrade from France," Whitney continued. The Abbé bowed.

"I'm not Lady anything," Magda said, presenting herself. "I'm Magda Maddingly." She extended her hand to Rowena.

"Magda is also a very important part of our team. She's a brave and loyal woman and we are fortunate to have her with us," Whitney said sincerely.

Rowena leaned toward Whitney. "Can you manage another flight of stairs? Erik has told me about . . ."

"About my leg? Please don't worry. I've climbed things a great deal more challenging than stairs."

"Shall we go up to the main hall?" Lord Hugh said, leading the way. "Don't worry about your things. Our men will take them to your rooms. Come along, now. We have made a hearty meal for the weary travelers."

The group followed him up the stairs, Whitney and Rowena bringing up the rear.

"Whitney, I can still hardly believe we are together again. You have grown even more beautiful."

242

Whitney squeezed her friend's shoulders. "You are a dear to say so, though I know it isn't true. We have so much to talk about. How is your Uncle Harry?"

Rowena smiled softly. "Getting on in years, I'm afraid, though still the main objective of every widow in the town. He rides each day, however, and manages to play his share of cards with his cronies. They're all Home Guard now and spend hours scanning the skies for enemy planes and marching about in their uniforms reminiscing about the trenches in France."

Whitney laughed at the thought. "And Swindon?"

"You do know that Colonel Donohue is using it in much the same way as our castle?"

Whitney nodded.

"But Frobisher, who is also in the Home Guard, runs it with an iron fist. I believe it looks better than ever. When we were last home, the gardens were in full flower. And your horses are fine. Burns is there as always, caring for them and making certain they are happy." She hesitated, looking at Whitney. "I can't stop myself from saying this. I hope it doesn't bring up any bad memories, but I wish so that Perry were still here. He would be so proud of you and of what you are doing."

"Thank you. And it doesn't bring up any bad memories, only a taste of sadness." She paused, then continued, "Which is more than overcome by being reunited with you again."

They reached the balcony over the entry foyer, then turned away, proceeding along a wide hallway to still another flight of stairs.

Whitney sighed at the sight of them, and Rowena giggled. "When I first came here, I thought I should never get used to living in a house where one could do nothing without using stairs. Now I hardly notice them until a guest, trying desperately to be polite, is confronted with the experience. We have just this last set."

Whitney chuckled. "I hope this is a very hearty meal. I've worked up quite an appetite."

* * *

243

The sky had grown gray and heavy with a strong wind from the North Sea. Although the fireplaces in each occupied room of the castle did their best to combat the effects of the wind, the cold managed to penetrate even the innermost chambers, forcing the small group to huddle close to the fire, their hands enclosing warm mugs of tea.

Sister Magda shivered, staring accusingly at the flames in the fireplace, challenging them to become warmer, then turned to Whitney. "He must have told you something about what we're doing here. And where is he? Are we just on a vacation?"

Whitney shook her head. "Answering your demands in order, Erik has told me nothing about the mission save that we will all find out this morning when the rest of the team arrives. At this moment, as a matter of fact, he's gone out to pick them up at the same landing field where we came in, and should be back shortly." She paused, then smiled. "Although it's not a tropic isle and has no glittering night spots, I almost feel this is a bit of a vacation."

Primrose nodded. "Indeed it is. I haven't tasted scones and marmalade in a very long time. And I haven't heard one word of anything but English in two days."

Magda shrugged. "I guess. Besides, the beds aren't bad." She shivered again. "But it sure is cold."

At that moment, the door swung open and Erik entered, followed by six people bundled like Eskimos until they began to remove the layers of warm clothing.

"Patrice," Whitney cried, jumping to her feet and hurrying to embrace her friend. "I can't believe it! Erik, you never told me!"

From one scarf-swathed face, a deep voice said, "As well he should not have."

"Colonel! What a wonderful reunion," Whitney said, helping to unwind the scarf from his face. "You look . . . cold."

"Not surprisingly," he said, unbuttoning the heavy wool coat and handing it to the butler, who waited patiently as people heaped clothing onto his arms.

The other four people were unfamiliar to Whitney, so

she'd given them little more than a glance as she and Patrice chatted happily.

"We have a lot to cover," Erik said over the din of reunion, "so please get some tea and get settled." He waited while everyone complied, then leaned against the mantel, cradling a mug in his hands. Donohue came to stand beside him.

"Perhaps a bit of history before we get to the matter at hand," Donohue began. "First, let me introduce the newest members of our mission. You may be aware of their work in Hollywood films, but no one is aware of how much they are doing to help. Alexander and Zoltan Korda." The two men nodded in greeting, and Donohue continued. "Vota Rajic on my left, and Jan Myjuszk on my right, are members of the Czech underground who have volunteered for this mission."

Whitney studied the man named Vota, wondering why his name was so familiar to her when his face was not. Suddenly she remembered. This man had been the lover of the woman who lay in a grave in Maryland in Whitney's stead. She wanted to tell him of the connection between them, but turned away instead, wondering if she would ever see life in an uncomplicated way again.

Donohue sipped at his tea. "In the past we have, for obvious reasons, been focused on the activities of Herr Hitler within the Nazi government. There are, however, others within the Nazi party who have the potential to be far more dangerous and destructive. Donohue ran his hand over his hair and sighed deeply. "As of two days ago, the United States is in this war."

A babble of questions tumbled over one another until Donohue held up his hand.

"I've brought some papers with me so you can read the details, but until then, the Japanese hit Pearl Harbor in Hawaii on the morning of December seventh, and Congress finally woke up."

"Hooray!" Prim said, then quickly held up her hands. "That is to say, hooray that the Yanks will be in to help us now. I'm not cheering an attack, you understand. Oh, now I feel terrible."

Magda sipped her tea, a pensive look on her face.

245

Patrice clasped Whitney's hand comfortingly. "I knew, but Donohue asked me not to say anything until we were all assembled. I'm surprised you hadn't heard it on the radio."

"Radio's broken," Magda said. "And what difference does it make? If we're in, we're in. Funny, nothing seems much different for us."

Whitney tried to decide how she felt about the news. Having been actively involved in the war and its preparations for four years, she had a sense of resentment that it had taken so long for her countrymen to awaken. But at the same time, she felt great sadness that, instead of being closer to resolution, the conflict was now broadened to include the whole world. No longer were the Germans the only force of evil to be defeated. "Have there been any other attacks on American soil?" she asked, fearing the answer might be Washington.

Donohue shook his head. "No." He snorted mirthlessly. "And it's very interesting how ready the military was for a war we weren't going to enter. There are American soldiers on their way to England right now and Eisenhower's in London setting up a command. But you'll have time to read the papers and talk about this later. Right now, however, we must return our attention to the war we've been fighting all along. If you recall, I was talking about shifting our emphasis away from the Führer toward some of his minions."

"Certainly Hitler's closest generals and advisors are well known to the Allies, even to civilians," Whitney said.

"Yes, but there are those who are not known, and one of them may prove to be more dangerous than all the others combined. Miss Rigby?"

Patrice stood. "His name is Reinhard Heydrich. Some of you may have heard about him."

Whitney nodded. "We've been monitoring his Russian communications. Or at least those of his operatives. He seems a cruel and highly active man."

Patrice agreed emphatically. *"Monster* comes immediately to mind. He has ordered the execution of thousands of people in Poland and Russia, and is as obsessed with the elimination of the Jews as Hitler, perhaps even more so. We have an operative who is very close to him who has told us details of his activities. She has also, however, given us something very valuable, something upon which this mission turns."

"Laurel?" Whitney asked, her voice flat with hatred.

Patrice nodded. "I have just returned from meeting with her in Berlin and she told me—"

Whitney held up her hand. "Forgive me for interrupting, but are you saying that we are planning what is obviously a dangerous and intricate mission based on information given to you by Laurel Smythe? Have you taken leave of your senses? Why in the world would she tell anyone anything while she has power among the Nazis?"

Patrice grinned. "Because—and I feel you will be delighted to hear this—Laurel's fortunes have changed." She proceeded to bring Whitney and the others up to date on Laurel's personal history.

"At any rate," Patrice went on, "Laurel has told me Heydrich is holding a conference in a small village in Belgium." She turned to Donohue. "Would you like to continue?"

He nodded, rising and moving to stand next to the fire. "We've had our eye on Heydrich for a while, and this seems the time to move. He'll be there to meet with a large group of Nazi officials and leaders from the occupied countries to tell them about his latest plans for the complete elimination of all 'undesirables,' as he calls them—Jews, gypsies, homosexuals, Catholic priests and nuns with a political conscience, the deformed, and the retarded, among others. He calls his plan 'The Final Solution,' and it is as ominous as it sounds. It's begun in Poland, according to our intelligence. We hear that his 'final solution' is extermination—genocide."

"My God," Prim whispered. "Then it is true. There have been stories. . . ."

"What is our role in this?" Whitney asked.

For the first time, Vota Rajic, who had been introduced as a leader of the Czech Resistance, rose. "He's been assigned to Czechoslovakia. We're going to kill him first."

16

PATRICE JUGGLED THE battered briefcase and cup of hot tea from her right hand to her left, tucking her elbow tightly against her side to keep the stack of newspapers under her left arm from cascading to the floor. Then she rummaged in her right pocket for the keys to her office, before realizing she'd already put them in the left pocket.

"Oh, bother," she muttered, reversing the juggling act, sloshing some of the tea onto the toes of her pumps in the process. "Damn," she muttered.

The door to her office swung open.

"Damn what?"

"Raven!" she said, surprised and delighted. "How wonderful to see you! Why are you wearing that uniform? Did you get fired from the RAF? Can you please take some of this before I spill the rest of my tea? When did you get here? And how did you get in?"

Mike Raven disentangled Patrice's fingers from the handle of the tea mug, then took the briefcase and stepped aside as Patrice hurried into the office, avalanching her desktop with the stack of newspapers.

"Well?" she said, retrieving the tea mug and briefcase.

Raven laughed, shaking his head. "Well, it's good to see

you, too. You look sufficiently harried to be running a London bureau."

Patrice settled into her creaking chair, feeling a familiar twinge of guilt at his words. With the increasing burden of work from Donohue, she felt it a wonder she hadn't been fired by *Sunpapers*. Thank heaven, she thought, for the fine cadre of reporters who managed to take what little direction she gave them and turn it into a steady flow of articles which streamed back to Baltimore.

"The bureau runs me more than I run it," she said, her response a bit too forced, a bit too late. "But I don't need to tell you about that. Now what's this change of fashion?"

He cocked his head and looked at Patrice quizzically. "Have you missed the news lately? Seems we're in this war up to our collective . . . oak leaves. I've been discharged from the RAF and made a light colonel in the United States Army Air Corps." His sigh belied his smile.

"What a promotion! That sounds wonderful for you. Why don't you look happy?" Patrice was glad the conversation had shifted away from her role in the bureau.

"Because they want me, but I'm too old to fly combat missions for America. I guess they don't put much stock in my RAF record—medals or no. They're sending me home, Rigby," he said, his face and voice sad.

"Back to the States? But the war is here."

He nodded. "True. The training, however, is there. I have to go to Kansas, of all places, to teach eighteen-year-old kids how to be fighter pilots. Kansas! America, for that matter! Christ, Rigby, I've lived in London for eighteen years. When the Army told me they were sending me 'home,' I thought they meant to Frogmore, not Kansas."

Patrice sipped at her tea reflectively. "I think this is called 'Lament of the Expatriate.' I'm sure they thought you'd be thrilled to get back to the land of baseball and apple pie." Her sigh mirrored his. "I live in constant dread of a letter from Baltimore, giving me the 'opportunity' to come back. Perhaps for a visit . . . But you must look on the bright side. The tricks you've learned flying for the RAF will benefit a great many young pilots."

Raven nodded. "And, just between us, a man of forty-five

249

doesn't have the reflexes this job requires. All I was doing was piloting a bomber—in and out. No dogfights. Lately the planes have been getting faster and the ground artillery better. It's a young man's war now, Rigby. Maybe that's what I'm really hating, not Kansas.''

"I'll step down and you can come back here just like old times," Patrice said softly.

He chuckled. "Not on your linotype, Rigby," Raven replied, his old gruffness emerging. "You're stuck with this."

"I wish I were doing it justice," she said, surprising both of them.

"Are you kidding? You're doing a great job here. I read the papers, Rigby, and you're still the best." He leaned forward, resting his elbows on his knees. "This job has to be the toughest one around. You can't print but ten percent of what you know because the Jerries are reading it. You have to sift through the prevarications and fantasies of government press releases and find stories you can run without being hanged for treason. You have to go places and do things that are dangerous and stupid in the context of real life, then filter everything you see and know through some narrow-minded censor who applies mystical standards and rattles chicken bones for all we know. And you not only have to do it for yourself but also for ten reporters."

"Well! Thank you!" Patrice thought for a moment. "I guess I just haven't been feeling as though I make enough of a contribution."

"Nonsense!" He rose. "I've got to get to the train. I'm off to Portsmouth and then onto a troopship to New York. From there, the wide-open spaces."

Patrice jumped up and came around the desk to give him a hug. "How do I thank you for all you've done for me?" she muttered against the wool of his uniform.

"Having had your job, 'damn you to eternal hellfire' would seem appropriate," Raven laughed, returning her hug. "Just keep digging, kid. Someday you may be able to write everything you know. And I want an autographed copy of *that* book." He released her, picked up his khaki coat, and plopped his cap on his head. Hesitating in the doorway, he

250

said, "Just one more thing for old times' sake," stepping back quickly and slamming the door resoundingly.

Tears streamed past Patrice's smile.

Paul pulled the headphones off and tossed them onto the table with a disgusted snort. "Nothing. Nothing. Nothing. What the hell is going on in Dubrovnik?"

Patrice picked up the earphones, slipping the contraption over her head and listening, her brow furrowed, to the squeals and static. She reached for the radio, turning the dial slowly through the bands.

"Three marches, a hundred languages, and a request to buy War Bonds, but no Morse. I wonder if it wasn't a bad idea to try to use commercial shortwave bands. Perhaps they're just getting lost in all the . . ." Her explanation faded and she set the earphones down.

"It's been eight days since their last transmission. What should we do?"

"You should stay right here and keep listening and trying to reach them. I'm off to Scotland." Patrice shrugged into her coat. "I'll try to get out tonight and be back no later than day after tomorrow."

"Following up on a story," Paul said. "Incidentally, I have a job offer."

"You already have two jobs. It would seem enough to keep you busy. From whom?"

"United Press. To go to North Africa." He grinned. "I turned it down."

"And you thought you wanted to be a lawyer." Patrice turned to leave, then turned back. "Fate may very well have given you a shove in the right direction, you know. You really are a good reporter."

Paul snapped a salute. "Thanks, boss. Have a nice trip."

The wind howled mercilessly across the moors and Patrice shivered uncontrollably, her teeth clattering, an amazed look on her face. "Where did all of this come from? I left here two weeks ago and this was empty, and now look at it."

Whitney clenched her jaw against her own shivering. "Just

don't touch it because it'll all fall apart. They're only façades."

"But it looks precisely like the village where the operation is to take place." Patrice turned around slowly, looking at the replicas of the houses along the cobbled street. "Even the flower boxes."

"Everything. And it grew practically overnight. The Korda brothers did it. It's a Hollywood set. I've learned enough about the magic of how movies are made to keep me from ever seeing another one. If you look closely at the photographs, then at the buildings, even things like the lace of the curtains and the worn spots on the doorsills are the same. But come with me." Whitney grabbed Patrice's hand and led her behind one of the façades and the illusion disappeared, replaced by leaning supports and framing. "Poof, the magic is gone."

"You're training here?"

Whitney nodded. "All sorts of exercises designed to make us function as a 'single organism,' as Erik so charmingly put it." Her smile faded a bit. "A single, deadly organism. This is a very big fish we're after."

Patrice nodded. "I know. I've met him. And from what Laurel says, he's a mean fish." She put her hand on Whitney's arm. "Please be careful. I think he has nearly psychic powers and he's well protected."

"I shall be. Careful and very well prepared. We train constantly, and the operation is more than a month away. By the time we get to Belgium, I shall be able to do it in my sleep." She took Patrice's arm, linking it through hers. "Now, let's get inside and warm up a bit. Wouldn't you know Heydrich would schedule a meeting in the dead of winter instead of at a more tolerable time. Ah, well."

Donohue looked disturbed as they entered. "We have secure radio channels and telephone lines, Miss Rigby. I don't understand why you came in person."

"The Butterflies, sir. They've been silent and unresponsive for eight days."

Whitney felt her stomach constrict. "Eight days! Nothing in eight days? What about the underground contacts? Have you tried them? What about the couriers?"

252

Patrice nodded. "Paul's tried everything. Except going in."

Donohue snorted angrily, pounding the desk. "I stopped the couriers after we lost three planes. Things were quieter, so I felt we could relay information through more standard, less expensive channels. Damn, I'm sorry."

Whitney leaned forward. "I'll go," she said quickly.

Donohue shook his head. "Impossible. We can't risk losing you during training." He leaned back in the chair, scratching reflexively along his jawline with his fingertips. "Ball's in North Africa, and I can't pull him out right now. Damn."

"What about me?" Patrice said, setting her hands on her hips. "I go in and out of Germany, so Yugoslavia should be a stroll in the park. No one knows me there."

"But you don't speak the language," Donohue countered.

"Nor do I speak German very convincingly, but I manage. And I do speak French. And Whitney doesn't speak Yugo-slavian or whatever they use. Or at least she didn't." Patrice set her jaw and feet firmly.

Donohue buried his face in his hands. "This is ridiculous."

"Actually," Whitney interjected, "it's not. Patrice could wear Primrose's habit quite easily and even travel with one of the Swiss passports we all have. She and Prim look a bit alike."

"I won't have her go in alone," Donohue said, retreating to a new stand. "And I don't have anyone to send along."

Patrice tried her best to hide her triumphant look. "Paul Sanders Stewart," she said, smiling brightly.

Patrice smiled sweetly at the Corsican customs inspector. "Humanitarian reasons," she replied, holding up the black medical bag she carried. "The Red Cross has been requested to investigate an outbreak of typhus in several of the mountain villages." She hoped he wouldn't question her further. She had no idea if there had been a typhus outbreak or if there were any mountain villages other than the one where she and Paul were to meet their pilot.

"If you are American, why do you have a Swiss passport?" the inspector muttered accusingly.

"All Red Cross workers carry Swiss passports," she replied, building her lie even further. "The Swiss are neutral, you know," she added.

"What is in this bag?" The inspector yanked the medical bag open, rummaging through the vials of medications and hypodermic syringes, then poured the contents out on the counter and thumped the bottom and sides of the bag. "There is no false bottom here," he said, obviously disappointed.

"Why should there be a false bottom?" Patrice said innocently. "I have nothing to hide."

The inspector waved his dismissal, and Patrice began to repack the bag, grateful beyond words for the insight Paul had shown in insisting it be legitimate.

"You are a physician?" the inspector turned to Paul, comparing his passport photo with his face.

"I am," Paul replied imperiously, obviously disgusted with the delay. "And this is my nurse. Your government has requested our presence."

"What kind of doctor?"

Paul sighed exasperatedly. "A good one," Paul snapped.

The man stared at Paul, then, to Patrice's astonishment, removed one of his shoes. "My foot," the man said, "it is most painful." He hoisted his leg up onto the inspection table, thrusting his filthy foot into Paul's face.

Paul adjusted his glasses and bent to inspect a grossly inflamed area. Finally he nodded and turned to Patrice. "Infection of the superior metatarsal colligula," he said with authority. "I shall lance it. Please clean the field with alcohol, then give me a scalpel."

Patrice was terrified at his audacity, but turned quickly to the medical bag, removing the bottle of alcohol and a large wad of cotton which she soaked with the liquid. Fighting back the bile rising in her throat, she scrubbed the infected area, trying not to touch the man's dirty foot.

Paul nodded. "That will suffice. Now, a scalpel and some iodine." He looked up at the inspector. "This will hurt, but we have no anesthetic. Why don't you bite on your pencil."

254

Without warning, he made a quick, deep stroke with the scalpel directly through the reddest portion of the wound, then stepped back as yellow-green fluid burst forth. "Hmmm. Appears to be a spongarina infectella infestation. Let me have the alcohol." Patrice gave him the bottle, and without warning, Paul poured a quantity of it into the seeping wound. The inspector howled. His pencil, bitten in half, fell to the floor. "Sorry, but this will heal it. Now, sulfa powder, nurse."

Patrice lowered her head practically into the bag, fighting for control over both her fear and her desire to laugh hysterically at Paul's flawless performance. Grateful for the clear labels, she handed him a can of sulfa powder which Paul sprinkled liberally over the bleeding foot.

"Now a roll of bandages, please, and we'll be done." He wrapped the man's foot in a huge wad of bandage. "Leave that bandage in place for ten days. Now, my good man, may we please pass and get on with our work?" Without waiting for an answer, he lifted his and Patrice's passports from the man's weakening grasp, snapped the medical bag closed, picked up their suitcases and turned away from the table. Patrice watched, open-mouthed, as the inspector's color faded from gray to white and he slumped forward onto the table, his eyes rolling up in his head.

"I'm glad he was on duty by himself," Paul said as he scanned the area outside the small airfield for the driver they'd been told to expect. "Vichy swine. That'll teach him to try to deflect the Red Cross from their duties. Ah, there's the signal."

Paul strode off toward a misshapen truck whose lights flashed in a quick pattern. Throwing the equipment into the back, he lifted Patrice in beside the driver before climbing in himself and handing the driver a roll of Vichy francs. The engine of the truck sputtered to life and they lumbered out onto one of the dark roads.

"Welcome Corsica," the driver said, his heavy accent nearly obliterating the words.

Patrice was staring at Paul, still in shock, but she managed to mutter, "Thank you," to the driver, who ignored her. Paul was watching the road, a slight smile on his face.

255

They left the edge of the small town and climbed into the mountains, the truck grinding its protests at the increasing grade of the road. Patrice was glad she couldn't see what lay beside the road, but was terrified the driver might not know.

"Is now," he said abruptly, jerking the truck around an impossible curve and into a surprisingly flat valley. The truck hesitated, the driver flashed his lights on and off, on and off, then waited. Suddenly a light responded in the distance and the truck lurched forward through the darkness. Finally, it hesitated. "Out," the driver said abruptly.

"Thank you for the nice trip," Paul said, pulling Patrice out of the cab and grabbing one of the bags from the back. "The medicine is here," he added before closing the door on the driver's grunted reply.

Before Patrice could speak, the truck was making a furious retreat in the direction they had come.

A man headed toward them. "Hi," he said, with an obvious American accent. "I'm Major Lewis. Fred Lewis. I'm your pilot. Let's get the hell outta here."

They followed him to the small plane which hunkered on the field in the darkness. Paul threw the bag into the back, then lifted Patrice in. "Comfy?" he asked as he climbed into the seat next to the pilot.

"Not very," she said, squirming around, fighting with the bag for space. "Now that we're comfortable," she said, tapping him on the shoulder, "I would like to know just what the hell you were trying to do back there—get us killed? I can't believe you operated on that man's foot. He might have shot you—and me." Her voice was filled with the residual of fear and agitation. "What is in this bag? Are you here on vacation? Is this your tennis racket?"

Paul laughed. "All in good time. First, Major Lewis, what route do you have in mind?"

The Major removed several maps from his pocket. "Basically, we're going right straight across Italy, across the Adriatic and into a small resistance airfield a bit south of Dubrovnik."

"Across Italy?" Patrice asked, horrified at the idea. "Won't they shoot us down?"

Major Lewis grinned. "Sure, but the Eyetie gunners stink,

ma'am. We'll just fly around their guns and into the mountains in the middle of Italy and they'll give up. They're not too interested in getting up in the middle of the night to chase one plane. Don't worry, I was doing this run about twice a week, more or less, until last month. Milk run!" he concluded confidently, returning the map to his pocket and turning his attention to starting the plane.

"Paul, I still want to know about that little medical act you pulled at the airfield when we arrived."

Paul turned in his seat to face her. "What else could I do? He obviously wanted to test me. And it did turn out to be infected. And it was hard for him to run after us." He shrugged, giving her a boyish grin. "And besides, I took first aid at summer camp one year."

Patrice covered her face with her hands, shaking her head. "So all those medical terms you were throwing around . . ."

"Well, they sounded authentic, didn't they? Who knows, maybe he'll actually get better."

The roar of the engine ended their conversation. The plane bumped and jerked along the rough ground, the darkness outside seeming all the more threatening as Patrice thought of the nearly vertical twisting road which had brought them to the field. The engines raced louder, and just as she was convinced they were going to taxi into oblivion, the plane lurched into the sky, wobbling on its wings as it climbed. Patrice could hear the pilot whistling and relaxed a bit. The plane stopped bucking and settled down.

But just as Patrice sighed with relief, they began descending. "What's the matter?" she yelled over the noise of the engines.

"Nothing," Major Lewis replied. "Why?"

"Because we're going down, not up."

He laughed. "Makes us harder to spot coming in over the coast. Really, lady, you don't have to worry. Why don't you just try to sleep. We've got four hours ahead of us."

Paul turned in his seat. "He's right. And, though I hope it won't be true, you may use up all your energy reserves in the next few days."

Patrice glared at the backs of their heads, but realized it wasn't worth arguing over, so she curled up around the

257

lumpy bag and rested her head on it. "I won't sleep, but I'll rest," she said to herself.

The series of bumping turns jarred Patrice awake. For a moment, she had no idea where she was. She shook her head, sitting up and moaning as her back protested vehemently.

"What are you doing? Are we landing?" she yelled, causing Paul to jump.

"Because we've arrived, Sleeping Beauty. We're in Yugoslavia. Or will be in a moment." As he spoke, the wheels touched down and the plane rattled violently as it sped along the grassy field. Patrice clung to the bag for dear life, biting her lips to keep from screaming, until the plane finally stopped.

"That was awful!" she said, trying to reorganize herself.

"Thanks," Major Lewis replied as he steered toward a flashing light. "Always try to please the passengers." He set the brakes of the plane and two men quickly began to refill the tanks. "Look, I'm flying right out of here again to Malta. You radio through your channels if you need me to come back for you. This is Vasili. He'll get you into Dubrovnik and stay with you." Major Lewis grinned. "Vasili is a good man."

Paul helped Patrice step down, then yanked the bag out of the plane. As soon as the space was empty, two men climbed aboard, their heads bowed.

"Hurry now, Missus," Vasili said, pulling on her arm, and she turned to follow him into the woods at the edge of the field. The engines of the plane roared to life, and soon Patrice could hear them accelerating, then fading.

"Now is safe," Vasili said, leading them to a dilapidated truck. Patrice climbed inside quickly, immediately followed by Paul and Vasili, who sandwiched her between them.

"I will taking you into Dubrovnik and give you there to someone other. I know nothing about Dubrovnik except Germans. Did you bring?" He spoke to Paul as though Patrice did not exist.

Paul nodded, opening the bag between his feet and pulling out a sack that looked like a flour bag. "Just add water t

258

this and you can shape it any way you like, perhaps so it looks like a loaf of bread. Put the fuse in before it hardens. Any charge will set it off. It's about three times as powerful as dynamite. And try not to let it get too hot; it gets unstable." Paul was also acting as though she weren't there.

"Excuse me, but what is that?" she asked, irritation in her voice.

Paul grinned. "They call it 'Aunt Jemima,' like the pancake mix."

"Explosives, right?" Patrice sputtered. "Explosives!"

Paul nodded. "Right."

"You jammed me into the back of a tiny little plane with a bag filled with explosives? What are you, crazy? We could have been blown to kingdom come."

"No, it's more stable than that," Paul said, returning his attention to Vasili. "Do you understand?"

Vasili grinned. "So will Germans," he muttered, starting the engine of the truck and pulling cautiously out onto the road. "Germans understand real good."

Patrice fumed as the truck rumbled down toward the sea along a cliffside road which led to a tiny village.

"Here is finish," Vasili said, stopping. "Now wait. Someone will come." He looked at them expectantly until they got out of the truck. "I come back here five o'clock today, five o'clock tomorrow, then finish."

Paul nodded. "Wait half an hour each time. Who will meet us now?"

"Someone come."

"When? When will someone come?" Patrice asked.

"Soon," he replied, engaging the gears with a loud grinding and pulling away.

"This mission is not going well," Patrice said, moving her back against the stiffness which still held it. "So far."

"I think it's going just fine. We're here. And a bit ahead of schedule."

"How can you say that? First you perform surgery on a customs inspector, then you make me sleep on a bag of explosives, and then that driver acted as though I didn't exist. We don't even know who is coming to pick us up. And

259

you say this mission is going just fine." She had a terrible urge to pout.

Paul put his arms around her, drawing her to his chest. "There, there," he muttered. "You're just having a bad time."

She sighed. "And behaving like a baby about it," she replied, her voice stronger as she pushed away from his chest.

"Goucher," said a gentle, accented voice behind them, and they both spun around, startled.

"Johns Hopkins," Paul replied to the small woman with the sad, serious eyes.

"I am Antonia. Please hurry. Something very bad has happened. You should go back now. This is not place for you now. This is not place for anyone now."

"What happened?"

"The Nazis. The SS." Antonia covered her face with her hands, sobbing.

"Take us into Dubrovnik, please," Paul said softly. "It is very important or we would not ask you."

The woman raised her head to look into his eyes, tears streaming down her face. "You will carry this the rest of your life. Please spare yourself this pain."

Paul shook his head. "We have no choice."

The streets in the outskirts of the city seemed empty as they hurried along. The people who were out walked with their eyes lowered, their pace quick and frightened. At the edge of the ancient walled city, Antonia pulled her small car into an empty parking place and motioned for them to follow.

The gate was a deep passage through ancient stone walls. In the center stood a Nazi soldier. Antonia presented her papers, and Paul and Patrice produced their Swiss/Red Cross passports.

The German guard sneered. "So the Red Cross thinks they can do something here. When will you learn not to waste your time and efforts?" He stamped their documents and stepped aside.

They emerged into a narrow, winding old street, cobble

260

and picturesque. Patrice was putting her Swiss passport into her pocket when she heard Paul gag. She looked up suddenly, then grabbed the wall next to her to steady her wobbling knees, stunned by the sight.

Stakes had been driven into the streets, and from each of them hung a mutilated human carcass. "Oh, my God," Patrice said, turning away sharply. Even with her eyes closed, she could still see the bodies, entrails dangling, nailed to the posts with huge spikes.

"I tried to warn you," Antonia said.

"We must go to the convent," Patrice said, reaching for Paul's hand. "Please take us there."

"It will only be worse," the woman said, turning to lead them down the street, "but I will do as you ask."

Paul put his arm across Patrice's shoulders. "They're animals. How could they do this?"

Patrice tried to keep her eyes lowered, repulsed by the dismembered bodies that lay scattered in the streets, and the stench of death that permeated the air.

Antonia hurried to the cathedral square, but hesitated before they entered. "Here it is the worst. Please, go no further."

"We must go to the convent," Paul said again, then stepped around her. "Oh, shit, Patrice. Don't look."

He was too late. Patrice had followed him into the square. Hundreds of bodies were heaped carelessly, slaughtered like sheep, stomachs slit open, blood and entrails mingling and flowing in the street. Some of the people still moved, still moaned.

Antonia, her face turned away from the horror, led them up the steps of the cathedral and into the dim interior. Patrice took a deep breath of the incense-scented interior, then looked around. The emptiness was almost as shocking as the scene in the square, stunning in its absence of carnage.

"Where did the sisters hide?" Patrice asked Antonia. "Do you know where we could find them?"

Antonia nodded slowly. "I do not know what has happened to them. I hope they are safe. Mother Luke is my sister." She took a deep breath then released it slowly, obviously struggling with a decision. Finally, she said, "Not knowing will not change things. Come."

"You are very brave," Patrice said. "I am so sorry we are putting you through this."

"It is not you who do this to me. It is the stupidity of all people who make war. It is the Nazi animals who come to our country, and for what? Why? Nothing changes. No one learns." She took another deep, ragged breath. "If they have killed my sister, I will have to become just like them. Do you understand?"

Patrice nodded. "All too well."

Antonia led them through the nuns' passage into the Mother Superior's chapel, then down the stairs into the catacombs.

Antonia called something softly in a language unfamiliar to Patrice, then stopped, waiting. They moved forward a few meters and she called again. This time there was a low noise in response, and Antonia turned into an intersecting room.

Patrice heard Antonia gasp as she entered, her heart heavy, knowing before she saw. Each of the women had been stripped and tied spread-eagled to crypts and posts. It was obvious they had been raped, but that was probably the least of the outrages committed against them.

"Eleni," Antonia cried, running to one of the women, throwing herself over the inert form.

"Antonia," Patrice heard the woman rasp and hurried to her side, quickly untying her hands.

"Paul, others may be alive," she said, but he was already rushing from one to the next as Patrice turned to the woman in front of her. "Is this Mother Luke?"

"Yes, my daughter," the woman whispered.

"I'm so sorry. We were too late. I'm so sorry," Patrice cried, draping a nearby habit over the woman's chilled form.

"You could have done nothing," Mother Luke said slowly. "You would have died with us."

"Sister Camille sends me," Patrice said.

A small smile changed the woman's face. "Our dear Camille. How I love that child. Tell her I am sorry about her Butterflies. We tried to protect them, but all have been killed. All of us."

"I promise you, we will take revenge for this," Patrice said, clutching Mother Luke's hand, tears streaming down her face.

"No, my daughter, God will take revenge. You must work for good only." Her eyes shifted to her sister's face and she said something in the same language the woman had called out in. Patrice withdrew to leave them in private.

"Paul?"

He stood, his face streaked with tears, shaking his head. "Not one. Not one. Why?"

Patrice put her arms around him and he enclosed her with his own. "Because of some damn political ideas," she said bitterly.

17

ALL THE BUTTERFLIES? And all the nuns? How could they do this?" Whitney thought of the gentle, caring sisters who had been such a part of her life for the past year. "Dear God, when will this stop?" she said, leaning her head into her hands.

Primrose's jaw was locked with rage. "When we stop it. When we stop *him*."

Whitney raised her head. "Or when I become less of a magnet. Remember, the obsession with finding me has to do with finding that microfilm. How can they believe that eighteen months have passed and I still have not discovered it and turned it over to my government?"

Donohue shook his head. "It's more than just the microfilm now, I fear. You, a supposedly frail woman with one leg who they had thought tidily in their thrall, have embarrassed the mighty Nazis, made them look like ineffectual fools, stolen their diamonds, and returned with a crack unit to embarrass them again. If I understand Heydrich, he does not manage defeat well. He's looking for revenge now, though the microfilm and/or diamonds would be a bonus."

Whitney's eyes became fiery. "So to take revenge on me, he murders not only my Butterflies but also innocent nuns

He's a pig!" She put her fingertips against her forehead. "I'm beginning to feel like the angel of death, as though I attract murder to anyone I care for. Well, I plan to get even for this. I'll have his head."

Primrose grabbed Whitney's hand from her brow then slapped her sharply. "Stop feeling sorry for yourself," she hissed. "You act as though this were planned entirely to make you feel guilty, to torment you personally. We have all suffered losses, Whitney, personal and national. We have all made sacrifices. If you cannot understand that you are but a tiny cog in the machinery of life, perhaps you had best retreat to the safety of your Maryland estate and spend the rest of your life weeping for the injustices you have suffered."

Whitney stared at her, astonished, her hand slowly rising to cover her crimson cheek. "How dare—"

Donohue interrupted. "She's right, Whitney. This can't be personal for you anymore or you will only bring disaster upon yourself and everyone else. What happened in Dubrovnik may or may not have had anything to do with you, but I think it's pretty unreasonable for you to assume you have such terrible powers as to cause the death of so many people. This is how the Nazis have been working in every country they've gone into. This is no different from what they have done in Poland or Russia or Czechoslovakia. It's Heydrich and his kind. It's what we are trying to stop. But it's not personally attached to you, or me, or Primrose. It took me a long time to convince you it wasn't a game. How long will it take you to learn it isn't a vehicle for anger, either? Wasn't it Shakespeare who said, 'Vengeance is a dish best served cold'? Whitney, you've got to be a professional, now more than ever."

Whitney looked from one to the other, then grabbed her jacket and stepped outside into the bitter wind of the moors, her tears stinging her cheeks with their cold tracks.

She turned up the collar of her jacket and crammed her hands into the pockets, hunkering down into the force of the wind, defying it to slap her as Prim had done. How could they be so certain this wasn't directed at her? Whitney and her damn microfilm. Why didn't they just make another

265

machine? Why murder people to get to her? Donohue and Primrose couldn't understand what it felt like to draw pain and misery from every quarter. They hadn't been there when Perry died. They hadn't felt the terror of running away from the SS. They simply didn't know how much she had to fear.

Whitney strode along the frozen ground through the dead grasses, climbing a hill which would hide the Kordas' replica village below once she'd crested it. Everyone on the mission had come to call the village "Hollywood," and normally Whitney liked it and found it charming. Today it represented everything that had hurt her, and she wanted it to go away and take all the lies and pain it represented with it.

The ground was stony, uneven, yet she walked steadily without really watching her way, her mind turning her anger and hurt into a meaningless babble of resentment.

She reached the crest and paused, glaring down at Hollywood. "As though you have all the answers," she muttered before turning her back. On the other side of the hill, the ground sloped sharply down to a stony, long-barren river bottom. Whitney kept her pace steady, choosing a path through the rocks, then turned to follow the course of the vacant stream.

Suddenly she stopped, halted by a thought: *Where would I be if not here; what would I be doing if not this?* "I don't know," she said aloud, lowering herself onto a gray boulder as she focused on the idea, ignoring the damp cold of the air, shielded from the wind.

With the toe of her "real" foot, she stirred a hole into a gathering of gravel the stream had stored in the lee of the boulder.

"What was it I expected my life to be?" she muttered. "If I'd wanted to stay in the Valley, why didn't I go back after Perry died? Why didn't I stay after escaping from the Germans?" She reversed the direction of her stir, examining the ideas.

"My God, I'm doing this because it's what I want. And Donohue is right. I'm not so powerful as to be the only reason things happen. This is my life, and things happen in people's lives. I don't want to be anyone or anything else.

Nobody's forcing me to make these choices. No one has ever forced me." Her foot stopped in the gravel and she stared down at the pattern she had made: a perfect heart.

She started back up the rocky slope feeling more certain and confident.

She opened the door to the control shack and strode inside. "I owe everyone an apology for letting my personal grief get the better of me." Prim and Donohue had been joined by Erik, and the three of them looked up, startled. "We have a very important job to do, and you have my full commitment. It's time we began to teach these Nazi animals that they don't have unlimited license in this world. And I have the feeling it was probably Mary Astor or Bette Davis who said 'Vengeance is a dish best served cold.' Now, let's get to work."

They sat in a semicircle around the glowing fire, the horizontal source of light making the shadows in the corners of the room the more distant, the colder.

"Considering the delicacy of the operation, I should be quite leery of using anything but the subtlest of signals and the most obtuse of codes," the new arrival said, his singsong accent irritating to Whitney for its monotonous, whiney quality. For all his dashing good looks, Whitney thought, Andrew Collins, the Raja Abichandri, seemed a very fey man.

"Did you have a question, Countess?" he said, and Whitney started.

"No," she said, regretting the guilt she could hear in her voice. "I was simply listening."

Collins nodded. "As I said, the code we have devised is useful, for it can be given in written or visual form. It is based on the sign language used by the Indians." His eyes locked with Whitney's. "The *American* Indians."

He doesn't like me any more than I like him, Whitney thought.

"I shall begin to teach you the hand signals and their written counterparts in the morning. We have two days before I must depart, but Tricycle is most familiar with the code and can assist you in the rehearsing of it."

267

Whitney glanced over at Prim and her husband, their shoulders and knees touching as though by accident. Whitney reached impulsively for Erik's hand, caressing it lightly, and he squeezed back.

Donohue rose as Collins resumed his seat. "Thank you, Andrew. Incidentally, Andrew has been able to provide independent confirmation that our target will indeed be in Belgium on the date planned. As you may have surmised, Tricycle has come to round out our mission. His contribution to date has been planning your arrival in Belgium. Dusko?"

"Parachute," Tricycle said.

Erik shook his head. "No, not Whitney."

"Wait a minute," she said, irritated at his assumption. "I can learn to do that. It can't be much worse than a hundred other things we do down in Hollywood."

Erik turned to her. "Jumping off a wall in Hollywood and jumping out of a plane, probably at night into ground you don't know, are very different. Dusko, isn't there some way we can go in by boat?"

Tricycle shook his head. "You've been into Europe, Erik. We all know the Jerries have it all tied up. The largest craft you can take in is a rowboat, and then it had best be filled with fish, of which the soldiers can take half."

Ross Robbins lit a cigarette, his Zippo lighter grinding into the tension in the room. "I don't know how thrilled I am to be leaping out of the sky with a bunch of explosives tied to my back."

"They wouldn't be tied to your back," Whitney said. "I am certainly capable of learning how to land properly on my good leg. You don't have to make special plans for me. I can hold up my end of this operation without special treatment."

Erik turned to her, taking both her hands. "I am sure you can. But if something were to happen to you, or to anyone else in the party, there is no provision for medical care in this operation."

Magda snapped her head around. "You mean if I get hurt or break my leg, you'll just leave me there?"

Tricycle shook his head. "No, my dear, of course not. We'll shoot you. We cannot afford to have this mission compromised by someone being taken prisoner."

268

The peat fire hissed into the silence.

"But if we came down from the north by land, using trains or available vehicles," Tricycle began softly, almost to himself, "split up into twos and threes, and each did not know the route of the others . . ."

"Then you wouldn't have to kill me," Magda finished, already satisfied.

"And I wouldn't have to blow up on impact," Robbins added, stubbing out his cigarette, then lighting another.

"Each group would still know the rendezvous," Whitney said. "We could still be betrayed." She shook her head. "Small groups would appear to increase the risk to everyone."

Donohue put his foot up on the rail around the fireplace, then leaned forward on his knee. "You have the unique advantage of all being right, so I shall make the decision. Magda, Lady Primrose, Abbé, Erik, and Dusko, you will go in by parachute. Whitney, you, Vota, Jan, and Ross will go in through the north coast of the Netherlands. We have some friends there who will help. You will carry the explosives."

Whitney caught Ross's eye and winked. "As long as we don't have to lay any priming cord," she said softly.

Donohue ran his palm across his hair. "This mission, briefly, is perhaps one of the most important you'll ever join. We've had a taste this week of the cruelty and power of the Germans, and Reinhard Heydrich is one of the biggest in the Nazi organization. He's a cruel, heartless man who has personally ordered massive executions, and from what we understand, his objective in this meeting is to present a plan more odious than anything he has thought of so far. He will propose the wholesale murder of all the Jews in Europe."

There was a gasp from several people in the room and a buzz of conversation, but Donohue held up his hand for silence.

"We must assassinate him before he can make his presentation in Brussels. Everything each of you does is significant and important. Don't let him get away. The man is a monster, and we are the only people who can stop him. If we don't, it is very likely he will succeed Hitler, and I am afraid he would be a far more terrible adversary than his mentor.''

"From now on, whenever someone says 'storm at sea,' I will know precisely what they mean.'' Whitney swallowed hard. "I always thought seasickness was psychosomatic.''

"In my country we do not have the sea,'' Jan Myjuszk said. "Now I know why.''

"Can we please talk about something else?'' Vota Rajic said, putting his hand gently over his stomach. "I can play saxophone, you know. Also accordion.''

"Well, then, if we get stopped, you're the one-man band who will have to perform,'' Ross replied.

"If they ask me to sing, we're cooked,'' Whitney said, settling down among the instruments in the back of the truck.

"No more than if they ask any of us to play this stuff.'' Ross pulled himself behind the wheel of the truck. "Still, this is one of Donohue's better efforts. Did you look at the contract and travel documents?''

Whitney shook her head.

"It's diabolical. We're supposed to be on our way to entertain at the Nazi Army Officers' Club in Brussels.''

"When did he give you that?'' Whitney giggled.

"Just before he left.'' Ross started the engine and ground the gears as he pulled out.

"I cannot imagine they would test us by asking us to perform. That wouldn't make any sense,'' Whitney said. "And the papers we have are legit.''

Ross nodded his agreement. "We'll only be in trouble if they want to search the equipment.''

"Or if we hit a bump and the instruments explode.''

"And today just north of Amsterdam an exploding xylophone killed four brave soldiers of the Reich,'' Ross said in his best German radio announcer impression, getting appreciative laughter from the other three, far heartier than the joke warranted. All four of them were, he knew, tense with pre-mission jitters which heightened not only the humor, but also the seasickness.

The flat countryside of Holland flowed past, the windmills

still standing sedate, fat sentry to the carefully outlined fields; the cows clustering in farmyards or huddling against the cold in the fields.

"It all seems so normal," Ross muttered, and Whitney nodded.

"As though they don't know about the war yet."

As Whitney spoke, they rounded a turn and encountered the first truck of a convoy emblazoned with the red-and-black flag of Germany. Whitney felt her back tense, certain one of the trucks would at any moment turn into the path of their vehicle, to stop them. She shuddered.

"I guess they must know about the war," Ross said, his voice disgusted.

"We should make all blow up," Jan hissed from the back seat.

The convoy must have contained two hundred trucks moving toward the North Sea. Whitney thought of the fat, contented cows and the tidy little farms and felt great sorrow for the people who had not chosen the life in which they were about to be immersed.

As their truck entered the small, tidy town of Deventer, Whitney glanced at her watch. "We're on schedule," she said.

"If it goes well, we will meet the others as planned. We should have only about another hundred miles to the safe house." Ross flipped a Lucky Strike out of his pack and lit it, then put the pack back into his pocket.

Whitney had watched him idly, then turned to look out the window at a charming little house. Suddenly she turned back. "Ross, your cigarettes!"

"You want one?"

"They're *Luckies!* And they're in your shirt pocket!" Whitney's eyes darted to the road, then back to Ross, and to the road.

"Oh, shit! Pardon, ma'am." He grabbed the packet from his pocket and began to throw it out the window.

"No! Don't! It would be an announcement of our presence. We have to get rid of them in another way. How about hiding the pack in the instruments?"

"Right. If the Jerries get to looking into the instrument

271

cases, we're finished anyway." Ross surrendered the cigarettes. "I've been meaning to cut down."

"I put in drums," Vota said, taking the pack. "None plays drums."

They used the darkness to hide their approach to the safe house Tricycle had arranged.

Leaning against the rough stone of the barn, Whitney strained to sort out the noise of the countryside so she would know when she heard the plane. The barren limbs of the trees creaked lightly in the breeze from the sea. She glanced again at her watch, the dial glowing dimly in the shadow in which she stood. It wasn't yet two in the morning and that was the earliest they could be expected.

She shifted her weight slightly, trying to keep the circulation in her foot moving, wiggling her toes inside the thick felt boot and heavy wool sock she wore.

"At least I won't have more than five toes get frostbite," she said to herself, then giggled quietly. "And they thought there was no advantage to having one leg!"

She had volunteered to take the watch outside while Ross, Vota, and Jan wired the bombs they would use during their planned escape as well as the rockets Ross had designed to use against Heydrich and his guards. Once the others arrived, the mission would proceed at breakneck speed toward their "rendezvous with Reinhard," as Whitney had dubbed it.

Whitney cupped her hand around her ear to filter out the wind. "Come on," she said, looking up at the clouds, wondering what it would be like to jump from a plane. "You were right, Erik. I had no business trying that."

Suddenly she heard it, a tiny buzz at first. She listened intently, then rapped a quick tattoo on the door. Jan slipped outside to join her, a lantern in his hand.

"I will go to meet. You go for warm. This night too short." He put an awkward hand on her shoulder. "I bring safe. You see."

Despite his reassurance, Whitney stood where she was listening to the buzz of the plane get louder until it remained

272

a steady drone, then recede before she slipped into the relative warmth of the barn.

Ross looked up, cupped his right hand into a symbol, and cocked his head. Whitney responded with three quick gestures, her hand moving confidently. He nodded briskly, then lit one of his precious Luckies and went back to work.

Whitney moved to the small pot of warming coals, bending to take some of the chill from her fingers and glance again at her watch. In six hours it would all be over.

The door opened and Erik entered, swinging his parachute to the floor and striding to encircle Whitney in his embrace. "Right on target," he whispered.

"And right on time," she answered, glad to have him safe.

Magda put her hands and face as close to the pot of coals as she could. "I've never been so cold in my life," she muttered. "I'm not sure this isn't worse than prison. Damn, it was cold and dark up there."

Prim joined her at the coals. "But you were wonderful. You just stepped out."

Magda tried not to look too pleased. "Once you've been sentenced to death, everything else seems pretty easy." Whitney could see she was proud of the compliment, however. "Besides, I owe it to the girls."

It was the first she'd spoken about the Butterflies since Whitney had told her of the attack at the convent. "We all do," she said softly. "And to the rest of the world."

The Abbé had joined Ross in his work, as had Tricycle. Primrose, Whitney, and Magda gave them food and coffee as they finished.

"It's amazing; it's Hollywood," Whitney whispered almost soundlessly to Primrose as they emerged from the back of the farmer's truck.

Primrose signaled for silence, then added the one for "I agree," as they found their way to their assigned spots.

Whitney, Magda, and Primrose were bundled in warm farm-wife clothing, each carrying a basket of eggs. Erik, Vota, Jan, and Tricycle had set up a barricade and began to dig a pothole which they could then appear to repair. The Abbé and Ross Robbins were stationed at the other end of the narrow street, serving as an advance lookout for Heydrich's car.

Tricycle had told them on the way in to the village that the driver of Heydrich's car was one of the OSS's deepest moles inside the SS. "Try not to kill him if you can, but he knows his risks."

Whitney stood on one corner with Magda, while Primrose took her basket across the street. As planned, Whitney had approached one door, and to her surprise, sold six eggs. It was the only thing they had not rehearsed, and Whitney suddenly realized the error. The woman took her time choosing the eggs, then told Whitney to wait. Magda stood at the curb, watching for Ross's signal.

The housewife had gone to get the money to pay for the eggs and was taking longer than Whitney wished when she heard Magda hiss. Whitney turned to look toward Ross and the Abbé and saw the car entering the street.

Quickly she put the full basket of eggs inside the house and pulled the door closed, then hurried down to the street, taking the bomb she was to use from Magda's basket. As she had rehearsed so many times, she had slipped around the corner to plant the explosive, blocking off the escape route, when she realized something was wrong. The streets were empty and much too quiet.

She stepped back to look again at the car, then shouted, "It's a trap!"

Suddenly doors all along the street burst open and soldiers in black uniforms poured out, guns blazing. Whitney lit the fuse of her bomb, counting as it burned, then threw the bomb toward a group of soldiers who were shooting at Erik, Tricycle, and the Czechs. She quickly dropped to the ground as she released it, and covered her head. As she fell, she saw Magda grab her stomach and crumple to the ground. Whitney began to get up, almost as a reflex, then put her head down, remembering Tricycle's rule: Save yourself. She felt the thud of the explosion, then looked up to see an SS man club Primrose with the butt of his rifle. She was astonished to see Tricycle disappear into a doorway under a Nazi flag, but had no more time to think about it as, in the next instant, Whitney was yanked to her feet and thrown ove

Erik's shoulder as he ran a zigzag pattern down a small alley. He hoisted her over a fence and quickly followed.

"Inside," he said, pushing open the door to a cellar under the house. Closing her eyes to adjust to the dark, Whitney felt her way down the stairs and along the wall, then waited for Erik, who, strangely, was running his hands along the floor.

"God bless the Belgians for their consistency," he said, and she heard a creak, then smelled an overwhelmingly foul odor. "Come on," Erik said.

"Where?" she asked as she followed his pulling hand.

"Into the sewer," he hissed. "Watch your step."

18

THERE HAD BEEN no noise in the house for more than an hour. Ross crept over to the cellar door and peered out. The slice of farmyard he could see was deserted. He pushed his shoulder against the door, lifting it slowly, scanning the wider field of vision before opening the door and stepping up into the farmyard.

Jan and Vota quickly emerged and Ross lowered the door as carefully as he had raised it. Silently, the three of them slipped through the shadows along the edge of the house, watching warily for any movement, then crouched low and ran across the farmyard into a small woods. Ross paused to remove his watch and unscrewed the back to reveal a compass. He took several readings, then replaced the back and led the others to the small road which passed the farm.

The shoulder of the road was smooth, allowing them to walk quickly, each man vigilant for the sounds of approaching vehicles.

Ross's fury kept off the cold of the night. It was obvious they had been sold out. They had felt so smug because no one entering had had any trouble, but the damn Jerries must have been laughing like hell, watching the little drama unfold. The only surprise they'd given the SS was that some o them had escaped. He'd seen Erik and Whitney disappear down an alley, but he knew Magda and the Abbé had been injured and taken. Jan told him Tricycle disappeared when the shooting started, and Vota reported that it looked as though Lady Primrose had been taken prisoner.

Now the three of them had to try to get out without another disaster. Ross was not about to try to make the rendezvous at Zeebrugge which Donohue had set up. It might be just another trap and they would still end up in the hands of the Jerries. But short of heading for the coast away from Zeebrugge, he had no plan, though he'd assured the two Czechs he knew precisely what they would do. They were headed roughly northeast, away from the closest coast but toward Antwerp, where they just might be able to rustle up something.

Jan tapped his shoulder and gestured toward the ditch, and Ross complied immediately. He didn't have to hear the car coming to take evasive action. The three of them scampered over a low dike of earth at the edge of a field and flattened against it just as the low lights of the car came into view. It ground and sputtered, and Ross could hear the occupants having a loud argument in German.

"Maybe the bastards will shoot each other and we can steal the truck," he thought, but soon it disappeared. They waited until the silence was complete, then re-emerged on the road.

They had walked silently, keeping a rigorous pace, for about three hours from the farmhouse when Ross heard something he couldn't define and held up his hand for them to halt. The sound seemed to ebb and flow on the wind, but finally he determined it was singing that seemed to be coming from the other side of a large hill to their right. The three of them left the road and climbed the hill, creeping over the top on their bellies.

The singing became louder and much more discernible, and its source more obvious. Ross grinned. Below the hill was one of the low countries' famous river canals, and the song was emanating from a canal boat tied up at the shore.

277

Jan wriggled over next to Ross and muttered in a very low voice, "Is folk song from Slovakia."

"This guy's a little out of his way, isn't he?" Ross murmured.

"We are also," Jan replied, listening intently, then grinning and rising to his feet. "Come, he is friend." He started down the hill as Ross grabbed for his leg and missed.

Vota immediately rose to follow, but Ross managed to snare his foot and he fell with a loud curse. "Why the matter?"

"The matter is we are in Nazi-occupied territory and they would just love to get their hands on us. This might be another trap."

Vota shook his head. "No. This song is from part of Slovakia which is home to us. It is song used by Resistance to know each other because is words in old speech not talk by outside."

As though confirming his words, Jan had reached the boat and called out something. Instantly the singer emerged, engulfing Jan in a huge hug. Jan motioned and Vota began to get up, but Ross held him back, suspicious of another trap.

After ten minutes, however, it became obvious to Ross that no Nazis were waiting for them, and he and Vota hurried down the hill.

"Why waiting?" Jan asked. "Is my cousin, Iwan. He also is with us."

Ross was completely befuddled. "But what is he doing here? Now? Just exactly where and when we need him?"

Iwan stepped forward, shaking Ross's hand. "Is luck of Irish. I bring load of guns to French underground fighters from England. Now going back. You want go with? Is much hiding in boat. I have good papers and," he stopped and grinned broadly, "much bribe in port."

Well, Ross thought, *I was looking for any opportunity that came along, even as preposterous as this one is.*

"Great," Ross said. "Let's just get back to England as soon as possible."

"Is good. You like scotch whiskey?"

*   *   *

278

Ross watched as Iwan and the Royal Navy patrol boat captain exchanged friendly greetings, then shook his head. The scene was almost a replay of the exit they'd made from Holland thirteen very bumpy hours earlier before crossing the English Channel. Iwan had an uncanny knack for making himself visible and invisible at the same time. He also had an amazing capacity for scotch, having consumed the better part of a fifth of the real thing since they'd left the canalside in Belgium. Ross shook his head. Iwan was the stuff of which war legends were made.

"I said right to London, park at dock of king," Iwan said as he returned from his conference with the Royal Navy captain. "My friend Fitzwilliam say okay, king expecting." He laughed uproariously, breaking into yet another of his Czech songs as he turned the boat into the Thames.

To Ross's infinite relief, Iwan chose to set ashore at a public quay. Ross left the Czechs to their parting and went immediately to a phone box, dialing the special number then giving a code phrase to the operator. As he waited, his eyes scanned the people and doorways reflexively.

"Ross, what the hell happened? Why didn't anyone meet the escape boat at Zeebrugge? We almost lost them in an ambush." Donohue sounded furious.

"Somebody sold us out," Ross replied. "I have the two Czechs with me. Where can we meet?"

Donohue gave him an address, and Ross motioned for Jan and Vota, who left Iwan with hugs and a babble of Czech. As Ross turned to find a taxi, Iwan called, "Good luck on you, Yank. You plenty good man."

Ross grinned, raising his hand in a wave. "You plenty good man, too, Iwan."

Patrice and Paul arrived just as Ross and the Czechs emerged from their taxi, and the five of them stood in silent tension in the lift of the office building where they were to meet Donohue. The sign on the office door said, "C. Dickens, Adoptions." Patrice rolled her eyes as she entered the outer office.

Donohue stood behind a rattletrap desk covered with papers. The receptionist's desk was deserted.

"Clever name," Patrice said.

"Believe it or not, it's legitimate. Carolyn Dickens is an old friend who is taking the afternoon off. Now let's get to work."

They drew up chairs around the desk. Donohue waited until everyone was settled, then said, "Ross?"

In a clear, dispassionate way, Ross recounted the catastrophe in the street at Aalst. "I saw Erik carrying Whitney down a small alley. I don't know what happened to them. I do know both the Abbé and Magda were hit, and Vota saw Primrose being taken prisoner. I don't know what happened to Tricycle. He disappeared when the shooting started."

Donohue ran his hand across his hair. "It definitely sounds as though they were expecting us. I should have been suspicious when there was no anti-aircraft fire on the plane. Damn." He paced across the office, then turned. "Jan, you and Vota were with Dusko and Erik. Did you see what happened to Dusko?"

Jan thought for a moment, then nodded. "I think he went into a house where Germans came out."

No one said anything for a long time. Finally Patrice muttered, "It would break Prim's heart."

Donohue cleared his throat. "I think we should wait to see what Dusko himself has to say before we leap to any conclusions. Let's find out what we can about who's been taken and who's on their way home. I'll get messages to my sources and we can begin looking."

"Is it worth trying Laurel?" Patrice asked. "After all, she told us where and when Heydrich's meeting. . . . Oh, that bitch."

"And then probably told Heydrich she'd heard something at the beauty parlor," Donohue said sarcastically.

"You don't know Laurel. She would make it sound plausible. And certainly someone betrayed the operation. We have no idea who it might have been. Maybe it was Tricycle. Maybe it was Laurel. Maybe they were working together. Shall I see if I can get her to reveal anything?"

"More than any other priority," Donohue replied.

*   *   *

280

"I probably don't want to know this," Whitney whispered to Erik as he came down into the tunnel beside her, "but when you use the word 'sewer' do you mean storm sewer?"

"You don't want to know," Erik replied, taking her hand as he moved along.

Erik carried a flashlight, but daylight filtered down through street gratings. Each time they reached a grating, Whitney turned her face upward and took a big gulp of fresh air.

They had been bearing constantly to the right whenever they had a choice of routes, sometimes through tunnels in which they could walk erect, and sometimes having to stoop closer to the rivulet of slime which ran down the center of the tunnels, making Whitney gag at the smell.

After nearly an hour, they emerged from one of the smaller tunnels into a large, domed passage. Erik hesitated at the mouth of the smaller tunnel, looking and listening.

"I believe we've become quite lucky. I think this is one of the main sewers leading from Brussels to the sea." He smiled. "It may smell a bit better. I think Brussels has a sewage processing area. We must be more careful, however, for sewers such as these in Paris have been used by the Resistance, and the soldiers patrol them. How do you feel?"

Whitney thought for a moment, then slipped her arms around him and pressed her cheek to his chest. "Scared, sad, betrayed, grateful to be alive and uncaptured, frightened for the others, and glad to be with you."

He returned her embrace. "But not tired? No pain in your leg?"

"No, I'm really fine."

"Good, for we must walk several miles."

"Toward the sea?" Whitney asked.

"No, into Brussels. I think they will be watching for us at the seaports. I am glad we are in local dress, for we will be more difficult to pick from a crowd in Brussels." He looked up and down the empty passage again, then jumped down to the dry stone of the larger tunnel. After looking up and down once more, Erik held his arms up and helped Whitney down beside him.

The tunnel seemed to have more light than the ones through which they had been walking, and what effluent

281

there was flowed inside a channel in the low center. The stone surface on which they walked angled slightly downward toward the center and Whitney realized she would have to bear her weight on her bad leg.

As though reading her thoughts, Erik picked her up and took a long stride across the center channel, then set her down. "If you get tired, we can change back," he said, tucking her hand into his and setting off.

The light coming through the gratings overhead was getting dimmer, and often the gratings seemed to be in basements or courtyards of large buildings. Whitney and Erik stopped more frequently to listen or to hide when they heard voices overhead. Several times Erik had climbed the rungs on the walls to peer out, looking for a landmark he might recognize. Other times they would have to detour around an outflow from a pipe or drain which had left a thick coating of mucky slime on the stones, but the smell was far less oppressive than it had been in the morning.

One such outflow bore a distinctly antiseptic smell, and Erik whispered, "Hospital," as he hoisted Whitney across the center channel. They had walked a few steps farther when he paused again to climb to a grating.

"We are under the basement storage room of a hospital the Germans have taken over. There are hundreds of uniforms hanging up there," he whispered, taking her hand to lead her along, but Whitney pulled back.

"Wait," she whispered. "Do you think you could climb up and steal a couple?"

A grin spread across his face. "What rank would you like to be?"

Whitney felt nervous down in the sewer alone after he had climbed up and pushed the grate to one side. It had become quite dark and she could hear rustling noises around her. She pulled up onto the rungs, uncomfortable in her position, but choosing that discomfort over a possible encounter with rats.

"I think we can get out through here," Erik said, startling her by grabbing her wrist. Whitney clenched her jaw hard to

282

keep from screaming before he lifted her above the grating. "What's the matter?"

"Rats," she squeaked.

Erik nodded matter-of-factly. "Probably big ones."

Whitney shuddered.

"These are all Luftwaffe uniforms. Here, see if this will fit." He extended a uniform shirt. Whitney removed her farm-wife sweater and slipped into the crisply pressed shirt.

"Just right," she said. She pulled on a pair of trousers which were too large, then found a smaller pair which fit not only around the waist but also in length.

Erik had finished dressing, tucking his pant legs inside the highly polished jackboots and buttoning the tunic as Whitney found boots which were not too large, then shrugged into a jacket. Erik came to assist her with the overcoat, putting on the finishing details, then stepping back to assess his work.

He shook his head. "There is only one problem," he said, surveying her.

"My hair," Whitney sighed and Erik nodded.

"I fear so."

She shrugged. "So cut it."

He pulled a knife from his pocket as she pulled her peasant skirt around her shoulders to catch the fallen locks. Erik ran his fingers through her hair, letting the strands cascade.

She caught his hand, turning to look up. "It will grow back."

When he had finished, he said, "Now it looks bad enough to be a German army barber's work. I'm so sorry."

She reached up to give him a quick kiss. "I shall be like Patrice and wear hats and everyone will think I'm terribly chic. Now shall we get out of here?"

Erik bundled up their discarded clothing and all the blond hair, throwing it down into the sewer. "Now you can be thankful for the rats, for they will eat the evidence." He pulled the grate back into place, then quietly opened the door, slipping out into the hallway with Whitney close behind. They scurried along the deserted passageway, trying doors as they went. Finally one of the doors opened, revealing a stairway.

They climbed the first flight, but the doorway was locked,

so they ascended another flight. They could hear voices and bustle out in the hallway, and Erik tried the door, finding it open.

"Hold your hat like this," he demonstrated, "until we get outside, and then pull it on low over your eyes. I'll talk, you nod."

He pulled the door open and Whitney followed him out into the hall. As they walked, apparently engrossed in a discussion, people seemed to ignore them. Whitney's heart pounded each time anyone glanced in their direction, but Erik didn't seem to notice.

They reached a junction where the hallway intersected another. Erik hesitated, allowing a wheeled cart to pass, and Whitney glanced at the occupant, then gasped. Erik turned quickly to follow her eyes, then put his hand on her shoulder and steered Whitney in the direction from which the cart had come.

"This way, Lieutenant," he said in German, then added, "There's nothing we can do now," under his breath in English. "At least now you know Magda's alive."

Whitney was afraid she would faint from the shock of seeing Magda lying on the cart. She had been very pale and her eyes had been closed, but it was obvious she was still alive. Whitney longed to turn back to save Magda, but she realized Erik was right.

They emerged from the front of the hospital and set their caps. Erik hesitated, surveying the parking area, then struck out toward a remote row of cars.

"*Herr Colonel*," a voice said behind them. Erik turned, a look of irritation on his face at the interruption. "May I bring your car around?"

"*Nein, danke schön*," Erik replied, turning back. "Since we don't know which one we're going to steal," he added under his breath to Whitney.

Aware that the man was probably watching them, Erik led Whitney around the corner of the hospital. A large black Mercedes sedan was parked in a space marked "*Doktor Braun*."

Erik looked around, then tried the door handle. When it opened, he slipped inside and fumbled under the steering

284

column for a moment. The engine roared to life and Whitney quickly climbed into the lush comfort of the passenger seat.

"Can't we make a plan to get Magda out?" she asked, feeling terribly guilty at their own escape.

"She was unconscious, Whitney. They will do their best to save her life so she can tell them what she knows. When we get back, Donohue will get her out."

He turned on the car's headlights and backed out of the space, then turned into the flow of traffic on the street.

"Have you ever been in Brussels?" Whitney asked.

"Once," Erik said. "I think I know where we are." He glanced down at the dashboard. "We can be grateful to *Herr Doktor* Braun. The gas tank is full."

Whitney had fallen asleep, exhaustion claiming her despite her efforts to help Erik stay alert, but she awoke with a start when he said, "Hot dog!"

"Hot dog?" she muttered, struggling to understand.

"Isn't that the American expression for something good? I hear Robbins say that sometimes."

"Perhaps in some circles," she said. "Now what is worthy of a 'hot dog!'?" She sat up, her back protesting the motion.

"That," Erik said, pointing across the road, "is a 'hot dog!' "

She nodded. "An airfield," she said, as though identifying it for him. Then a grin spread across her face. "An airfield," she said with delight. "And we're wearing Luftwaffe uniforms."

"And I know how to fly a plane," he reminded her.

"Hot dog!" Whitney said, throwing her arms around his neck, then sobering. "But how do we get one of the planes without papers?"

"Arrogance," he replied confidently. "German soldiers respond very well to arrogance."

He pulled the car in beside a small shack which served as an airfield office. As Erik emerged from the car, a soldier appeared from inside the building. Whitney wished she could hear what they were saying, but she didn't know if it would be proper military protocol for her to get out of the car before being summoned. She watched the exchange intently, Erik standing with his feet slightly spread, his gloves in one hand, in control. The soldier stood at attention, listening and nodding. When Erik finished speaking, the man turned and scurried away and Erik returned to the car, sliding in behind the wheel.

"I suppose he's going to warm up the plane and stock it with champagne for you," Whitney said with a nervous giggle.

"Not quite. I've given him a fool's errand which will keep him busy for a few minutes. When he returns, I have a more complex one which will keep him occupied while I steal a plane."

"But why two?"

"The first is to verify that I am an officer. Then he will give us a plane, and by the time he radios for verification, we will be out over the channel." He squeezed her hand. "Just believe me. I know my own people."

As he had predicted, the guard appeared with a lieutenant in tow. Erik stepped from the car, again in obvious control of the situation. Whitney held her breath, then let it out slowly as the two men saluted and Erik motioned to her to join him as he strode to the plane.

Whitney scrambled into the seat behind the pilot's. Erik followed into the pilot's seat, strapping himself in, then confidently turning dials and flipping switches. The engine coughed, coughed again, then caught, roaring as Erik signaled and the two young soldiers removed the blocks from the wheels and turned the plane.

As they taxied along the dark landing strip, Erik shouted, "They think I will be back because I have left my Mercedes."

He turned the plane quickly at the end of the runway and pushed the throttle forward. The ground sped past and Whitney willed the plane into the sky. Finally it complied, lurching away from the ground, climbing higher and higher into the clouds which would hide them out over the channel, past the batteries of antiaircraft guns aimed at England and the RAF.

"You must be so tired," Whitney said as she leaned forward, rubbing Erik's tense shoulders. "How do you know where we are?" she asked, scanning the mysterious dials.

"I don't," he said. "At least not precisely. I know we are headed toward England, though." His hand came up to cover hers. "We will be home soon."

Whitney dozed again, her head leaning against the back of Erik's seat. In her dream, they were sailing on Chesapeake Bay in her father's boat. Erik, however, was at the helm, and her father was sleeping. Patrice was swimming alongside, grinning and waving even though the seas were heavy. Whitney was laughing at her antics.

Suddenly they were hit by a heavy wave that made Whitney scream, waking abruptly to find the plane tilting wildly to the right.

"We're hit," Erik yelled as he wrestled with the control stick. "Brace yourself. We're going down."

"But where are we?"

"England, I hope," he shouted.

They were enveloped in a shroud of clouds and Whitney stared out the windshield, expecting the clouds to part to reveal storm-tossed waves or German guns below.

The plane pitched and bucked, as Erik tried to keep it steady. There were two more thuds and bright flashes, but neither hit them.

"I think they're ours, judging from the angle," Erik said, his voice as tight as his grip.

Suddenly the clouds parted and Whitney could see a grassy field below, hemmed by tidy rock walls.

"It's England," she shouted, excitedly.

"Brace yourself," Erik yelled back as the plane descended rapidly.

There was a thunderous crash, then a terrible grinding noise as the plane rotated to a stop.

"Erik," Whitney called, leaning forward. "Erik, darling?"

He moaned and she squirmed forward, quickly noticing the bleeding gash on his forehead.

"Oh, no. I smell gasoline. Please, Erik. Wake up." When he showed no response, she retreated to her seat, then wormed forward on his other side, grabbing for the door handle, which was just beyond her reach. "Sorry, darling," she said, releasing his harness and pushing the seat forward, then wincing when his head thudded against the windshield. She grasped the door handle and pushed. The door opened and she yanked herself past Erik's seat and out onto the wing.

Outside the smell of gasoline was stronger. She pushed Erik and the seat back, then grabbed his tunic and yanked with all her might. He slumped to the side, his upper body outside the plane but his feet still inside.

"Come on, damn it," she shouted at him, grabbing his belt and hauling backward.

Suddenly whatever held his legs released and they both tumbled off the sheared wing and onto the frozen field, Erik landing on top of Whitney, pinning her with his unconscious weight.

She lay there for a moment, trying to catch her breath, then smelled smoke. She grabbed his shoulder with her free arm and rolled him away. Struggling to her feet, she saw flames filling the cockpit.

"Oh, God, why won't you wake up?" she said to his inert form, but he didn't stir. Quickly she ran to his legs and tucked one knee under each of her arms. "I'm sorry, darling. I hope I don't kill you, but we must get out of here." Digging in with her good foot, she pulled hard and he began to slide along the ground. She tried not to think of his bleeding head bouncing along on the frozen earth. She kept pulling until they were about thirty yards from the plane. Quickly she yanked off her overcoat, then lay down beside him and covered both of them.

The explosion sent a wave of searing heat and rained clumps of earth down on the coat, but the fire didn't reach them. Whitney waited until the rattle of dirt stopped, then threw back the coat and turned to inspect Erik.

"Righty-o now, Jerry, you just stay put," said a voice directly over her head. She looked up abruptly and smiled broadly into the apple-cheeked face of the Home Guard who held a 1915 vintage rifle on her.

"Oh, thank God we're home," she blurted and the man's face became puzzled. "Please, call an ambulance immediately. Please hurry. This man is badly injured."

The Home Guard just stared down at her. "You're a Yank. And a woman. What'll the ruddy Jerries think of next?"

19

"How do we know they're even alive?" Ross Robbins had tilted his chair back against the wall and was tapping rhythmically at the front legs with his heels, staring up at the wall, avoiding the eyes of the others.

"Magda was alive when we saw her being taken into the hospital," Whitney said, then winced as she moved her arm in the sling and her shoulder objected.

"Five days ago," Ross said tonelessly.

Whitney turned to glare at him. "If you don't want to save them, simply say so and leave it to the rest of us," she snapped.

He pushed away from the wall and the legs of the chair thudded against the floor. "How many lives are you willing to risk to maybe get four people back?"

Donohue held up his hand. "Whoa, you two. First, Whitney, if you please, you are not at liberty to include yourself in any rescue mission until your collarbone mends. And Erik and his leg cast also are out of play at the moment. Which means if—and I stress the if—there is to be a rescue mission, we must be certain there is a willing team on this side and, as Ross points out, someone to rescue."

"I'm sorry, Ross," Whitney said. "I just feel so powerless."

He nodded. "Me, too. And I'm not saying we shouldn't give it a go, but I don't want to risk my neck so we can give them a nice memorial service."

Erik pulled himself up in his hospital bed, using the bar that supported his broken leg. "Nor do you know for certain either that they are being held together or where to find them." He shook his head. "As far as I can judge, there is no rescue mission until more is known."

The door to the hospital room burst open and a large bouquet of flowers entered, followed by Patrice. Paul set the flowers on a table, as Patrice closed the door, then waved a piece of paper.

"We've got something. Karl Foch has never responded so quickly. Listen." She unfolded the letter. " 'I surmise from your missive that your friends were responsible for the attempt on RH. The foiling of same has elevated his status and he's making AH alternately happy and wary. His plan to begin shipping the victims to camps in Poland is already in action. The worst of it is that they're making the victims choose among themselves who goes on the trains. AH is euphoric. His writings sicken me. But they have yielded something I know you need. He talks about three who were captured in the attempt on RH and has ordered them kept alive because he thinks it's a way to remind RH who still has the upper hand. Two are in a hospital in Brussels and the third, a woman he calls 'The Nun' is somewhere he hasn't named. I will keep watching for further references in the diaries and let you know. Tell the people you work with that these terrors are madder than they ever suspected.' " Patrice looked around the room at each of the faces.

Ross leaned the chair back against the wall again, then lit a Lucky. "If they're badly injured, we can't take them out through the sewer," he said contemplatively. "We do have those uniforms you got out." He took a deep drag on his cigarette, then didn't continue.

Donohue ran his hand across the top of his head. "I don't like it. It's too much risk for too little reward. I regret if this sounds heartless, but none of them has any knowledge o future plans, for there were no future plans. The Butterfly operation has been decimated and they know little of any of the resistance groups we help. I'm sorry, because they are my friends as well, but I can't see any reason to take excessive risks to pull them out. Particularly when we don't know who is where and what condition they are in."

"Three," Whitney said pensively. "We know one is Magda. Perhaps she is the one they're calling 'The Nun.'"

"And perhaps it's Primrose," Patrice said.

"Which would mean, since they are calling one of the women by that name, they have associated whoever they have with the Butterfly operation. And with Whitney," Erik added. "Which means the reward is far greater than it would seem at first glance, because they all know where Whitney can be found. My guess is the three would be Primrose, Magda and the Abbé. Tricycle has been functioning as a double agent long enough to protect himself."

"Or to sell us out," Whitney replied. "He knew the whole plan, and we walked into an ambush that was set up perfectly."

Donohue held up his hand. "Wait a minute. I have known Dusko Popov for a very long time and I would hate to think my judgment so bad that I would have trusted someone who would betray us."

Erik's expression showed both the physical and mental anguish he felt. "Dusko has been a friend and partner to me as well, Colonel. He's saved me more than once. But I stood right next to him and watched him do nothing except save his own skin. Who knows what was going on in his mind? He probably saw how much trouble Primrose was in. Maybe it just froze any action he might have taken."

Ross picked at his fingernails. "I've worked with him too, you know, and I would hate to think he'd be a traitor, but somebody sure as hell sold us out. It could have been the guy who was supposed to be driving the car. None of us knew what he looked like, so how would we know if the driver was our guy or not? Maybe one of the folks who live at that castle up in Scotland saw a way to make a few bucks. What about those guys from Hollywood? What I'm trying to

291

say is not to hang Popov before he gets a chance. It might just be happenstance."

"I would prefer to believe Dusko got out and will come drifting back just as you five did. And we still are not certain he isn't a captive. Which brings us back to that question, one we are more able to discuss at this time. Though I do not like the idea, I think we have to go after the two in the hospital, no matter who they are."

Whitney turned, puzzled. "Excuse me, Colonel, but a moment ago you were saying it wasn't worth the risk. I find this a bit confusing."

"Erik's right. If they are calling one of the women 'The Nun,' they know there is a connection with the Butterflies. Either they know more than we expected, or whoever sold us out told them, or the one they're calling 'The Nun' has already given everything away. We need to get everybody out before the Germans learn anything about Whitney or her cargo. Which means I hope Primrose, who knows the whole story, is not 'The Nun.' " Donohue paced.

"I'll go," Patrice volunteered.

"Me too," Paul said.

"I'm in," Ross said.

"I hate the whole idea," Donohue said.

Patrice smoothed the white uniform and settled the navy, red-lined cape on her shoulders. As Ross helped her off Iwan's boat, she said, "I hope this works. These people are not stupid, and what we are trying is."

Paul buttoned the white orderly's uniform jacket. "The reason it will work is because it's so obvious."

Ross, remarkably convincing in his SS uniform, joined them. "And because if it doesn't, we're all cooked." He turned and waved to Iwan, who moved the boat away from the river's edge as the three of them moved into cover along the riverbank to wait.

Patrice was moving from one foot to the other, trying to keep her circulation going when Ross suddenly touched her arm. She stopped, holding her breath, listening to the approaching engine, her fists clenched with tension. Donohue's contact in Belgium had known enough about the disastrou attempt on Heydrich to have been the one to sell them out. Now he was the one they were depending on again. She closed her eyes. She opened them abruptly as Ross grabbed her hand, pulling her forward toward the boxy white vehicle with a large red cross painted on the side. Paul jumped into the back and helped Patrice in before Ross winked and closed the door.

"Phase one," she said quietly.

Paul and Patrice stood behind Ross as he presented the wad of credentials and documents. The guard at the hospital desk looked at each of the papers with interest, sucking his teeth loudly as he turned each page. Ross kept his hand lightly on the gun holstered at his belt.

"We had no request from Berlin to release these prisoners," the guard said.

"You hold the request in your hand," Ross snarled. "Unless you would like to telephone *Obergruppenführer* Heydrich to confirm his written instructions."

Patrice's German was sufficient to appreciate the courage of Ross's strategy and to be terrified by the audacity of it. The man stood next to a telephone.

The guard shuffled through the papers again, studying the seals and signatures.

"Is it your intent to delay the SS?" Ross asked, the threat in his voice obvious.

The guard stared at him for a moment, his hand on the telephone, then looked once more at Reinhard Heydrich's name on the orders.

"The prisoners are in Ward Three and Ward Seven," he said, saluting.

Ross gave him an expert Nazi salute. *"Heil Hitler."*

Patrice and Paul followed Ross and the guard. "The woman first," Ross said and Patrice held her breath, hoping the guard wouldn't answer, "Which one?"

"Yes, sir," the guard said, turning at the next intersection and leading them down a long, crowded hallway, finally stopping outside a locked door. He removed keys from his pocket and released the catch.

Patrice hurried into the room. Magda, pale and emaciated,

was the only occupant. Her eyes were closed as Patrice bent over the bed. "Magda," she said, her voice low,

Magda's eyes opened slowly, the lids fluttering. "No," she muttered, her words slurred. "I don't know anything. More medicine? The pain." Her eyes closed again.

Patrice signaled and Paul entered with a cart. Quickly they bundled Magda in the bed's blankets and shifted her to the cart. As they left the room, Ross said, "Take that one to the ambulance, and I shall see to the other."

The driver of the ambulance helped them transfer Magda to one of the pallets inside the coach, then stayed with her as they returned to retrieve either Tricycle or the Abbé.

Ross followed the guard, their boots a threat in the hallway. The guard halted abruptly, unlocking another ward. Ross brushed past him and quickly approached the bed.

The Abbé was barely recognizable, his face badly swollen and bruised, his body and head swathed in bandages and casts.

"Mon ami," he mumbled through broken teeth, "I have told them nothing."

"Just relax. We're here to get you out and back to England," Ross said, reaching to take his friend's hand, but the Abbé shook his head.

"My good friend, I am not capable of such a feat, even on the Ile de France. But you can send me on a journey I want very much to make. Do you have one of those pills?" Ross could hear the great pain in his friend's voice.

"Yes. Do you want it now?"

The battered mouth twisted itself into a smile. "Yes. Put it in my teeth, then leave me to make my peace with God."

Ross placed the small capsule between the Abbé's jaws, in the back where there were still teeth intact, then squeezed his hand. "Good-bye, my good friend, *adieu,*" he said softly before turning away from the bed.

"The nurse will return for this man," he said to the guard. "Be certain the door is kept locked until that time. No one is to enter."

The guard saluted and Ross hurried to intercept Patrice and Paul. He was relieved to see them just as he entered the

294

lobby. Glancing around to be certain they wouldn't be observed, he said, "We're too late for the Abbé. Let's get outta here."

As the ambulance pulled out of the hospital's drive and onto the main road, Ross slid the window open between the driver's cab and the compartment. "How is she?"

"Weak, drugged, and I think she's had surgery. How do I know? I'm not a nurse," Patrice replied irritably. "And I don't know how well she will do on that horrible boat."

"Donohue's sending a plane," Ross replied. "We'll be home in time for breakfast."

Patrice curled into her comfortable chair, the lap robe tucked in around her knees, and looked across the room at Whitney with a gentle smile. "Seems like the old days at Goucher."

Whitney chuckled. "Just exactly. Well, perhaps a few changes."

Patrice held up her hand. "Just for the fun of it, don't list them. Let me go on being delusional for a moment longer. It's not as good as the bathtub stuff we used to guzzle, but would you like some gin, just for memory's sake?"

Whitney grinned, then nodded quickly. "But only if you promise to serve it in a cup stolen from the school dining room."

"A tall order, but since we're pretending . . ." Patrice set her lap robe aside and took out two of the bone china cups she'd bought at Harrod's when she'd first come to London, then poured the make-believe Tanqueray and delivered a cup to Whitney before resettling with her lap robe.

"To all the girls of Goucher, wherever they may be," she said, raising her cup.

"And to all the men of Johns Hopkins and Annapolis who did their best to corrupt us," Whitney added.

They laughed and drank.

"I'm going home next week," Patrice said abruptly.

Whitney looked up. "For how long?"

"Not for long. *Sunpapers* likes to haul the bureau chiefs back every so often for meetings, but I suspect it's actually to make certain we're not spending their money on liquor and wild parties. Of course while we're there they do manage to have a few wild parties. I'll be glad to see Monkton and Reisgarten again.''

"Are you going up to the Valley?" Whitney asked, and Patrice could hear something beyond the question in her friend's voice.

"I think so. Do you want me to look in on your mother?"

"Please." She took a long drink from her cup. "I wish you could tell her I'm alive." Patrice started to reply, but Whitney shook her head. "Oh, I know that's out of the question. I wouldn't want to burden her with either the shock or the knowledge. Since I'm such a high item on the Germans' agenda, they might put pressure on her. Of course, since they already know I am alive . . . Oh, the whole thing is so gothic."

"I raise my cup to that. But wouldn't life be dull without it?"

"May I give you a pillow and blanket?" the stewardess asked in a quiet whisper, bending forward so as not to disturb the man sleeping in the seat in front of Patrice and Cesar Ball.

"Perhaps a blanket, if you please," Patrice replied.

"And some coffee," Ball added.

"My pleasure," the stewardess said, surrendering the blankets she carried over her arm. "Would you like something to snack on as well? We have cheese and crackers, oranges, or sandwiches."

"Cheese and crackers and an orange for me, please," Patrice said, her mouth watering at the thought of a fresh orange.

"Fine," Ball added, and the stewardess disappeared.

The inside of the Pan Am Clipper was almost dark, the plane chasing the night across the Atlantic, engines droning hypnotically.

"Did you have a pleasant time on your vacation?" Patrice inquired.

"It was quite an adventure," Ball replied, craning his neck to watch the passengers around them. The seat in front was occupied by a heavyset man who'd fallen asleep before

296

they'd taken off. The two seats behind were unoccupied, and across the aisle was an elderly woman and her nurse, who fussed over the woman in a constant patter of French. Content they were not being overheard, he lowered his voice still further. "My recent vacation produced some very interesting and most unexpected information," Ball said, then paused as the stewardess returned with their coffee and food, bustling with lap trays and napkins.

When she finally departed again, Patrice turned her attention back to Ball. "You were saying?"

"It seems Mr. Greene and Mr. Smythe, with whom you are acquainted, have continued their associations despite the war, working within government circles to promote their views despite the position the United States has taken." He paused to take a sip of his coffee.

"Isn't that rather foolish?"

"They are viewed as foolish men and have been ignored by those in power. However, my contacts in North Africa have uncovered information which make them far more ominous than we originally thought."

Patrice hesitated, listening to the rumbling, regular snore in front of them and the patter of conversation across the aisle, then asked, "In what say? Certainly they can no longer have their former business associations. And what damage could they be doing in the Valley? It's hardly a nest of government secrets."

Ball raised his eyebrows. "Our friend the Countess, as you know, was entrusted with a very valuable document. The document she carried was the only existing copy. The people who trusted her would do anything to recover it, and it is their belief that somehow she gave this item to her father, the Senator."

"That's ridiculous. He was killed in an accident before she . . ."

"The original possessors of the document had no way of knowing that, for they could not locate her, if you recall."

Patrice suddenly felt dizzy. "We had suspected this before, but are you now certain her father's death was not an accident?"

Ball nodded. "According to my sources, Greene and

Smythe were in disfavor with their associates and were told that the recovery of the missing document would restore them to their former positions."

The dizziness became bile in the back of her throat. "They killed the Senator?"

"Very probably."

"And the attack on his wife?" Patrice was stunned.

Ball nodded.

"But we all grew up together. We were all friends. How could they?"

"It is unlikely they were the actual murderers or attackers, but certainly they helped set up both situations. I'm sorry, but part of what we must accomplish during this visit is to see what threads of truth we can find which might support this."

"Does . . . Mrs. Baraday . . . know?" Patrice thought back to her conversation with Whitney the previous week.

"No. Outside of the Colonel and myself, you are the only one. We decided not to tell you until this trip to spare anyone else undue concern. And perhaps we will not be able to uncover anything."

Patrice felt the full weight of the chain of events bearing down on her. "And perhaps we will," she said with cold rage.

20

PATRICE HAD BEEN irritable for two days, almost from the moment she had stepped off the Clipper in New York, and certainly from the very instant she'd entered Baltimore. She couldn't quite explain it, but she seemed not to be able to stop herself from snapping at people who were being perfectly courteous.

She ordered breakfast from room service, then returned to finishing her makeup and hair, patting a bit of rouge onto her cheeks and moistening the tiny brush for her mascara. She filled in the generous curves of her lips with bright red lipstick.

She had surrendered to her hair's strong will years before, allowing the impudent curls to take their own way, but keeping them fashionably bobbed. She brushed her hair and stepped back to give herself an inspection. Approving her image, she set her hat on the dresser next to her purse and gloves, and laid her suit jacket carefully across the back of the chair, then glanced at her watch. What was taking them so long with her breakfast?

"You are a sourpuss," she said to the mirror just as the rap came at the door.

"Room service," the elderly man said as she opened the

door. Patrice stepped aside and he wheeled the cart in. "Here? Next to the windows?"

"Yes, thank you."

He removed the covers from the plates then poured the coffee and laid the folded *Morning Sun* to the left of her plate. "Will that be all, ma'am?"

"Yes, thank you," she said, slipping a quarter into his hand. He bowed slightly and turned to leave. "No, actually," she said, hearing the Englishness in her accent and feeling very much out of place.

"Ma'am?" He stopped, turning back to her.

She looked over at the plate he'd uncovered. It was filled with an unseemly pile of scrambled eggs and bacon, three pieces of toast and a generous bowl of butter pats on another two dishes, half a grapefruit, and steaming coffee. She turned her eyes back to the gentleman. "Does anyone here know about the war?"

The man smiled broadly. "Yes, ma'am. They're all signing up. I'm too old, or I'd be down there myself. I was in the last war, though." His smile disappeared. "We thought we'd taught the Germans a lesson, but now, so soon, they're back, and worse than ever. Yes, ma'am, we surely do know about the war. You folks in England have had it longer, of course, but we're coming over now, and we'll save you just like we did in my day."

Patrice bristled at his attitude of superiority. "I'm an American," she said testily.

"Really? What part of the country? Boston?" The man seemed genuinely surprised.

"Baltimore, Greenspring Valley." She was becoming more irritated by the moment.

The man looked at her curiously, then suddenly burst out laughing. "That's a good joke, ma'am, but your accent gives you away. You almost sound like one of those girls from out in Greenspring Valley, but you can't fool an old soldier like me, ma'am. I served in the trenches with some of the Brits, and you sound just like them. Yes sir, I know a British accent when I hear one. Fine boys they were, too. But if you'll excuse me now, I have to get back downstairs. There

300

aren't many to do the work, so we keep hopping. I hope you have a nice visit to America."

Patrice sat down at the table, angry with the man and his insolence in not believing her, and angry at the amount of food which was more than enough for two people. She hadn't realized how much her posting and the war had changed the way she saw the world—and, obviously, the way she sounded to it! A British accent, indeed.

"Tommyrot!" she said aloud, then covered her mouth with her hand. Maybe she had more of an accent than she'd known.

She stabbed her fork into the eggs and took a bite, then slowed down. Real eggs, scrambled with real milk and cooked in real butter. No matter how displaced she felt, these were to be savored.

"After all, if I don't eat this, it will just go to waste," she said, trying to salve her guilt as she loaded the toast with butter and preserves.

She unfolded the paper and scanned the headlines. Yes, they did indeed know about the war here, she realized. What had been making her so snippy was that the war here was suddenly new and bright, something which, to Americans, had only been a small skirmish before the Japanese chose to wake them up. Now it was an *American* war, as though that somehow meant it could truly be fought.

She felt embarrassed at her countrymen's attitude, more so because it seemed America was the only hope Europe had to rid itself of Hitler. The room-service waiter had said it: now the Yanks were coming to save Europe again. More than ever, Patrice felt the dichotomy of her life, the British side of her embarrassed and angry, the American side proud and filled with nationalism.

"Still, no matter how split my personality, I must stop taking it out on others." She opened the paper again, this time really reading.

VOLUNTEERS CLOG LOCAL DRAFT BOARD.
RED CROSS COLLECTING FOR WAR EFFORT.
WAR BOND SALES BEGIN.
GERMAN SUBMARINE SIGHTED IN CHESAPEAKE BAY.

"In Chesapeake Bay!" Patrice quickly skimmed the article, then chuckled at the familiarity of it: a new generation of the Home-Guard who would be ever-vigilant against the menace.

Patrice glanced at her watch, then turned through the rest of the paper.

BALTIMORE CONCERN SOCIETY PRESENTS ANDREW COLLINS IN RECITAL caught her eye.

Andrew Collins' exceptional gifts on the pianoforte will be demonstrated this evening at the Lyric, 8 P.M. The concert is to benefit War Relief for Refugees. Mr. Collins will greet his admirers at a reception to follow at the Lord Baltimore Hotel. Known in his native India as the Raja Abachandri, Mr. Collins took his early classical training at the London Conservatory of Music and the Berlin Conservatory. Believed by many to be one of the great child prodigies of his time, he has maintained his brilliant style and fluid classicism while building his repertoire to include many less-recognized composers whose technical demands often eliminate them from the usual concert. Mr. Collins now makes his home in London, but because of his concert schedule in America, also spends time at his pied-à-terre in New York. Ticket information may be obtained by contacting the Lyric.

"Interesting," Patrice muttered. "I must mention this to Ball."

". . . and try to self-censor. By now you know what will and what will not get past. Frankly, if we do the job, we can maintain freedom of the press and national security without having to constantly defer to the military." Thornton Gholson ran the bureau in Honolulu, and Patrice could imagine he'd been bombarded with military censors.

Mark Mausen, former Bureau Chief in Tokyo, now operating out of Hong Kong, leaned forward. "My biggest problem is trying to decide what's true and what isn't of what I'm being fed from the military—our's and the Allies'. It's not so much managing the news as trying to make the best of what is obviously a very bad situation. I think our war coverage seems to be reflecting this ambivalence. On the one hand, we want to be optimistic and patriotic, but we cannot, on the other hand, ignore the horrors of what our reporters are seeing and experiencing."

"How much do the readers believe in what we write? The Blitz, for example. How sympathetic were Americans to what was going on in London during that time?" Patrice looked at Reisgarten.

"First, yes, they do believe what you write. But think about it for a minute. If you hear about a tornado wiping out a small town in Kansas, you feel sympathy and perhaps even some of the fears the residents would feel, but nothing is like experiencing it. The residents of that town think it's the worst thing that ever happened and, to them, it may very well be. I listened to the reports from Honolulu and read the wires, and it still isn't real to me."

Monkton broke in. "You are not complaining about anything unknown in the last war. You do your best to keep the military censors happy while still passing on the only thing you can: information and understanding. Stop worrying about it and worry about how you are going to keep your own soul intact." His eyes caught Patrice's. "It's a job for the young."

She put her hands palm up in surrender. "Can't blame a girl for trying, Monkton. With all due respect to my colleagues, you're the best one ever."

"Bullshit isn't getting me to London, either, Rigby," Monkton replied gruffly, covering his obvious enjoyment of the compliment with lighting a cigar.

"It's an open offer, Monkton," she added. "I never give up."

"So I remember," Reisgarten said. "So I remember."

"Darling girl, why did you not let us know you were coming? I feel as though I never know where you are these days. And I do so worry about you with all that business going on in Europe." Patrice's mother swept her into the

303

house, hugging her crooked. "Charles, come quickly," she called in the direction of Patrice's father's study.

"What is it now, Jeanette? I told you I'd be occup—Patrice, my girl." He held out his arms and Patrice ran to be enfolded. "You look wonderful, my girl. Wonderful."

Patrice patted her father's expanded stomach. "And you look prosperous, Daddy," she said.

"How long will you be with us this time—and don't you dare say 'a few days,' " Jeanette Rigby fluttered.

"Then I can't say anything. I must be back in London no later than Tuesday." Patrice wished she could stay longer. Being in the Valley again made her see how much she missed her parents and how much she wished she had more time to spend with them.

"But ⌐day is Friday!"

Patrice planted a firm kiss on her mother's cheek. "So we shall have nearly three days. And the weather is wonderful. It's been so cold in Europe." She deliberately put a smile on her face and a happy tone in her voice.

"Do they call this Indian Winter, Charles?" Jeanette asked in her dear, distracted way.

"No, my darling, they do not. Now what do you want to do while you are with us, my dear girl?"

"I want to ride. And make some social calls. I'd like to see Mrs. Baraday. But most of all, I want to spend time with both of you." She sighed. "I do so wish this didn't have to be such a quick trip."

"Poor Lucille," Jeanette Rigby cooed. "She would be so glad to see you, I feel certain, though we all know she . . . well . . . oh, you know I do not approve of gossip, but Lucille Baraday seems to have retreated into herself. She just is not the spirit she used to be. Oh, do go see her, dear."

"I shall. I would also love to see Howland and Tessa Kenney."

"I am certain Tessa would be glad to have you visit. Howland has signed up and she's terribly worried about him. He's in one of those western states learning how to be in the Army. Tessa is hoping Howland will be able to be a veterinarian in the army, but I cannot imagine that much of this war is going to be fought on horseback. And no one car imagine what will happen to the animals in the Valley with Howland away at this war business." She took a deep breath as though she had much more to say on the subject, then closed her mouth only to open it again. "But that's all just silly when one thinks of what is going on over there. How I do go on."

"Indeed, my dear, but always with something to say," Charles Rigby said lovingly, before giving Patrice another hug. "Now, dear girl, why don't you visit with your mother or do whatever you please, and I will finish this tiresome bit of business. Tonight I shall take you and your mother out for a lovely dinner, but you must excuse me now." He retreated into his study, closing the doors.

Jeanette sighed. "He's been working much too hard lately. It's all this war business, you know. Everything is turned all topsy-turvy." She sighed again. "But we only have such a short time together. Do tell me what you've been doing. How is that young man of yours who works in the mountains and treats the refugees? Oh, why can't I recall his name?"

"Stephen, Mother. I suppose he's fine. The last I heard he had accepted a position in Canada, working in a hospital that rehabilitates injured pilots." Patrice tried to keep her tone light.

"The last you heard? That doesn't sound as though things are very close anymore." Her mother looked very concerned.

"We haven't declared anything to one another, but it's obvious to me that we are star-crossed." She saw the sadness on her mother's face. "But don't misunderstand. I think we were star-crossed from the beginning, and although it may not be a traditional choice, I am very happy with my career and my life as a . . ." She'd been off guard and had almost said "spy" at the end of the sentence. She could just imagine her mother's reaction to that bit of news. "Reporter and bureau chief," Patrice hastened to finish.

Jeanette reached to take her daughter's hand. "I think you assume we are not proud of your achievements. My dear daughter, your father and I are so proud when we read your articles and understand the influence you have on how this country thinks. We would have liked you to marry and have children, but we also understand that is not the choice you've made." Jeanette squeezed her hands and Patrice felt the sting of tears in her eyes. "We love you no matter what."

Jeanette pulled Patrice into her arms and both of them burst into tears. After a moment, they stepped back, each reaching for her hanky.

"Well," Jeanette said, obviously embarrassed, "I hardly meant to get so carried away with myself."

Patrice blotted at her own eyes. "I'm glad you did. Now let me call Mrs. Baraday and ask if she's receiving callers this afternoon. Then we can decide where we shall go to dinner."

WINFIELD FARMS. The sign at the stone gates looked the same as it had since Patrice could remember, and the oaks along the drive looked still as majestic. The stables were shuttered and empty, the paddocks overgrown. The house, however, was as stately and elegant as always, only now seeming more aloof without Whitney's presence.

A tall black man answered the door, reminding Patrice of the attack on Mrs. Baraday and the murder of the butler. "Miss Rigby," she said, depositing her calling card on the silver tray.

"Won't you come in," he said, stepping aside. "Might I take madame's coat?"

As she surrendered her coat and followed him into the drawing room, Patrice had the distinct impression the war would never be known in this house.

"Patrice, how good of you to come by."

Patrice turned to face her hostess, then had to refrain from staring rudely. Where once Lucille Baraday had been tall and elegant, she was now gaunt and fragile, almost translucent. Her white hair was carefully marcelled, but her stylish dress seemed as vacant as her eyes.

"It's really lovely to see you," Patrice lied. "I'm only home for a couple of days and I wanted to . . ." *To come tell you your daughter is alive and doing very courageous work*

306

she longed to add, but instead said, ". . . be certain you were still doing fine."

"Won't you sit down, dear. Will you have tea?" Lucille lowered herself gently onto the settee as Patrice sat on one of the petit-pointe–covered Chippendales that flanked the unlit fireplace.

"Thank you. One lump. Thank you." She took the tea, wondering if she'd ever have the courage to tell Whitney not only about her mother but about the involvement of Laurel's father and Boyleston Greene in the Senator's death. Looking at the fragile woman who had once been so strong, Patrice ached for the innocent victims of the war.

"How do you find London?" Mrs. Baraday asked.

"It was most peaceful after the Blitz stopped and before the Americans came. Now it's bustling again. There isn't a hotel room to be had and everything is rationed."

"I suppose the ballet and theater seasons are abandoned," Lucille said wistfully.

"Quite to the contrary. West End and Covenant Garden have never been busier. You see, we've adjusted. I mean, those of us who live in Britain. The war isn't so new to us."

Suddenly Mrs. Baraday looked up at Patrice and the weak, broken woman was pushed aside by the Lucille Baraday Patrice remembered. "For some of us, this war has been going on for a very long time, Patrice," she said, her voice clear and firm. "And it is high time for it to be over." She seemed to shrink, the curtain falling, covering her again. "And how is your mother, dear? I don't see her often."

"She's fine. Just fine." Patrice couldn't wait to escape.

Patrice waited patiently for the groom to bring a horse around for her. It seemed a little strange not to have a horse of her own now, to be riding a mount with whom she hadn't spent hours becoming friends.

"Miss Patrice, I believe you will enjoy Ariel. She comes from quite good stock and young Miss Kenney has been riding her in competitions."

"Young Miss Kenney? Do you mean Clarice?"

"Oh, no, Miss Patrice. Miss Clarice is now married and living in New York City. I'm speaking of Dr. Kenney's daughter, Jessica. She is quite the young rider. Reminds me a bit of Miss Whitney, God rest her soul." The groom held Ariel as Patrice mounted, then adjusted the stirrups for her.

"Jessica. My goodness. Dr. Kenney's daughter. She must be quite young to ride in competitions."

"She's ten now, I believe. The only caution I'd give you about this horse, Miss Patrice, is that she spooks at water jumps."

Patrice held up her hand. "So do I, Roger. So do I." She tapped Ariel lightly with her heels and the horse slipped into an easy trot, responding to the lightest direction from knee or rein. Patrice relaxed, letting herself merge with the horse's gait and timing.

When she reached the edge of the fenced paddock area, she leaned down to open a gate, allowing them to pass into the fields where the horses would graze and nurture their foals in summer.

"Okay, you've got me. Let's run a little." Patrice leaned forward in the saddle and tapped Ariel's ribs lightly with her heels. The horse increased her gait, passing from a trot to a canter and finally to full gallop, as Patrice sat easily in the saddle. They approached the edge of the field and the stone wall and Patrice began to rein Ariel in, then stopped herself. "What the heck," she said, hoping her body would remember clearly what her mind did not.

Ariel coiled and Patrice leaned forward over her neck, feeling the horse leave the ground in a graceful stretch, landing firmly and squarely on the other side.

"Oh," she said, patting Ariel's neck, "that was glorious. Of course, I may not be able to walk tomorrow, but that was worth it."

Patrice steered Ariel to the road, entering the gate of the Smythe house and trotting up the driveway. It had always seemed rather a small house, as though it were drawn in on itself, and Patrice found, as she rounded the curve in the driveway, that it had not changed.

A strange man came to take her horse, and she didn't recognize the man who answered the ringing of the doorbell.

"Miss Rigby, coming to call on Mrs. Smythe if she is at

home." Without waiting for an invitation, she brushed past him and into the house.

"I shall see if madame is receiving," the man said, his accent unmistakably German.

Though the butler hadn't offered the courtesy of a chair or a room in which she might be received, Patrice wandered about the foyer, looking into the rooms which were open, wondering at the activity she could hear behind the closed doors and wishing she had the temerity to simply open them and go in.

"Patrice, is that you?" Mrs. Smythe's little voice floated down from the stairs above her head. "I do so wish you had called ahead, dear, for I can only spend a moment with you."

Patrice returned to the middle of the foyer just in time to see Mrs. Smythe look nervously over her shoulder before she came down the stairs.

"Please forgive my breach of manners, but I was out for a ride and came past your gate and wanted to say hello. I am only home for two days and came by for just a moment."

Mrs. Smythe gave her a quick, nervous embrace, kissing the air beside her cheek. "You look so well, dear. Are you still in London?" She didn't offer to take Patrice's coat nor to move them from the foyer.

"Yes. I fear I have become a true expatriate. I adore London. I'm almost afraid to ask, but has Laurel stayed on in . . ."

Mrs. Smythe's face became clouded with worry. "Indeed she has. She and Helmut, however, seem to be quite safe, and her letters, when they come through, are cheerful and filled with good news. This is a difficult time for . . . for everyone," she finished lamely.

"I am certain Laurel will be fine," Patrice said, wanting to reassure the woman, who was so obviously frightened, wondering if she were lying about Laurel and Helmut or truly did not know that Laurel's husband had been murdered. "My mother knew nothing of Boyleston Greene, that old wag. He was always so amusing, and I know he and Mr. Smythe were engaged in business at one time. Have you seen him?"

"Boyleston?" Mrs. Smythe's voice quavered. "Not . . . ah . . . not for . . . for several . . . several mon—ah . . . years."

"Oh. I wonder how he is. I shall never forget the hunt where he appeared on the back of a donkey with a poodle dressed up in pinks. I think the master nearly died that morning."

Mrs. Smythe's eyes darted to something over Patrice's shoulder and Patrice could see the fear in them. "And how is Mr. Smythe? Does he still spend so much time in his office in Baltimore?"

"Yes," Mrs. Smythe replied quickly. "Yes, he does. As a matter of fact, I was preparing to go in to Baltimore to meet him just now when you arrived." Her words tumbled out of her mouth as her eyes danced over Patrice's shoulder again.

"Oh, then I won't keep you another moment. Please give him my regards." Patrice turned suddenly, hoping to see what Mrs. Smythe had been looking at, but saw nothing.

"Good of you to come by. Do stop again," the woman said with a complete lack of sincerity. "Is this your horse?" she asked as the door opened to reveal Ariel being held by a groom at the foot of the front steps. Patrice was astonished. Mrs. Smythe might as well have taken her by the seat of her pants and thrown her out.

"How convenient. Thank you so much," Patrice said, trying to exit with as much noise as possible. "Good to see you again, Mrs. Smythe," she said loudly. "Please let me know if you plan to be in London. I shall be happy to entertain you in my home. Keep in touch, now." Patrice mounted Ariel. "And have a nice time in Baltimore," she called as she pulled away. "Give my best to Mr. Smythe," she yelled, waving gaily and urging Ariel into a canter.

As soon as she'd rounded the curve and entered the small woods, she reined the horse in and slipped from her back, tying her hidden in an evergreen hedge. Removing opera glasses from her jacket pocket, she crept forward until she had a view of the driveway.

As she focused the glasses a car pulled up to where she had mounted Ariel and the door of the house was opening. "Haven't seen Boyleston for years, you say," she muttered as the man himself emerged from the house and descended the steps to the driveway. "Oh, and going into Baltimore to meet Mr. Smythe, are you," she said as Mr. Smythe appeared in the doorway. He was talking to someone behind him and hesitated in the doorway.

Patrice focused the glasses on his face, wishing she had more powerful binoculars and could read lips, when suddenly Mr. Smythe's face blurred with movement and was replaced. Patrice gasped.

"Andrew Collins? What in hell is Andrew Collins doing with Harold Smythe and Boyleston Greene in Greenspring Valley in Maryland?"

21

"Your father has made me angry," Heydrich said, as he read something he'd taken from his briefcase.

"My father? What has my father to do with anything?" Laurel blew on her fingernails, encouraging the polish to dry.

"Your father has become much too comfortable." Heydrich reached over and took her hand, closing his fingers over the wet nails.

"Now look what you've done. It's bad enough I have to do my own nails without having to do them over!" Laurel tried to jerk her hand away, but his fingers tightened, bending her knuckles. "Ouch. Ow. Stop that. Reinhard, that's not funny."

He let go of her hand, pushing her fingers away, wiping at his palm. "It was not meant to be funny. Look at this mess."

"Look at *this* mess," she snapped back, extending her hand. "And you still haven't answered what my father has to do with anything."

"Your father and I have an arrangement. A deal, as you Americans say. He and his partner Greene agreed quite a long time ago to provide something I need, but they have taken my money, and they have taken too much time, and now I find they have nothing for me. This makes me very angry."

Laurel kept her eyes down, scrubbing at her ruined nails with the acetone-soaked cotton. "Why tell me?"

"Why . . . do . . . you . . . think . . . I . . . have . . . kept . . . you . . . around . . . for . . . so . . . long?" His words were slow, verbal assaults. Suddenly his tempo speeded up. "Do you think I am in love with you? Do you think it is because you are such a wonderful mistress? Do not flatter yourself. I have kept you as an insurance policy to make certain your father did not lose what little courage he had." He grabbed her wrist. "Which he seems to have done. So you are going to encourage him."

She shrank from him. "What do you mean?"

"Why are you pulling away? Do you think I would hurt you?" His eyes gleamed. "No, of course not. I have arranged for you to be able to talk with your father on the telephone to encourage him to renew his efforts on my behalf." He picked up the receiver and said, "Make the connection," then replaced it in the cradle. "I have gone to a great deal of trouble so you can speak with your family."

Laurel tried to pull her hand away, wanting to run out of the apartment, to flee from him, but she was stunned by his revelation. No wonder she had been able to survive an SS jail with nothing more than a better figure. Now she understood why she could say or do anything and he kept coming back. What could be so valuable? What did he want from her spineless father and his drunken friend? And what would he do to her to get what he wanted?

The phone rang jarringly and Laurel tried once more to pull away, but Heydrich closed his hand, bending her fingers painfully. He lifted the receiver and put it into her hand. Laurel raised the instrument to her ear.

"Hello?"

"Laurel, is that you, darling?" Her father's voice sounded as though he were at the far end of a large tunnel. Or, she thought, a dungeon.

"Hello, Daddy. How are you? How is Mother?"

313

"We miss you. We're fine. It's been a pretty mild winter, not much snow, and now spring is coming."

"Good," Laurel said, certain she would never take another full breath, her eyes on Heydrich.

"Ask him if he's had any success," Heydrich said.

"Daddy, have you found anything for my . . . friend Reinhard?"

The line crackled and she waited for it to clear, finally hearing, ". . . yet, but tell him we're working on it."

"He says they are working on it."

Heydrich shook his head, then grabbed the phone. "Time is running out. I must have it and I must have it now. My future depends on it, as does your future and the future of your daughter. Do you understand?"

Laurel was listening to Reinhard's side of the conversation, worrying about what he might do now that there were no more pretenses, when suddenly he grabbed her little finger and snapped it back over the top of her hand. She heard the noise quite clearly, like a twig or a wishbone snapping cleanly before she felt the searing pain. "Oh, my God," she whispered, reaching for her hand.

"I don't think your father can hear you," Heydrich said, tugging sharply on the broken finger.

Her shriek reverberated across the telephone lines. Heydrich let her scream for a moment, then hung up, releasing her hand at the same time.

"Now perhaps he will understand how important his work is," he said, picking up his hat and coat. "And perhaps you will understand how precarious your situation is as well. Do not defy me. And do not betray me. I am very powerful and I have very long arms."

Laurel rapped the fingernails of her hand without the cast against the cold glass of the windowpane, staring out at the gray sky of winter Berlin, gray streets, gray buildings, gray cars, gray uniforms. Petulantly, she stuck out her tongue at the scene, then turned away from its monochrome, hugging her wool chalais robe around her.

She crossed to the script which lay scattered on the table, but as soon as she sat down, she stood again, pacing around the room, her hand fluttering from one object to the next, grazing the back of the couch, touching the smooth walnut surface of the table, sliding quickly across the wooden case of the radio, resting for an instant on the bookshelf.

It's a fine mess now, she thought for the thousandth time, clenching her fist. Reinhard had told the story about the attempt on his life until she was bored senseless, gloating at having outwitted his adversaries. Laurel had congratulated him, acted as though she thought he were magical and wise, all the time feeling sickened, knowing everything was ruined. Patrice would never believe she hadn't somehow been the one to tip him off, even though Laurel truly had known nothing about their plans and wouldn't have said anything even if she'd known. If she could only tell Patrice how much she wished they had succeeded in their attempt. At least she assumed it was Patrice and her friends, especially since Karl Foch had been asking questions about prisoners taken in a raid just after the attempt on Reinhard. If she could only do something to get revenge on Reinhard for breaking her finger and threatening her family. Damn him and his disgusting ways.

Now it was all ruined. Instead of being a dead hero, Reinhard had proven just how invincible he was. Patrice would probably donate her half-million to some fool charity just for spite because Laurel had been friends with Reinhard and Reinhard hadn't died.

Laurel stamped her foot. *Damn him,* she thought then shuddered. He was so loathsome. How could she ever have thought him attractive? Now when he touched her, it made her flesh crawl. Laurel cradled her hand in its plaster cast, the little finger protected but still uncomfortable.

At least he didn't seem to be Hitler's fair-haired lad anymore. She thought about that for a moment. It was so strange. Hitler had originally behaved as though he thought Reinhard a favorite son, and now he treated him more like a threat. And Reinhard didn't seem to care, because he kept challenging Hitler even though it was obvious the Führer didn't like it one bit. She sniffed. Reinhard should be more careful about whom he insulted if he didn't want to be

315

"Reich Protector of the North Pole," instead of Reich Protector of Czechoslovakia.

She drummed her fingernails on the table, her thoughts drifting in another direction. Perhaps she could keep her half-million dollars if she could produce something for Patrice—a token, but better than just information about where he would be or when—this time, beyond suspicion of compromise.

Laurel turned, surveying the room. Reinhard had gone back to Prague the day before, but had left some scripts for her broadcasts. She moved to the desk, sifting through the pages, considering each one more carefully, looking for something to appease Patrice. She sighed. How she hated to have to read these words now, ever since America had gotten into the war. It was one thing to speak for an adopted nation, but now she realized it had become a matter of speaking *against* her own country, and she hated it more every time she did a broadcast.

"Such lies," she muttered to herself, scanning the words he'd written for her to speak. "Does he actually think anyone in their right mind would believe any of this? The 'glorious Reich'—murderers led by a madman." Disgusted, she flipped the script across the desk, and a photograph fluttered to the floor. Laurel pounced on it.

The woman had been tortured, starved, and bruised, it was obvious—but she was alive. Reinhard had been showing it off two nights before at dinner, she now remembered, but at the time she had ignored what he had to say about the prisoner. It offended Laurel's sensibilities to see what they were doing to people in the obsessive pursuit of their victory. Laurel tapped the photo against her cast. What had he been saying about this woman?

Laurel nodded, the memory returning. "The Nun," he had called her, and he had been gloating about how much the Führer wanted to take this prisoner away from him. If Hitler wanted this woman, why would Reinhard not only not give her to the Führer, but also brag about keeping her in Prague, out of the Führer's grasp?

"Oh," she said, the details becoming more clear, the puzzle starting to emerge. "I'll bet this woman might be someone Patrice very much wants to find. Which means my money is safe if I get this to her.'' Two tears slipped from her eyes. "And maybe she'll be so happy that she'll help me come home.''

Keeping the photograph as close to her as possible, she dressed quickly. Karl would know how to send this out to make certain Patrice had it as soon as possible—before she gave the money away. Laurel grabbed her purse and coat, then hesitated. If she were stopped and asked for papers or searched, they might wonder why she would be carrying such a photograph.

She drummed her fingers impatiently for a moment, then folded the photo and slipped it between her cast and her arm. If they found it there, it would be because she was already in deep trouble.

She hesitated as she went out the door, looking once more to see if there were anything else she could use to hang Reinhard. After all, since he had threatened her and her family, she might as well make it really worth his while to come after her. By now she was getting used to being in deep trouble.

The photograph, crumpled and cracked, had arrived as Patrice was leaving her office, and she'd rushed to Dono- hue's office at U.S. Army headquarters, which he'd inhab- ited since the OSS acquired official status when the Ameri- cans entered the war.

"It *is* Primrose.'' Whitney studied the photo closely be- fore she surrendered it reluctantly to Donohue, vividly reliv- ing her own imprisonment, knowing the desperation Prim- rose must feel, the sense of abandonment, the fear that the next person who came in would be the one who killed you, and eventually the prayer for death.

Tricycle jumped up, rushing around to peer over Dono- hue's shoulder. "Yes, yes, it is. Oh, thank God. Do you think she's still alive? Where did you get this? When was it taken?''

Patrice studied him coldly, then gestured toward Dono- hue, indicating that the answers, if any, would come from him. Donohue raised his eyes from the photo.

"Patrice has a valuable resource in Berlin who supplied this. What does your source say? Is she still alive?"

Patrice skimmed the letter, written in Karl's flowing script without benefit of code or hidden-ink precautions. "Apparently she is. Obviously my resources felt it was urgent to get it here, considering the risks that have been taken."

Donohue set the photo down deliberately. "Read the letter aloud, Patrice."

"But . . ."

Donohue sighed. "But you are still concerned that Dusko may have been the one who betrayed the assassination plans."

Patrice squared her shoulders. "*Someone* did. And the circle has narrowed. There were only a limited number of people who knew about the operation in the first place, and now three of those are injured, one is dead, and one is in prison. That leaves very few others."

"But it leaves more than one," Dusko said quietly. "I know you have not known me for a long time, but how could you think I would endanger my own wife? Why do you suspect me still?"

Patrice felt uncomfortable with the confrontation, but stood her ground. "Because you have been a double agent. How do we know they didn't capture you and torture you until you had no other choice? How do we know you haven't had to make some sort of deal to keep her alive even now?"

Popov shook his head. "You do not know these things. I understand your suspicions and cannot deny they sound possible. Perhaps if our situations were reversed, I would think this of you." He smiled in a gentle way. "Colonel Donohue has found a good agent in you, I think. I will not be innocent in your eyes until I have been proven not guilty. That may never happen." His eyes met Patrice's, then Whitney's, then he turned to look at Erik and Paul, then finally at Donohue. "I can only give you my word."

"Good enough for me. Now can we please set all this aside? What is done and over is done and over. Somebody sold us out, but now we have other things to accomplish. Please read the letter, Patrice," Donohue said.

" 'L has been by, demanding this get into your hands

immediately. She says you may be looking for this poor woman. According to L, she is being held in Prague in the custody of RH.' Heydrich!'' Patrice looked up at Donohue, who was staring out the office window, rubbing his chin.

"Perhaps we need to get in touch with Jan and Vota," he finally said softly. "We have a score to settle with Mr. Heydrich. And we have an agent to retrieve."

Laurel flexed her stiffened hand again. Four weeks did not seem long enough for the bone to have healed, but the doctor had assured her it was fine when he removed the cast. He hadn't been very gentle about it and the finger had ached, but now it only throbbed.

She fumbled for her keys, leaning against the door, which swung open, nearly throwing her onto the floor of the apartment foyer.

"Oh, hell," she sputtered, stumbling into the hallway, fighting to recover her balance. "Damn." She rapped her recently unveiled hand as she caught herself. "Reinhard, are you here?" she called out irritably, examining her hand for damage.

"No. Where is he?"

Laurel looked up, startled to hear English being spoken, accented or not. "Oh, it's you," she said, not trying to disguise her dislike for The Concertmaster. "I have no idea where he is. How did you get in here?"

The man simply looked at her, his dark eyes blank. "Do you enjoy your life here? Are you comfortable?"

Laurel was taken aback. "Yes, why?"

"Because the reason I am looking for my friend is to warn him that his life is again in danger."

Suddenly everything seemed very clear to Laurel. The man said, in English, "again in danger," which meant he had known before. She began to walk around the couch and bumped her leg against his briefcase, knocking it over. "Oh, sorry," she said, stooping to set it right again. Harrods, the embossing under the handle said clearly—London. Laurel wanted very badly to have a look inside that briefcase. "He might be back soon if you want to wait. Would you like a drink?"

The Concertmaster nodded, surprised at her unusual hospitality. "Yes, perhaps. How long do you think it might be?"

Laurel smiled merrily. "Who knows, with Reinhard? Now let me make you a cocktail." She slipped into the small kitchen, rummaging in the drawer until she found the sleeping capsules the doctor had given her. She ground three into the bottom of the glass, then made a sweet Manhattan. ". . . a delightful chat, of this and that, and cocktails for two," she hummed to herself as she stirred the drink, making a quick and very light highball for herself and returning to the living room.

"Here's to the glorious Reich," she said, touching her glass against his. "Are you here for a concert?"

He shook his head then took a sip. "No, just for Reinhard. This is very good."

"Reinhard manages to get real liquor. Drink up, and I'll make you another. I'm certain he'll be here any moment." *Or he might still be in Prague,* she thought, smiling winningly at the dusky-complected man. "Drink up, now."

She put four of the tablets into the next drink. His voice slurred badly when he asked for a refill, so she put five tablets into the third Manhattan, which he only had a sip of before slumping to his side.

Laurel watched him for a few minutes to be certain, then grabbed the briefcase, put it on the table, and fumbled with the locks until it opened.

"Music," she said disgustedly, rifling through the papers. "All music." She hesitated. "Just like the music he has sent to Reinhard. Music which was never played, just studied." She lifted the papers out, then sorted through the matchboxes and pens and pencils in the bottom. "There has to be a passport," she muttered, then ran her hands around the lining of the briefcase, hesitating when she felt a lump, digging at the leather with her fingers until a corner of the lining came up.

Triumphantly, she withdrew a Swiss passport, but the lump remained. Laurel glanced over her shoulder at the couch, but he remained very still. She withdrew a second passport, this one Canadian. "You seem to get around quite a bit," Laurel said, withdrawing a third, British, passport

"Quite a bit. And I know someone who will probably be very interested in all of this." She hid the passports, then returned the lining to its place and repositioned the music, closing the briefcase and returning it to its spot beside the couch.

She stepped around. "Can I get you another drink?" Laurel pushed at his shoulder, but there was still no response. She stepped closer, leaning down to look at him. The Concertmaster was very still. Hesitantly, she reached out to touch his shoulder again, her hand brushing against his cheek. Quickly she yanked it back from the cold flesh.

"Oh, God. Wake up now, please," she whispered, looking at the door. With revulsion she reached out slowly, probing with the tips of her fingers along his very cold arm, searching vainly for a pulse. "I'm sorry, but I think I might have given you too much phenobarbital. Oh, God." She stood up, then took a deep breath. "I think I might deliver these in person," she said, scurrying into the bedroom to gather up all the money she had in the house and the small collection of jewelry she'd managed to get from Reinhard.

When she came out of the room, she looked once more at the man on the couch, watching him, hoping he would move or stir, but he remained in the same position as she had left him, his colorless face still.

"I suppose you won't be needing this case," she said, "so I'll deliver the music, too."

"Karl, do you remember when Patrice left you that passport and disguise?" Laurel bounced up and down with nervous energy as he nodded slowly. "I need it now. I've got to get out of Germany tonight."

"Why are you so edgy?" he asked, his voice teasing. "You act like you've killed someone."

"I have, and I've got to get out of here before Reinhard finds out." She shifted from one foot to another, breathing quickly.

Karl's face became very serious. "You aren't kidding, are you?" She shook her head and he quickly left the room, then returned with the wig and passport in his hands.

Laurel tucked her hair up under the blond wig, then, looking at the photograph, applied her makeup hurriedly.

"There is a plane," he said, returning from the telephone. "It goes to Lisbon. I made a reservation for you, but you must hurry. I have phoned for a taxi."

"You are taking a great many risks to help me. I hope it doesn't make trouble for you."

He shrugged. "I have learned to be a very good liar. Don't worry about me, just get out safely."

"There," she said as she finished filling in her enlarged lip line. "What do you think?"

He put his arms around her. "I think I will miss you very much."

The taxi driver flirted with her all the way to Templehopf, but she ignored his advances, pretending not to understand his motives. As they approached the field, she could see an airplane sitting on the runway, its door open. She took a deep breath before overtipping the taxi driver and rushing into the terminal.

"I have a reservation on the flight to Lisbon," she said as she approached the desk.

"Do you have travel documents? I must see an exit visa." The uniformed guard at the counter stepped toward her.

She produced the Swiss passport, handing it to him with exaggerated flirtation.

The guard smiled, brushing her hand with his as he took the passport. "You have been in Berlin for quite a time, Fraulein," he said.

"Who can resist Berlin?" she said, touching his arm with her hand. "Victors are so appealing to me."

"But now you must leave?"

Too much, too much, she said to herself, lowering her chin and looking up at him through her eyelashes. "My mother has become ill in Portugal and I must bring her home to Geneva for medical care." She tilted her head slightly, wondering if it was working.

"Why is your mother in Portugal?"

"For the sea air," Laurel lied again, brushing her exaggerated bosom against his sleeve. "She thought it would help but it hasn't, so now she will go back to mountain air."

The guard looked at the passport photo again, turned to a new page in the document, and stamped several symbols with several different stamps before he returned it to her, his hand straying deliberately to her breast. "And when will you return to Berlin?"

"Very soon," Laurel whispered. "Will I find you here?"

He cupped his hand openly around her breast. "You will, Fraulein. I will wait for you."

"Good," she said, turning to the ticket agent. "It will be soon." *As soon as hell freezes solid,* she thought as she paid for the ticket, then waved to the immigration guard as she left the desk.

"Do you have anything to declare?" the customs agent asked. "Where is your luggage?"

"I am traveling in an emergency," Laurel lied, "so I have nothing except my briefcase. It has my music in it. It's an opera I am writing about the glorious Reich."

The customs official opened the case, glanced at the music, then closed it again. "An opera?"

"Yes. For the glorious Reich." She wondered why men would believe anything a blond woman with an enlarged bosom would say.

"Good. I would like to hear it, but the airplane is ready to leave."

Laurel grabbed the briefcase. "Thank you," she said over her shoulder as she hurried out into the chilly night air, presenting her ticket to the stewardess and hurrying up the steps to the plane. *Almost there, almost there,* she kept saying inside her head as the stewardess directed her to her seat.

Laurel fastened the safety belt and stared out the window at the men filling the airplane's gas tanks and loading the luggage. *Almost there, almost there, almost there.* The door of the plane closed and the engine just outside the window began to whine as the propeller started to turn.

Laurel began to relax, leaning back in the seat as the plane began to move away from the terminal and taxi out to the end of the runway. She even smiled at the man across the aisle, who had been openly staring at her since she'd sat down.

The plane reached the end of the runway and turned onto the strip, but instead of roaring, the engines were suddenly shut down. Laurel looked out the window, then craned to see two vehicles approaching, red lights flashing on their tops.

Oh, please, no, she thought. *Please don't let me get this close and then take it away. I'm sorry for everything and anything I've ever done in my whole life, and I won't do any of it again if I can just leave here. How could they find him so quickly? And how could they find me?*

She heard the door opening and her heart thudded. She could see the red lights flashing off the wing and closed her eyes, waiting for the rough hands to grab her and take her to prison.

She felt the weight of someone sitting down beside her, and wished she had brought enough of the phenobarbital to kill herself.

"Well, little *Liebschen,* are you frightened of flying? Is that why you have your eyes closed? Do not be afraid, I will protect you."

Laurel didn't want to open her eyes, but was certain she had to. Her lids fluttered open to see the twin silver lightning bolts on the shoulders of the man who was speaking. An SS officer.

"Yah," she muttered, squeezing her lids tightly shut as the engines revved to life and the plane began to move.

The man reached over, squeezing one of her breasts as the plane left the ground. "Fritz will take good care of you all the way to Portugal," he growled in her ear.

I hate your guts, she thought, gritting her teeth, *but soon I will be rich and rid of all of you. Soon I will be home with my own people.*

22

". . . AND SAINT PETER said to the *Swedish* correspondent, 'Sven Jensen, for your sins on earth, you must spend the rest of eternity with her,' and he pointed to the really fat one with the gargoyle face. By this time the guy from *The New York Times* was grinning and leering at Betty Grable, since they were the only two left, when he heard Saint Peter say, "Betty Grable, for your sins on earth you must spend the rest of eternity . . .""

Patrice sagged into the doorway, holding her head. "Paul Sanders Stewart, I cannot believe you kept me standing here for fifteen minutes for that punchline. You are hopeless." But she couldn't help laughing.

"The UPI stringer told it, though not half so well, at Churchill's press conference today while we were waiting for the old boy to arrive. He told several others, but they were of the traveling salesman–farmer's daughter ilk, and . . . are you inviting me up for coffee?"

"As long as you promise not to tell any more jokes." Patrice turned to the stairs, pleased not only at the comfort of their friendship but also at the respite his silly jokes had given her from the constant pressure of her work at the bureau and their training with Donohue.

She rounded the curve at the top of the stairway, then stopped abruptly, motioning for Paul to come up beside her, pointing silently at the figure huddled beside the doorway to her apartment.

The person seemed not to have heard them, so Paul slipped past Patrice, withdrawing the small gun he carried. He crept forward silently, Patrice following. Still, the figure remained motionless.

Paul leaned close, then grabbed the person, yanking upward. "Put your hands against the wall," he commanded.

"Are you trying to give me a heart attack?" the woman said as she complied. "Who are you? Where is Patrice?"

Patrice stepped around Paul, looking quizzical, then said, "Laurel! What happened? Why are you here?"

Paul stood back. Patrice escorted the woman inside her apartment.

"Just a minute, and I shall tell you the whole thing. Who is he?"

"Paul Sanders Stewart, this is Laurel Smythe Pugh." Paul extended his hand and Laurel brushed it imperiously with her fingers.

"I've heard your broadcasts," Paul said, his tone ironic.

"Well, you won't hear them anymore," Laurel replied, turning to Patrice. "I can never go back now. I killed a man."

"Heydrich?" Paul asked, hopeful.

"Of course not," Laurel replied. "The man Reinhard called 'The Concertmaster.' I have his things here with me because I thought you would want to see them." She opened the briefcase, tossing the sheet music onto the table, then clawing at the leather lining. "This music means something, I think, but these are what is important." She fanned the three passports like a bridge hand and Patrice reached for them.

"Oh, my God . . ." Patrice said, handing one of them to Paul. "Come with me." She scooped the music and documents into the briefcase, then handed it to Paul and pulled Laurel up off the chair.

"Do I really have to do this? I'm so tired, and it was such a strain getting out of Germany. You can't imagine what I've been through in the last forty-eight hours. If you had one ounce of human compassion instead of being your usual selfish—"

Paul opened the door to his car and pulled the seat forward. Patrice put her hands on Laurel's hips and pushed, transforming the tirade into a yowl as Laurel was launched into the back seat. "How dare you do that to me?"

"Laurel, please. Don't complain and don't whine, for once in your life. I should think you'd be relieved just to be here in one piece. Just think, you're about to be reunited with your money."

Laurel brightened considerably, then her eyes narrowed. "Providing that I cooperate, I suppose."

"This isn't Germany, Laurel. You don't have to make deals. What's yours is yours." Patrice paused as Paul started the car, then continued, "Of course, there is the small matter of your treasonous behavior, but I'm certain you could find a lawyer who would be more than happy to represent you. Unless you truly believe what you have been saying on your broadcasts, in which case you might just want to wait until your friends invade."

Laurel's voice quavered. "Why are you being so mean, Patrice? Here I risk my life to bring you something which you obviously think is valuable, and you're just being nasty."

Bletchley at night seemed more Victorian and forbidding than during the day, Patrice thought as they wound their way through the mill side of the town and to the house which housed the Baker Street Irregulars, the code-breakers headed by Alan Turing, and where Donohue had gathered the remnants of the Butterfly force. Paul hesitated at the gatehouse and a guard emerged.

Paul offered his ID and Patrice's and asked, "Is Colonel Donohue in the house?"

"Where are the papers for the passenger, sir?" the guard replied.

"She's a prisoner. Is Donohue in?"

"I'm *not* a prisoner," Laurel sputtered. "I'm on *your* side."

"What is the prisoner's name, sir?"

Patrice could feel Paul's frustration building and put her hand on his arm. "Please tell the Colonel we have Laurel Pugh with us and she has something very important."

"What is this place?" Laurel asked from the back seat.

Patrice and Paul both ignored her, watching the guard on the telephone. He hung up, nodded briskly, then raised the gate.

The door was open by the time they reached the house, and Donohue, clad in an Irish sweater and khakis, stood in the dim frame of light, his arms crossed across his chest.

"It's a pleasure to see you again, Colonel. I believe we last met at—" Laurel bustled up the stairs, her hand extended.

"I recall," he replied, giving her a cursory handshake before leading them into the conference room, indicating they should take chairs at the large table.

Patrice set the briefcase in front of Donohue while briefly recounting Laurel's appearance at her door.

"Well, that's not the whole story," Laurel said when Patrice had finished. "No one has even asked me how I killed the Concertmaster, and no one is being very nice to me. Maybe I should have just stayed in Berlin."

"How did you happen to kill this man?" Donohue asked, and Laurel smirked smugly at Patrice before beginning.

"You see, I knew I could no longer continue to live in Berlin. I realized what I had done was wrong and I should never have spoken against the brave and valiant efforts of the Allies against the evil Nazis." She looked at each of their faces, trying to convey sincerity. "This man, the owner of this briefcase I brought to you at great personal risk, called himself 'The Concertmaster.' He has been coming to visit Reinhard as long as I have . . . have been around. With Reinhard."

At least, Patrice thought, *she has the grace to stammer, if not blush.*

"You see, Reinhard plays the violin, and rather well, I think. Anyway, The Concertmaster has been sending music to Reinhard for a long time, or sometimes bringing it, but always thought it was strange that Reinhard never played it

He'd just look at it for a long time as though he were reading it or playing it in his head. You see, I really don't know very much about music, so I believed Reinhard when he told me it was a symphony they were working on together." She shrugged, seeking support, then, getting none, continued. "As you may know, Reinhard isn't living in Berlin anymore; he's down in Prague now, but he's really back and forth. Last night The Concertmaster showed up in Berlin and wanted to see Reinhard right away. At first I was going to tell him that Reinhard was in Prague, but then I wondered if he might know something or have something which would be valuable to you since I wanted to prove just how loyal I am to America. So, I made him several cocktails and I put a lot of phenobarbital in each one, but I think he had at least four before he finally fell asleep. Once I was positive he was really out, I opened his briefcase and found all this music, and then I felt the lumps under the lining, and that's when I found the passports."

Patrice pointed to them and Donohue opened the top one. "Oh, hell," he said, opening the others and shaking his head. "Are you certain he was dead?"

Laurel wrinkled her nose. "Well, he wasn't breathing and his skin was really cold. I didn't think it would be such a good idea to call a doctor, but he really looked dead. I mean, it is sort of hard to tell in people of his color, but he was really pale and pasty-looking, and he didn't move or anything during the time it took me to get out of there."

Donohue reached for a telephone and mumbled something into it, then motioned for Paul. Paul nodded, then slipped out a side door. The room was silent as Donohue stared first at the passports, then at the music. Suddenly the sliding doors opened and Alan Turing, wearing a plaid bathrobe with his hair flying in several different directions, came bursting in. As he strode to Donohue's side, he nodded with detached recognition at Patrice and glanced at Laurel.

"Alan, have a look at this," Donohue said, extending the sheets of music.

He shuffled through the stack, then looked closely at the top page again. "This is Andrew Collins's work," he said, his brow furrowing. "But I thought this was a secret project of his. How do you happen to have it? Also, where is the boy? I expected him back from some deuced concert in Zurich today. Did he send this along?"

Donohue tossed the three passports onto the table. "Not intentionally."

Turing picked up the passports, his brow furrowing even more deeply. "What the devil?"

"Apparently Andrew Collins has been suffering from divided loyalty for quite a long time. We have evidence he's been using the music code to give a lot of information to one particular Nazi for at least a year. One of our agents in Berlin picked this up last night. Collins is dead."

"Dead! If he was giving us to the Nazis, it's what he deserved, I guess. Now at least we know where the leaks have been coming from. Turing turned to Laurel. "Are you the one who intercepted this?"

She nodded.

"Are you certain he was dead? I mean did you *see* that he was actually dead?"

"You people are such ghouls," Laurel said, wrinkling her nose. "I am not a doctor and I haven't seen that many dead people, but I think he was dead. And why is it so important?"

The four of them stared at her. Finally Donohue said, "It's a logical question. We just want to be certain."

Laurel tossed her hair. "Well, I think you don't trust me, and I don't like it. Here I risk my life bringing this to you, and all anyone does is question me. I didn't have to come here, you know." She rose, picking up her purse. "As a matter of fact, I might just leave."

"Sit down." Donohue's voice was ominous, and Laurel immediately returned to her chair. "And let me clarify something. You are not in a bargaining position, Mrs. Pugh. You may consider yourself to be under arrest."

"Under arrest? Perhaps you aren't aware of the contributions I've made."

"I think we are all very much aware of the contributions you have made, Mrs. Pugh."

Paul reappeared in the doorway, a leather-bound book in his hand. "I'm afraid we hardly know any of them," he said as he crossed the room to give the book to Donohue. "You were right. Collins kept a journal. Why it isn't in code is beyond me, but what I've seen just glancing at it . . ."

Alan Turing had spread the music sheets from the brief-case, plus the files he'd found in Andrew Collins's quarters, across one end of the table and had become completely absorbed in deciphering the code. His hair seemed to have grown even more wild and unruly with his tugging at it while he contemplated the contents of the scores.

Donohue had been sitting at the other end of the table reading the journal and making notes. Every so often he would glare at Laurel, who had curled into a chair and gone to sleep.

Paul was pacing quietly, alternating his attention between Turing's work and Donohue's expressions. Patrice glanced at her watch, surprised to find it was nearing eight in the morning, suddenly conscious of the noise of daytime and work which had begun outside the conference room.

The doors slid open and a uniformed man entered carrying a tray laden with a large coffeepot and cups. He was followed by another man whose tray was stacked with covered dishes. As the smell of coffee filled the room, Laurel stirred, then sat up.

Patrice glanced toward Laurel, then to the door beyond which Whitney stood silently watching. When she caught Patrice's eye, she shook her head, waiting.

Laurel scurried to pour herself coffee, then turned back, when she stopped abruptly. "So you really are alive," she said, looking Whitney up and down. "You look better than I'd expect."

Whitney smiled slightly and shook her head. "Gracious as always, I see, Laurel." She turned to leave, but Donohue called after her.

"Whitney, maybe you should join us. And please close the doors."

She settled into a chair and Patrice immediately came to sit beside her. Laurel had begun to join them at the table, then backed away and returned to the armchair where she had been sleeping, sitting with her back straight, her hands clenched, suddenly wary.

"Mrs. Pugh, you and your family have made some, shall we say unfortunate, choices of companions and allegiances. In a world of absolutes, my decision here would be obvious. However, the circumstances of your arrival and the attendant information you have brought, as well as your earlier contributions, have put me in rather a difficult position." Donohue tented his fingers. Laurel didn't breathe. Paul, Whitney, and Patrice watched both of them intently. "And what I have read over the past four or five hours only makes it more complex."

Laurel's eyes shifted to the door, and Patrice nudged Whitney, who raised her eyebrows in response. They had seen this behavior since in grade school, when Laurel had fled from any class in which she'd been in trouble.

"How much do you know of your father's involvement in German politics?"

Laurel looked puzzled. "German politics? My father has . . . rather, had . . . some German business interests, but I have never heard him say anything about politics—American or German."

Whitney leveled her icy gaze at Laurel. "That's patent nonsense and you know it. Your father has been in business and political maneuvering for the Germans since the last war. He's tried to sell his own soul to the Germans, and he has sold you. Laurel, you and your endless deceits disgust me."

"It was what he believed in," Laurel replied defensively.

"Money and greed are what your father believes in, so much so that he would betray his friends and his country and his own family in exchange for money. My father protected him for years from the other people in the Valley, and I regret that more than you could ever know." Whitney leaned forward and Laurel shrank back from her frigid eyes "And what I regret most is that my father, a man o principles and honor and loyalty to his country, is dead while your father, the traitorous scum, not only lives bu prospers from his sedition."

Patrice put her hand on Whitney's arm, stroking her soothingly.

Donohue rose and poured a cup of coffee for himself, then came back to the table through the palpable silence of the room. "Whitney, from what I have been reading, you are understating the case," he said quietly, his voice filled with regret. "Andrew Collins has apparently been betraying our operations to the Nazis for a long time," he began. "Mrs. Pugh has apparently killed him with an overdose of phenobarbital, and has brought us some evidence of his activities, but in his room we have found his journal." He paused and picked up the leather-bound book, glancing at his notes, then opening it.

"Mr. Collins was quite a meticulous record-keeper. This journal begins in May, 1940, so I feel we will probably find diaries for times prior to that, but I'm afraid this contains damning enough information." He sighed. "In June, 1940, Andrew Collins records a meeting in Greenspring Valley, Maryland, with Boyleston Greene and Harold Smythe. The topic of this meeting was an investigation on the part of Senator Baraday of American businessmen who were making deals with German industries to supply materials which had been strictly excluded from commerce with the Germans. One of the businesses under investigation by the Senator's committee was the one owned by Mr. Smythe and Mr. Greene which was brokering certain raw materials to Pugh Industries in Germany. This was not, however, sufficient to make them feel concern about the Senator, for he was investigating many businesses. Their concern with the Senator had to do much more with what he might or might not know about his daughter: the fact that she was still alive, and more importantly, that she carried something of great importance to the Nazis and their war effort."

Whitney was leaning forward, her back straight with tension, staring at Donohue intently. "Please continue," she said, her voice flat.

Donohue sighed. "The decision was made by the three of them, under the direction of Reinhard Heydrich, to whom Collins reported, that the Senator's knowledge must be investigated." He turned a few pages. "In July, they broke

333

into the Senator's office in Washington, looking for the microfilm or something which would indicate he knew Whitney's whereabouts."

"I was in Paris in July," Whitney said softly. "Hiding with the French underground. I think you knew I'd gotten out, William."

He nodded. "And was frantically looking for you—in Switzerland."

"Did my father ever know I had survived?" Whitney asked quietly.

Donohue shook his head. "I don't believe so. I think he wished it were true, because he put enormous pressure on the State Department to get Turkey to present your body, but I don't think he ever knew. Your mother does not know to this day."

Whitney nodded. "Ironic, isn't it? The people who know I'm alive want me dead, and the people who think I'm dead wish I were alive."

Donohue drank from his coffee cup. "The break-in was futile, as were their efforts to intercept his mail and telephone calls, but Heydrich was convinced Whitney had somehow managed to be in touch with him and to pass on the microfilm. At the end of July," he continued, paging forward in the book, "the three of them made the decision, augmented and encouraged by Heydrich, to question the Senator directly."

"And they killed him," Whitney finished, shifting her furious look to Laurel. "They murdered him. And I suppose they were also responsible for trying to murder my mother later that fall." Her hands clenched the edge of the table, her knuckles white.

"Collins actually did the work," Donohue said, trying to keep his voice calm and keep Whitney from exploding.

"My father never would have gone anywhere with some one he didn't know." Whitney's eyes never left Laurel' face. "Someone had to set him up. It was Harold Smythe wasn't it? My father would never have trusted anythin Boyleston had to say."

"Under orders from Heydrich," Donohue said.

Whitney got up slowly from the table, turning her back ⊂

Laurel, walking to the other end of the room. Suddenly, she turned, and the gleam of a knife appeared in her hand. Before anyone could move, she threw the knife toward Laurel. With a loud thunk, it imbedded itself in the leather chair in which Laurel cowered, stopping a hair's breadth from the side of Laurel's neck.

"If I ever lay eyes on you again, Laurel, my aim won't be so careless." She turned her back and left the stunned room.

"She tried to kill me!" Laurel screamed.

Donohue shook his head. "No, if she'd meant to kill you, she would have. I suggest, however, that you take her advice and stay out of her way."

"That's fine with me. If Patrice will just give me my money, I'll be happy to leave."

Donohue shook his head. "Mrs. Pugh, we still have the small matter of treason to discuss. Not to mention that you are now privvy to confidential information. No, I think we shall have to hold you in our care for the time being."

"But Patrice promised me . . . ."

"I promised you nothing, Laurel," Patrice said evenly. "And now that I know what your father and your lover have done, I would renege on any promises anyway."

"Mrs. Pugh, you will be the guest of the government of the United States for the time being, held in an area where your knowledge will be of use only to our side."

She jumped to her feet, grabbing the knife from the leather of the chair.

"If you touch me, I'll kill you," she screamed, backing toward the door and directly into the arms of Cesar Ball. He put one huge arm around her, removing the knife from her and with the other.

"Now, now, Mrs. Pugh. Let's not make things any worse for ourselves, shall we?" he said smoothly, turning her into the waiting hands of two uniformed guards.

"We have one chance and one chance only to get him." Erik looked at each of them in turn: Patrice and Paul sitting next to the fireplace on a small bench, Regina leaning against the mantelpiece, a cigarette dangling from her lips, Dusko Popov sitting on a rough chair, leaning forward, his body reflecting his tension, Whitney and Ross Robbins at the small table, and Vota Rajic and Jan Myjuszk, who stood next to the door.

"And to get Primrose," Dusko added quickly. His eyes darted to each of them in turn. "You must believe me. You must. I stayed in the village to try to get her myself. I used every SS contact I could without betraying all of us. I tried to devise a rescue plan that would only involve me, but I was outsmarted and outnumbered at every turn. Can't you believe me? Don't you know how much she means to me?" His fingers picked unconsciously at the splinters on the chair.

Whitney rose and moved to his side, putting her arm across his shoulders. "Dusko, none of us believes that our Tricycle would betray us. I understand better than most the frustration and fear you feel at the way things appear and the way they really are." Her eyes rose to meet Erik's.

Erik nodded. "Of course." Since his vindication, Dusko had been a strong presence, but Erik could see the changes in his old friend and wondered how much longer he would be willing to subject himself and his wife to the risks of their careers. "The biggest difference from the last time we tried this is that I am the only one who knows the plan until this moment. And from now on, we are always together. There will be two groups: one to rescue Primrose, the other to get Heydrich. Group one will be Patrice, Ross, Dusko, Regina, and Jan. Group two, then, is made up of Whitney, Paul Vota, and me. Just remember what we really want to do here. We want to get Primrose back and we must kill Heydrich. Now we must get to work, for we have less than twelve hours. Vota?"

"Through our comrades we have discovered the Lady Primrose is held in the building where the Protector has his office, and his torture chambers."

Patrice felt the bile rising in her throat and swallowed hard, turning away from the intense anger on Vota's face. It was too much pain almost to imagine, too personal to watch. Her eyes fell on Whitney's face, and Patrice shivered at the cold fury in her friend's eyes which had not abated since her confrontation with Laurel.

Vota continued. "We have found out that Lady Primrose is alive and not too much tortured. The Protector Heydrich has her in a place by herself on one floor. His office is two stairs up from this. The outside is guarded at the front door by many soldiers." He stopped and his eyes twinkled. "But the Protector has not all the cards in his pocket. There is another way inside."

Patrice leaned toward Paul and whispered, "Why do I find that so ominous?"

Vota unfolded a map of Prague on the table and everyone gathered around. "Here is where lives Protector. He has taken very nice castle for himself. Here is where is office and prison." Vota stubbed at the map with a short finger. "Now is come to mistake of death. I think Protector believe after Belgium that he could not be killed, so he now is careless. You see here, where road comes from castle." Everyone leaned closer, watching the movement of Vota's finger along the map. "This road very steep from castle, with much walls until come this corner, where road go two ways. First goes down mountain with still walls. This way goes shorter, but no walls. Sometimes Protector takes one road, sometimes other—it cannot be known." He looked up and grinned. "But can make him take road we want."

"Which road is that?" Whitney asked.

"This one. The one with walls. Here, at this place, car must turn around sharp corner with high walls. He thinks walls make safe, but always two sides to knife. This time we have knife."

Patrice stuffed three bundles of dynamite into the grating at the foot of the prison wall. Then, gathering the priming cords together, coiling them as Ross had told her, she edged along the wall to where he was working. Dusko approached from the other direction, his coil of wires as large as hers. Jan stood, the Sten gun braced and ready, his eyes scanning for guards, while Regina guarded the other direction.

Robbins worked quickly, stripping the ends of the wires bare and fusing them into the single detonator cable. As soon as he screwed them onto the posts, he stood up, glancing at his watch.

"Just in time. This oughta blow the Jerries outta their

socks." He picked up the coil of detonator cable and eased along the wall. "Remember, keep shooting, keep shouting, and try to sound like a battalion, or they'll bump us off quick. Keep it confusing."

Patrice slung the gun down from her shoulder, making sure the reserve clips were still in her pocket. She rubbed her hands together and held the gun tightly. Dusko put his hand on her shoulder.

"Thank you for coming. You didn't have to."

"Yes, I did," she replied. "Not only for Prim, but also for Senator Baraday and for the thousands of other people this animal has killed."

"Everybody ready?" Ross asked, and they all nodded. "Well, brace yourselves." He raised the plunger on the box, then pushed downward sharply.

Nothing happened. Patrice, crouched against the building, clutched her gun, and steeled herself against the concussion she knew she would feel. Instead, a bird whistled into the stillness of the morning. On the wall high above their heads, she heard two men speaking rapid German, but it was gossip about a woman. She turned to look over at Ross, but his head was lowered over the detonator box.

Patrice was about to ask if there were something she could do when suddenly the entire world turned red.

"Let's go," she heard a male voice shout above the din, and felt someone grab her arm and pull her along the base of the building. A huge hole had blossomed at the grating and five of them clambered through the dust into the prison.

"This way," Jan yelled, leading them to a staircase, then up into a long corridor.

Patrice heard a noise behind them and turned. Five soldiers in SS uniforms were running after them. She clutched the rifle against her shoulder and squeezed the trigger. A deafening burst of noise filled her right ear and the five soldiers scattered or fell. One soldier kept coming and Patrice pulled the trigger again. The man's arms flew up and he screamed as he fell.

She turned and raced down the hall after the others. When she reached the top of the stairs, Jan was removing a ring of keys from a soldier whose head lolled backward, a surprised look on his face.

Jan used the keys to open the door to the cell block, then scurried along, opening the cells, calling out something in Czech. People emerged from the barred rooms, running down the hallway to the stairs. The first took the gun from the dead soldier, and the others were searching for weapons as they ran.

"Come with me," Dusko said, grabbing Patrice. "We will find Primrose."

Patrice pulled away, firing at three approaching SS guards, then quickly removing the spent clip and inserting a new one. "Yes, let's do go find her now. All this noise must be frightening her."

Dusko hesitated, looking back at Patrice. "Or very reassuring."

Whitney placed the mirror against the bottom of the wall which faced the direction from which Heydrich's car would approach. Then she walked across the road, making certain she could see the lights as soon as the car rounded the corner. When she was satisfied with the angle, she retreated to her hiding spot. Vota and Paul had gone on up the hill with the borrowed hay truck and she had heard a grinding crash not long ago which meant they had overturned the truck in the mouth of the shorter, nonwalled road. Vota's brother was with them, and had rehearsed a very convincing hysterical farmer on their way in from the safe house.

Whitney smiled with anticipation. This would be her kill, she knew. Certainly Vota and Paul and Erik would be in position with weapons, but she had chosen a spot where, as the car came around the hairpin turn, she and Heydrich would be almost face to face. She wanted him to know with unquestioned certainty that it was she, the Limping Lady, the daughter of Senator Nelson Baraday, who was taking his life. *An eye for eye,* she thought. *Your life for my father's, you bastard.*

Vota and Paul came running down the hill. Paul vaulted up, scrambling over the top of the stone wall as Vota came to stand down the hill from Whitney, backing her up. Erik, she knew, was already hidden on top of the wall, his high-powered rifle, with its telescopic sight, trained on the spot they knew the car would cross.

Vota would take out the motorcyclist who always preceeded Heydrich's car, and Paul was to shoot any trailing soldiers or escorts. Erik would first aim for the driver and guard in the front of the car, leaving Heydrich to Whitney.

Whitney cocked her head, listening, then smiled again at the distant rumble of thunder which rolled up the hill from the prison. "Good luck," Erik said in a hoarse whisper, and she looked up at him. "I love you," he added, and she brushed her lips with her fingertips, then angled them toward him.

Suddenly they heard the whine of a siren starting at the top of the hill. The sound echoed and bounced off the walls, but Whitney kept her eyes locked on the mirror, ignoring the confusing message of the sounds.

"Now," she said as the headlight of the motorcycle illuminated the wall of the curve above where they waited. She heard the three rifles cock and pulled the slide back on the hand-held automatic she carried, bracing herself against the wall, the gun in both hands, her eyes on the mirror.

The motorcycle headlight bobbed into view and she watched its cyclops lurching toward her only until the headlights of the car appeared. The sound of the sirens increased, tormenting and abrasive as the car and escort came closer.

The motorcycle engine screamed as the driver downshifted to control the speed of the vehicle as he rounded the sharp curve. Whitney had expected the man would look up, but he was concentrating on the curve of the road. Vota waited until the motorcycle came even with him and the front of the Mercedes appeared before he opened fire.

Whitney heard the scream of the motorcycle rider as she raised her gun, leveling it at the height she expected the windows of the car would be. From overhead, she heard the sharp report of Erik's rifle and watched as the driver crumpled to his side. The car drifted forward and the faces in the back came lazily into view.

It was his eyes that surprised her. She had expected crisp blue, but they were washed out and soft. It was obvious he was neither surprised nor frightened. Whitney pulled the trigger and the window between them shattered, but Heydrich scrambled to the other side of the car as Whitney pulled the trigger again.

She heard Erik and Paul firing from above, but Heydrich scrambled out of the car and up the hill. She moved quickly around the corner and began firing after him. She saw him grab his back, but he still kept running.

"No, damn it, you're not getting away," she yelled, and began to run after him, firing again and again. "Die, damn you," she shouted, pulling the trigger.

Suddenly Heydrich's arms flew up in the air. He stopped abruptly, then turned and began to come back down the hill toward her.

Whitney was so surprised, she held her fire for a moment, watching Heydrich, soaked with blood, stagger toward her, a huge grin on his face.

"You can't kill me," he rasped, lurching close to her.

Whitney clutched the gun in her hands, staring into his mad eyes.

"You can't kill me because you fear me," he rasped.

"Go to hell," she said, firing into his smile. He stood, facing her, the grin still in place, and she began to pull the trigger again when suddenly Heydrich crumpled to the ground.

Whitney turned, expecting to find Erik standing behind her, then gasped. "I thought you were dead," she said.

Raja Abachandri, Andrew Collins, shook his head slowly with a smile. "She couldn't even do that right," he said, then gestured with his gun. "Drop your weapon, Countess."

Whitney looked for reinforcements as she dropped her gun. She realized she had run a long distance after Heydrich, and now none of them were in sight.

"Why did you give up your nation to its enemy?" she said. "I really need to know."

"*My* nation? My nation is India, the jewel in the crown of the British Empire, a nation indentured to the ignorant British, who treat us as though we are slaves or fools. How could I pass up a chance to contribute to the downfall of those pompous old fools? In Hitler's world I am an Aryan,

341

a member of the chosen race, not some brown man that you and your kind sneer at. That fool woman gave me drugs and stole my codes, but it doesn't matter, for now I am the Assistant to the Reich Protector of Czechoslovakia. My future is assured. It's a pity you won't be able to tell all this to Colonel Donohue, for he should know the truth, but now I must kill you."

Whitney held her breath, bracing herself for the bullet, wondering how death would feel, when his chest exploded, covering her with chunks of bone and gore. He crumpled and Erik appeared, stepping over the fallen cryptographer to take Whitney into his arms.

"Are you all right?" she asked into his chest.

"Yes. Are you?"

"Yes. Now let's get out of here before anyone else comes along who wants to kill me."

Epilogue

OH, TEA. How lovely. I really missed tea," Primrose said, taking the cup from Whitney and sipping at it with her eyes closed.

"Dusko says he's taking you to Nassau for a vacation. And then to Cuba and perhaps Miami," Patrice chimed in. "I think you need a chaperone. Or a private nurse. I'm really quite good at being a private nurse, you know."

"You're also quite good at being a journalist," Whitney said.

"And not such a bad rescuer," Primrose added. "I have never been so happy to see two people in my entire life." Her brow furrowed. "Are you positive Heydrich is dead?"

Whitney shuddered. "I thought he would never die. He just kept coming at me. It was terrifying. And then to turn around and find Andrew Collins! I felt as though I were in a terrible nightmare." Her hand went to her face and made an absent brushing gesture. "Erik and I are going back to the valley for a visit with my mother. It's time she knew the whole story."

"While you are there, please see Mrs. Smythe. The poor woman," Patrice sighed.

"I had planned to, but I thought you were coming back to the States as well. Have you changed your mind?"

Patrice shrugged. "Someone has to stay in London. You see, Magda was offered a full pardon by President Roosevelt, but she's decided that she'd like to stay on with us. Donohue has asked me to sort of take her under my wing to teach her some of the finer points of the business. After all, when you come back from lounging and loafing, there might be a bit more to do. The war isn't over yet, you know."